A LAND NOT THEIRS

Also by David Marcus

TO NEXT YEAR IN JERUSALEM
THE MIDNIGHT COURT
(translation from the Irish)

A LAND NOT THEIRS

David Marcus

BANTAM PRESS

NEW YORK · LONDON · TORONTO · SYDNEY · AUCKLAND

TRANSWORLD PUBLISHERS LTD
61–63 Uxbridge Road, London W5 5SA

TRANSWORLD PUBLISHERS (AUSTRALIA) PTY LTD
15–23 Helles Avenue, Moorebank NSW 2170, Australia

TRANSWORLD PUBLISHERS (NZ) LTD
Cnr Moselle and Waipareira Aves,
Henderson, Auckland

Published 1986 by Bantam Press,
a division of Transworld Publishers Ltd
Copyright © David Marcus 1986

British Library Cataloguing in Publication Data

Marcus, David
  A land not theirs.
  I. Title
  823'.914 [F]   PR6063.A624/

ISBN 0–593–01228–3

Printed in Great Britain by
Mackays of Chatham Ltd.

For Ita and Sarah

And the Lord said unto Abraham, know of a surety
that thy seed shall be a stranger in a land
that is not theirs.

The Haggadah

1

DAWN was still a full hour away, but Colonel Windsor was already at his post. His presence in the pitch darkness was marked only by the dull glow of a cigarette, its red tip pulsing into light every few moments to reveal the black pencil of the Colonel's moustache as he sat, immobile behind his desk, reflecting on the previous day's visitor.

He had not expected to run across Tubby Walters again, not within only two years of their end-of-war farewells in London, and certainly not in Ireland. Somehow he had missed the announcement that Tubby was in command of one of the Dublin Black and Tan units – he had enough to do maintaining the morale and the strictly military role of his own division in Cork without spending time scanning the lists of appointments elsewhere in the country. Besides, he had no sympathy with the Black and Tans' methods – they were only making a bad situation worse. So when Tubby was shown into his office wearing the already infamous khaki and dark green uniform the shock almost bowled him over. Tubby, like himself, had been a career soldier, with an army record second to none – India, Malta, then France and the Somme. What was he doing as a Black and Tan officer? How could he possibly be associated with the excesses of such a raggle-taggle outfit?

7

An even greater surprise was Tubby's appearance. It wasn't merely that he had lost stones in weight – dash it, the man's sobriquet was a libel now – but that his whole demeanour was that of a soldier completely confused, completely disorientated. Shell-shocked was almost how the Colonel would have described him. His eyes were lack-lustre and bloodshot, the cheeks of his moon face had collapsed into wan saucers, and the generous tyre of flesh on which the face used to ride was little more than a slack tube. Even worse, Colonel Windsor's sharp glance detected a tremor in the hand that avidly accepted the whiskey and soda he had poured out to celebrate the unexpected reunion with his old comrade-in-arms.

'To the future!' the Colonel had said, raising his glass.

Tubby had made no response but drained half his drink in one quick swallow and, as if the Colonel's toast only then reached his ears, replied: 'No, Eric, not the future. Not that. Let's say "To old times".'

The Colonel was not normally one whose nerve or self-confidence could be shaken by a comrade's torment – he had seen too much and, besides, a soldier in the field made his own luck – but sitting now in the darkness, hardly aware of the familiar sounds of a barracks coming to life, the hollow ring of that dead voice seemed to re-echo in his ears. Could there be a warning for him in the circumstances of Tubby's decline? 'There but for the grace of God ... eh?' he muttered. No, he couldn't really see himself ever reduced to such a state. Even so, he lit the lamp on his desk, put a fresh cigarette in his holder and firmly affixed his monocle – all as if to reassure himself, as if to confirm both his identity and his authority: Colonel Eric R. S. Windsor, DSO, Colonel-in-Chief of His Majesty's 16th Infantry Division, currently stationed in Cambridge Barracks, Cork. He was glad he hadn't gone on to the Reserve after the Armistice, as Tubby had – though, if he had, he would have stayed retired. Old soldiers should never return to the colours – except in cases of dire necessity. Conditions in the Army were changing – had changed – so quickly that unless one were continuously involved there was no hope of keeping up.

Ironically, it was change that had driven Tubby back to active service – change in civvy street and in the set ways of the pre-war world he had been used to.

'It was gone, Eric,' he had explained, his eyes fidgeting to every part of Colonel Windsor's crammed office as if seeking some corner which would not awaken images of once familiar surroundings. 'It was all gone. Nothing the same. Children grown up and away. Wife an old woman before her time. No sap in her; too much waiting, y'see, waiting and worrying.'

He broke off, apparently only to finish his drink, but then as he sat hunched in his chair contemplating his empty glass some overpowering depression seemed to crush him into silence. The Colonel frowned. Tubby's speech, he noted, still bore all the marks of his military training and background – clipped, precise, factual – but the note of self-pity was totally out of character.

Colonel Windsor coughed, and Tubby looked up sharply. As if suddenly remembering where he was and why he had come, he resumed.

'What was left for me? Elevenses in the garden, *The Times* over my face, pension at the end of the month – and not a damned thing I wanted to buy with it. I was bored, Eric. You were right to stay on. I missed it – the only world I ever really knew. God, how I missed it. So when the chance came to get back....'

'Well, wasn't that just what you wanted?'

Tubby Walters held out his empty glass without a word. Colonel Windsor refilled it, and Tubby took a large swallow before gathering himself together to reply.

'Oh, yes, it seemed the very thing. When I got the nod that the Government was looking for ex-army officers to form a new force for service in Ireland, I tell you, Eric, I thought my prayers had been answered.'

'And hadn't they been?' Colonel Windsor had to prompt when Tubby relapsed once again into a brooding torpor.

'My God, man, don't you know?' Tubby flashed, his cheeks suddenly going scarlet with passion.

'Know what?'

'They're thugs, Eric. These Tans are just hired killers.

9

That can't be news to you, man. You've had plenty of incidents in your own area.'

'But, damn it, Tubby, you're the boss. You're in command of your unit – surely you can control them?'

The Colonel was startled by Tubby's reaction. What had seemed an innocuous and perfectly reasonable suggestion was answered with a moan as of a child in pain. There was a crash as Tubby's empty glass fell to the floor and he covered his face with his hands.

'Easy, old man, easy,' Colonel Windsor urged, momentarily at a loss. If it had been any other soldier, he would have told him sternly to pull himself together and be a man. But not Tubby, not an old friend. Besides, they had been through enough together for Colonel Windsor to know that Tubby *was* a man – or, at least, he had been.

Bit by bit the Colonel had pieced together Tubby's story. According to him, the Black and Tans were a terror force, hastily recruited from ex-soldiers to carry out a policy of naked and bloody reprisals against the IRA. They had been put nominally under the command of ex-army officers like Tubby, to give them a cloak of respectability, but Tubby pointed out that they weren't army units or subject to army authority. They were attached to the Royal Irish Constabulary yet had no police training, and, knowing the British Cabinet would turn a blind eye to their activities, they had quickly proved uncontrollable. They wreaked havoc in the country villages, looted and burned at will and were drunk more often than sober.

None of this told the Colonel anything he hadn't already known. Black and Tan outrages had drawn only lame excuses, even denials, from the Government, and it was becoming more and more difficult to contradict the widespread assertion – by the local newspapers, by the man in the street, even by the RIC themselves – that the whole purpose of the Black and Tans was to crush Sinn Fein and the Irish Republican Army and cow the population. It was hard to credit that a British Cabinet would pursue such a policy but, then, there were plenty of hard men in the Government. They knew the RIC couldn't be relied on; they knew they had no hope of persuading the Army to go on a reign of terror; so a new force with *carte blanche*....

'But what happens when you arrest these men?' Colonel Windsor had asked. 'You *do* arrest them, Tubby?'

'If I arrested all of them who deserved to be put under arrest, then I'd have no one left,' was the reply. 'Oh, I did at the beginning. But Dublin Castle quickly had them released.'

'What about the Secretary for Ireland? Did you complain to Greenwood?'

'Complain to London?' The venom in Tubby's voice confirmed the worst of Colonel Windsor's suspicions. 'It was a waste of time, Eric, a sheer waste of time.'

'Why? What happened?'

'Nothing. Absolutely nothing. "Complaints being studied", et cetera, et cetera. But no action, no support. The blind eye, Eric. Don't you see, man? They're all in it together.'

'You're sure of that, Tubby? It wasn't just red-tape delays, Home Office routines, that sort of thing?'

There was a brief silence, and then 'There's a village by the name of Balbriggan, just outside Dublin,' Tubby said, his voice unnaturally low.

'Wasn't there a policeman shot there a little while ago?'

'Yes, the Head Constable. Assassinated in broad daylight. A dastardly act. I don't hold with it. I don't excuse it. But....'

His hands clenched and unclenched.

'Go on,' Colonel Windsor urged. He could see that whatever was agitating his friend had pushed him to the limit but he judged it better to let him get it off his chest than keep it bottled up.

'That night, in Balbriggan, the RIC and the Tans looted four public houses. Then they burned them down. Then they burned down a factory and forty-nine other houses. Then the RIC picked out men they said were Sinn Feiners. Six of them. Two were bayoneted. God knows where they got the bayonets. They're not even supposed to have them. The other four were shot by the Tans. Just shot

11

without trial or question. By my men, Eric. Men supposed to be under my command.'

'But surely you reported *that*? Surely you told London?'

'Oh, yes. I reported it. I certainly reported it. Names, places, time, every detail.'

'And?'

'Nothing. Except. . . .'

'Except what?'

'Don't know if it's true. But it came from a reliable source. I was told that when the Cabinet got my report of what the Tans had done Churchill said he could see no harm in it.'

Colonel Windsor's initial reaction had been to discount that, no matter how trustworthy the source; but now, as he reflected on it, he felt it could well be true. Churchill was a particular hothead and, after all, if the Cabinet didn't condone what had happened, why hadn't they authorised an enquiry? Why had they just ignored Tubby's report?

'What can I do, Eric?' he had pleaded. 'I can't stop such outrages but I can't just stand by and let them continue. These men are supposed to be my responsibility, and I'm powerless. Just a figurehead. Not even that. A puppet. I'm ashamed, so ashamed. I never thought . . . after the career I've had, the service I've given. . . .'

'I know, Tubby, I know. It's not your fault. It's not something you, personally, have to be ashamed of. You're just being used. It's not really your disgrace.'

'But it is. I *feel* disgraced. And what can I do about it, Eric, what can I do?'

The panic in Tubby's voice alarmed Colonel Windsor. He poured his friend a fresh drink and pressed the glass into his shaking hand.

'Drink that and I'll tell you what to do.'

Tubby took one swallow and then looked up at the Colonel.

'What?' he asked.

The Colonel put a hand on his shoulder and said quietly: 'Resign.'

12

The response did not greatly surprise him. The light of hope that had flickered in Tubby's eyes died and he shook his head wearily.

'I've thought of that. I can't do it. It would be like deserting.'

Colonel Windsor resumed his seat.

'Nonsense,' he replied. 'You must resign.'

'On what grounds? On the grounds that I can't control my men? That would look fine on my record. What an end to my career – to my life.'

'No,' Colonel Windsor explained. 'You resign on medical grounds.'

'But I'm not sick. I'm not, Eric, am I? Do you think I'm sick?'

It was a flash of the old soldier, the true grit of a seasoned campaigner who refuses to leave the field of battle despite his wounds. That ingrained courage, the belief that he must continue to fight on – the ability to fool himself into thinking that he *could* fight on – was all that was left to Tubby, and Colonel Windsor realised that to take it away from him could precipitate the final breakdown. Equally, however, he saw that, unless Tubby did resign, breakdown was inevitable.

'No,' he assured him, 'of course you're not sick. You know what you're doing – you know what you're saying. You're under pressure, that's obvious, great pressure. But you're not sick yet. What I mean, Tubby, is that if you continue like this you'll end up sick. And for what? For the empty command of a gang of thugs and for a government that's just using you.'

He paused to see what effect his words were having. Tubby was sitting up straight, shoulders back, head raised, looking for the first time in his visit like the confident soldier he had been. Pride – that's all he needed, Colonel Windsor recognised: restore his pride and he'll see sense.

'You don't want any of this charade, Tubby,' he went on. 'You don't want to have anything to do with it. You're too fine a soldier to be dragged down. You have your record to consider – a sterling record, old chap, I don't

13

have to tell you that – and you have your self-respect and your pride. These are things you can't afford to lose, not at this time of your life. So you resign on medical grounds.'

He stubbed out his cigarette in the already half-full ashtray, inserted another into his holder, and slowly lit it.

'It's the only dignified way out. It's the only dignified way of telling them that you're not going to be made a fool of any longer and you're not going to be dragged down to their level.'

It had been the right advice – Colonel Windsor knew it was – and Tubby had promised to take it. That at least was something to congratulate himself on, but there had been nothing else in the encounter to afford the Colonel any consolation. The implications of the Black and Tans' behaviour and of the complicity of the Government in their reign of terror had been clear for some time, but Tubby's experience had brought it all into sharp focus. Ireland had been slipping out of Britain's grasp – Sinn Fein had almost swept the board in the local elections, they had set up their own provisional government in Dublin and in some areas of the country theirs was the only authority recognised – and, on top of all that, in September alone there had been over two thousand IRA arms raids. The Colonel knew there were only two possible answers to that situation: massive repression or get out. The Government had in its wisdom decided on the former – hence the Black and Tans. Colonel Windsor was a soldier, not a politician; he mightn't like the choice, but his duty was to make the best of it.

He lit a fresh cigarette, screwed his monocle more firmly into his eye, and took out his pen. His only concern was for his own men and for the standards and traditions he expected them to live up to. The British army garrisons had stayed aloof from Black and Tan outrages; and the IRA, in concentrating their attacks on the Tans and the RIC, had seemed on the whole to recognise that. But already there were signs that the mood was changing, that to the people all uniforms were alike; the Army was now being tarred with the same brush as the Tans, and its

14

patrols – as his own men had recently learned – were no longer immune from IRA attacks.

Colonel Windsor took a sheet of paper from his desk and wrote out the day's Orders:

Friday, 12 November 1920
To all section commanders

Special General Order

Section commanders are warned that the severest disciplinary measures will be taken against any sign of looting or retaliation. These are breaches of conduct which would merit the death penalty if the Army were on active service. If police operating with troops begin to engage in reprisals, the commander of the troops will withdraw his men, after giving the police due warning of his intention.

(Signed) ERIC R. S. WINDSOR
Colonel-in-Chief
16th Infantry Division

That, the Colonel felt, was the most he could do.

As Colonel Windsor laid aside his pen, dawn was breaking murkily over the County Longford village of Granard, some 150 miles north of Cambridge Barracks. Longford was far from Owen O'Clery's usual haunts in the south and east. It was a county he wasn't familiar with, and Granard he didn't know at all. Not all that distant from the rocky stretches and barren wastes of Mayo and Connemara, Longford mightn't be the most profitable place for a wandering fiddler, Owen thought. And if it wasn't profitable it mightn't be welcoming, either. Not that he was inclined to blame its inhabitants for that. Struggling peasants they'd be for the most part, trying to keep body and soul together in difficult times. It wouldn't be their fault that there wasn't enough to go round. They

15

had always had it hard. Wasn't it in the first cousin of just this sort of place that two centuries earlier another wandering fiddler, the blind poet Raftery, had composed his famous lament about 'playing music to empty pockets'? God be trusted, Longford and Granard wouldn't be as bad as that. Still, if there were villages in Ireland these days where a man might be in danger of meeting the same ill-fortune face to face, Owen feared he was getting near them.

Not but that he ever needed much. For bed a roadside ditch in the summer, a barn or hay-loft in the winter was all he sought, while for food and drink a farmer's wife never begrudged him the plate of bread and potatoes washed down by a mug of tay. And it was seldom his tunes failed to draw the odd penny from a shopkeeper's pocket or, indeed, a bottle from the publican to sustain him to the next village. The open road was all he knew; he had spent forty of his fifty-five years tramping it in every kind of weather with only the fill of his pipe for company.

He wouldn't stay long in Granard. The way things were, it was best to keep on the move. But where could he go? Dublin had the richest pickings and the south was hospitable, but they were too disturbed for his liking, and getting worse. He had seen enough terror there to last him the rest of his days. He had seen fear, and bravery, too, and savagery and oppression, homes burned down, wheels smashed off carts and farm implements so that the land could not be cultivated, crops ruined – he had seen it spread everywhere and he didn't want to see it any more. Even if there mightn't be much for him in these parts, be it without strife that little would have God's blessing on it.

He couldn't complain, anyway, about his first night's lodgings in Granard. He had reached there late after a long tramp from Ballyjamesduff in the next county. It had been a cold evening, heavily overcast, not a splink of moonlight to pierce the darkness of his last few miles. Still, he had been treated fairly in Ballyjamesduff, so that he didn't need to go seeking his next bite before breakfast. Just as well, for with the state the country was in people would be wary of a stranger who'd come knocking on

16

their door at an hour when they might be warm and snug at the gates of dreamland. Time enough and soon enough to greet them in the morning's light when the men would have said their prayers and the womenfolk would have been to Mass and a stranger with a fiddle might be a welcome diversion from the day's chores. Until then a safe shelter under a dry roof would be Owen O'Clery's sufficient address and a good night's rest would fit him to take Granard's measure.

The safe shelter he had found on the edge of the village could not have been more comfortable, for all that on awakening and having his first lightsome look it struck him as a mite strange. But the shed at the side of the road had been unlocked, and when he peered into it the outline of the covered carriage he had been able to make out in the darkness promised adequate protection and a degree of comfort. A degree of comfort it had certainly provided. He had climbed in and settled himself down with a sigh of contentment at the way the softness and smoothness of the upholstered seats favoured his weary limbs. He felt he might have been a lord, or at least a prosperous shop-keeper about to be driven to his mansion – except that there was no horse. The horse, he reflected, was probably asleep in his stable. 'And so should yourself be, too, Owen O'Clery,' he had muttered as he laid his fiddle-case on the opposite seat, curled himself up and was immediately transported to his own dreamland.

Now, in the reluctant dawn light, he stood eyeing the carriage and rubbing his grizzled chin. The gleaming black exterior with the polished silver lamp-brackets and the forbidding curtains within that could be drawn to hide its occupants from prying stares told him it was a mourners' carriage he had spent the night in. He smiled to himself. 'Better that than a coffin,' he whispered, adding as he leaned in to retrieve his fiddle: 'And if my coffin is half as comfortable 'tis a smooth journey I'll be having to Paradise.'

Straightening up, he heard a sudden peal of church bells cleave through the silence. It was a welcome sound. The village would be awake, he could get Mass himself

17

and no doubt his breakfast, too, from a kindly worshipper. It looked as if St Christopher, the patron saint of travellers, had been watching over him and had guided his steps to Longford and Granard. He might linger a while in this village after all. And if he did itself, he thought, as he doffed his cap to the carriage and shook hands with one of its shafts in mock farewell, at least he had reserved select accommodation where no one was likely to disturb him.

Pulling open the shed door he poked out his head to see if anyone was about. He sniffed. He sniffed again. There was no mistaking the smell. Burning. There was a fire somewhere. Was it some other traveller, camping nearby perhaps, and brewing his breakfast mug? The presence of a rival could blight his own prospects, and if he happened to be from the locality, then Owen O'Clery told himself he might as well be moving on immediately.

He looked around. There was no one in view. Twenty paces or so beyond the shed the road twisted out of sight, and it was from that direction the smell of burning was being carried by the breeze. Above the bare-branched trees on the edge of his vision he could see clouds of smoke. That came from more than a few crossed twigs and dry leaves. That was a real fire. Tucking his fiddle-case under his arm he set out to find it.

'Mother of God!'

The words, both exclamation and prayer, were forced out of him as he reached the bend in the road and came on the village of Granard.

The sight that met his eyes sent a spasm of horror through him. He took a few steps, then suddenly weak with shock he reeled and collapsed on the road, his fiddle-case falling from under his arm.

'Oh Jesus!' he groaned. 'Oh Jesus, Mary and Joseph!'

At the other end of Granard's single short street, cottages on both sides were ablaze. Black smoke gushed out of open doors and through windows and roofs only to be suddenly consumed by tongues of fire that licked heavenwards, raising up their flaming fangs like the arms of satanic dancers placating some obscene god. Beyond

18

the twin pillars of fire eating their way towards him and throwing billowing curtains of smoke across the road Owen could fitfully see the gathered villagers clinging to each other in terror. Their wails and screams rose above the crackle of their burning homes and were made even more blood-curdling by the clangorous din of the church bells that frantically appealed to heaven for aid. Some of the womenfolk had turned away, unable to look. Others had drawn their shawls across the faces of their children to shield their eyes from the sight. A straggling line of men feverishly passed to each other splashing pails of water from a roadside pump where a perspiring youth, naked to the waist, was madly working the handle to keep the chain of buckets supplied. But what struck like an ice-cold knife into Owen's heart was the group of six or seven men standing in the middle of the road, between him and the fire, laughing and jeering at the villagers' puny efforts to save their homes. He knew only too well their dark trousers and khaki coats.

'The Tans!' Owen breathed. 'Oh Jesus, the Tans!'

Suddenly one of them turned and saw him. Owen tried to rise, but his legs were like lead and kept getting entangled in his long coat. It was no use – even if he could have got to his feet, he knew he'd never be able to escape. Already the Tans were running towards him, guns being waved menacingly in case he tried to get away.

As they surrounded him, eyes red-rimmed and faces glistening from the heat of the flames, their whooping cries added to the pandemonium and it seemed to Owen as if he had already died and retribution for the sins of his life was about to be exacted by Satan's minions. Weakly he crossed himself.

'Hi, Captain, there's some old bastard here sayin' his prayers. What'll we do with him?'

One of the Tans raised his rifle, and Owen closed his eyes, cringing away from the blow. The weapon descended with a thud. But it was Owen's fiddle-case, not his skull, it was aimed at, and as the lid flew open the Tan pounced on the fiddle and bow.

'Wotcher!' he shouted as he scraped on the strings.

19

'How about a little victory dance? Come on, take your partners there.'

Gleefully two of his companions linked arms and cavorted around Owen, drawing their guns with their free hands and wildly shooting into the air. Their maniacal screeching, the exploding bullets, the crackle and thunder of the approaching flames, the hammer-blows of the still booming church bells and the nerve-rasping wailing of the fiddle whirled around Owen's head, but even that maelstrom of noise could not drown the cries of the villagers.

'You can't bleedin' play that thing,' a prancing Tan shouted, grabbing the instrument and throwing it onto Owen's prostrate body. 'Come on, you. Give us a tune there, a proper tune,' he demanded. A wave of his gun made Owen reach desperately for the fiddle. He struggled to his knees, but the menace of the leering faces surrounding him drained the strength from his limbs, so that when he tried to draw the bow across the strings the result was a tuneless scratch.

'Come on, up! Get up!' one of the dancers ordered; and then, turning to another of the group, he said: 'No malingering allowed. Right, Captain?'

For answer the Tan addressed drew his gun and fired into the ground at Owen's feet.

'On your pins, Nero,' he bawled, taking hold of Owen and jerking him upright. 'Give us a tune. A good dancing tune now, or else you might be dancing yourself on the end of a rope.'

The fear which before had turned Owen's limbs to water now suddenly galvanised him. If he didn't want a beating, or worse, he'd have to pander to these monsters. He rose to his feet and struck up a reel.

The Tans immediately began to prance around him, laughing and howling. One of them broke into a war-dance like a Red Indian and the others followed suit, but their captain quickly intervened.

'Hey! We don't want any of your bleedin' Irish jigs! Give us some real music, something civilised. That right, lads?'

'Right,' the others shouted, echoing his demand.

'Give us a good old English tune,' came from one of them.

'I don't know ... I don't know any ...,' Owen stuttered. The circle of grimacing faces thrust themselves at him, guns and fists roughly bruising him as the calls for something English were repeated. The approaching flames were nearer now, and beyond them he could see the villagers trying to peer through the smoke to make out what was happening. A few of the men were pointing at him, struggling as if to go to his aid but being restrained by their companions and womenfolk. It was an awesome sight to Owen – the charred and burning cottages almost totally engulfed, the huddled families powerless before the wanton destruction of all they possessed, their torturers still encircling him, screaming out the names of tunes he had never even heard of. But, even if he had known one, he still wouldn't style these beasts by playing it. The fear was banished from his heart by pity for his fellow-countrymen and anger at what was being done to the little village of Granard that he had thought would be a haven of peace. He'd play – yes, but he'd play for *them*, for these stricken people; he'd play something *they'd* know, something that might lift their hearts in their plight and strengthen them to defy their oppressors.

He stiffened his legs, put the fiddle under his chin, and sounded the first notes of 'The Manchester Martyrs', a song in praise of three Fenians who had been captured in England and hanged over fifty years before. It was a ballad that since then had been sung and played in the streets and pubs of Ireland. That was a tune they'd be familiar with – oh, by God they would. It was a tune to give them heart and remind them that they were not alone in their suffering.

Owen played with all the strength and passion at his command. He saw the knot of people beyond the flames gazing at him in puzzled amazement, but they made no response. Then he realised that his music was being drowned by the noise of the conflagration. Without hesitation he started to walk towards them, despite the searing heat of the flames now only yards off. The shouts

21

and jeers of the Tans battered against his ears. He ignored them. He could feel the perspiration stinging his eyes, and his hands became wet and clammy as he strode on. Now he had drawn level with the fire, and as the villagers caught the air of his song he was quickly rewarded with the sound of their voices – men, women and children – lifted in unison.

'Attend you gallant Irishmen and listen for a while
I'll sing to you the praises of the sons of Erin's Isle –
It's of those gallant heroes. . . .'

Suddenly there was a shout from one of the Tans behind him. 'Jeez, Captain, listen to them. The bastard's playing a rebel song' – and immediately a shot rang out. The violin flew from Owen's grasp as the force of the bullet jerked him upright. For a second he stood, his arms extended towards the horrified villagers, before staggering a few steps and collapsing into the flames. With his last ounce of strength he tried to stretch a hand to his fiddle, but it was already burning fiercely. He heard its strings twang, snapped by the heat, and then he heard no more.

2

AS THE FIRST chimes of noon from the bells of Shandon broke over the pavements and washed into the busy shops, the people of Cork halted in their step or turned from what they were doing to cross themselves and murmur the Angelus prayer. For those few moments life seemed not to be quite the noisome beast it had become of late – the pale November sun was a warming coin in the palm, fear was forgotten, bloodshed cleansed away, losses solaced. The swell of responses seemed alone to fill the crisp air, even the rasp of soldiers' boots on the paving-stones went unheard. Then the sound of the bells faded and, like water suddenly released from a dam, vigour and brawl and bustle flooded back into the scene.

The revived activity made North Main Street whole-some once more to Boxer Sullivan. He was perched on the seat at the front of his open cart – the sides of which declared in now weatherbeaten letters 'JAS. SULLIVAN, VICTUALLER' – and alternately reined in his horse and then with his whip prodded its jittering rump. The fitful progress that resulted was the most the overcrowded state of the narrow roadway allowed. On each side were stalls heaped with fruit, vegetables, fish and other staples, behind which strapping black-shawled women bawled produce and price, oblivious of the packs of snarling dogs

23

and ragged children lunging in and out between them for whatever scraps they could scavenge. In both directions – south towards the Grand Parade and Patrick Street, and north to the quays – other horse-drawn vehicles threaded their way, wheels screaming, drivers cursing and cracking whips, the while throngs of Friday shoppers darted from one side of the unpaved road to the other, dodging between carts and traps and under horses' necks as if they weren't there at all. And every now and again a Crossley tender carrying a company of Black and Tans, their guns held at a threatening angle, would butt its way through the press, its progress retarded – sometimes even brought to a halt – by as unlikely a variety of breakdowns and traffic jams as the doggedly obstructive citizens of Cork could improvise this side of outright rebellion.

The bedlam in no way flustered Boxer Sullivan. The return to normality after the Angelus hush made him feel that the all-seeing spirit which had for a while hovered doubtfully over his actions had now moved on. Reality's raw challenge, especially if it engaged muscle and pluck, was his more favoured companion. His nickname, his flattened nose, a crossed scar like an emblem beside one eyebrow had all been won honourably, in and out of the ring, and whatever suspicions he might have about the feelings – even about the suitability for the present assignment – of Denis Hurley, sitting back-to-back with him on the cart, he knew that *he* would be man enough for anything, *his* nerve would not fail.

The confidence of this self-knowledge sounded a note of cockiness, amounting almost to elation, as he remarked over his shoulder: 'It's tricky enough here. Probably be like this until we're past Wellington Barracks.'

'Well, just go easy. Don't take any risks,' answered Hurley. Advice rather than command, apprehension riding authority was dominant in the urgent tone.

There was a third passenger in the cart, but he said nothing. He was lying on his back at Hurley's feet, hedged in by fruit-baskets, potato-sacks and bags of meal. His body was completely buried under a dirty rug, part of which Hurley held with one hand, ostensibly to cover his knees from the wintry air, but more particularly to hide his other hand in which was a gun pointed straight at his prisoner's head.

The gun troubled him. He had been in the unit over six months now and this was the first time he was seeing action, the first time he had been entrusted with a weapon – apart from a few training sessions. It was too long to go without being blooded. The right time would have been immediately after he had joined, when he was still almost dizzy with anger at the way the city's Lord Mayor, Tomás MacCurtain, had been murdered. A squad of armed and masked men had broken into MacCurtain's home one night in March and shot him dead in front of his wife and children. The assassins had never been traced, and the British authorities had said they were Sinn Feiners; it was a stupid accusation, for MacCurtain had been a staunch Republican himself, so nobody had any doubt that the killers were Black and Tans. The coroner's jury had even brought in a sensational verdict, that 'the murder was organised and carried out by the Royal Irish Constabulary, officially directed by the British Government, and we return a verdict of wilful murder against David Lloyd George, Prime Minister of England. . . .' It was a verdict which had fired many a nationalistically minded but hitherto passive young Irishman to join the IRA, and it had prodded Denis into convincing himself that the time had come for him to stop wavering and take an active role in his country's struggle. Since joining his local unit, however, he had been given nothing to do but monotonous night drilling in almost inaccessible fields with shovels or hurleys as substitute rifles, dire shortage of arms and ammunition having restricted the unit to only two sessions of real firing practice.

The months of frustration had begun to drain his enthusiasm, until the arrest of Terence MacSwiney, MacCurtain's successor as Lord Mayor, and his death in Brixton Prison after seventy-four days on hunger strike banished at a stroke his returning doubts. Even so, two meagre sessions of firing practice in all that time were of little help in strengthening his nerve or stoking up his fighting spirit. Anyway, practice was different. It wasn't the real thing. *This* was. And the gun he held now, pointed at an unarmed man's head – its menace was chillingly different from those few target practices. Then it just shot bullets at a tin can. It missed mostly; when it did score a hit there was a screaming ping and no more. Not like a human scream. And no blood. No gasps. No pleading eyes. He had hardly noticed its weight before. Now it was leaden in his hand. It threatened him as much as it did his victim. It would kill at the pressure of a finger on the trigger. *His* finger.

He stirred himself and shivered into alertness. He'd need to keep his senses sharp and try to put any such callow thoughts quite out of his mind. It was probably the tension that had him jittery. Most action was bound to be like this – a span, long or short, in which one did nothing – could do nothing except be at the mercy of one's nerves – and then the moment, the test....

He shook himself again and nudged Boxer.

'What's it like ahead?' he asked. Sitting with his back to the way they were going was unsettling. He was supposed to be the leader in this assignment, but how could a man lead going backwards? Hardy should have thought of that and found them some more suitable conveyance.

'Much the same as it is behind,' Boxer replied. 'Don't worry, we have bags of time.'

They were passing over North Gate Bridge, and below them the River Lee flowed on to Cork harbour and the open sea. Denis loved the river, had loved it as long as he could remember. As a child he had been taken by his father for walks every Sunday always along the banks of the Lee. Sometimes they would stroll under the leafy canopies of the Mardyke, where the river was not a river at all but a stream – his father used to say that you couldn't even call it a branch of the Lee, perhaps a twig at best – often dried-up in summer and so narrow that he could nearly have jumped across it if he had been allowed; at other times their route would take them down the Marina where the river was a broad rink-like expanse that copied in shimmering reflections the haughty hills of

26

Montenotte drawing themselves up from its other side. Ships – two- and three-masters – would frequently glide by as if on skates, coming from or going to the river's mouth. The city's motto came to mind: *Statio bene fida carinis* – 'A good and safe haven for ships'. For ships maybe; not for people. Not nowadays anyway, be they Irish or British – or even neither. He resisted the temptation to look under the rug and see how his prisoner was getting on. They weren't out of the woods yet – far from it. There were still soldiers patrolling, and as the cart turned right into Pope's Quay they came under the scrutiny of a Royal Irish Constabulary man on duty at the corner. Boxer Sullivan chose that moment to pull an apple from his pocket and polish it on his coat.

'I'll save you the heart,' he joked.

Denis didn't answer, but 'Wouldn't doubt you, boy,' the local catchphrase denoting approval, rose silently to his lips. Lucky Boxer! This assignment was eating and drinking to him. But, then, Boxer not only had no nerves, he also had no qualms; the morality of their actions – of any action in the national struggle – was not a question he ever weighed. Not that he was stupid, just uncompli- cated. He believed in doing, and came into his own when he was free to renounce the responsibility of reasoning anything out and could trust himself entirely to his own reflexes. Denis envied him. If only *he* could accept things without question. But how could he possibly feel happy about the role he had been given? Kidnapping an old man for ransom was demeaning, sheer gangsterism. It had nothing to do with the struggle; it wouldn't help beat the Black and Tans. Hardy had said it would – not that Denis would believe a word from Hardy, even if he *was* the unit Officer-in-Command. 'Headquarters in Dublin has OK'd it,' Hardy had assured him, but Denis did not believe that, either. 'HQ need the money for arms, and this is the safest way.' Yes, Denis knew how precious arms were. What guns the unit possessed had been captured in raids on isolated police barracks or ambushes on convoys in which men – his comrades – had willingly risked their lives. Certainly without guns they had no hope, they might as

27

well give up. The more weapons they could capture – or preferably beg, borrow or buy – the better their chances. And it was known that some of the Royal Irish Constabulary were ready to do business if the offer was tempting enough. That made money in a way as important as guns – if they could find enough. But kidnapping for ransom.... The whole exploit had all the marks of Hardy's twisted mentality. 'Old Josh, Iron Josh, he's your mark. As rich as Rothschild. And, anyway, it was from the British he made his money, selling them scrap iron during the war, so it will be an extra pleasure to make him cough up that sort of loot.' It had been useless for Denis to protest that Iron Josh was an outsider with no involvement in their cause one way or the other. Not even an Irish outsider, but a foreigner – a Jew. Why kidnap a Jew? 'Because he's rich. He won't miss the money. And it's an old Jewish custom – buying their safety with their wealth. Jews never fight; they just pay up. You'll have no trouble with Josh Cohen.'

Iron Josh had certainly given them no trouble when they had driven into his yard at the back of Old George's Street and ordered him to climb into the cart. Few words had been spoken – Denis had been glad of his gun's eloquence as he found his own voice suddenly unreliable. He had made Iron Josh lock up before they left – Hardy had told him that on winter Fridays the Jewish sabbath commenced in the afternoon, so no one would be surprised if the store was closed extra early. Oh, Hardy was a crafty planner all right, you'd have to give him that. But Denis had been totally unnerved by the complete lack of fear or even concern the Jew had displayed at the sudden sight of the gun. Calmly he had removed the black skullcap from the back of his head, replaced it with a bowler hat, and donned a heavy overcoat. He might, indeed, have been finishing his week's work and locking up to go home and celebrate his God's sabbath. Denis didn't remember what happened to the bowler hat after the old man had laboured to haul himself up into the cart and, in response to a wave of the gun, had carefully stretched himself out on its messy floor. He supposed it was somewhere under the rug, perhaps held on to by old Josh as some sort of comforter.

Boxer had been steadily bowling along the quays, where the traffic was less congested. They passed lock-up stores, splendid Georgian terraces, and the stern front of St Mary's Church with its massive columns which had always seemed to Boxer like the fingers of an upraised hand ordering him to halt, enter and say a prayer. A touch of restraint on his horse's reins to reduce its gallop and an extravagant sign of the cross were the best amends he could make this time for his inability to comply. Once out of its range, however, he quickly whipped the animal on again and was soon able to announce: 'The Barracks coming up.'

Denis tightened his grip on his gun. This was a danger-point. With the city in such a ferment, they could be stopped on a whim by police or soldiers. He looked hard at the outline of the body under the rug. Its only movement was a regular tremor in unison with the rhythm of the cart. Still, he couldn't take any risks. If Cohen showed the slightest inclination to get up or cause a commotion, he'd have to knock him out – swiftly and silently. To forestall any such eventuality he bent his head down towards the rug and growled into it, as loudly as he dared, 'One move from you and you're a goner,' underlying the threat by prodding the body with his boot. There was no response. It appeared that Josh Cohen had no intention of giving them any trouble – just as Hardy had predicted.

Boxer was forced to reduce pace at this point by the congestion of traffic in and out of the Barracks. Police and army vehicles were interspersed with civilians' traps and tradesmen's carts, the latter having to submit to careful scrutiny before being allowed to enter the Barracks square. There was even a gleaming newfangled Ford tractor, the racket of its engine filling the air and little jets of steam spurting from its radiator like the darts of hot breath expelled from the nostrils of the horses in the street.

'I suppose that's from above in the Marina,' Boxer commented.

Denis nodded. The building of the Henry Ford factory on the Marina had been started a few years before; and Denis, whose regular walks to Blackrock – solitary now that his father was no longer there to accompany him – took him past the site, had watched its growth from the first brick. He knew that what he was seeing meant jobs for Cork, wage-packets for its workers, money for its shopkeepers, business for its tradesmen; but, more than that, more even than the commerce that would result on a national scale, he saw it as history in action. Henry Ford's family had been born just outside Cork city and had emigrated to America, he himself had become a multi-millionaire and now, as a national benefactor, was perpetuating his name in his ancestral home town. Already it had its place in local balladry. Denis smiled to himself as he thought of the jingle going the rounds:

> There was a little man and his name was
>   Henry Ford,
> He took a bit of rubber and an old piece of
>   board,
> He got a pot of glue and an old tin can
> And he stuck them all together and the damn
>   thing ran.

How many other exiles like him would his example encourage? Ireland would have need of plenty of 'money from America' when its day of freedom dawned. And yet, if it had not been a conquered repressed country from which so many of the flower of its youth were forced to escape, would Ireland have been able to produce sons like Henry Ford? It was almost a treasonable thought, and Denis was relieved when Boxer, observing that the tractor was a 'queer-looking contraption', drew him back to the present.

They were proceeding at no more than walking pace past the numerous hut-like structures around the peri-meter of the Barracks, and Denis kept his gaze resolutely in front of him. It was a building he didn't particularly want to see, though he didn't imagine he could ever succeed in burying its memories and associations.

'You know that place well, I'm told,' Boxer ventured.

'What do you mean?' But Denis knew what he meant, and Boxer's comment brought home to him the fact that even if he were able to blot out its significance he wouldn't be allowed.

'Wasn't your oul' fella stationed there?'

It was a statement rather than a question, more information-seeking than accusation.

So you know, Denis reflected resignedly. You all know, the whole unit. He wasn't really surprised. He had guessed that Hardy wouldn't keep that titbit to himself. Denis had had to reveal it when applying to join – they'd have found out anyway that his father had been in the RIC. And of course that was why Hardy had taken against him, why he had left him on the sidelines any time he picked a team for some action, why he had now given him a job that he knew anyone else in the unit would have balked at. But he didn't need to give it to anyone else – no one else was flawed in the way Denis was, no one else's loyalty gave grounds for doubt and therefore for the most unsavoury of tests. 'You wouldn't want to fail first time out, would you?' Hardy had urged as he signed out the gun and ammunition to Denis. 'You know what to do. I'll expect you back with the money. Or without the Jew.'

Denis wished that his father was still stationed in Wellington Barracks. Far better even that than where he was now – stretched six feet deep in a foreign grave. Boxer hadn't pursued his question, so he must know that, too. Of course he did. Denis could imagine Hardy telling the others in the unit about Hurley's old man, such a reliable, dependable, loyal, *Irish* subject of King and country that he answered His Britannic Majesty's call to arms and fought across the seas under the British Crown for the rights of small nations! That was just how he'd tell it; Denis could hear the tone of sarcastic relish in his voice.

Reliable, dependable, loyal – what did such labels mean? They could be turned inside out, like those optical-illusion drawings of a cylinder that could be made to

31

appear either concave or convex, depending on how one focused one's gaze. And love? Admiration? The rhythm of the cart, moving once more at a steady pace, rocked the kaleidoscope of memory. He could recall – how old was he then? ten? eleven? – regular visits to the Wellington Street Barracks canteen where, list clutched in his hand, he did the weekly shop while his father was in the orderly room. Things were cheaper there than outside – butter, sugar, candles, tea, fruit – and he felt grown-up, puffed with self-importance, at being allowed with all those policemen, seeing them taking their ease, sitting at table, drinking, smoking, laughing, playing cards, some with their coats off and braces showing. They were friendly, jolly men, his father's comrades. They asked him how he was doing at school, made up questions to test him, twitted him about imaginary girlfriends, and there was always someone who wanted to know if he was going to be an RIC man like his dad when he grew up. Of course he'd join the RIC. It was his dad's world, everything in it happy and unclouded, and Denis saw himself and his father patrolling its streets together.

After the shopping Denis would sit in the orderly room, watching his father write in ledgers twice as wide and twenty times as thick as his school exercise-books, or he'd gaze longingly at the Royal Irish Constabulary uniforms of his father's colleagues with their shining buttons and belts hanging neatly from pegs on the wall, the caps, the spiked helmets and the little pill-box hats of the cavalry police lined up, as if on parade, on a table along with whistle-chains, handcuff-cases and batons. He would touch the menacing batons very gingerly, withdrawing his fingers sharply from their hardness and flinching as he imagined the solid *clump* sound as a baton descended on someone's skull. That was a time when young and old had thronged the streets to welcome in a new century and, though anything with the 1800s about it was already as dead as history, it still took some years before the magical 19 in the date lost its strangeness and one could write it without a slight hesitation. That was a time when the proudest moment of Denis's young life had been being brought by his mother to Fitzgerald's Park to see his father, brave and bold and handsome in his dress uniform, standing firmly to attention with his company as His Majesty King Edward VII – who seemed to Denis like a huge teapot with his cigar puffing steam like a spout – and Queen Alexandra moved sedately among the flower displays at the Great Cork Exhibition. He had been proud of his father then, had admired him, had loved him – and had not needed to understand him. Now? Now he mourned him – but secretly. He hadn't dared take part in yesterday's Armistice Day service in the city in case he'd be seen by any of his IRA comrades. He didn't doubt there were many others also who had brothers, fathers or sons among the fifty thousand Irishmen slain in the Great War and who had to swallow their grief and mourn in private. The irony of it, considering the hundreds of fellow-Irishmen who attended Armistice Day ceremonies in the smaller towns throughout the country only because the Black and Tans had forced them to shut their businesses and turn out.

'How are we doin' for time?' Boxer's question suddenly shook the kaleidoscope again, and Denis was back in the present. He glanced at his watch and looked around. They were out of the suburbs now, skirting the graceful slopes of Montenotte on one side, the level river on the other.

'Not too bad. It's safe enough to put a bit of speed on from here.'

'Right enough, then' – and a ferocious crack of the whip electrified the horse into a gallop.

'That's funny,' Denis mused.

'What's funny?'

'That whip of yours. Wouldn't you think that a sudden noise like that – like a rifle-shot, I'd say – would startle a man if he wasn't expecting it? Yet there wasn't a move from our friend here.'

'Jesus, Denis, you don't think he's died on us? His heart could have given out.'

Denis lifted the rug and put his face near to Cohen's.

'Well, is he all right?' There was a note of real anxiety in Boxer's voice. 'Is he breathing?'

33

'Oh, he's breathing for sure,' Denis laughed. 'Would you believe it, the bugger's fast asleep, like a newborn babe.'

'Thank God for that,' Boxer grunted in satisfied relief. Denis, however, had his doubts. He bent low to examine his prisoner's face even more closely. Yes, he wasn't shamming; he was certainly asleep. Hardy had said he'd be no trouble. Jews don't fight, he'd said. They just pay up. Perhaps. But what sort of a man was it who could be kidnapped, bundled into a cart and made to lie on the floor under a rug with a gun at his head while being driven halfway across the city on a cold November afternoon – and then just calmly and quietly fall fast asleep?

3

'Soon. Very soon. Soon now. Soon.'

Abie Klugman's week's work was done. He was going home.

He relaxed his roly-poly figure in the cart and let his piebald pony, who knew the way home as well as he did, trot ahead through the darkness of the berry-lined road.

'Yes. Very soon. Very. Soon now.'

Abie spoke little to anyone apart from himself and various personages from his past and his future. The people in his past had been real once but, although that was a very long time ago, he had never been able to forget them or what they had done to his life. The people in his future were imagined, but to him not imaginary. They existed, too, somewhere, seeking him out in every corner, and if they ever found him they would surely drag him back to the terror from which he looked forward to escaping, finally and permanently, soon.

'Very soon. Soon now. Soon.'

But as the pony trotted on under the cloud-filled November sky the voice that soon stole into Abie Klugman's mind was not from his past or his future, but from his present.

'Klugman! Klugman! That's a good joke, Abie. You know what *klug* means?'

It was the voice of Mickey Aronson, who lodged in the small attic room next to Abie's in Ada Neumann's home at 17 Celtic Crescent. Celtic Crescent wasn't a crescent, and it was a long time since it had been Celtic. Built in 1881 to accommodate the employees of the nearby Rocksavage railway station, it was a straight terrace of some thirty tiny one-storey houses, each fronted by a strip of grass and hedged railings betokening the gentility of its original occupants. That gentility had, however, suffered a sea-change, for Celtic Crescent was now the centre of Cork's 'Jewtown'.

'Ada,' Aronson would insist to his landlady, *'you* know what *klug* means. "Clever". *Klug* means "clever". Would you say that Abie was clever?'

Abie Klugman had long grown used to the taunt – it was Aronson's stock joke for all of the ten years they had been lodging with Mrs Neumann, and he no longer minded it. He knew he was slow-witted; so many things that were simple for other people quite defeated him, and he was aware that this made him different – he had even heard himself referred to as 'not all there'. But, dull and wanting though he might be, he at least had dignity, consideration, *mensheskeit*. Never would he have committed the outrage of addressing his landlady by her first name.

'Mr Aronson,' she would respond in her mixture of Yiddish and English on hearing Abie taunted, 'don't be annoying Mr Klugman. *Luz em alein.* Let him eat his food. You like? Special *kugle ich hub gabakt. Ess.'*

To Ada Neumann her lodgers were not grown men but children, the only children she had ever had. Left penniless when her husband dropped dead suddenly one Monday morning as he was putting his horse between the shafts to go to the country on his weekly door-to-door round, her pride had not allowed her to accept for long the charity of the community's Board of Guardians.

'But you're entitled, Mrs Neumann,' Zvi Lipsky insisted, his watery eyes almost overflowing with frustration at finding someone evidently intent on undermining his whole function as Hon. Treasurer of the Board. 'You're entitled. Your husband was a member. Sixpence a week he paid. He never missed a week. You're entitled.'

Mrs Neumann shook her head. 'Keep it for those who need it. *Gott tzu danken,* I have my health and strength. I won't starve. I'll always have *tzu essen. Nu'* – and she searched in her purse and found the Treasurer a coin – '*he* paid every week; *I* pay every week.'

Treasurer Lipsky, the community's dentist, ground his teeth as he bowed to her adamantine will. Writing out a receipt he bethought himself of the verse from the Book of Proverbs: '*Eishes chayil....* A woman of virtue is a price above rubies.' A trial, too!

As soon as the *Shivah* days of deep mourning were over, Mrs Neumann converted her small front parlour into a shop selling basic foodstuffs and domestic items and set up a camp-bed for herself in a corner of the kitchen by the range so as to rent out the two attic rooms to lodgers. The dormer windows faced a high wall which hid railway storerooms and repair sheds, but the absence of dwellings on that side of Celtic Crescent helped to give the wider roadway an open aspect. Other Jewish families living in the warren of neighbouring streets where the rows of cramped houses confronted their twins at almost arm-stretching distance had no such suggestion of exclusiveness and seemed to encourage the natural ebullience of their inhabitants as well as confirming their more straitened circumstances.

To Abie Klugman, Celtic Crescent was more than just board and lodgings. It was a place where he was protected by the known and familiar, a refuge where each week the Sabbath, like a bride embraced, renewed his strength. While there, he was able to forget the ritual of Monday morning when, in the darkness of winter or the bright light of summer's early dawns, Celtic Crescent and the streets of Jewtown would be clamorous with the noise of horses being led from nearby stables and harnessed to carts, of men shouting instructions and calling to each other in Yiddish and English as they struggled under the weight of trunks and knapsacks stuffed to overflowing with clothes, fancy goods, kitchen articles, holy pictures, enlargements of family photographs – anything that

37

might be suitable for selling from door to door on a weekly-payment basis. Some of them would make their way to the railway station, but a few, having no horse and trap and unable to afford even the train fare, would travel on foot the whole week, often sleeping rough in the fields or in barns or farmhouses. Then on Friday they would stream back to Cork from all over the province of Munster to clean themselves up, don their best clothes, and go to synagogue to greet the Sabbath.

For Abie this Friday meant something special; there was even more than the Sabbath to return to. As he journeyed home in the early-morning gloom, he tried to fix it in his mind with words. Words made things whole for him, words were what he always aspired to.

'He is coming,' he muttered to himself, almost tentatively. Then again: 'He is coming.' After a pause he asked himself: 'Who?' The answer rose eagerly. 'Karlinsky. An important man. Berel Karlinsky. From the Jewish National Fund. To tell us about *Eretz Yisroel* – the Land of Israel.'

He rested for a minute, weighing Karlinsky's impending visit, dreaming himself into the spell of its promise. His eyes closed. A smile slowly puffed out his fat cheeks. The cart bounced on over the rutted road. He opened his eyes again and saw a vision of the land of milk and honey to which he and a small band of pioneers led by their Rabbi had for so long planned to emigrate. Anticipation was like a fever bursting through his very pores.

'To take me to *Eretz*!' he shouted to the empty fields round about.

He looked sharply to all sides, searching the banks and hedges, protesting 'Not! Not!' in a loud voice. To give the dream words would warn his pursuers. They might be waiting – waiting to snatch him from salvation at the very last moment.

Abie trembled, more angry now than afraid. Familiarity with the voices that had haunted him down through the years had encouraged a bravado that was little like his real self. The imaginary conversations he held as he travelled the country roads were not simply distractions to while away his lonely journeys but rehearsals of the arguments he would use to outsmart the hunters and send them back home empty-handed. But how would he know them? They might be dressed as soldiers – he had noticed with growing suspicion that there were far more soldiers on the streets in recent months – or they might just be posing as ordinary officers of the law.

Abie peered fixedly at the way ahead. In the half-light that was not yet day, roadside trees could conceal – could even be – the dreaded pursuers, caught up with him at last. He kept his gaze on one particular tree. Was it a tree? Were these branches or . . . ? Abie did not bother to make a closer scrutiny. It looked like a policeman. *Nu*, let it be a policeman. He was ready.

He drew in the horse's reins and waited silently, his eyes momentarily tightly closed. Words tumbled through his mind, and inside his head he could see himself – as if on a stage – daring the figure to make its business known. What new trap could it lay for him?

POLICEMAN: I'll have to search your cart, Mr Klugman.

ABIE: You have a warrant? (He didn't know what a warrant was but he had often heard locals use the phrase when the RIC came to search their houses.)

POLICEMAN: I don't need a warrant, Mr Klugman. By law I can search your cart if I want.

ABIE: What for?

POLICEMAN: I think you may be carrying arms.

This made Abie grip the reins tightly; the muscles of his neck knotted and grew as all his worlds – past and future, real and imagined – became jumbled together and in his confusion the voice in his head rushed out of his mouth.

'Who told you that? It was that *meshuggeneh*, Aronson. He's always at me. Every time I see him he says he's going to the police.'

There was no answer to his outburst. The wind in the trees and the whistle of his horse's breath were the only sounds to break the silence of the night. But Abie did not hear them. He had closed his eyes again and was once more listening to his voices.

POLICEMAN: And why should he go to the police?

ABIE: To tell them about my gun.

POLICEMAN: So you *have* a gun, Mr Klugman.

ABIE: Of course I have a gun. I had a gun before you were born.

POLICEMAN: But it is against the law for you to have a gun, Mr Klugman.

ABIE: My gun is not against the law – it is against the Russians.

POLICEMAN: Russians? What Russians?

Here Abie threw up his hands at the ignorance of policemen. He got down off the cart to pick a leaf from a roadside bush, and hoisting himself back into his seat resumed his journey, sucking on the leaf as he started to explain.

The story of the gun was the story of the most important part of his life, but it was a part too painful for him to describe coherently. Silence quickly overtook him as memory tried just to keep pace with the tumbling images.

The gun was a rifle, Russian military issue, assigned to him when he was conscripted into Tsar Alexander III's army on 17 August 1881. He remembered how he had been taken by force from his home in the Lithuanian village of Akmeyon when he was sixteen; how he was beaten and spat upon by the officers because he was a Jew; how he was forced to eat *treif*, and how his life in the regiment had been such a hell that he decided to desert.

Abie urged his pony on. The image of the policeman had faded back into the trees, the fear of pursuit was momentarily forgotten as he relived the saga of his escape. Stealing from the camp one night with only his rifle and iron rations, wading the river at the border, finding a sympathetic ship's captain to take him to Sweden, working there for a while and then making his way down through Poland and Germany and the rest of Europe, village by village, *shtetl* by *shtetl*, always moving west, America the ultimate goal, until he reached Cork. There he stayed, exhausted by his years of wandering, his mind unhinged by the daily terror of the sudden hand on his shoulder. All he had by then were the rags he stood up in – and his gun. That was something he would never yield up

– it was his protection if the Tsar's soldiers ever tracked him down and tried to drag him back to his regiment to be court-martialled and shot, which was what Mickey Aronson said would happen. So the gun went with him to the country every week, wrapped securely in sackcloth and tucked under the seat of his cart. It went into the farmhouses where he lodged overnight and where he was known and befriended. The farmers' wives indulged him in the harshness of his religious practices, never minding that he brought his own delph and cutlery and would eat only boiled eggs and bread. They thought it was all part of his evident 'foolishness'. 'Sure God save us,' they would say, 'isn't it soft in the head the poor man must be to be carrying round an old gun for to fight the Rooskies?' And out of compassion they would always buy something small from his stock of knick-knacks and fol-de-lols to help distract his thoughts and put some money in his purse. But nothing erased the images from Abie's mind. Even if it were true that the Tsar was long dead, as people said, Abie knew that no army ever gave up the hunt for a deserter.

Soon, however, that would all be over. He would go to Palestine with the others leaving the community. He had no skills – but what skills did *they* have? What skills did they need? Strength of limb, willingness of spirit – that would be sufficient. Abie was no youngster any more, but that much he had and he would accept any task he was given – eagerly and gratefully. Only let him reach *Eretz*; Palestine was his star of hope, his refuge. He would take nothing there, for he had nothing to take but himself; he would leave nothing behind – nothing except his gun. There he would need no gun, there no one would ever find him. Only let him reach *Eretz*. That was all he prayed for. Only let him reach *Eretz*.

'Jish ish my shixth jish morning, Mishish Cohen.'

The knife gripped between his teeth slightly distorted Rev. Levitt's articulation but did not inhibit his chatter, which rose above the shrieks of the fowls beating their

41

wings in panic against the coop and the even more frenzied squawking of the hen imprisoned in his hands. He pulled the bird's neck straight, smoothing away the feathers, then deftly swept the knife from his mouth and with one clean stroke severed the gullet. The squawking continued for a moment before dying out in a final gurgle as Rev. Levitt recited the prescribed blessing. Then he eased himself up from his straddle-legged posture over the small backyard shore, holding the cut artery open while the blood drained away.

'Finished?' Bertha Cohen asked as she emerged from the kitchen. The weekly ritual slaughter was too gory a ceremony for her to watch, though every time it took place she was reminded of how it always fascinated her daughters when they were children.

'Finished,' the minister confirmed as the last red drops fell. He balanced the warm bird in his hand, testing its weight, put his head on one side and suggested: 'Eight? Eight and a quarter?' His eyes danced behind their heavy spectacles, and the neat square of his moustache twitched with anticipation.

Bertha Cohen nodded, and Rev. Levitt smiled in self-congratulation. A man of small but many prides, he regarded the accurate guessing of a bird's weight as proof of his expertise. 'All part of the service, Mrs Cohen. All included in the charge.' The charge was reasonable enough – a few pence per bird – and with a community in which many families kept hens or whose menfolk were able to buy them direct from the country farmer Rev. Levitt's qualification as a slaughterer of fowls brought him a regular, if modest, bonus on his salary. Other extras were the fees received for circumcisions and for officiating at burials and weddings. Such events, however, were not very frequent – a whole year might pass without one – and so the only additional earnings he could usually rely on were his winnings at the weekly bridge school. They'd never amount to a fortune – not at a penny a hundred points – but at least they paid for a few packets of cigarettes. And soon Miriam Levy and Reuben Jackson were getting married; that was certainly something to

42

look forward to. Luckily for him they had decided to be married in Cork before going out to Palestine. A wedding was a great earner, for on top of the handsome fee which was traditionally the obligation of the bride's family the exuberance of the occasion invariably resulted in his being tipped quite generously by the groom's family as well. The thought of the forthcoming windfall reminded Rev. Levitt that his last wedding had in fact been that of Mrs Cohen's elder daughter.

'And your daughter, Mrs Cohen, how is she?' he enquired. 'Keeping well, I trust.'

'Which one? I have two.'

The minister was not put out by the note of impatience in Bertha Cohen's voice. He had long marked her down as a less than sociable woman who appeared to nurse some secret grievance.

'Ah, yes,' he smiled, 'but I know Judith is well. I saw her at the butcher's this morning. I meant Molly, the girl in Leeds. My last *kallah*.'

'She's all right,' Mrs Cohen grudgingly conceded.

'The happy event is very soon, yes?'

'Next month.'

'Please God everything will be fine and you'll be a grandmother.'

Bertha Cohen snorted as if to convey that she expected as little from grandchildren as from children.

Rev. Levitt finished washing his knife under the tap. He dried it, slid it into its sheath, and accepted the coins Bertha Cohen drew from her apron pocket.

'Well, Mrs Cohen, I won't keep you,' he said, not wishing to delay himself when he had more money to earn and no prospect of any worthwhile gossip from this quarter. As he tapped a cigarette on its box preparatory to departing, the front door – always on the latch – was opened and Judith Cohen came into the small kitchen.

'I'm finished, Judith,' Rev. Levitt told her. 'Just leaving. Good morning to you, Mrs Cohen.'

Bertha Cohen nodded briskly from the scullery sink where she was cleaning the blood from the dead hen's neck before plucking its feathers.

'"Good morning," he says,' she complained as Judith returned from accompanying the minister to the front door. ' "Good morning"! It's nearly afternoon already. What kept you?'

Disgruntlement always led Bertha Cohen to exaggeration. It was not yet eleven o'clock, but Judith did not argue. She knew her mother's moods; she recognised the strain of annoyance that drew the long delicate features of her face into a severe mask.

'Oh, it was the butcher's,' Judith replied. 'There seemed to be more people than ever there. And I was a bit late, so I had to wait a long time to get served.' Soft answer, she felt, might turn away wrath – whatever it was that was making her mother grumpy.

'There's a letter from your sister.'

So that was it. Judith glanced up at the mantelpiece above the range where letters were always left and saw the familiar blue envelope. It was over three weeks since Molly had last written, and the delay had angered her mother.

'What has she to do?' Mrs Cohen had been protesting with increasing frequency as day overtook day with no news. 'She has a husband who makes a good living. She has a fine home. She has a *shiksah* to do the housework. Yet she's too busy to write to her mother.'

'But she's having a baby, Mother,' Judith would point out. 'Her first baby.'

'She's having a baby! She's having a baby! What has that to do with it? It won't be for another month. Is she the first woman to have a baby? I had babies, too. Your sister was *my* first baby. Has she forgotten that? But she'll need me some day. You mark my words. She'll need me some day and then she'll be quick enough to write to her mother. Children I should have? Stones I should have!'

As Mrs Cohen sat herself down on one of the wooden kitchen chairs, a basin between her feet, and commenced with some savagery to pluck the feathers from the hen's carcass, Judith made no comment. She presumed there had not been enough news in the letter to compensate for

44

its late arrival. Better not read it immediately so – that might only start off another litany of complaints, and a strained atmosphere on Friday morning was one thing Judith wanted to avoid. Her regular shopping trip to get the food for the Sabbath was something she always enjoyed as the prelude to the best part of the week with its special evening meal, its rituals, her *zeide*'s stories of his life in Lithuania – no matter how oft repeated – and of course not having to go to work in her father's store. She hated even the slightest shadow to be cast over these few days. So better give her mother time to cool down and not stoke her anger further by trying to defend Molly. She knew it would be no use. What did it matter anyway? Molly had got out – got away from all the criticism and tantrums. Judith knew how relieved her sister was to have escaped. Molly said so in her letters – not those she wrote home but the ones she addressed to Judith at the store. Of course her father saw them arrive but he never mentioned them. Joshua Cohen was a man able to keep his own counsel – and other people's, too.

Those secret letters were in a way Judith's lifeline. She and Molly had always been close until Molly's marriage to Sol Stein, owner of a thriving factory in the rag trade in Leeds. Their closeness was less due to their nearness in age – though with only eighteen months between them it had been easy for them to grow up with similar interests and shared confidences – than to the fact that neither of their parents had ever made much of them. Their father had wanted a son – he had got one eventually, their young brother, Jacob; their mother had wanted aristocrats – attractive, shapely, superior ladies, royalty without crowns. Such a progeny she could have looked upon simply as reproductions of herself, who, when they grew up, would be sure to marry distinguished professional men. She would have basked in the reflected glory of their marriages; she could have boasted of her sons-in-law for ever more. But what had she got? As the years progressed and the girls grew from babyhood to childhood and on into girlhood and womanhood, Bertha Cohen could not prevent her early hopes from first wilting and then

45

withering: what she had got were two daughters who were replicas, not of herself, but of her husband. The same pugnacious jaws, the same steely eyes and, worst of all, the same muscular thickset build – they answered to nothing in their mother's self-portrait. By the time Judith was seven, it was quite obvious to Bertha Cohen that if she was to have any hope of achieving the enlargement of her life that she dreamed of she would just have to try again.

Jacob was still not the daughter she had set her heart on, but even though he was a male child he was, at least, physically recognisable as *her* offspring, and as he grew up he displayed artistic tendencies of a kind which she was sure could have flowered in her had she been given the chance. In his early teens he turned to reading poetry, then to writing it – and, though he showed his poems to his sisters, he kept them secret from his mother. Now, at seventeen, he was bowing to Mrs Cohen's wish and had entered University College to study medicine. One way or another there would be a professional man in the family.

If his mother's ambition for him was not discouraged by any of the family, neither had it occasioned much more than a passing interest. Joshua Cohen had long ago recognised that Jacob would never make a businessman and had quickly abandoned his dream of having his son join him in his scrap-iron store. Joshua's father, Moishe, the community's Rabbi, cherished his grandson and would have devoted what was left of his life to guiding him through the intricacies of Talmud and Gemara to the Rabbinate if Jacob had shown any vocation. But the patina of religiosity his demeanour had acquired through attendance at Hebrew classes and preparation for his bar mitzvah was quickly shed when the classes and his bar mitzvah had passed and early manhood overtook him. He found the teenage years confusing – college would at least provide a different background, new faces, fresh distractions and, eventually, the chance to shake off ghetto restrictions, to escape.

Escape was something Judith could not see in her own future. Marriage, of course, would be a way out but there

46

was no prospect of that. Besides, she didn't want to take such a step merely for escape's sake and perhaps find herself ending up as a prisoner in just another house in just another town. 'You were lucky,' she wrote to Molly once in answer to her sister's repeated urgings that she should come over to Leeds where there were plenty of young Jewish men who were starting businesses and wanted wives to help them. 'You took a chance and it has worked out and I am so happy for you. But I don't want that sort of marriage – no disrespect to your Sol, sister dear! Don't ask me what I *do* want. I wish I knew. I sometimes (no, often) feel that you are much more than eighteen months older than me. You are mature. You're a realist, like Daddy. I shall probably still be here when you're a *buba* sending your grandchildren over to spend their holidays with me!'

Now, as Judith started to help her mother prepare the Sabbath-evening meal, she continued to avoid mention of Molly's letter.

'The butcher's was so full, and of course nowhere to sit down while you're waiting. And that butcher gets ruder every week.'

Her mother's contemptuous sniff meant, Judith knew, 'What can you expect from a *goy*?' but that was too familiar a piece of bigotry to provoke her into argument. 'I'm always amazed,' she continued, 'that someone in the community doesn't open a kosher butcher shop. Then we wouldn't have this nonsense of having to get our meat through a Christian butcher twice a week. We could get it as and when we like. Planning meals would be so much easier.'

'Oh, what a *chachem* you are! Where's your sense? Do you think Watson could live just on what this little community buys from him? In two days we get everything we want and for the rest of the week he has his Christian customers. But a kosher butcher wouldn't have *goyim* coming into his shop, would he? And do you imagine he could make a living from our little community alone? *Ai*, what brilliant thoughts you have. A fine businesswoman you must make!'

47

Judith was well aware of the economics involved in the provision of kosher meat for Cork's forty or so Jewish families, but it was worth submitting to a lecture on it from her mother if it helped to make her more amenable.

'Dora Klein was there – more fussy than ever. Asking for extra liver for her visitor.'

'Ah, Karlinsky,' Bertha Cohen said. There was an edge of disdain in her voice which Judith presumed to be a comment on Mrs Klein, wife of the community's President, with whom Karlinsky would be staying. She watched as her mother spread newspaper on the kitchen table and swung the hen on to it with 'Here. It's ready for you.'

Judith rolled up her sleeve and commenced to clean out the hen's entrails preparatory to stuffing the carcass.

'Your *zeide* says he's a big man in the Jewish National Fund – that Karlinsky. A *baaleboss*,' Mrs Cohen observed.

'I suppose he's coming to make the final arrangements for the group going to Palestine.'

'Well, he certainly isn't coming to collect the Blue Boxes.'

'That reminds me. I didn't put my penny in yesterday. I'll do it as soon as I've finished the hen.' Judith glanced up at the blue and white JNF money-box, with the map of Palestine embossed on its face, standing on the mantelpiece next to Molly's letter. For the first time they struck her – both letter and box – as symbols of escape. Was that why a handful of Cork's Jews had decided to emigrate to Palestine? To escape? Of course no one gave that as a reason – except for Abie Klugman, and poor Abie didn't really count. No, they were Zionists, they were believers, they were responding to the call or answering a challenge. But Judith wondered if it was really as clear-cut as that. Perhaps Reuben and Miriam were secretly not happy with the prospect of raising a family in Cork. Perhaps Benny Katz didn't want to spend the rest of his life as a *viklehnik* – a weekly-payment collector. Who could blame him? And Sam Spiro – he had been like a lost soul since his wife died. Maybe he dreamed of finding

48

another wife in Palestine. Had they all in fact something to escape from, perhaps something they didn't even acknowledge to themselves? Was there a secret reason that made them hanker for a new life in a new world? But what about her *zeide*? Surely his determination to go to Palestine, at his age, was an example of pure Zionism. From what could *he* possibly be trying to escape?

As Judith finished cleaning out the hen for the next day's dinner, she made room on the kitchen table for her mother to prepare the Friday-night traditional meal of *gefilte* fish.

'Another month and they'll be gone.'

'So your *zeide* says,' agreed Bertha Cohen as she spread the hake, thoroughly washed and cleaned, on a wooden board and cut it into thick pieces which she liberally sprinkled with salt.

'I wish *zeide* wasn't going,' Judith said. 'It seems madness at his age.'

'You know how stubborn he is. If he says black is white, black is white. He's made his mind up.'

'But he's seventy-six. What can he do in Palestine?'

Bertha Cohen, judging that the salt was by now sufficiently absorbed, took the pieces of fish to wash under the scullery tap. As she returned, carefully drying each piece with a towel, she answered Judith's question.

'I'll tell you what he can do in Palestine. He can die in Palestine. To him that would be like dying in heaven.'

'That's something I just cannot understand. Why should he want to die in Palestine – away from his family and people?'

'You can ask such a question! What's his name? Moishe. What was Moses? A leader. He led the People of Israel out of slavery in Egypt, led them through the Red Sea, led them forty years in the wilderness and brought them safely to Palestine, *Eretz Yisroel*.' Bertha Cohen spoke slowly, as if recounting something by rote, her hands intent on the job of scooping out each piece of fish without breaking the enclosing skin. This operation, so delicate, captured the concentration of both mother and daughter and the conversation was temporarily

49

suspended. As each piece was released, Judith took it in charge to chop it up finely on the wooden board, then season it and return it to her mother.

'But, for goodness' sake, that was thousands of years ago,' Judith resumed. 'I don't see what connection there is.'

Bertha Cohen was silent as she restuffed each empty piece of skin, assembled the whole fish again, with the tail, in a dish, and put the dish into the range oven to cook. Then she sat down and shook her head from side to side at her daughter, disbelief in her eyes.

'You don't see what connection there is! Have you forgotten what it says in the Haggadah, what you read every Passover? Each Jew must imagine that he personally was brought out of bondage in Egypt and taken to the Holy Land. You can't imagine that, can you? To you that is all in the past, someone else's past, long ago. But to your *zeide* it is *his* past. You were never a slave in Egypt, but your *zeide* was.'

'You mean Lithuania?'

'Of course Lithuania. Who brought us here? Your father and I would still be in Akmeyon if it wasn't for your *zeide*. And most of the *Yiddin* in Cork – you know them, you know them all. Ask them. Ask them who brought them here. Who begged and argued and fought for them until they were free to go?'

Bertha Cohen turned her head aside, and Judith knew she was fighting back tears for her own family – her parents, her brothers and sister – who had not escaped. To Judith they were just faces in a photograph. Her mother had kept in touch with them for years, and Judith remembered that when she was a child her father had sent them money to have that photograph taken. Months later it had arrived in the post and since then it had stood, in its velvet frame, beside her mother's bed. The photograph was there, but where now were the people who had posed for it, stiff and unsmiling, in their clothes all washed and ironed for the occasion? Not long after it was taken, her mother's letters went unanswered. Had she had a premonition? Was that why she wanted a memento of her

50

family? Because she knew that now they would never escape and might not for long even survive?

'That was your *zeide*'s Egypt,' Bertha Cohen said as she packed her memories away again, blew her nose and determinedly rose from her chair. 'More than that I don't have to tell you. You've heard it all before and you'll hear it again.'

'So now for him it's really *Leshana habaa b'Yerushulayim.*'

'Yes. "To next year in Jerusalem." For him. That, too, is in the Haggadah. That, too, you say every year.'

'But it's only a prayer,' Judith suggested.

'Does a person pray for what he doesn't want?'

'But there are prayers and prayers. Some are just – well, just words and phrases. We don't actually mean them.'

'Speak for yourself, *mein kinde*,' Bertha Cohen said. It was an admonition more than a reprimand. 'Some mean them. Only by meaning them can you make them happen. To you it is a phrase because you've lived all your life at peace here in Cork. No suffering. No want. But other Jews ... the ones who have suffered like your *zeide* ... for centuries they have been praying "To next year in Jerusalem" and meaning it. Your *zeide* is a rabbi, a holy man. What every holy Jew prays for is to end his days in *Eretz Yisroel*. Now for many of them it is possible. Your *zeide* is blessed.'

Is that being blessed? Judith asked herself. To be allowed to choose where to die. Perhaps it is – for some. For holy men and patriots. Not alone Jews. She remembered a phrase from her Irish history lessons in the convent school most of the girls of the Jewish community had attended. What was it? Something the Wild Geese used to say – the Irish soldiers who had fled Ireland after that big battle at the end of the seventeenth century – when they were dying on foreign battlefields they used to say: 'Would that this were for Ireland.' *Bás in Éirinn*: 'death in Ireland' – the fervent wish of every true patriot, Sister Assumpta, their history teacher, had called it. How unexpected to find both the Jews and the Irish nourishing the same sort of dream. Yet it wasn't all that surprising,

51

was it? Two persecuted races. But there, Judith thought, the similarity ended. It seemed to her that the reason the Jews of Cork got on so well with their Catholic neighbours was because they were actually poles apart. There would hardly have been harmony between them if they had the same desires, if their interests coincided, if they were a threat to each other.

Bertha Cohen went out to the yard to release the hens from the coop, calling to Judith to bring some meal for them. Outside the air was cold, and in the small space almost entirely surrounded by walls there was little light. As Judith scattered the meal here and there, calling out 'Chook, chook, chook,' to the hens, she heard the Angelus bells ring. All over the city, all over Ireland, now, people would be pausing to recite a prayer. She didn't know what that prayer was but she wondered if they meant it or if to most of them it was ... just words and phrases?

Maybe she should say a prayer herself. But for what would she pray? Love? She had no idea what love was like and, if she didn't know what it was like, how could she know if she wanted it? There truly seemed to be nothing she really desired. Escape? Not even escape. She wasn't ready for that yet. If she had been, if she really hankered after it, she would have prayed for it long ago. But, then, while Molly was at home Judith had little cause to feel discontented. With Molly gone, it wasn't the same. Something – something more than just missing her – had been vaguely unsettling. Perhaps it was that being monotonously grumbled at by her mother and taken for granted by her father were becoming irksome when there was just herself. Or perhaps Molly's departure had in fact sown the seed of restlessness in her and the prospect of others – especially her *zeide* – emigrating to Palestine was beginning to nourish that seed and make it grow.

The Angelus bells ceased ringing and, the spell broken, Judith shook off her doubts. Returning to the kitchen she heard the sound of a horse and cart in Celtic Crescent and she went to the front door to look out. Just as she expected. It was the same every Friday: Abie Klugman was home for the Sabbath, always the first to return.

52

4

THEY HAD ALREADY BEEN almost half an hour inside the
barn. Disused, ramshackle, and whistling with draughts,
both its windows had been boarded up, and to obtain some
light Denis had had to leave the door open after persuading Joshua Cohen in by pressing the gun firmly into the
small of his back. Farm machinery covered what little
space there was, but it all seemed to be derelict or broken
beyond repair – rusted scythes, mould-encrusted harness
leathers, cracked buckets, discarded plough-pieces, an
axe-blade that lacked a handle. One corner of the barn
had already been cleared to make room for two kitchen
chairs placed facing each other, with an old tea-chest in
between. To Iron Josh, stiff and bruised after the discomfort of his journey in the cart, even a kitchen chair
had looked inviting. Without waiting for direction from
his captor he had sat down, his overcoat, muddy and
stained, pulled around him for warmth, and his bowler
hat, the crease of a dent in its crown, clamped on his head.
Denis had turned the other chair round and now
straddled it, his arms crossed and resting along its back,
the gun on the tea-chest within easy reach.

'It's a lot of money, two hundred pounds,' Joshua Cohen
was saying in a voice that was warm, amicable, almost
paternal.

'Don't be messing me about,' Denis warned as harshly as he could. 'Sure two hundred pounds is nothing to you.'

Cohen's eyes flashed with a sudden steely glint, and his eyebrows shot up. 'Oh? You know how much money I have, do you? You've counted it? Or perhaps you have friends in my bank, eh?'

Denis cursed to himself for his indiscretion. He took the gun and went to the door, checking that the horse and cart were still safely tethered. Boxer came out from the nearby farmhouse carrying a bag of oats and waved. Denis made no acknowledgement but before turning away he looked up at the sky, now completely hidden in dark cloud. There wasn't much time left – certainly not enough time to be taking the wrong tack with old Cohen and antagonising him. Anger tended to drown fear – that was a lesson he had learned himself. But what in the name of God was the right tack with such a man? It was easy for Hardy to say Josh Cohen would give him no trouble, that the Jew would come through without a murmur. He obviously didn't know Iron Josh. He couldn't ever have met him or else he'd have recognised the calibre of the victim he had selected. If he *had* known him.... But speculation wouldn't help. Denis just couldn't fall down on this job; he'd have to get the money somehow. After all, he had a gun and his captive was no tough aggressive youth who might be foolhardy enough to try to disarm him. Cohen had no means of protecting himself; he was an elderly Jew – well, perhaps not elderly but clearly past his prime – and it was most unlikely that he'd have the guts or the strength to attempt physical resistance. His obstinacy up to now might be all bravado. It *must* be all bravado. What alternative could the man possibly have to paying two hundred pounds for his life and freedom?

Denis returned to his seat, but before he could frame a new approach Josh Cohen started to drum his fingers on the tea-chest, looking about him and nodding his head in a calculating manner.

'I'll make a bargain with you,' he said. 'I'll give you twenty pounds for the lot.' He gestured around at the

54

conglomeration of abandoned implements, hardly any of which he could put a name on. 'It's a fair offer, believe me. Most of it isn't even scrap iron, but there may be a few pieces I could use.'

Denis almost gasped aloud in astonishment. He didn't know whether to laugh or scream. Such cheek! Was the man mad? Or bluffing? Or trying to be funny? But there was obviously no point in wasting any more time expecting to get results the easy way. If Cohen wouldn't co-operate, Denis would simply have to get tough.

'That's enough of this cod-acting,' he barked, pointing the gun at his prisoner. 'I want two hundred pounds and I want it now, or else....'

'Or else?' Cohen echoed.

'Or else you'll be locked in here until you decide not to be so stubborn.' The threat just might make him see sense. It was worth a try anyway.

'And if I still refuse?'

Jesus, how far would the maniac push him? Well, there was no going back now.

'If you still refuse' – and Denis levelled the gun at Joshua Cohen's heart – 'I'll just have to shoot you.'

He tried to keep his voice firm, but the thought of actually having to kill the man in cold blood numbed him. Up to now the possibility had seemed so remote as not to need consideration – an order given by Hardy as a matter of course, accepted by Denis as a standard instruction in an operation of this nature. But it had been inconceivable that it would really come to such a point.

In the silence that followed Denis was suddenly aware, for the first time since arriving at the barn, of farmyard noises nearby. Cattle lowed, there was a jingle of harness and the rhythmic suck-slurp of a horse's hoofs crossing muddy ground. The creak of a pump-handle and the answering gush of water made him feel his own thirst and taste his tongue's rancid dryness. He envied Boxer Sullivan waiting for him in the farmhouse, as like as not with a bottle of beer in front of him or at the very least a cup of tea. God in heaven, he seemed to do nothing on this job but envy Boxer and his easy role.

55

'Come on, come on,' he rapped out despairingly, conscious that – gun or no gun – he simply had no control of the situation and was struggling to stave off panic.

Josh Cohen was quick to respond. He raised his hands resignedly, nodded as if to himself, and then drew his wallet, along with some letters and documents, from the inside pocket of his suit. Methodically he straightened the collection of papers to fit it back into the pocket, and then opened the wallet and inspected its contents. He took from it a ten-shilling note which he placed on the tea-chest, smoothing out the folds to make it lie flat. Then, his expression quite impassive, he dug a hand into a trouser pocket and carefully, as if trying to hold fast to quicksilver, brought up a fistful of small change. He arranged the coins neatly in their denominations on top of the note, halfpennies and pennies at one corner, sixpences and shillings at another, two florins at a third, and a half-crown covering the last unanchored corner. It was a ludicrous ceremony to Denis, but he was mesmerised by it, powerless to interrupt. He looked at old Cohen. Silently Joshua returned his stare, then made what sounded like a snort which quickly became a chuckle until finally he exploded into outright laughter.

'What the hell is the joke?' Denis shouted at him.

'*Oi vey! Oi vey!*' Joshua gasped as his heavy frame shook. He started to wipe the tears from his eyes with the back of his hands. 'Why didn't you tell me before we left that you wanted two hundred pounds? I haven't brought much more than two hundred pence.'

'Shut up! Shut up!' Denis screamed as Cohen was about to go into a renewed bout of laughter. 'Don't try to make a fool of me. You don't think I expected you to have two hundred pounds on you, do you? What sort of a gom do you take me for? You have a chequebook. Write out a cheque and we'll take it back to town. There's time to cash it before the banks close. Come on now! Don't give me any more trouble.' He waved the gun menacingly.

Joshua smartly became serious again. He collected up the coins and put them back into his trouser pocket. He took out his wallet once more, along with the assorted papers and documents, and restored the ten-shilling note to its place. From among the papers he extracted a chequebook and, drawing his chair close to the tea-chest, he rested the chequebook on it, took out his fountain pen and looked up at Denis.

'Two hundred pounds?'

Denis nodded, almost unable to believe that Cohen was, after all, giving in, having had his little joke.

'Payable to?'

'Never mind that,' Denis urged him, anxious to get the whole business over with quickly before Iron Josh changed his mind again. 'Leave the name blank. It'll be filled in later.'

Joshua nodded. He took his bowler hat off and placed it on the chest. Then he screwed the top from his pen, opened the chequebook and wrote in it, quietly dictating the words 'Two hundred pounds' to himself. He tore out the cheque and handed it to Denis.

Denis, leaning over, half-raised from the chair, grabbed it in his hand and read it. He remained poised in that position as he jerked up his head.

'But you haven't signed it!'

Joshua Cohen calmly closed his chequebook and put it back, with his wallet and papers, into his inside pocket. He screwed the top back on to his pen and clipped that in beside them. Then he lifted his hat from the tea-chest, rubbed some dirt off it with his sleeve, placed it on his head and stood up.

'That's right,' he said. 'I haven't signed it. And I don't intend to. Now, my young friend, let us go home.'

Denis was furious; rage and humiliation at being toyed with like a small child drove out all caution. He rushed at Cohen, digging the gun into his ribs.

'Sit down. Sit down and sign that cheque,' he commanded, 'or you'll be bloody sorry.'

Joshua looked into his eyes, as if weighing up the strength of his anger and calculating the possible effect of even further defiance. The searching gaze was too much for Denis. To escape it he pushed Iron Josh back into his chair and resumed his own seat. He mustn't give in; he mustn't allow temper or panic to take over; he just mustn't break, no matter how great the provocation.

'Look, Mr Cohen,' he appealed, 'I'll give you one last chance to sign that cheque. If you don't, I'll just blow your brains out. I have my orders – come back with the money or without *you*. I have no alternative. It's up to you.'

Cohen smiled. 'If you blow my brains out, you'll have to do without the money.'

'If I have to do without the money,' Denis answered civilly in an effort to match his adversary's self-control, 'I'm likely to want the satisfaction of blowing your brains out. Besides, I told you my orders: the money or – a bullet.'

Joshua's demeanour changed again and he threw up his hands impatiently. 'You keep on talking with your gun. What do you think you have in your hand, Aaron's staff? I'm telling you, it is useless to you. Throw it away. It cannot make me change my mind, so if you intend using it use it and shoot me now. Otherwise you're wasting your time.'

Denis was frozen to his chair, the gun held fast in his hand. He could neither move nor think, as if all power had at a stroke been cut off from both body and brain.

Suddenly there was a step outside the barn and Boxer Sullivan appeared in the doorway.

'Are you all right?' he asked anxiously, seeing the gun pointed at Iron Josh. When Denis made no reply he asked again: 'Are you all right? Did you get the money?'

'No,' Denis barked back – and then, forcing himself out of the nightmare of his paralysis, he added: 'Not yet.'

Boxer was about to remind him that time was getting on but then thought better of it and withdrew. Denis's 'Not yet' might have been a hint that he was nearing success and didn't want any interruptions.

Left alone again the two men faced each other, but Joshua gave Denis no time to think about his next move. He pulled his overcoat about him, shivered exaggeratedly and, as if resuming a friendly conversation, complained mildly: 'It's cold in here. Don't you feel the cold, Mr ... eh?'

'No, I'm not cold.'

'Ah, it must be hunger, then. I had my breakfast at half-past seven. I get up at half-past six every day. An old habit. It's a long morning' – and he pulled out of his overcoat pocket a neatly tied brown-paper package. Ignoring Denis and the gun still pointed at him, he opened the string to reveal a mound of sandwiches, wrapped in greaseproof paper.

Jesus above! The man was having a picnic with a gun in his ribs. But Denis was past being surprised by anything Cohen did. Maybe he should try humouring him. He certainly wasn't going to get anywhere making more threats.

'Half-six?' he said. 'Why so early? And what do you do for an hour before you have your breakfast?'

'Morning prayers. Jewish morning prayers are very long,' Joshua explained, taking a sandwich in his hand. 'You are hungry, too? There's enough for both of us.' He leaned forward to offer the package to Denis.

'They're very good,' Iron Josh assured him. 'Cold meat. And Jewish brown bread. You've never had Jewish brown bread. My wife made it. She's a good cook, my wife. She bakes good bread. It's strong – like your beer. And mustard. I hope you eat mustard?'

Denis recoiled, as much from the sudden flood of talk as from the sandwiches which were now almost under his nose. He stared at the unfamiliar brown bread, dark brown with an even darker, almost black crust. When he still made no move to accept Cohen's offer, Joshua put the package on the tea-chest, held up his sandwich and uttered a short Hebrew prayer before putting it to his mouth. He chewed away for a few moments and then nodded with pleasure. About to bite into the sandwich again he stopped suddenly, as if only just realising that Denis still had the gun pointing at him.

'You wouldn't shoot me now, while I'm having my lunch, would you? At least wait until I've finished. I'll have a better stomach for it then.' Overcome by his own joke he broke into a fit of choking laughter until tears sprang from his eyes.

Denis flung down his gun in disgust. The man was

impossible. It was useless; there was no way he could master him, not at the moment anyway. He might as well let him finish his sandwiches.

Joshua, wiping his eyes with a snow-white handkerchief, continued eating and gestured to Denis to help himself.

'Try one. Tell me what you think of it.'

Denis hesitated for only a moment before surrendering to his instinct to meet kindness with kindness. Having discarded his gun it was awkward having nothing to occupy his hands, and he would feel even more foolish sitting like a dummy just watching a man he was supposed to shoot eating his lunch. Besides, he *was* hungry himself.

He took a sandwich as casually as he could, covering the embarrassment of his capitulation by asking: 'What were those foreign words you said a moment ago?'

'That was the Grace Before Meals – in Hebrew. "Blessed art Thou, O Lord our God, King of the Universe, Who bringeth forth bread from the earth." Short and sweet, no? Sensible. Who wants a long Grace Before Meals? Ah, but our Grace *After* Meals – now, that's another business altogether. Half an hour – at least: songs, prayers, loud prayers, silent prayers. By the time you've said the last blessing your food is digested.'

Iron Josh finished his sandwich and took another. 'What do you think? Good, yes?' He didn't wait for Denis to answer. 'Tell me, my young friend,' he went on, 'those orders you have to shoot me – if I don't give you the money you want – who gave you such orders?'

'Oh ... my boss,' Denis replied evasively.

'Your boss?'

'Well, my unit OC.'

'OC?'

'Officer-in-Command. Irish Republican Army.'

Cohen laughed. 'Army! How many men in your army?'

'Every patriotic Irishman is in the IRA – or supports it.'

'And you think you can beat the British by ambushes and blowing up police barracks?'

'We *are* beating them. And if we had more arms we'd

60

finish them off. We have them on the run,' Denis insisted. 'Why do you think they brought in the Black and Tans? If you read the newspapers, you'll see that we're winning.'

'I read more than the newspapers. I've read your history. The fighting Irish, you're called. Isn't that so? If you haven't anyone else to fight, you'll fight among yourselves. But you're wasting your time – and your blood. You can't beat the British Army.'

Denis was stung by Cohen's dismissive tone.

'Ireland is our country. Why should we be ruled by a foreigner?'

'I'll tell you why,' Joshua answered almost patronisingly. 'Because the foreigner was stronger than you and conquered you. And you're not strong enough to throw him out. It's not fair, but you have to put up with it. If you read more history instead of newspapers, my boy, you'd realise that's the way it has always been.'

'So you think we should do nothing,' Denis said, remembering Hardy's conviction that Jews don't resist.

'If you can get out of Ireland, find somewhere else to go to start a new life, then go. Others have had to do it – other people in other countries. Why not the Irish? If you don't, then you must make the best of living here. At least it would be better than throwing your life away.'

'But we can't do that, man. We just can't give up. This is our home. Wouldn't you fight for your home?'

'For my home, yes, if I had to. But what is my home? My home is my self, my body. I live in my body, in my family. That's my home.'

'And your country?' Denis asked.

'What's that? A piece of land where I happened to be born. A piece of land ruled by tsars, kings, princes, politicians – people I have never met. People I don't know and cannot influence. People who don't care about me – or about you. Is that what I should fight for? Is that all my life is worth?'

Denis was taken aback by the passion of Joshua Cohen's argument – and also by its bitterness. But, then, Cohen didn't have a country to fight *for*. He was a wandering Jew, a refugee, driven out of the land he had been born in. You could hardly expect him to be ready to defend it, or give his life for it. You could hardly expect him to regard it as his home. He didn't have a country, so how could he understand what Denis felt for Ireland? But what about Palestine? Wasn't it called the Land of Israel?

'Would you fight for Palestine?' he asked. 'Isn't it the place all Jews look on as their home?'

'Biblical home. Spiritual home. Something to pray for. It might have been that a long time ago, when people believed in prayer. But these prayers haven't been changed for centuries. Fight for it? How? The British rule it, just as they rule this country. How could we beat them? How could we even fight them? There are only a handful of Jews in Palestine. We would have even less chance than you and your IRA. It would be madness.'

Denis shook his head in denial and disbelief. Perhaps Hardy was right after all – Jews just aren't fighters. Money, not resistance, was their weapon. But, if that was so, why had Cohen resisted the threat to his own life? Why had he refused point blank to buy it off with money?

'You don't make sense. You say your life is too precious to give it up for any country and yet it's not valuable enough for you to pay me two hundred pounds not to shoot you. I don't understand.'

Cohen gave a self-satisfied smile. 'Of course I would pay two hundred pounds – two thousand pounds – every penny I have – to stop you shooting me. But you aren't going to shoot me, are you?'

'Who says I won't? I wouldn't be too sure of that.'

'No, my young friend, you won't shoot me. Not because you've shared my lunch – it's not a very big bribe, is it, a few sandwiches? But I don't think you've ever shot anyone, have you?'

Denis hesitated. The question was a trick. He couldn't answer yes because it wouldn't be true – and he didn't feel confident of being able to deceive Iron Josh; and he couldn't answer no because that would reveal him as the beginner he really was. He ignored it and said: 'What makes you think I wouldn't shoot you?'

Cohen stood up. 'When we reached here,' he said, 'I was

getting out of the cart and my hat fell to the ground. You picked it up and gave it to me. Perhaps you don't remember that, my boy. But that was your real nature, and it told me that nothing would make you kill an innocent man, a complete stranger, who had done you no harm. Not money, not orders, nothing.' He took the sandwich wrapping off the tea-chest and shook out the crumbs before folding it neatly and putting it into his pocket. 'Now let us go back. It's very cold here and it is getting late. It will be dark soon. Shabbos – that's the Jewish Sabbath – will be commencing. If I'm not home for it, my family will be looking for me. You don't want them to go to the police, do you?'

Denis did not move. This time, however, it was not indecision that held him, but relief – relief at not having to play a role any more. He knew he would do as Cohen had directed. That he had failed miserably in the role did not worry him – yet.

He looked down at the gun lying by his feet on the ground. Joshua, anticipating him, bent to retrieve the weapon and handed it to him.

'I'd better take it back,' Denis said, blushing at his carelessness. 'We're very short of guns and ammunition. That's what we wanted the money for.'

He went to the door, shouted, 'Boxer! Boxer!' and led Cohen out to the cart.

Boxer, coming at a run and seeing Iron Josh, took success for granted. 'You got it, then? Wouldn't doubt you, lad.'

Denis let the question pass. He'd have enough explaining to do later. 'Let's get back,' he said. 'And hurry. It's late.' He helped Joshua into the cart, sitting him on the floor again but this time leaning up against a wing, and tucked the rug under his legs. As he was about to sit down himself on the cross-seat, Joshua caught his arm.

'What's your name? I'd like to know your name.'

Denis hesitated.

'Don't worry,' Cohen assured him. 'I won't report you to the police. I give you my word.'

'Hurley. My name is Denis Hurley.'

'All aboard?' Boxer called over his shoulder, cracking his whip as they moved off.

At first Joshua took an interest in their route, peering into the gathering darkness in an attempt to identify some landmark. After a while he seemed to recognise his whereabouts and closed his eyes. Denis was slumped in his seat, his chin sunk into his chest. The abortive kidnapping had left him drained – too exhausted even to contemplate the consequences of his failure. Boxer alternately whistled and sang above the noise of the cart, familiar songs and ballads the words of which Denis allowed his mind to echo in a silent duet.

A tug at his trouser leg awakened him from his reverie. Iron Josh beckoned him down, and Denis knelt beside him in the cart.

'We're nearly at Tivoli. Put me off there. I'll walk the rest.'

When Denis started to remonstrate, Joshua interrupted him. 'I must. You see, it's very nearly the Sabbath, and a Jew is not allowed to ride on the Sabbath. Do not worry – it's not far to my home. Anyway, in case the police or the soldiers stop you, better for both of us if I'm not your passenger.'

Denis nodded and leaned forward to speak into Boxer's ear. As the cart came to a halt he jumped out to help Joshua down.

'Do me a favour,' Iron Josh said as he stepped on to the road. He opened his coat and got out the ten-shilling note from his wallet and the coins from his trouser pocket. He lifted Denis's hand and placed all the money in it.

'That's another thing a Jew cannot do – carry money on the Sabbath.'

'But what will I do with it?' Denis protested.

'Well, it won't buy a gun. Perhaps a few bullets? But give it to charity. If you don't take it, I will just have to throw it away.'

'I hope you'll be all right,' Denis said as he put the money in his pocket. 'Are you sure you'll be all right?'

'Yes, I'm sure, Denis Hurley. I'm sure. Now you must go.'

64

Denis jumped back into the cart, and Boxer immediately urged the horse into a trot. As they drew away into the darkness, Joshua Cohen stood and looked after them. Denis waved to him, and he returned the wave. The Hebrew blessing of thanks for deliverance from danger sprang to his mind, but without the requisite *minyan* of ten males to make the obligatory responses he was unable to recite it. That was another thing a Jew could not do!

He buttoned his coat and with firm long strides began to walk.

5

Though Father McGiff admitted to himself that he was no longer a youngster, he knew it wasn't his age that had him suddenly welcoming autumn and winter far more than he had ever welcomed spring and summer. There was nothing aesthetic or spiritual about his unexpected response: it was simple gratitude. He would stand at his study window before the open curtains, his bespectacled eyes blinking into the night and his lips parted, but motionless, until after an interval they would shape a soundless 'Amen'. Such oblations to the darkness of the early evenings had not been necessary in previous years when, whatever the season, bright hour and night hour had been dedicated to the service of his flock – there were Masses to be said, sick to be visited, meetings to be chaired, burial services to be conducted, bereaved to be comforted.

It had been an exacting treadmill, not at all what he had envisaged when, as a young priest, newly ordained, he had arrived in Cork from his County Longford village of Granard. His resolve had been to give himself up every evening to a period of deep meditation. It was a resolve he had fulfilled for as long as he could, relishing settling his mind on sacred thoughts and holy themes in an effort to make himself spiritually equal to the demands of his calling. But that had been all of thirty years ago, and very quickly these demands had multiplied, absorbing more and more time and energy, so that the moments of evening meditation were soon subsumed into the preoccupations and stresses of an active Christianity. Yet the exchange had been all gain, for this became the happiest, the most rewarding period of his life, when to lose himself utterly in God and His Work was truly to find himself. This was a time of real communion, and it was not long before his parishioners began to think of him, as well as to address him, as Father Brendan rather than as Father McGiff, and he began to look on them as his family, and on Cork, their city, as his only home.

He had returned once to Granard – to bury his widowed mother beside her husband in the hillside cemetery – and he knew that that would certainly be his last visit to the place of his birth. There would be no more family graves to warm the soil beside those of his parents, for no more was the name McGiff to be found in Granard. His sister was a member of an Order in Scotland and his five brothers, all senior to him, were scattered in various parts of Britain and America, and so the little village had nothing left to hold him. Too small even to be found on many maps, too hidden for any of its innocent affairs to be worthy of attention, Granard seemed no longer to be part of the priest's past. So far removed was it, both in time and in temper, from the realities of a large city parish and the growing bewilderment and tribulation that the first two decades of the new century had visited upon its inhabitants that his birthplace and its memories became as insubstantial as the tales of Cuchullain and the Red Branch Knights that he had read about in school. It was a faery world, a faery past, and for many, many years Father McGiff had given it neither thought nor tongue.

Time and its buried hoard, however, had only been waiting in the wings, and it was now that the priest was discovering just how perfidious Time could be. He began to notice how people deferred to it, seeking to mollify its tyranny: this business, for instance, of praising the compassion it displayed in healing old wounds. But it didn't always *heal* old wounds. What about the ones it reopens, he reflected bitterly, the old memories that, long dormant, it gratuitously stirs up until nostalgia becomes a pain that no balm can alleviate? *Perfidious* was certainly the word for the way it operates. First, it blots out the past so that a body can face up to the present. And then, when you think you have everything under control, when you're certain you're in complete command of it all – your thoughts, your life, your world and your work – what does Time do? Nothing dramatic, nothing sensational. It just slows you down so that there are no longer enough hours in the day, and then some things get put off and other things are only half-completed and you're told you need help – an assistant priest, no less, to concentrate, as the Bishop with his unfailing instinct for the wrong word put it, on 'the donkey work' (well, perhaps after all I *was* only a beast of burden, Father McGiff conceded) to give you 'a chance to relax, take life more easily, think a bit more, pray a bit more, meditate'. At least that was some consolation: meditation. Yes, indeed. Now, Father McGiff told himself, I'll be able to resume my old evening routine when I can stop my ears to the world outside and listen only to God within me. It was a prospect the priest found both exciting and soothing. That it turned out to be neither was because of Father McGiff's discovery that there was more to Time's perfidy than just the simple ruse of slowing him down. Oh, yes, that boyo had a much better trick up his sleeve. Slowing him down had been merely the preparation for the real poisoned phial.

Early that summer the new curate took up his duties, and Father McGiff at last was able to sit at his desk of an evening and compose himself for his planned period of meditation. He wasn't too upset when at first his mind rebelled at the change of pace – a cluck or two was sufficient to make his straying hand release an unanswered letter, a firmer reprimand put aside his list of tasks for the next day. But after a week of total failure to concentrate for more than a minute he had to acknowledge to himself that nothing was going right. It was the view from his study window opposite his desk that was distracting him, and he thought fleetingly of sitting somewhere else. But then he'd have to take the desk with him if he wasn't to be completely disorientated, and he'd never be up to manhandling such a heavy piece of furniture. No, it was too late to change places at this stage of his life. Besides, what he saw outside the window had too much potency, too much spell-binding sweetness for him to turn his back on it. That old devil, Time, was what he saw there, Time at his insidious work, leafing through the picture-album of his past and using the sky outside the window to throw long-forgotten images onto its evening brightness, each disposition of cloud-shape and colour-tint magically re-forming into a scene from his Granard childhood.

At first the memories intrigued him, then they amused him, then they entrapped him. Landmarks he had completely forgotten seemed to materialise before his mesmerised gaze – like the moat of Hugh de Lacy's twelfth-century castle, now overgrown and weed-filled, the castle itself a ruin, and in front of it at the end of Granard's gently curving single street the already greying walls of St Mary's Church that his labouring father had helped to build. He remembered the brackish stream where he had fished for pinkeens with – who was it, Tommy Murtagh and Seánín Carty? – and the mercifully short walk to the National School that in good weather he made in bare feet over stony roads, with in winter a sod of turf for the schoolroom fire crushing the jam sandwich in his satchel. He couldn't dismiss the images, he couldn't stay Time's hand as it turned page after page of that memory-album until tears flooded his eyes at the scenes recalled: his mother, her brown hair screwed into a bun at the back of her head, taking him to see a house at Edgeworthstown where she said a famous woman writer had lived; he hadn't paid much attention, not being interested in books then, but when he grew older he read Maria Edgeworth's novels and went again for himself to gaze at her home. His mother – God rest her – had got more of a spark out of him when they went to nearby Ballymahon and Oliver Goldsmith's birthplace, but that was only because he had already at school learned off by heart the whole of 'The Deserted Village'.

Evening after evening Father McGiff sat at his desk, ashamed of his indulgence, upbraiding himself for his inability to drag his eyes away from the window which, like some perverse crystal ball, conjured up only ghosts of the past instead of promises of the future. It was enfeebling, it had killed off his efforts at meditation, and there was something almost sinful in allowing his imagination to feast on these buried years when he considered the present turmoil and growing anarchy engulfing the city that had made him one of its own. That should be his concern – Cork and its agony. If his mind was too restless to maintain any hold on the spiritual, then didn't he have something far more immediate to face up to rather than to be wallowing in daily bouts of nostalgia?

It wasn't, however, until summer had faded that he could at last feel he was his own man again and was able to address himself to the present. The bright evening skies that had served as a backdrop for the parade of revenants had been blotted out by a darkness which entombed them once more in the grave of the past. But as the priest stood at his study window, fingers joined in thanksgiving to the night sky for his release from the bitter-sweet torture of reliving what was dead and gone, his mind quailed before his new dilemma. He was a man of God – and a man of God was surely a man of peace. His whole inclination was against the violence all around him and against the insurrection it bred. Not that he didn't know its history – he had been part of it, if only as a silent witness of his brothers' refusal to join the Fenian organisation which had started trying to recruit the young men of their day. 'You can't solve Ireland's problems with a gun,' their father had told them and he had repeated so often the words of Archbishop Paul Cullen, one of Ireland's great clerics, that they were still fresh in Father Brendan's mind. 'Those who engage in and encourage secret plans and conspiracies may think they are patriots, but they are the worst enemies of their country.' And, in case that wasn't enough to show the people where their duty lay,

70

hadn't the Church's ban on Fenianism been reinforced later by a papal decree? How could any Catholic – much less a priest – argue against that?

But that had been half a century ago, and now most Catholics and many priests *were* arguing against it. Father McGiff turned from the window and wearily sat at his desk. Was he going to be chained here for evening after evening, tearing his soul to pieces with a moral dilemma to which he was no longer sure there was one certain simple answer? He had already spent months like this in one sort of mental prison and here he was again in another. Past and present – Time, the old enemy, again. Time never stops – he had learned that much. And, if it never stops, it must evolve; things must change. Things *did* change, God knows that was true – facts, events, circumstances. But principles? Moral truths? There was the Bishop of Limerick defending the Easter Rising, a man who thirty years before had been speaking out against resistance to civil authority. Why had he changed his mind? And only the previous week the head of the Irish College in Rome – a widely respected Monsignor – had said that illegal resistance was the natural protection against immoral laws and that 'the Catholics of Ireland rightly disowned what force made them endure'. Who was right? Where did truth – God's truth – lie?

Father McGiff sighed heavily. There was no answer anywhere, no solace for him anywhere, not in the pronouncements of the other clergy, nor in the speeches of politicians, and certainly not in the daily litany of murder and worse than murder that the newspapers carried.

He took up that morning's *Cork Examiner*. It had lain there all day, still unread, for he knew that just to look at it, just to scan its heavy headlines announcing further death and destruction would only make him sink deeper into the bog of doubt. But it was his duty to suffer, if only vicariously, with his people, and as long as he had any strength left he would fulfil his duty as he saw it.

He opened its news page. As expected, another instalment of the seemingly never-ending agony – the same as yesterday, the same as the day before, the week before, the

71

month before. No matter where he searched in the page, the same, the same. And then his eye was caught by a smaller heading in one corner: 'Granard tragedy. Bizarre outrage in Longford village.' His hands trembled as he read the report.

'Oh my God!' he moaned. 'Oh Jesus, Lord above.'

The words choked in his throat as the newspaper slipped from his grasp. Sinking to his knees, the priest put his head in his hands and sobbed. For a full minute he was bent double, like a stricken animal. Then slowly Father McGiff raised himself back to a kneeling position and, taking off his spectacles, he made the sign of the cross before closing his eyes in prayer.

6

THE CORK SYNAGOGUE was much younger than the Cork Jewish community. No more than ten minutes' walk from Celtic Crescent, in a wide drab street that was unserved by any tram route, its tall aspect, railed forecourt and large Star of David hewn out of the brickwork over the doors drew attention to its foreignness. Although its walls had been painted a self-effacing grey, it still stood out like some exotic folly among the neighbouring tenement houses. Within view was the River Lee, curving around Morrison's Island and the busy South Mall in its circle of the city, conveniently providing the flowing water beside which, each Jewish New Year, Rabbi Moishe and the devout turned out their pockets as they murmurously recited *Tashlich*, the prayer symbolic of casting one's sins into the river.

The affairs of the community were managed by an Executive Committee headed by an annually elected President who habitually was one of the community's more long-established and successful businessmen. The office called for a thick skin, a loud voice and an aggressive personality – qualities which the pressures of competitive life in an unfamiliar environment tended to develop.

Max Klein, its incumbent for going on ten years,

revelled in those qualities. A squat chunky man whose face was stitched by tiny red veins, his head rested on his shoulders like a box on a shelf, and the rasp of his voice could drill through any argument. Originally a resident of Celtic Crescent, he had found that even with the occupancy of two adjoining houses there it was becoming impossible for him to accommodate his growing family along with the near and distant relations from Dublin and England who availed of his hospitality in a constant procession. So he had moved away from Jewtown to a considerably larger and more imposing semi-detached house in Blackrock – a suburb which, though no more than a mile beyond Celtic Crescent, was undeniably middle-class and rising. Its nearness to his original Cork roots meant that he could easily retain his contact with the main body of the community, and it also kept him within fairly comfortable walking distance of the synagogue – an important consideration because of the religious law forbidding riding on the Sabbath or on solemn festivals. Max Klein's wife, Dora, however, had recently begun to tolerate this prohibition with definite, if unexpressed, ill-grace, finding that it greatly restricted her opportunity of parading before the community Max's newly acquired Ford motor-car.

Whatever his faults, the President himself was not one to flaunt his wealth or success. Boast he occasionally might, but that was part of his childlike pride in the continued expansion of his wholesale fancy goods business; from a weekly round of nearby villages it had grown over the years into a limited-liability company with an extensive warehouse and a solid share of the city's and province's retail market. What his co-religionists sometimes found it difficult to put up with, however, was his abrasive personality and haranguing manner, a combination which ensured fiery exchanges and injured feelings in the frequent communal meetings. Still, Max Klein's steamrolling tactics, accompanied as they were by after-battle embraces and chucks under the chin of opponents young and old, in the end always proved irresistible. And his *tzedaka* – the performance of

74

charitable deeds enjoined on him by his religion – won him the gratitude and loyalty of many of the young men and their dependants, for it was as his travellers that they made their weekly Monday-morning trek to the country, secure in the knowledge that, no matter how erratic the week's takings might be, their basic wage was guaranteed by Max Klein.

The Saturday evening of Karlinsky's address provided Dora Klein with the perfect opportunity of drawing attention to her status as the President's wife. That the other women had never shown any deference to that status was a perennial aggravation. Now, however, her husband had a motor-car – the first Cork Jew to possess one – and as they drove to the synagogue, their distinguished visitor, Karlinsky, beside her in the back seat, she felt she had at last come into her kingdom. 'Drive slow, Max, drive slow,' she urged, anxious that none of her friends walking to the meeting should fail to notice her in the darkness. As she hitched up the fox fur draped about her neck, she was tempted now and then to give them a regal wave but decided that to sit back in dignified hauteur was more fitting to her role.

Fortunately for the walkers, the drizzle of the morning and early afternoon had ceased and the sky was clear. The evening air had its accustomed November nip, but the groups making their way from Celtic Crescent were impervious to it. They strolled along, bidding *goot vuch* – 'good week' – all round, and heightening with chatter and speculation the excitement they all felt about Berel Karlinsky's visit. It was an event which no one wanted to miss. Here they were, a tiny outpost in the Diaspora, and someone from the very heart of Jewry had come to address them, someone so important that his coming all that way proved they were important, too. But, more than that, it made them feel involved at last. *Chaverim kol Yisroel* – 'All Israel are brothers' – was what went through many minds. Indeed, Percy Lovitch voiced the thought to Rev. Levitt as he strode past the minister and his wife. Levitt smiled polite agreement, no more; he was privately jealous of Lovitch whom he looked upon as little more than a huckster – though it was a well-stocked music shop that Lovitch owned. Rev. Levitt's antipathy sprang from the fact that when he was ill or needed a break in the non-stop Day of Atonement services it was Percy Lovitch who deputised for him, his tall corpulent figure seeming to fill the small pulpit and his exquisite tenor voice quite outshining Rev. Levitt's pedestrian baritone. What if the man *had* for years been an opera singer in England – it was a *chillul hashem*, a profanation of the Divine Name, to mix operatic arias in with the traditional sacred melodies. The minister was not an opera-lover himself, but many of the congregation were, and such blasphemies distracted them from their devotions into vying with each other to identify the operatic intrusions. But, true enough, all Israel *were* brothers; and as Rev. Levitt looked ahead and behind him at Cork's Jews, in ones and twos or groups and households, converging on the synagogue to hear Karlinsky, it was indeed like going to take part in a family meeting. Years – was it four or five? – had passed since Rabbi Moishe first suggested that they should set up their own settlement in Palestine. It had seemed an impossible dream at the time; but to have an impossible dream was a harmless comfort, and their love and respect for Rabbi Moishe made it difficult for them to grudge him their co-operation. Besides, the Zionist fever was gripping Jewry everywhere, and even if the dream did not come true for them – well, their regular donations would redeem some small plot in the Holy Land which could provide a home for other less fortunate brethren.

The fact that the dream was, after all, coming true quite bemused the community. Earlier in the year – fittingly, during Passover, the festival which celebrates the Israelites' escape from Egypt and the beginning of the journey which eventually took them to the Promised Land – Rabbi Moishe announced with quiet satisfaction that their contributions had mounted up to a sum sufficient to buy three hundred *dunams* of land in Palestine, that the purchase was in the process of being arranged on their behalf by the Jewish National Fund, and that he himself would lead an advance party of settlers from Cork before the end of 1920. Anyone who wished to accompany him was welcome.

It took some time for the first volunteers to come forward. A few weeks passed before the initial shock wore off. Then those who felt attracted by the idea of emigrating discussed it among themselves to see if it was at all feasible for them – there would be their affairs in Cork to liquidate, there might be family ties to take into account, there was even the question of whether they could endure the change of climate. But with Rabbi Moishe's encouragement, with advice and co-operation from the Jewish National Fund leading to a visit by one of their emigration experts to answer questions, resolve doubts, fill in forms and outline all the preparatory steps – by summertime fourteen members of the community had responded to the call and committed themselves to going. Before the year-end would be their departure date, the official had confirmed as he shook hands with each one of the party before he left. Now, with hardly more than a month of 1920 remaining, they were being honoured with the presence of the JNF's top secretary, who would make the final arrangements, tie up the loose ends, perhaps name the day. Above all, Karlinsky would tell them – those who were going, those who weren't going, those who were still undecided – what Palestine was really like, what living there entailed. Karlinsky was the harbinger of their Promised Land, their Jewish National Home.

Inside the synagogue long wooden bench-seats facing the curtained Ark of the Law were filling up, and the high roof made the din of conversation echo loudly. The men called to each other across the floor or wandered from group to group, while their womenfolk exchanged their own news in undertones. Their restraint was mainly due to their feeling of strangeness – it was unique for them to be sharing the seats with the men, their usual place being in the high gallery around the side-walls. From there they were accustomed to having something like a bird's-eye view, seeing their husbands and the other male members of their families not as the tall figures they were familiar with and on whom they relied but as the busy little children they often privately felt them to be. To be imprisoned side by side with them in the male domain made them look forward beyond Karlinsky's address to the regular Saturday-night social in the communal hall next door when they would be able to get together, relax and talk without constraint.

Joshua Cohen, sitting with his wife and daughter at the back of the synagogue rather than in his usual seat near the Ark of the Law, kept glancing up at everyone as they passed him. Bertha Cohen felt his anxiety and shared it. She knew it was not her father-in-law, Rabbi Moishe, he was searching for – the Rabbi would be in a waiting-room with the President's party – but for their son, Jacob. She was worried about her husband; it had been obvious for the past few days that something was preying on his mind. It would be useless to ask him; she had learned that much from experience. Whatever problems he had faced in their life together he had kept to himself. He would tell her about them afterwards of course, when he had overcome them, but share them he wouldn't. Was it Rabbi Moishe's imminent departure to Palestine that was making him more withdrawn than usual? That must be disturbing him greatly; for, after all, though the Rabbi was not her blood relation and she had known him only since her marriage, even for her it was an intolerable wrench. What must it be like for Joshua? They had never been parted before – they had never even lived in different houses. So how could he not be far more upset than he would admit at the thought of the gap it would leave in his life and the prospect of probably never seeing his father again?

Bertha Cohen wished she could believe that that was the explanation, but in her heart she knew it wasn't. Her instinct told her that it was something far more worrying. And she wasn't depending only on her instinct – yesterday he had come home too late to go to the Sabbath commencement service and looking very tired. And all he would say was that he had been delayed. That had never happened before. What could have delayed him? Business? No, he wouldn't let business make him late for Shabbos. A visit to the doctor? She was afraid to consider such a possibility. She had stolen many a glance at him since yesterday to see if perhaps there was anything that might show, but it was difficult, she did not want him to feel he was under examination, and anyway today the tired look was gone. But there *was* something important troubling him – that much Bertha Cohen was sure of.

Iron Josh also had his instinct and it told him that, no matter how much he had tried to hide the fact that he was worried, Bertha had guessed. He had caught her looking sharply at him when she thought he wouldn't notice. But how could he tell her? He could have told her about the IRA kidnapping him, but that would have alarmed her and the whole household. And what would have been the point? It was over, he was unhurt, and it hadn't cost him a penny apart from the few pence in his pocket – and as the kidnapping wasn't what was eating his heart out he knew he couldn't pretend it was. It wouldn't fool her. But to tell her the truth? He might as well get a gun – like Denis Hurley's gun – and put it to her head and shoot her. He almost wished Denis Hurley had shot *him*. But that would have solved nothing. They'd have found his body and gone through his pockets and discovered the letter. He had received it in the post almost a week ago, and the moment he read it his heart had frozen – he had actually felt himself go ice-cold. He remembered every word:

Dear Mr Cohen,
Do you know that your son Jacob is going with a Christian girl? He meets her every day in college.
A WELL-WISHER

He had read it again and again, scores of times, since then. He had examined it minutely – written on a sheet of white copy-paper – but there was nothing he could learn from it about its sender. Anyway, what did he care about its sender? He cared only about what the letter said. Was it true? Could it be true? He had no idea, for the letter forced him at last to admit to himself that he knew nothing about his son, that he had lost touch with him, had allowed him over the years to drift further and further away so that now they were virtual strangers. His own flesh and blood! As he sat waiting for Karlinsky to appear, looking around him he could see other men's sons, boys of Jacob's age, sitting with their fathers. But Jacob wouldn't be joining them; Josh Cohen was quite certain of that. No matter how long he waited or how often he looked up to see who the latest arrival was, he knew in his heart of hearts it wouldn't be his son. And where was he? Out with his Christian girl? But no – he mustn't condemn him. He mustn't think of him as guilty. He had no evidence – nothing but an anonymous letter which might easily be the work of some anti-Semite. He must wait until he could find out the truth. But where would he start? Whom could he ask? Jacob himself? No, he couldn't confront his own son. And, even if he did, would Jacob tell him?

He took his gold watch out of his waistcoat pocket and snapped it open. Six o'clock. So that the meeting and the usual Saturday-night social that was to follow it could end before curfew, proceedings had been due to commence at six but, even so, no one really expected a punctual start. Joshua shifted uneasily in his seat and wished they would hurry up.

Iron Josh wasn't the only one made fretful by the delay. Zvi Lipsky, the Burial Society Treasurer, had spent the whole afternoon trying to rid his mind of the annoyance of Arnold Wine's advertisement in that morning's *Cork Examiner* and now there was Wine himself, as bold as brass, sitting up in the front seats if you please, instead of at the back where he should be. To Zvi, Wine was an upstart – an interloper who had suddenly appeared in the community a year ago (real name, Zvi had been told, was Benny Wineberg from Brighton), set up as a dentist, and by charging ludicrously low fees had been taking clients from Zvi. It was a *chutzpah*; Zvi Lipsky had taken thirty years to build up his practice and reputation. Only in the last ten years or so had he been able to give up going to the country towns and villages for uncomfortable, if lucrative, one- or two-day visits; only then had he found it

80

possible to move from Jewtown to commodious rooms in Patrick Street, Cork's main thoroughfare, where he could live as well as have his surgery. Now that he was getting on in years he wanted to take things just that little bit easy, not see patient after patient, cramming in as many as possible, but space them out – eight, ten a day was enough – for with his practice so long established and his clientele so solid he couldn't imagine any reason to fear blanks in his appointments-book.

'A fly-by-night,' Zvi hissed into his wife's ear, his angry breath making her pearl ear-ring shiver in response.

'What's that?' Myra Lipsky asked.

'Wineberg. Over there. His ad was in the paper again today. With his photograph as well.'

'Oh! With his photograph!' Perhaps Zvi should put *his* photograph in, too. After all, he was a handsome man. At least, he had been when she married him. Of course that was thirty years ago – he had lost most of his hair since then, and his jaw muscles were beginning to sag noticeably. She hadn't yet seen his own advertisement in that morning's paper, but he had told her he was putting one in. Zvi couldn't remember how long it was since he had last found it necessary to advertise, but with Wine telling the *Cork Examiner*'s readers for the last three weeks that 'owing to the great increase of my practice' he was moving to larger premises Zvi felt he had no alternative. And the photograph was especially annoying. It had obviously been touched up, exaggerating the waves in his dark hair, making him look a masher and younger than he was – just the thing to attract the lady patients. Perhaps Zvi could put his own photograph in next time – an early one. But no; if he did that, he'd have to face the laughter and ridicule of the community.

'Remember Rosenstein?' Zvi reminded his wife.

'Rosenstein? Who's he?'

'Don't you remember?' Lipsky repeated impatiently. 'Soon after I started here. Rosenstein used to go to all the country villages before me doing fillings and extractions for half-price.'

'Oh, yes. My God, that was years ago.'

81

'Yes, but what happened? He ruined people's teeth. And then he disappeared. Another fly-by-night.'

Myra didn't remind her husband that Rosenstein's butchery had made more business for Zvi.

'It's terrible that all these quacks can come along without proper qualifications,' Lipsky complained, forgetting that he himself had set up as a dentist without qualifications, there being as yet no legal requirement for special training as there was for doctors. 'As soon as Wine has made enough, he'll be off somewhere else.' But that was Zvi Lipsky's wishful thinking. His real fear was that the interloper might set down roots and eventually steal the bulk of his clientele.

His morose ruminations were interrupted by Benny Katz, who wanted anyone he could find to listen to his tale of woe. Why he should think there was anything special about *his* troubles, Zvi couldn't imagine. All the men of the community who had to travel to the country every week to sell their goods – at least, any who didn't have his own means of transport – had for months been finding it increasingly difficult relying on the railways. Zvi's own practice had been affected by the strike. Quite a few of his country clients had been late for their appointments, or had failed to turn up at all, and the story was always the same: British troops had boarded the train as passengers so the driver or the fireman or the guard or ticket-collector – sometimes all four – refused to work and the train never moved.

'I had to rush around trying to find a farmer with a cart who might be going where I wanted,' Katz lamented, his woebegone countenance matching his sorry tale. *'Oi vey*, in the country it's a real *tzuriss* getting from village to village. I couldn't see half my customers – and then I had to leave early to be certain of getting back.'

Lipsky, however, wasn't very interested. *Viklehniks'* worries were no concern of a professional man like him.

'Buy a horse and cart,' he advised gruffly.

Katz made a face. 'Animals, animals, I don't like animals.'

'Beggars can't be choosers,' Zvi said with a snort, but there was no silencing Katz.

'I got the ten-thirty from Mitchelstown yesterday morning,' he insisted. 'Listen, listen. Would you believe it? Just as the train pulled out of the station a lorry load of soldiers drove in like maniacs. But they were just too late to get on. We got away. We just got away,' he was repeating loudly to his neighbours when he realised that the noise of conversation had ceased and people were all sitting down. He turned to find the President, Max Klein, leading his party up the aisle and he hastened to take his own seat.

The President, freshly shaved, his Sabbath suit replaced by his High Festival suit, was wearing his special spats, and on his head was a new Homburg instead of the white *yarmulkah* he usually sported in the synagogue.

'He's like a lighthouse,' Mickey Aronson whispered to Ada; and, indeed, Mickey's comparison was well chosen, for the smile of pride Max Klein could not suppress at being the *baaleboss* for such a momentous occasion seemed to reach his lips only after first puffing out his chest. He strode ahead of Karlinsky, upon whom all eyes were fastened, and a few steps behind Karlinsky came Mrs Klein. She was followed by Rabbi Moishe, his sallow face with its rippling white beard inclining first to one side and then to the other as everyone did him honour by rising until he had passed, and just behind him came another black-garbed figure, a bespectacled priest, greying head covered by a *yarmulkah*. '*Vee is der galach* – who is the priest?' a few were heard to ask, but they were more recent settlers who did not live in Celtic Crescent. Those who did live there all knew Father McGiff and they were able to inform the ignorant that he had been a close friend of the Rabbi ever since the Jews had arrived in the city.

The President ushered his party into seats which had been kept vacant in the top bench and then he turned to address the community.

'I don't have to tell you why we're here tonight,' he commenced, almost threateningly, so that some of the

83

men turned to their wives or neighbours with the prediction: 'That means there'll be a collection afterwards'.

'We've come to listen to a very distinguished visitor, Berel Karlinsky, a famous man we've all heard of. Earlier this year we had a visitor from the Jewish National Fund who told us how badly they need men – and women, too – in *Eretz*, as well as money. Well, we've always given money for *Eretz* and now we're giving men and women, including our beloved Rabbi. I don't have to tell you how much he'll be missed. But this is not the time to talk about that. We all want to hear our distinguished visitor who has come to us to make the final arrangements with those going to *Eretz* – and with any others who might want to go, too; there's still plenty of time, it's never too late. But I'm sure our distinguished visitor has a lot to say to us, so I won't say any more.'

He motioned Karlinsky forward and with a generous flourish directed him up the three steps on to the small platform in front of the Ark of the Law where a lectern had been placed. To loud applause Karlinsky shook hands with the President before ascending the steps where he put his face against the blue and white silk curtain with the gold braid which hung before the doors of the Ark. He lifted the curtain to his lips, kissed it tenderly, and then turned to his audience.

Berel Karlinsky was a striking figure. His thick white hair and silver-streaked goatee beard gave him a look of experience and authority, while soft blue eyes and a hint of wryness in his smile suggested a mortal to whom disappointment was a familiar companion. Wherever Jews were to be found – whether in the Holy Land or in the far-flung Diaspora – his name had become a household word as one of the select band of zealots whose spirit had never relinquished the hope of one day setting up a Jewish state in Palestine. Certainly it was the British who now ruled the land but they ruled it not as owners or conquerors, but as trustees for the League of Nations. And the British Government had already, two years earlier, issued the Balfour Declaration formally recognising the Jewish right to a National Home in Palestine.

Never since the Lord's promise to Moses to bring the Israelites to a land flowing with milk and honey had Jewish hopes been so high, Jewish dreams so wild, Jewish spirits so elated. And in the creation of all this euphoria Berel Karlinsky had played a leading role. The Jews of Cork hung on his words.

'But everything is still to be done!'

Karlinsky's opening sentence was followed by a brief silence and then a restrained buzz of conversation. 'What did he say?' 'He said "But everything is still to be done".' 'Yes, yes, I heard that. What did he say before that?'

Karlinsky stroked his beard and smiled. 'Do not be puzzled, my friends, I will explain. For some time now, we, the Jewish people, have had joy in our hearts because the British Government has committed itself, by the Balfour Declaration, to the establishment of a National Home in Palestine for the Jewish people. We have celebrated all over the world – in the Diaspora outside Palestine, and inside Palestine too, in the Yishuv itself. But the celebrations in the Diaspora and in the Yishuv have very often had a different spirit behind them. In the Diaspora, our Jewish people has been inclined to sit back and think that the battle has been won and that in a little while we Jews will have our National Home in our Promised Land. In the Yishuv we know that is not so. The Balfour Declaration is there, yes, but in *Eretz* we know that nothing will change unless we ourselves change it. And that, my friends, explains why my first words to you, my first peculiar words, were "But everything is still to be done".'

The listeners turned to each other, each anxious to assure himself that his neighbour appreciated the speaker's remarks and the wisdom of his approach. Rabbi Moishe nodded energetically, and Father McGiff took it on himself to applaud – a lead which the rest of the audience immediately followed.

Karlinsky waited for the applause to die away. He sipped at the glass of water on the lectern and then resumed.

'Before me I see you, the Children of Israel; behind me' – and he put a hand on the braided curtain – 'is the Torah,

85

the Law of Israel. It is two thousand years since the Children of Israel have been able to follow the Torah of Israel as citizens in their own land. Yet to bring them together – the people and the Torah – in *Eretz Yisroel* is what we in the Jewish National Fund intend to do. We are mad! Of course. We are attempting the impossible! Of course. We have no army; we have no institutions; we have no seat in the councils of nations; we have nothing to trade. We are trying to populate a land which has been derelict for two thousand years with a people which has been scattered for two thousand years. We *are* mad, ladies and gentlemen. And so are you. For you sit here, thousands of miles away from Palestine, a land which most of you will never see, and yet which you will certainly pay for – with your money, yes, and some of you with your blood and sweat – you sit here and you listen to me as I tell you about this impossible, this ridiculous dream, and it doesn't occur to you that we are all mad, you and I and all our people?'

There were ripples of self-satisfied laughter, as if to have such a mad dream was something for which they could congratulate themselves. Mickey Aronson could not resist nudging his landlady beside him and whispering: 'Now I know why Klugman is going to Palestine. With all these madmen he'll feel at home.'

'Hush! That's a cruel joke to make.'

Ada Neumann shook her head in resignation and once again concentrated her attention on the speaker.

'Twenty years ago the Jewish National Fund was established for the purpose of purchasing land as the inalienable property of the Jewish people. Land costs money. We all know that. You have given money. I know that in every one of your homes there is a JNF Blue Box and I know that wherever it is in your homes it is not gathering dust. But land costs people, too. Money alone will buy land but money will not clear the deserts, move the rocks, turn the soil, plant the seed. Only people can do these things, and people we need as much as we need money. We have not come to you before to ask for people, but we are asking for people now. And just as you have in the past answered our call for money, so you are now ready to answer our call for people. I have come to you tonight as much to thank you for that answer as to explain to those of you who already plan to make your home in *Eretz* – and to any others who may make such a decision in the future – what lies before you.'

There was a rustle of excitement as the listeners exchanged expectant looks and then shifted for more comfort on the hard wooden seats. This was what they had come to hear.

Karlinsky painted a grim picture – endless hardship, unceasing toil and sweat, back-breaking labour in hostile climatic conditions, some of it in malaria-ridden areas. Their habitations would be huts, which they would have to build themselves, in desert land away from the few cities; their diet would be healthy and sustaining but it would be monotonous, and they would have to do without delicacies which many of them might have become used to in the Diaspora. Family life would not be the family life they knew now. Meals would be taken in common. Parents would not see their children for most of the day, and when they finished their daily work they would be too tired for much except rest.

'It would not be so bad,' Karlinsky continued to his now rapt audience, 'if there was nothing else to worry about but the hardships and difficulties I have described to you. But there are others. Often worse than these hardships and difficulties. I will hide nothing from you. How could I? I am sure you read the papers and know the stories. There are dangers to life. Even though your settlement may not be in a known danger area, no one can be sure. Few of the settlements in Palestine have any means of protecting themselves, and so they are sometimes attacked by armed Arabs. These attacks might only be cattle raids – that's bad enough – but sometimes they might be more hostile.

'In February of this very year there was the attack on the settlement of Tel Hai when six of its defenders were killed by marauding Arabs. And even in the big cities one must always be prepared for danger. You will ask "Is not the British Army protecting the people of the cities?" and

87

I would have to answer "Yes, that is part of their duty". Yet only last Pesach, in Jerusalem itself, there was a pogrom. I am sure you read about it, so I don't have to say much more. Except that in the capital city of Palestine, a city covered with soldiers, it was possible to have Arab riots in which six Jews were slain and no soldiers around to prevent it.

'That, my friends, is my story of Palestine today and *Eretz Yisroel* of the future. I have ended the story with killing and bloodshed because I want to leave that picture before your eyes – a picture which stands for all the anguish and hardship and disappointment and dangers anyone going to *Eretz* must expect. Those of you who have already said you will go – and any others who may wish to join them – I will talk to privately later. But now, before I finish and let you commence something more enjoyable, I will do my best to answer any questions you may have.'

Karlinsky sipped water and waited while the people looked around, each encouraging the other to ask a question. For a few moments no one spoke and then there was some activity in one corner where a young man was trying to persuade the girl beside him to stand up. At his urging she raised a tentative hand as if at school, and Karlinsky smiled down at her.

'You have something to ask me?'

The girl was pushed to her feet. 'My name is Miriam Levy,' she said, her strong voice belying her embarrassment, but before she could continue Karlinsky interrupted her.

'Ah, yes, Miss Levy. You are one of the brave young women who have already put forward their names for *Eretz*. What can I tell you?'

'Well, I would like to know – well, what would I be doing there? What would my work be?'

'Yes, of course, that is important,' Karlinsky began, addressing the whole audience as Miriam Levy resumed her seat and her fiancée, sitting beside her, squeezed her hand.

'I am sure you know', Karlinsky went on, 'the high place – the very high place – that the Torah accords to

88

women in the direction of Jewish family life. In *Eretz* family life will not be the same as you have known here in Cork or anywhere in the Diaspora because in the settlements women are involved in communal work just as much as the men are. Nevertheless, the high status of the woman's influence is in no way diminished. But what work is it you will be doing?'

Here Karlinsky turned to Miriam Levy, drawing momentary blushes to her cheeks.

'Well, you will be doing the sort of work women do in the home anywhere – cooking, cleaning, minding children, laundering – all those tasks to which women are no strangers. That doesn't mean that you would be engaged in the same boring work all the time. These tasks rotate – a month in the kitchen, a month in the laundry, a month in the vegetable gardens, things like that. But also women work in the fields – if they wish to and are physically fit for it. Sowing, threshing, tobacco-farming, citrus-planting, even building – no activity is closed to anyone. And if you have any special skills or knowledge that can be made use of they would be more than welcome. Does that answer your question?'

Miriam blushed again and nodded. As Karlinsky waited for any other questions, the President stood up to turn and survey the congregation. '*Nu? Nu?* Anyone else?' When there was no reply he went on: 'Then I shall ask Father McGiff to propose a vote of thanks to the speaker.'

There was polite applause and some surprise that the priest should be asked to speak. Father McGiff, however, did not himself seem to share the surprise and it was clear that his participation had been decided on beforehand.

'My very good friends,' he commenced, 'I won't keep you long. I'm sure many of you would prefer to get your weekly social started rather than listen to me. Not that I'd blame you, not that I'd blame you. But to be serious for a moment' – and he hitched his spectacles up higher on his nose. 'I may not be of your persuasion but tonight I have been persuaded that the world is reaching a turning-point in its history and that the ancient biblical promise to your people is about to be redeemed. I believe it is. I hope it is.

Because it would be a miracle, you know, a sure sign of the grace of the Lord Who created all of us. But when that miraculous day dawns and your wanderings are over' – another hitch of the spectacles – 'I hope you won't all leave Cork. I have been a friend of your wonderful Rabbi and of many of you for a very long time. I cherish his and your friendship, and I can say in all sincerity that Cork would be the poorer without you. But I'd better not keep on like this or I'll be accused of queering Mr Karlinsky's pitch. It's a privilege and honour for me to thank him, on your behalf, for coming here tonight and addressing us in the way he has. I wish him and all of you good luck in all your hopes and endeavours.'

The priest went and shook hands with Karlinsky. As soon as the applause died down Max Klein called out, 'Well, what are you waiting for? Go and enjoy yourselves,' adding, with a gravelly laugh, as if he knew they were expecting something else: 'There'll be no collection tonight.'

Banter and mocking cheers greeted the announcement as the drift to the communal hall commenced.

Already in the hall, having slipped out while the priest was speaking, Judith Cohen had lit the gas under the tea-urn and unwrapped the sandwiches. Drawing the curtain across the windows she looked out on the gloomy, almost deserted street. Drizzle was falling again, and she saw two RIC policemen patrolling past, their capes gleaming. They would be based in Union Quay barracks just around the corner; that would be their home. The word stirred her, and she recalled what her mother had said to her the previous day: that Cork had been her home all her life, with no suffering and no want – a safe and secure home. What home was safe these days? The policemen's homes weren't – their barracks were being attacked almost daily all over the country. The Irish people – their homes weren't safe, either – the papers were full of reports of houses being burned by one side or the other. Jewish homes? When were they ever anything but targets – real or potential? Even in Palestine – Karlinsky hadn't tried to hide it – they had to be on their guard. And Cork? She had never felt in danger before, at least not from the sort of attack that menaced the settlers in Palestine, the RIC in their barracks, the Irish in their homes. Her home might be secure, but was she herself? Suddenly she knew that, without her having noticed it was happening, her sense of permanence, her feeling of stability, had already begun to crumble. At the realisation, a shiver ran through her body. Fear or anticipation? She could not tell.

She heard voices, laughter, the sound of hurrying footsteps approaching the hall, and she quickly wound the gramophone and lowered the needle on to the record.

7

EVEN IN THE BEST OF WEATHERS the view from the officers' mess of 16th Division's Cambridge Barracks was dispiriting. At seven o'clock on a chilly Saturday evening in November, the shroud of darkness enveloping it was a kindness as far as Captain Roddy Simcox was concerned. As he gazed out over the still wet cobblestones, all he could see was the glimmer of lights – lights on the barrack square, lights on the sentry posts at the main gates, lights in the barrack huts, and beyond them the lights of the hospital's east wing. There was a hint of menace about the scene, an unnatural stillness in which the Captain was aware of his body's answering tension. He felt that something was waiting out there, that to venture beyond the lights' pale embrace for whatever reason – necessity, whim or duty – was to take one's life in one's hands.

'Stuff and nonsense,' Captain Simcox muttered to himself as he threw back his head, downed the last of his whiskey and dried the ends of his thick red moustache with finger and thumb. What a ruddy nightmare the whole blasted show is, he thought.

He tapped his empty glass, then shrugged his shoulders as if too indifferent to meet some sort of challenge and almost defiantly poured himself another large measure. He knew he was drinking too much but, damn it all, what else was there to do when a man was off duty and his wife was hundreds of miles away? It was too early yet to go to his lodgings and he had already made his visit to the hospital to see how Byford was getting on. Poor bugger had caught a bad one in an ambush outside Blarney the previous day. He'd probably have to lose a leg, was the MO's report.

'They came from nowhere, Captain,' Byford kept repeating. 'One minute the road was clear, and then....'

'I know, Corporal, I know how it is,' was all Roddy could offer. 'You just rest and try not to think about it.'

Captain Simcox knew very well how it was. He had himself frequently led patrols along the narrow roads and boreens that ran like veins through the countryside about Cork, and before that he had spent more time than he cared to remember in the muddy trenches and dug-outs of France with shells screaming overhead. Touch wood, he had been lucky and come through it all unscathed, but it would be no consolation to Byford to tell him that *he* had been *un*lucky, that it was the RIC and their Black and Tan recruits rather than British army patrols that were the main IRA targets. Byford had only to read the newspapers or listen to the barrack-room talk to know the figures: over 400 police stations destroyed so far in 1920 alone and two senior police officers assassinated. As if that wasn't enough, what about the 2000 arms raids on RIC depots all over the country in the past two months? And now, to cap it all, poor Byford had to be the first army victim of the latest IRA tactic – Flying Columns – compact bands armed only with a few rifles and automatic pistols, moving soundlessly at night along country lanes on foot or on bicycles, and waiting behind roadside hedges – waiting for hours, days if necessary – for a patrol to come along. This time it had been Byford's patrol, not the police or the Black and Tans. 'You pays your money and you takes your chance' – that was war.

Privately Captain Simcox hoped the IRA would be a match for the Tans – well, perhaps that was expecting too much – but it would be something if they could put some manners on them and give them a bloody nose now and again. Contempt was what every man in the barracks felt for them. Even Windsor, their Colonel-in-Chief, made no secret of his belief that they were only licensed thugs rampaging through the countryside in drunken gangs, shooting indiscriminately at passers-by, looting shops, setting fire to farmhouses and stock. The Government might fool the British public by denying the atrocity stories, but the Army in Ireland knew the truth, the newspapers knew, the people knew. It was obvious that the Tans had been given *carte blanche* by a panicky Cabinet. Why, so hasty had been their recruitment that there even weren't police uniforms ready for them when they were rushed over to Ireland and they had to make do with some rag-tag-and-bobtail hotch-potch of khaki tunic and dark green trousers, supplemented with the black leather belts of the RIC.

Well, maybe the IRA would be a match for them after all. They could be just as ruthless and at least they had most of the military advantages: a thorough knowledge of the countryside, the support of most of the people, and a cause to fight for. Plus a British-trained commander! Intelligence had reported that the Flying Columns were directed by a soldier named Barry who had fought for Britain in the Great War! If Intelligence was right, that would be a fitting irony. After all, in the war Barry would have been told that he was fighting to uphold the rights of small nations, so what could be more logical than that he should now fight for the rights of his own country, Ireland, a small nation if ever there was one!

The sound of the mess door opening made Roddy turn from the window, but whoever it was closed the door again and disappeared. Thank goodness they're not looking for me, he thought as he crossed the room. Checking his watch, he poured himself a last drink and sank into one of the easy chairs before the fire. He should have enough time to finish his drink and be away before his fellow-officers started to drift in. He'd be just as pleased to avoid them. Especially Campbell – 'By-the-book' Campbell as he was known – a nickname he was secretly proud of, though he publicly deplored the practice of addressing officers of the British Army in any other way than by proper rank. He was the only one in the mess who complained about Roddy's preference for outside lodgings rather than barracks quarters.

'It's not the right example, Captain Simcox,' he'd say aggrievedly, the musical Scots burl belying the complaint in his voice. 'The officers are a team and all the members of the team should stick together. Ye know what I mean.'

Roddy knew but did not care. King's Regulations allowed an officer to have outside accommodation and, if the Colonel-in-Chief didn't forbid it, it was none of 'By-the-book' Campbell's business. There was a time when Captain Simcox had fitted comfortably into the officer class – but that was before the war and his marriage to Elizabeth. What he wanted now was a normal married life away from uniforms, fighting, and the whole insanity of men being paid to kill their fellow-men. He lived for his reunion with Elizabeth; all that sustained him until then was the daily letter from his new wife waiting for him in his lodgings. He still thought of her as his 'new' wife even though the wedding was now a two-year-old memory. He had been serving in France when he met her, they had married as soon as the Hun had been finished off, and after the honeymoon it had been back to the colours for him and straight over to Ireland.

The two years in the Cork posting had seemed like twenty years to Roddy. If he *had* to be shifted to Ireland, why couldn't it have been Dublin where he'd at least have been nearer to Elizabeth and might have managed to hop over to England more often. Since being stuck in Cork he'd had only two brief periods of leave with her. Still, to look on the bright side: if they had been together all this time, by now they might already be a dull settled couple, instead of which the long separation had preserved the thrill of courtship in their marriage, with letters passing between them constantly. And with a baby on the way there would surely be some compassionate leave for him soon. He'd have to stick it out until then. Somehow. Despite the fact that he had come from a long line of soldier forebears, even the combination of breeding,

95

upbringing and training no longer made it easy for him to bear the tedium of army life with good grace. He had something to live for now, something infinitely more worth while than the seemingly mindless routine of military discipline and the risk of pointless death or – what was often worse – horrible mutilation. As he put the glass to his lips to wash out the thought, his eye caught the soldierly portraits all around, the Divisional insignia above the mantelpiece, the roll of battle honours flanking them on each side, and he had a sudden vision of the mess walls decorated not with these trumpery monuments to man's stupidity but with the torn and mangled limbs of countless unfortunates and, in the place of honour, Corporal Byford's shattered, still bleeding leg.

'Ugh!' Captain Simcox shivered and rapidly swallowed the last of his drink. He bent to throw a few pieces of turf on the fire and was reminded that the locals called them sods of turf. The word seemed to him to describe perfectly the smelly, often damp cakes of earth they were forced to burn since coal supplies had been so reduced by the constant cancellation of goods trains.

'Sod it all,' he muttered, the fire and whiskey combined sending a flush of warmth through his body. He forced himself out of the chair and fastened his tunic. If he didn't get away now, he'd only be waylaid by the others, there'd be more whiskies, and it would be all hours before he'd get to his lodgings and the letter from Elizabeth.

He threw his greatcoat over his shoulders and then, remembering 'By-the-book' Campbell, donned it properly. At the main gate he acknowledged the sentry's salute and turned to face the short hill up Southern Road to his rooms. As he strode out into the darkness, the gloom and chill of the evening only served to sharpen his anticipation, so that he had no eyes for the RIC men on patrol, the few pedestrians hurrying along, or the horse and cart just moving off beside him on the road, the barely discernible name JAS SULLIVAN painted on the cart's side and a burly figure with a flattened nose and scarred face hunched on the driver's seat, desultorily twitching the reins.

8

SATURDAYS the Jews of Cork spent with their families and their God, Sundays they spent with each other. On Sundays three or four houses in Celtic Crescent and its neighbouring streets – always including Rabbi Moishe's – would be the venue for morning prayers. There groups of men along with youths over the bar mitzvah age of thirteen would gather at eight o'clock, and to the muttered accompaniment of the special blessings each would kiss his phylacteries, wind one around left arm, palm and second finger, encircle his forehead with the other, and then join in reciting the ritual prayers. More intimate and relaxed than synagogue services – whoever felt inclined could take it on himself to lead the responses – these *minyanim* were held in the front rooms of the tiny houses and anyone passing along the street at the time would be assailed by a chorus of incantations like the sound of bees swarming in a hive. In fact the only pedestrians abroad then were early churchgoers on their way to second Mass at St Joseph's, its echoing carillons summoning them to *their* house of God. Prayers in Jewtown over, the men would drift out onto the street, each separate group mingling with the others in a leisurely trading of news and gossip before eventually they entered their own homes where breakfast awaited them.

In Rabbi Cohen's the exodus followed very soon after the last Amen, for the Rabbi spent little time in idle conversation and his withdrawal from the room was the signal for the other worshippers to leave. But outside the house on this Sunday morning the usual gossip was forgotten, for Max Klein's new motor-car was parked at the Rabbi's front door and it seemed that half the community had gathered to wonder at it. Many of them had seen it at the synagogue meeting on the previous night, but now in the daylight they were able to examine it more closely and exclaim at its resplendence. The black wings and running-board set off the sober mole colour of the body, and the President glowed as he proudly explained the working of the controls and gear lever, opened the doors to display the interior with its adjustable foot-rests for the rear-seat passengers and obliged a request from one admirer to see how much space there was in the luggage compartment at the back.

'That must have cost a pretty penny,' Mickey Aronson declared, not really expecting to be told the price. To his surprise Max Klein announced: 'Two hundred and fifty pounds. The latest model on the market. This year's.' There were gasps and whistles at the magnitude of the figure.

'*Kein aynhoreh! Mazeltov!*' the admirers congratulated the President, who almost blushed. He hadn't meant to boast of his wealth, but he couldn't resist rejoicing in it and basking in his friends' appreciation. But when someone tried to test the security of the spare wheel attached to the side of the body by pulling at it roughly and then, intrigued by the pair of leather driving-gauntlets resting on the front seat, fitted them on and passed them around for general examination he decided it was time to leave. He took the crank-handle, inserted it in the hole at the bottom of the radiator and, encouraged by a chorus of 'One, two, three, heave!' swung it energetically until the engine sprang to life.

'Did you remember to cut a few inches off the exhaust-pipe?' Mickey Aronson shouted as the President sat in behind the wheel.

'What for?' Max Klein shouted back above the engine noise.

'To circumcise it, what else?' Mickey Aronson replied, delighted at the ribald laughter that greeted his witticism. But not for nothing had Max Klein spent the best years of his youth and early manhood at country fairs and markets learning to give as good as he got. He waited for the laughter to die down and then, ignoring Mickey Aronson, he leaned his head out of the window, gave his gravelly laugh and confided to the other men: 'A bigger ignoramus I never met; he doesn't even know that ships and cars are always female.' The exchange put him in excellent mood for his breakfast.

Rabbi Moishe, too, was looking forward to his Sunday breakfast. For him it held a special appeal: the one day of the week he could break bread with his family and not have to feel that they were only loaned to him for the while – his son Joshua had no business to go to, his grandson Jacob no college lectures. The Sabbath meals, of course, were family occasions also, but they were invested with the day's solemnity and holiness. If the Sabbath was a day of rest from labour, Sunday, Rabbi Moishe sometimes thought – but it was not a thought he voiced for fear of being misunderstood – was a day of rest from the Sabbath. And breakfast was not only a leisurely start, it was also the only Sunday meal when he could be sure that all the members of his family would be together at table. Jacob, increasingly since he commenced going to university, might be missing for the rest of the day; Joshua, particularly in the summer, would go out for·long walks in the country, following, he said, the course of some *meshuggeneh* game in which young men threw an iron ball along the road and ran after it – could there be such a game? Molly and Judith frequently went visiting other girls in the community after dinner and as often as not did not come home for tea; and, since Malka had married and left Cork, Judith spent even more Sundays out of the house. Bertha, of course, never went anywhere, but Rabbi Moishe sometimes wished his daughter-in-law had a little more – humanity? no, no, he mustn't judge – a

99

little more inclination to mix with the other married women; he respected his daughter-in-law, she was holiness itself, as *frum* as an angel, and as for housekeeping.... But there were times, when they were alone in the house together – and even though the Rabbi might be in his own room teasing out a *bissle* Talmud – his attention would suddenly stray from the holy words and he would become uncomfortably aware of some *dybbuk*, some spirit of unhappiness, brooding in the kitchen.

Still, on Sunday mornings there were no such worries and the Rabbi could look forward to the family breakfast – and to *bagels*. At five o'clock in the morning Ada Neumann would have been in her kitchen, simmering the dozens of doughnut-shaped rolls in hot water for a few minutes before baking them in the oven, glazing them with egg-white and then showering them with sesame seeds. After the *minyanim* the men would collect them to bring home, sweet-tasting harbingers of the new week. To Rabbi Moishe, however, they were more than just delicacies, more even than symbols of the hoped-for good week to come – they were remembrances from the past, taking him back forty and more years to his distant home in Lithuania. There his family, like all those in the village, had been too poor to eat anything but black bread, and so *bagels*, baked with expensive white flour, were the rarest of luxuries. He had come a long way from there to this home in Ireland. God willing, he would soon go on a final long journey to another home, his real home, in *Eretz*. Karlinsky's visit could almost be regarded as the signal for the journey to commence. Rabbi Moishe felt that at last the past was about to bear sweet fruit. This Sunday morning, as he broke a piece from the *bagel* to pronounce over it the Grace Before Meals, there was a special fervour in his voice, his blue eyes were full of love and good humour, and he refused room in his heart for the sorrow he knew he would feel on leaving his family. Here and now he was with them and while with them he would enjoy.

'Karlinsky, he was at the *minyan*?' Bertha asked. She lifted a large saucepan of eggs from on top of the hot range and gave one to each person. 'There's more if you want them. You'll have two?' she urged her husband. Joshua distractedly waved the second egg away as the Rabbi answered his daughter-in-law's question.

'*Nein, nein*. He left early this morning, to catch the first train to Dublin. The President drove him to the station.' Then as he broke off the top of his egg he grimaced and tugged at his beard.

'What is it? *Vos?* A blood spot? Here, take mine; there's plenty,' Bertha Cohen said, passing her egg to the Rabbi and taking his to the yard to throw it in the rubbish-bin.

'When will you know about *Eretz* – about your departure date, I mean?' Judith enquired. 'Did he say?'

'He will write me a letter immediately he gets back to London. He still has some details to arrange. I'll know this week – in a few days perhaps.'

'But it will be soon, before Christmas?' Bertha Cohen remarked. 'You'll be leaving soon?'

'Before Christmas,' the Rabbi agreed. 'I hope not before Malka has her child. I would like to be here for that.'

'Here – there – what's the difference?' his daughter-in-law grumbled, pouring out cups of tea. She hoped the departure would be as early as possible so that she and Joshua could go over to Leeds for the birth of their first grandchild.

'If I'm here,' Rabbi Moishe replied, in the sing-song voice he would adopt to explain a point in the Torah, 'I'll know about it sooner. When the Almighty makes an old man a great-grandfather, better he should learn of it quickly.'

'Will it make you feel any different? Will it make you feel any younger?'

'*Ai, mein kinde*, let me tell you a story.' He paused, a spoonful of egg halfway to his mouth. 'About old Mrs Rubinstein who went to the doctor.'

Jacob nudged Judith; this was one of his grandfather's chestnuts – he told it at least once a year, unfailingly on his birthday.

'The doctor examined her and said: "Mrs Rubinstein, organically you are in perfect health." "So", Mrs

101

Rubinstein said, "*vos iz de meisa mit mir?*" "What is wrong with you? Something, Mrs Rubinstein, that medicine cannot cure. It cannot make you younger." "Who wants to be younger, Doctor?" Mrs Rubinstein answered, "I want to be older." The same with me – the older I grow, the better my chance of becoming a great-grandfather.' Pleased with himself, he returned to his egg and *bagel*.

The laughter was dutiful, except for Joshua who merely grunted and shrugged his shoulders.

The Rabbi brushed some crumbs from his beard and turned to his grandson.

'*Nu, Yankeleh,* how do you feel about becoming an uncle?'

Rabbi Moishe was the only one of the family who had always called his grandson by his Yiddish pet name. Jacob now only vaguely remembered childhood days when his grandfather had loved bouncing him on his knee until the boy's tiny *yarmulkah* almost slid down over his eyes, while chanting '*Yankeleh, Yankeleh, geb tzu zein zeide a bonkeleh*'. '*Vos iz a bonkeleh?*' Jacob's father once asked. In sing-song came back the reply: 'A *bonkeleh* is a *greisa kuss*' – accompanied by a noisy demonstratory kiss on the child's forehead. 'I never heard of that,' Joshua answered. 'I think you just made up the word.' '*Ai, ai,*' Rabbi Moishe crooned to Jacob, 'your *tata* is such a *chachem*, such a wise man! "You just made up the word," he tells me, as if that is forbidden. How does he think words are made? Does he think a boy-word meets a girl-word, they get married, and in time another word is born? *Ai*, is that it? No, *Yankeleh*, you tell him: people make words. *Yankeleh, Yankeleh, geb tzu zein zeide a bonkeleh.*'

As Joshua sat, unconsciously shepherding the crumbs on his plate into a neat pile as if they were pieces of scrap in his store, he listened to the Rabbi talking to Jacob, heard the warmth in his voice, and felt a pang of envy at the bond that existed between his father and his son. He wished he had been able to act as unaffectedly, but some reluctance that he could never understand always held him back. Was it just shyness? Or was it because he had had two daughters before the son he wanted eventually arrived and by then he was too old, with all the eagerness and spontaneity of early fatherhood dried up? Or perhaps it was that he had not wanted to turn Bertha's disappointment with her daughters into bitterness by seeing him show too much interest in his son. Whatever the answer, it was too late now to turn back the clock, too late to understand anything about Jacob. Yes, he did envy the affection that flowed between the boy and the old man. He envied it, but he feared for it, too, for when the Rabbi departed to *Eretz* who would show Jacob the same affection? Not his sister, Judith – the gap between them was too wide; not his mother – it would not fit her image of the man she wanted him to become; and not his father – not even his father. Jacob would have to look elsewhere for it. Perhaps he already had.

'*Oi, gevald,*' Joshua murmured to himself, unable to suppress the age-old cry of suffering and despair as he momentarily covered his eyes with his hand. But Bertha, sitting across the table from him, saw the involuntary action and the slight movement of his lips, and her heart ached to share her husband's burden – whatever it might be.

Whenever Jacob was meeting Deirdre outside college hours he waited for her at the bottom of Patrick's Hill where it joined King Street. It wasn't King Street any more of course – at least, not officially, for some months earlier the Cork Corporation had defiantly renamed it MacCurtain Street in honour of the city's martyred Lord Mayor. But the sign on the wall still said King Street, and Jacob presumed that as yet only members of the IRA and their supporters would call it by its new name. Perhaps that meant most of the city's population – it certainly included Deirdre.

He kept his eyes fixed on the crest of the hill over which she would appear freewheeling down on her bicycle, black hair streaming and her long skirt ballooning out on either side like a bat's wings. Patrick's Hill was so long

103

and steep that even pedestrians found it an excessive strain, and its footpaths had been layered with sets of steps at regular intervals to make the ascent tolerable. Coming down, especially on a bicycle, was exhilarating, even dangerous if the handlebars developed a wobble. One's impetus was such that, provided there was nothing in the way, one would be carried through Bridge Street, right over Patrick's Bridge, and halfway into Patrick's Street, Cork's main thoroughfare, before having to put foot to pedal once more.

At ten o'clock on a Sunday morning traffic was almost nonexistent, and as soon as Deirdre came into view Jacob began to cycle towards the bridge. He was only halfway there when she passed him at full speed, shouting 'Slow coach!' as she flew ahead. He did not hurry to catch up with her. For him these first moments of meeting each day were so exciting an elixir that he always tried to make them last as long as possible, and the sight of her in full flight on her bicycle never failed to set his blood tingling.

She came to rest beside the statue of Father Mathew, the Apostle of Temperance, and as Jacob drew up to her he joked: 'You wouldn't want to get too close to him. You'd never know what way he'd take you, being without a drink for so long.'

'Safer in his arms than some I could mention,' Deirdre joked back.

The veiled allusion of her reply, the intimacy of her tone of voice, reassured Jacob. Having known her for less than two months, he was not yet confident of any strong hold on her affections, despite the fact that she seemed quite willing to accept his embraces and kisses. But he did not feel that she looked upon their amorous exchanges as more than innocent dalliance. If her beauty, her year advantage in age, and her casualness were not completely deterring, they often induced in him a tentativeness and an uncomfortable awareness of his own inexperience.

'Come on, let's go,' Deirdre said. 'There are too many policemen around here for us to be hanging about.'

Pairs of RIC men were patrolling on each side of the

wide thoroughfare and, though to Jacob they were of no more account than any other pedestrians, he realised that Deirdre could not feel so unconcerned. He glanced at the basket on the front of her bicycle. As usual it was full, her handbag plonked on top of bags of fruit which on the outward journey were reserved 'for my grandmother in the country', but which, her assignment completed without incident, they would eat on the way home. The assignment was the distribution of *An tÓglach*, the banned IRA newspaper, hidden beneath the fruit. If they were stopped by the police and her basket was searched, he was to say that he knew nothing about the newspapers – she made him agree to this arrangement if he wanted to accompany her on her clandestine journeys. His acceptance of the condition was made with an easy mind – he didn't feel that distributing a newspaper, even a banned one, would be considered a particularly heinous offence for a young girl, and anyway he could not imagine that he would be in any danger himself if he admitted knowledge of the basket's contents.

'Where to today?' he asked as they set off, weaving between the trams drawn up at the Statue terminus and careful to avoid getting their tyres caught in the tramlines.

'Gougane Barra.'

'Gougane Barra! But that's miles away,' Jacob expostulated. 'We couldn't possibly cycle there and back in a day.'

Deirdre laughed at his alarm. 'No. I only said that to wake you up. We'll go as far as Coachford – that's on the way to Gougane. Do you think your lordship could manage that much?'

'I think so,' Jacob replied and then, in a fruity voice, declaimed:

> 'There is a green island in lone Gougane Barra
> Where an allua of song rushes forth as an
> arrow.'

'What's that?' Deirdre asked.

'A poem. Called "Gougane Barra", by John Joseph Callanan.'

'Who's he when he's at home?'

'Shame on you,' came the bantering reply, 'not to know one of your own local poets. Admittedly he *is* rather obscure and it's nearly a hundred years since he died. But you wouldn't approve of him anyway.'

'Why not?'

'Because at one stage of his life he joined the British Army.'

'Oh, a renegade,' Deirdre commented.

'Not exactly. He was just too poor to do anything else.'

'There you are.' There was a note of triumph in her voice. 'Why was he poor? British oppression.'

'Yes, that's true,' Jacob agreed.

'But it doesn't disturb *you*. It doesn't affect you.' As they cycled along side by side, Deirdre put a comradely hand on Jacob's shoulder, as if to deny any accusation in her words. 'After all, you're not Irish – or so you keep telling me.'

They had reached the end of Patrick Street and were turning into Grand Parade. Jacob pointed to an elaborate fountain a hundred yards ahead of them in the middle of the road, the distance making the play of water seem frozen in mid-jet.

'See that?'

'What? You mean the fountain?'

'Yes, Berwick Fountain. Do you like it?'

'Like it?' Deirdre echoed in puzzlement. 'I don't know. I never thought about it. It's just a fountain.'

'Just a fountain. And Patrick Street is just a street. And that lovely shop we just passed – Queen's Old Castle – is just a shop. Oh, beggin' your pardon, ma'm, but with a name like *Queen's* Old Castle I could hardly expect *you* to like it.'

'What *are* you ramaishing about?' Deirdre laughed.

'Listen to me, Deirdre. I'll tell you.'

Jacob, however, wasn't sure what he had to tell. He had never been able to grasp it himself, never been able to assemble the jigsaw pieces of his identity into a clear

106

recognisable picture. There was no form of words he could quote to define himself or his purpose, like a lodestar or a motto an ancient family would bear on its coat of arms. The whole puzzle became even more tantalising whenever he tried to fashion it into a poem. But he was encouraged by his feelings for Deirdre, by his desire to impress her, perhaps also by some vague idea that to excite her sympathy would automatically make him more attractive to her. Most of all, she was the only person he knew to whom he could talk without embarrassment, and it was a help that cycling side by side he didn't have to look at her as he tried to explain.

'You and I were both born here, in Cork, but you think of it as Cork, Ireland, while I think of it as just Cork, where I live.'

'It's more than that,' Deirdre interrupted. 'It's where you were born – as you said – with all that that implies.'

'That's just it. What does it imply for me? Cork is where I *happened* to be born. Where did my family come from? Lithuania. They happened to end up in Cork but it might just as well have been Hamburg or Paris or London, or America, as so many other Jews did. Where were your people born?'

'Father Cork City, mother County Cork, grandparents different parts of Ireland.'

'There you are,' Jacob said, giving his bicycle bell a ping as if to reinforce his point. 'And probably – no, almost certainly – your great-grandparents were born in Ireland, too, and their parents before them. You. Are. Irish. I'm not. Oh, technically, officially, I am. But I can't *be* Irish. I can't *feel* Irish.'

'You're talking about roots, aren't you?' Deirdre asked.

'Roots and what grows from roots. Involvement, commitment.'

There was a pause while Deirdre considered this. Then, as if she had found a flaw in his argument, she pinged her own bell and announced: 'But you love Cork. You've told me you love it. You know so much about the city.'

'Yes. But that's the very point I'm trying to make,' Jacob threw back at her. 'Cork is as deep as my roots go.

107

Remember, I never mixed with Christians until I went to college and met you. You're the first non-Jewish girl I've ever said more than "Nice day" to. I've lived my life in a ghetto – Jewish people, Jewish friends, Jewish history, Jewish affairs, Jewish concerns, that's been my world. And that world, that ghetto, happens to be in this city, in Cork. It's all I know, or feel, of Ireland – my physical surroundings. They appeal to me emotionally, aesthetically, but not – not – viscerally.'

'God above, you're using horrible-long words,' Deirdre laughed.

'Sorry. Blame my medical training – all six weeks of it. But, seriously, to me Cork is a beautiful city. I love its buildings, its river, its setting, its atmosphere. While I've grown up in it, it has grown in me.' Jacob paused, and then with a side-glance added light-heartedly: 'Oh, and I love some of its people, too.'

'Now, don't try to change the subject,' Deirdre admonished him with a smile.

They had reached the beginning of Western Road and were passing the Cork & Muskerry Railway station. From there the single line emerged onto the road, and along one side of it the train to West Cork would puff and blow at a brisk but not incautious pace, its smoke staining the leaves of the roadside trees, the guard ringing his bell almost without stop until they were approaching Carrigrohane and could reasonably expect to be out of range of busy pedestrians, excited children, and messenger-boys on bicycles plaguing the engine-driver by trying to outspeed him.

'We don't have to worry about bumping into the train today,' Deirdre commented.

'Why not? It runs on Sunday, doesn't it?'

'Not at the moment. The British have closed it down. Didn't you read it in the *Examiner* last week?'

'Oh, yes,' Jacob recalled, 'and there was talk of it at home. Some of my father's friends who have their "weeklies" in West Cork were having an awful job getting there.'

'Well, shouldn't that make you feel more Irish?'

'If you mean anti-British, no, I don't feel it has anything to do with me. It's not my fight.'

'But it should be,' Deirdre insisted. 'You and the other Jews live here. You found refuge here. Don't you feel you owe the country something?'

'Do you mean me or the Jewish community?'

'Either. Both.'

By now they were in open country. Far behind there were the church spires, the woodlands, the houses and buildings on the hills surrounding the city of Cork, postcard size but still plainly visible in the clear morning air. On either side and ahead of them were endless fields, uncultivated, unfenced, broken here and there by boreens, and populated by nothing except occasional tinker settlements with their smoky caravans, wild-looking ponies and the disorder and abandon of their ragged encampments.

'Let's rest awhile,' Jacob suggested. 'I can't think properly on the move.'

Deirdre did not object. They dismounted, leaned their bicycles against the bank by the roadside and hoisted themselves onto its grassy top. Bending to remove his bicycle clips, Jacob's hand brushed against Deirdre's ankle. He saw a white edging of petticoat escape from under the hem of her dress without quite concealing the swell of her calf muscle. Even the incongruous recollection of the butcher's-slab-illustrations in his anatomy textbook failed to arrest the flutter his heart gave at the sight.

'Well,' Deirdre persisted. 'Do you or don't you feel you owe Ireland something?'

Jacob plucked a blade of grass and rolled it between his hands for some moments.

'I can't say what other Jews might feel,' he answered eventually.

'Yourself, then.'

'Do I feel I owe Ireland something? What you mean is *shouldn't* I feel I owe Ireland something.' He heard his voice instinctively adopt the sing-song cadence of the *Yeshiva bucher*, the rabbinical college student, who

109

would spent all day reading the Talmud and elucidating its knottier points in the traditional chanted inflections that distinguished between problem and solution.

'In the first place,' he continued, 'what is Ireland? Is it "an island entirely surrounded by water" as I learned at school, or is it the Irish people? We can't be talking about Ireland, the physical land, because how can I owe its – how many? thirty-odd thousand square miles, is it? – how can I owe a piece of land anything? And if we're talking about the Irish people – well, it wasn't the Irish people who let the Jews into Ireland, it was the British government in Ireland. So, according to your reasoning, it's really the British I should support, not the Irish.' His laughter was meant to show that he didn't take his argument seriously, but he felt quite pleased with his own cleverness and hoped it would impress Deirdre.

'Go 'way with you,' she replied, pushing him almost off the bank in horseplay. 'Are you sure it's a doctor you should be and not a lawyer? You're only evading my question. It's the Irish people who have accepted you – or the Cork people, if you like. They are your neighbours. You depend on them for your living. It's their country. How can you not owe them something in return?'

Jacob was beginning to feel impatient at Deirdre's persistence – or was it really that he was impatient with himself? He recognised the logic in her question; he was aware – uncomfortably aware – of its logical answer.

'You're right of course. My grandfather – the Rabbi – has often told me about his arrival in Cork, when he and my father and mother and some other Jewish families came to live in Celtic Crescent, about thirty years ago. The day they moved in, a crowd began to gather outside their houses, and as more and more people joined the crowd my grandfather and his companions got very frightened. You see, they didn't know any English, so they couldn't understand what the people were saying. But this was the way pogroms had started where they came from – first, hostile neighbours taunting and shouting, then bricks and stones, and then breaking down their homes and setting fire to them. So all my grandfather and

110

his companions could do was lock their doors and windows as securely as possible, push boxes up against them because they had no furniture, and pray.'

Deirdre interrupted to say quietly: 'The Irish used to have to do that, too, when they couldn't pay their rent and the English landlord would send in the bailiffs to eject them.'

'Well,' Jacob continued, 'this went on for some time until they heard a knocking on the window. They looked up and saw it was a priest. My grandfather opened the door and somehow the priest was able to tell them, able to make them understand, that the people meant no harm. It was just that they had never seen a Jew in their lives and they were anxious to know what Jews looked like. So my grandfather and the other Jews came out and stood together to let the people see them. They were a bit afraid at first, but after a while, when they could see that what the priest had said was true, there was great relief and laughter and handshakes all round. The crowd looked into their houses, satisfied themselves that the Jews were ordinary mortals like themselves – just men, women and children, with no furniture and little possessions – and then they just quietly went away. Later on some of them came back with gifts of food and some stools to sit on and small ornaments and an old mattress – and one woman even brought a framed picture of Jesus! These neighbours and the Jews became firm friends from that day. There aren't many of the original Christians left because in time they moved elsewhere and other Jewish families came to live in their houses. But that priest is still there – Father McGiff. He's one of my grandfather's most intimate friends – probably more intimate than any of the Jewish community because, I suppose, my grandfather, as the Rabbi, has to be the same to all his flock. But Father McGiff visits us regularly, especially on Sunday nights. Most Sunday nights he and my grandfather play two-handed solo together.'

'And the moral of all that?' Deirdre suggested.

Jacob shrugged. 'I suppose it would be surprising if the Cork Jews didn't feel sympathetic to the Irish and their

111

cause. If I had to take sides myself, I'd probably be in favour, too. But as to owing them anything.... What, for instance? What am I supposed to do about it? I don't feel Irish – I told you that – at least, not Irish enough to know the answer to that question.'

'You're the proverbial Wandering Jew,' Deirdre commented. 'But if you don't know whether you owe the Irish anything why do you help me distribute a paper about our fight, and a banned one at that?'

'I help you because I – I. . . .' Jacob did not dare to use the word he wanted, so he ended tamely: 'Because I like you. I like being with you.'

'Thank you kindly, sir, she said,' Deirdre whispered. She was silent for a moment before saying briskly: 'Come on. I'm feeling cold. We'd better get going.'

Emboldened, Jacob put an arm around her, feeling the swell of her breast beneath the thick cloth of her coat and wishing he might somehow, some time, get the chance of being alone with her indoors, rather than always having to embrace where any passer-by might see them.

'Let me warm you,' he urged.

'What! At this hour of a Sunday morning! And out in the open for the world and his wife to see!' She gave him a swift light kiss and jumped off the bank. 'We have miles to go and I've seven calls to make.'

Reluctantly Jacob put on his trouser clips, slid down off the bank and mounted his bicycle. Deirdre already was twenty yards ahead, ringing her bell, laughing, and taunting 'Slow coach, as usual!' as he overtook her.

'I heard ye had a great meeting last night in the synagogue,' Mrs Burns announced in her high-pitched jokey voice.

Late on Sunday mornings she always dropped in to Ada Neumann's little shop to buy some of Mrs Neumann's special *pletsls* – thin crisp rolls garnished with onions – and to listen in on the gossip of the Crescent. She knew all the inhabitants of Jewtown intimately, having lived in

112

the last house in the street since the first arrivals. Her red-cheeked, wrinkled face smiled out from beneath a bulky hat – her Sunday Mass hat – secured by a large pin to her grey hair, and around the spotless frilled blouse buttoned over her ample bosom right up to her neck she wore a black woollen shawl. The blouse she had cut and sewn herself – she was an accomplished dressmaker who had made all her own children's clothes and, now that most of them were grown up and away, she had plenty of custom from her Jewish neighbours. She was especially favoured by the young unmarried girls who found her enthusiasm for the new fashion of shorter-than-ankle-length skirts as welcome as it was unexpected. 'Sure, what harm?' she told their mothers. 'Isn't it great to be young and romantic? Sure if we had our time again wouldn't we be the same? They're great girls altogether, ye have no fear of them.' The Jewish mothers, however, tut-tutted mildly or smiled without comment, preferring to keep their daughters as decorously dressed as possible and not wanting to encourage Mrs Burns's chatter. They were well used to her interest in their doings, and it was no great surprise to Ada Neumann that she already seemed to have gleaned some report of the Karlinsky meeting.

'Ye're off soon,' she was saying. 'A whole crowd of ye. To the Holy Land. The Rabbi an' all. I'd love to visit the Holy Land, but sure it's the other end of the world, isn't it? And the cost of it! Aren't ye grand to be able to afford it at all. C'm here to me, though' – and she leaned forward conspiratorially – 'is it true ye're going for good? Miriam says ye are. She's goin', too. Miriam Levy, that is – I'm making her wedding dress. It's gorgeous altogether. Wait till ye see it. She'll be a picture. An' ye had a big pot over from London last night to tell ye all about the Holy Land!'

She rearranged her shawl meticulously as she awaited the replies of the customers in the shop. The Jewish delicacies available here were only part of the attraction, for Sunday mornings in Neumann's had long been established as mainly for men, a time when as well as buying their weekly supplies of cigarettes, tobacco and snuff,

113

along with Mrs Neumann's kosher titbits, they could pass an enjoyable hour of gossip and banter.

'That's right, Mrs Burns,' Percy Lovitch agreed. 'We had a big pot over from London.'

'Sure don't I know,' Mrs Burns reiterated, ready now to reveal her source. 'The priest told us all about it.'

'The priest?'

'Father McGiff it was. Who else! He preached a sermon about it at Mass this morning.'

'*Nein!*' Ada Neumann exclaimed in mock disbelief.

The word and its nuance was a familiar expression to Mrs Burns, and she hastened to assure her listeners. 'He did. Preached his sermon about the Jews leaving Cork. As God is me judge' – and she crossed herself energetically.

'And what did he say in his sermon?' someone asked.

'Sure didn't he tell us that ye were after buyin' a huge space in the Holy Land and ye were goin' out there farming and fighting? Farming and fighting for what the Lord promised your people. Well, I never! Sure aren't ye the brave ones? And whisper – Father McGiff said that more of us here should take an example from the Jews and fight for our country. Isn't it true for him?'

'You mean he told you to join the IRA, Mrs Burns?' Mickey Aronson asked, his eyes twinkling with suppressed amusement at the thought.

'Well, now, I wouldn't say that. Not in so many words. But he said quite plainly that if more of us had as much fight and spirit as some of our young boys Ireland would soon be free. He made no bones about it. You could have knocked me over with a feather. Father McGiff never preached about that sort of thing before. Sure isn't he the mildest of men? And the holiest. He's a saint, he is. You're not goin' with them yerself, are yah?' Mrs Burns asked Percy Lovitch. 'To the Holy Land, I mean.'

'Would you miss me?' Percy joked back.

'Ah, go 'way with yah,' Mrs Burns laughed, leaning against his side for a moment as she pushed her way out. 'Sure I'll miss ye all.'

'*Nu*, Tevyeh,' Benny Katz, who had just entered the

shop, asked the customer in front of him. 'What did you think of Karlinsky's address?'

'You know, there was a talk about the Holy Land in the Assembly Rooms the other night,' Tevyeh replied in his mock-cultured accent. 'By a Protestant minister, a Rev. Allen or Alley, some name like that.'

'You were there?'

'Yes. I thought it might be interesting. "My Visit to the Holy Land", it was called. He spoke a lot about the Holy Places and about the Arabs. A lot of slides.'

'Holy Places! Arabs!' Mickey Aronson grumbled. 'What about us? What did he say about the Yiddin?'

'Very little,' Tevyeh answered. 'Nothing that isn't in the Bible. And nothing about Zionism and the Jewish settlements. It was ancient history mostly.'

'Mr Rosenberg,' Ada Neumann interrupted. 'I've kept some *pletsls* for you. You want?'

'Yes, yes, Mrs Neumann, I'll take them. *Nu*, Percy, I see your friends are coming tomorrow.'

'Who's that? Who's coming tomorrow?' Benny Katz enquired.

'Yes, I hope so.' Percy Lovitch smiled broadly and rubbed his hands. 'The Carl Rosa Company. The Carl Rosa *Opera* Company.'

'*Ach*, opera,' Mickey Aronson taunted. 'Tra-la, tra-la! *Vee a feygela* – like the birds. Only the birds don't dress up in silly costumes.'

Lovitch, used to Mickey Aronson's habit of making fun of everything, ignored his remarks.

'I hope they don't cancel their trip. I had a letter from their manager last week. He told me that some of the Company were worried about their safety in Cork – they're mostly English, of course.'

'And what about the trains?' Benny Katz interjected. 'If the train from Dublin is on strike.... I have to go to Midleton tomorrow. I don't know how I'll manage. There's more cancellations every day.'

'Well, I'll be at the station to meet them,' Percy Lovitch said, blowing his nose like a trumpet as if he were clearing his air-passages before launching into song. 'It'll be a

115

tragedy if they don't arrive. A great disappointment.'

'Are you singing with them this time, Mr Lovitch?' Ada Neumann asked.

'I won't know till they're here. I expect they'll have something for me to do. They usually have. For old times' sake, you know.'

'Maybe Pinkerton in *Madame Butterfly*,' Tevyeh Rosenberg said, laughing at the idea of portly Lovitch as the handsome young American lieutenant.

'You needn't laugh,' Percy rebuked him. 'When I was young I sang Pinkerton often.'

'They'll be doing *Butterfly*?' Rosenberg asked.

'Yes. Tomorrow *Bohème*. Then *Carmen*, *Cav* and *Pag*, *Mignon*, *Tannhäuser*, Saturday matinée *Tales of Hoffman* and *Butterfly* in the evening. A great programme, a great week.' And Percy hummed a few bars of 'Your Tiny Hand Is Frozen', but *sotto voce* – he had to save his voice and, anyway, why give such a small audience a treat for nothing!

On Sunday afternoons Rabbi Moishe's home was always open to anyone with a personal problem, a religious query or even a disagreement on a point of Torah or Talmud that needed adjudication. Traditionally the women did not trouble him on Sundays – they had every weekday morning when the men were away at work to bring their questions, which more often than not revolved about the dietary laws – was this new food kosher, was that one a *pareveh* brand that could be used either with a meat or a milk dish? As the years passed, however, the Rabbi was presented with fewer and fewer queries – either from the women or from the men – but he still sat alone in his front room every Sunday afternoon studying Talmud and ready to receive any caller.

This Sunday, however, as he bent over a large volume of Commentaries on the Torah, forgetting to call for the gas-mantle to be lit even though the light was dying around him, he did have a visitor. There was a timid knock on the front door, and Bertha Cohen went to open it. Abie Klugman stood there, half turned aside as if changing his mind.

'Mr Klugman! Come in, come in. No need to knock – the door is always on the latch.'

'The Rabbi ...,' Abie whispered.

'Inside, inside. By himself.'

She urged him before her to the small front room. He hesitated sheepishly on the threshold, his clean white shirt almost shining in the gloom, and the straining buttons of his Sabbath suit, which he had put on specially, leaving no doubt that it had been made many years before for a far less rounded Abie Klugman.

'You'll have a cup of tea, Mr Klugman, and some sponge cake, yes?'

Abie, too shy to take anything although his throat was dry, and too embarrassed to say either yes or no, merely mumbled and shook his head.

'Are you sure, Mr Klugman?' Bertha Cohen pressed.

When Abie made no answer, she shrugged her shoulders at the Rabbi as if to commiserate with him – he always liked a Sunday-afternoon cup, but she knew he would not partake of it while his visitor stayed empty-handed. He motioned his daughter-in-law to shut the door and led Abie Klugman to a chair.

'*Koom arein*, Mr Klugman, *koom arein*. Come in and sit down.'

Abie sat carefully on the edge of a chair, clasping his hands around his knees.

'*Nu*, Mr Klugman,' said the Rabbi, anxious to put him at his ease. 'And how is business?'

When Abie took no notice of the question but remained stiff and tongue-tied, Rabbi Cohen nodded sympathetically as if an answer, which he fully understood, had indeed been made.

'You are lucky, Mr Klugman. At least you have your own transport. If you were depending on the trains these days, as so many of the community are ... *ai.*...' And he threw up his hands in resignation.

'Rebbe ...,' Abie said, almost inaudibly. His brow

117

furrowed, but no further word came. Still, it was at least a beginning, Rabbi Cohen consoled himself, and he nodded his head and stroked his beard. Daylight was now all but gone and the two men, merging into the shadows of the small room, were like figures in an old oil painting. Rabbi Cohen looked out the window and saw that the lamplighter, with his long gas-taper, had just entered Celtic Crescent. The street-lamps, however, would throw little light into the room – a relief to the Rabbi, for he knew that the darkness was more likely to encourage his visitor to unburden himself. Father McGiff, he recalled, had told him he had the same experience in hearing Confessions – but of course Abie Klugman hardly had come to him with any story of transgressions.

'Tell me, Mr Klugman,' he resumed, 'what will you do with your horse and cart when you go to *Eretz*? Will you sell it before you leave?' Rabbi Cohen knew the horse and cart belonged to Max Klein, but it was wise to speak of something close to Abie Klugman and to ask him a question which, since he must know the answer, might make it easier for him to start talking. Certainly he was very slow, the Rabbi told himself, slow to collect his thoughts, slow to gather his courage, but he was a good man, a *mensh*. And, indeed, the Rabbi's question seemed to release whatever had locked Abie Klugman's lips.

'Rebbe,' he said, leaning forward anxiously, 'Mr Karlinsky – he is a great man.'

'Yes,' Rabbi Moishe agreed, 'an important man, a *baaleboss*.'

'But, Rebbe, soon I go to *Eretz*' – the Rabbi nodded – 'and last night . . . Mr Karlinsky . . . he said nothing to me.'

Rabbi Cohen smiled understandingly.

'Mr Klugman, you had a question for Mr Karlinsky?'

'*Nein*,' his visitor answered. 'Me! What could *I* ask him?'

'If you had asked a question, he would have answered you. You were with us after his address, in the side-room?'

Klugman nodded.

'So. He answered anyone who had a question. Otherwise what he said was for everyone.'

118

Abie Klugman nodded again, but Rabbi Cohen could see that he was still ill at ease.

'What is troubling you, Mr Klugman?' he asked quietly.

'Rebbe, I am not a *ga lernta mensh* and ... and ... I am not ... *du veist*, you know ... I get *tza mist*, mixed up ... my mind ... slow....' He paused, then all in a rush burst out: 'Rebbe, I must go to *Eretz*. I must go to *Eretz*, but Karlinsky did not tell me ... he did not speak to me ... perhaps they will not let me go....' Tears welled in his eyes. 'A fool they will not want in *Eretz*,' he forced himself to say, his head sinking to his chest in shame.

Rabbi Cohen rose from his chair.

'Mr Klugman, Mr Klugman.' He put a hand on the man's shoulder. Abie Klugman immediately got to his feet – *mensheskeit* required him not to remain seated once the Rabbi had stood up.

'Mr Klugman,' Rabbi Cohen said to him softly, looking into his eyes. '*Eretz* is the Land of Israel, the land the Lord promised to all Israel. Not only to the *greisah*, the *klugah*, the *baalbatish*, the *raich*, but to every Yid. Karlinsky has your name, yours and mine, and the others – and anyone else who might still decide to join us, a place will be found for him.'

He took Abie Klugman's hand in his and felt it tremble. All fear and doubt had not even yet been dispelled.

'Mr Klugman, you have my promise. *Eretz* is there for both of us. It waits for both of us. If *you* don't go, *I* don't go. *Ga nug?* Enough?'

Abie took the Rabbi's hands in his, enveloping them as if they were no bigger than a baby's. His face, like a balloon suddenly filled with air, swelled into a beaming smile and his head nodded convulsively. A Rabbi's word was God's own promise.

'*Ga nug*, Rebbe, *ga nug, ga nug, ga nug*,' he muttered over and over as he backed into the now dark hall and let himself out into the street.

Rabbi Moishe stood for some moments in silence. *His* head was nodding too – in compassion for Abie Klugman and in gratitude to God Who in His mercy was bringing them both to *Eretz*.

119

By evening the Rabbi was tired but looking forward to Father McGiff's usual Sunday-night visit. He tried not to think of how much he would miss his old friend, but their imminent separation filled him with sadness. It had been a long friendship – over thirty years: thirty years of conversation, philosophical speculation, religious discussion, reminiscence, mutual history lessons, tea-drinking and two-handed solo in the front room of No. 1 Celtic Crescent. Rabbi Moishe's early wariness had long been forgotten, though his intimacy with a priest of the church which for so many centuries and in so many lands had sought to root out Judaism still sometimes surprised him. It was an intimacy, the Rabbi was certain, based on their mutual love of God reflected in their mutual love of God's creatures. There was no rivalry between them, no fishing for souls and no scoring of points. There was not even – and this was something the Rabbi was glad of – a single joint experience in which their reactions and performances might have been compared, by others if not by themselves. Indeed, the previous night at the synagogue meeting was the first time they had found themselves together in any place apart from this small room where they had first met and which held all the memories and echoes of their years of friendship.

Rabbi Moishe, resting in his armchair beside the hissing gas-fire, suddenly thought of so much else the room meant to him. He opened his eyes and looked around at all the familiar objects, the companions of his second life. In the glass case were the *becherim*, the silver goblets for the Kiddush prayer to sanctify the Sabbath, and the rows of holy volumes and prayer-books for all the Jewish festivals, the gold print on their dark pimpled spines like beacons of truth guiding him in the path of the Lord. On the mantelpiece were family photographs flanked by the two Sabbath candlesticks and in the middle the many-branched *menorah*, which – unless Karlinsky arranged an unexpectedly hasty departure to *Eretz* – in three weeks' time, come Chanukah, he would be seeing lit for the last time in this house. His gaze fell to the floor, to the corner facing east towards *Eretz*, where morning, afternoon, evening, and again at night before retiring, he had recited the daily prayers if there wasn't a synagogue service. A smile creased his face as he noted how the linoleum there had been worn away by the ritual of the Amidah prayer. This silent private prayer to God always ended with three symbolic steps backwards to signify one's withdrawal from the presence of the Lord, the same three steps also being necessary before the prayer to make sure that there was nothing in the way. This little room had been the fulcrum of his life for so long – a simple life, a *richticha Yiddisheh* life. What would it have been if flight had not changed it? What would it yet be when flight would, presumably, change it once again? But it was not the flight from Akmeyon, his birthplace in Lithuania, that he wanted to think of, or the impending one from his family and community in Cork. It was the flight *to* somewhere that now lifted his soul. He had eaten his bread of affliction. Like the first Moses he had wandered – well, maybe not in a wilderness, no, Corkileh was not a wilderness, even Akmeyon had been better than a wilderness – but, then, his wanderings had been much longer than Moses's forty years, if he counted from the day of his birth. Seventy-five. Three score years and ten – and a bonus. Of course that other Moses had lived to be a hundred and twenty – but he was not complaining. God had been good to him. If he could have just a little longer. . . . But he would not importune the Lord; God would grant what He would grant. Still, a little longer, and *Eretz*, and a great-grandchild. . . . He looked up at the low ceiling and through it to heaven on high. In whatever order might suit You, O Lord. . . . He smiled to himself and shook his head. '*Ai . . . ai*,' he murmured, '*ai . . . ai . . . Gott iss goot.*'

The sound of Father McGiff pulling the latch-string on the front door made him rise from his chair in anticipation.

'Welcome, my friend. Welcome, Father.'

The two men shook hands and the Rabbi guided the priest to the easy chair beside the glowing gas-fire. Before he could sit down, Bertha Cohen, who had heard him arrive, appeared in the doorway. Her smile of welcome

121

was sincere even though she had never felt completely at ease in his presence. Her husband might deal almost daily with non-Jews, and the Rabbi had his Father McGiff, but Christian friendships had no part in her life. *De veldt* to her meant the Jewish world. Any thing and any person from outside that world could become a threat. A priest? There had been priests, too, in Akmeyon, priests with blood on their hands.

Still, Father McGiff was Rabbi Moishe's friend and had been a friend to the whole community for a very long time. She conceded that. And very soon these Sunday calls would come to an end.

'Good evening, Father.' She made her customary awkward half-bow.

'And good evening to you, Mrs Cohen. You're keeping well? You are, thank God. And the Rabbi, too. He looks great altogether, doesn't he? I think it's all the excitement that agrees with him.'

In fact Father McGiff had immediately observed the lines of tiredness in the Rabbi's face and he wondered about the effect the strain of all these arrangements for his departure, and the journey itself, might have on the old man. But, then, he'd be sure to perk up once he reached Palestine – wasn't that all he was living for?

Bertha Cohen had silently departed and she reappeared almost immediately with a tea-tray.

'The very thing, Mrs Cohen. Aren't you great? I see those delicious biscuits of yours. Ah, you know my weakness. You're very kind.'

'They're different biscuits, Father. My daughter Judith baked them. She can cook very well – when she puts her hand to it.'

'And why wouldn't she, Mrs Cohen, with a teacher like yourself? None better. And tell me, what news of Molly? Everything taking its normal course, I've no doubt.'

'Yes. We had a letter on Friday.'

'God be praised. Sure it won't be long now. Next month, isn't it? You'll never notice the time flying, what with all the excitement here and the good Rabbi getting ready to leave us. Ah, don't you be bothering now' – as Bertha made her ritual motion to pour out the tea – 'you can leave that to me. I'm quite used to doing the honours for myself. Let me not keep you. Sure aren't you always busy.'

Bertha Cohen gave a small smile of acquiescence and left the room, glad to get out of range of the priest's clattering tongue. The Rabbi nodded sympathetically to his friend. Father McGiff was never garrulous with him, and he recognised that the chatter was a disguise to hide his shyness with women. In the early years of their acquaintance Rabbi Moishe had secretly been appalled at the priest's unworldliness. He appreciated his sincerity, his devoutness, his very holiness – but how could he minister to men and be so inexperienced in the real problems of life? The Rabbi was himself, he hoped – he certainly tried to be – sincere, devout and holy; he knew that he spent most of his time with his head sunk in Torah or Talmud or Gemara, but he had been a husband and was a father, so he was in touch, no, more than in touch – he was part of life. Father McGiff was the one who was in touch – no more than in touch – with life. Life was family – a world in microcosm. When a man had a wife and family, he had – what was it they said? – given hostages to fortune, but Rabbi Moishe never worried about that aspect of living. These so-called hostages *were* a man's fortune. As Rabbi Moishe's friendship with the priest warmed over the years it was a subject they often discussed.

'Worldliness breeds prejudice,' Father McGiff had argued, adding: 'No, that's the wrong word, Rabbi. Bias. That's it. It breeds bias. How, in ministering to your fellow-man, can you approach near to God's truth if you're swayed by bias? And there's nothing to sway a man to bias so much as emotional involvement. You say I need worldliness. I'm flesh and blood. That's worldliness enough. But I'm more than that. I'm soul and spirit, too – other-worldliness. Checks and balances, Rabbi, checks and balances.'

The Rabbi thought of that now as he sat with Father McGiff and waited for the priest to speak about the sermon he had preached that morning. He *would* speak about it – Rabbi Moishe knew he would – in his own good time. Strange how their paths were diverging in so many ways so late in their friendship – the Rabbi off to a land where he could rest for whatever years were left to him, rest and study and praise God, with no other commitment; the priest to stay at home and become, it seemed, more committed than ever before.

Father McGiff poured the tea, first the Rabbi's, slowly through a strainer into a tall glass that rested in a filigreed silver holder, and then his own into a rose-rimmed china cup. He milked his and took a few sips before resting back in his chair, one of Judith's biscuits in his hand. Rabbi Moishe kneaded with a long spoon the slice of lemon already in the bottom of his glass and then, putting a piece of lump sugar behind his teeth, sucked the black tea through it.

'That was a good meeting last night,' Father McGiff mused. 'That Karlinsky – a real live wire.'

'You spoke well, Father. I appreciated your words.'

'I spoke what I felt.' The priest paused for a moment before continuing. 'But it can be self-indulgent, you know, Rabbi.'

'You mean?' the Rabbi asked as he put a fresh cube of sugar into his mouth.

'I mean that once you start it's like a crying fit – hard to stop. I did a bit more of it this morning – in my sermon.'

'Yes,' Rabbi Cohen nodded. 'I heard about it.'

'You heard already!' the priest exclaimed in surprise. 'That wasn't long getting around.'

'I believe the news came from one of your parishioners – Mrs Burns.'

'Ah, the *Shabbos-goy.*'

It was the Rabbi's turn to be surprised. 'I didn't know you knew the word, Father.'

'Ah sure, God love you, Rabbi, wouldn't it be hard for me to live with Jews for so long and not learn a little of their ways. A *Shabbos-goy* is a Christian who goes into Jewish households on the Sabbath and does little tasks like lighting the fire, drawing the water, little things like that, that they are forbidden to do on their Sabbath. And

124

Mrs Burns does it for most of the houses in the Crescent. She's their *Shabbos-goy*. Am I right? Do I go to the top of the class?'

'You do, Father. And I must congratulate you on your accent.'

There was a silence, but Rabbi Moishe refrained from prompting the priest.

'They're great biscuits,' Father McGiff commented, helping himself to another. 'Very tasty. Congratulate Judith for me. Women like to be praised for their womanly accomplishments, I'm told.' Then he went on: 'Yes, I preached a sermon this morning. I suppose you'd call it – I mean they'd call it – a seditious sermon.'

'In what way?'

'Ah sure didn't I as good as tell the people to join the IRA and fight?'

'You never suggested that before?' the Rabbi asked.

'I did not. I've always kept pulpit and politics separate.'

Father McGiff rested his cup in its saucer and then, as if searching for something to do, poured himself more tea. Rabbi Moishe sensed his bewilderment at his own actions, his need to have them, if not endorsed, then at least understood by some independent judgement.

'And now you have changed your mind? You no longer think the pulpit and politics should be kept apart?'

'But, damn it, man,' the priest exclaimed forcefully, 'that's the point. It's not politics – it's freedom. A different thing altogether. And since the Lord created Man free what better place to preach freedom than in the House of God?'

'True, true,' the Rabbi said, nodding his head while running a hand through his beard as if to register a hint of reservation in his agreement. Freedom, yes – but violence?

'Tell me, my friend, what made you change your mind?'

Father McGiff hesitated. Then 'Two things did,' he said. 'You, for one.'

'I!' Rabbi Moishe's eyes widened.

'Yes. You and your people. Last night the scales fell from my eyes. I thought, if *you* could fight for

125

what you believe is yours, then should I not fight, too?'

Rabbi Moishe's hands went up in horror. 'Fight? Who spoke about fighting? Do you mean the stories of the settlements in Palestine being attacked by wandering Arabs? But that is self-defence. The Jews in Palestine are not soldiers. They are not resisting the ruling powers.'

'Not yet, Rabbi, not yet. But it's early days. What do you think all those Jewish settlements in Palestine amount to? They're the first step in your fight for your homeland.'

'No, no,' Rabbi Moishe contradicted. And then he was brought up short by the implication of his friend's suggestion. Was that really why he was going to *Eretz*? Was there anywhere in his mind the smallest idea that he was the vanguard of an army? No. Never. No such thought had ever occurred to him. And yet ... if the Jews were some day to have a home of their own in Palestine – the Jews as a nation, not merely scattered bands of settlers – could it be purchased with Blue Box pennies and appeals and collections? Countries are not chattels to be bought and sold. What about the people living there? What about its present rulers? Even if there was enough money for a homeland, who would be willing to sell it to them?

'*Ai ... ai*,' Rabbi Moishe uttered in consternation, swaying from side to side. How simple he had been! How foolish not to have analysed his own emotions. 'A fool they will not want in *Eretz*,' Abie Klugman had said. And hadn't Father McGiff always warned about the danger of being swayed by emotions?

'I can see you're surprised, Rabbi,' the priest said. 'I know what you're thinking. You're thinking that as men of the cloth we must preach love of our neighbour, peace, friendship. And I know it's in that spirit you're going to Palestine. Maybe I exaggerate. Maybe you or your people won't have to fight for your home. Perhaps you'll get it by peaceful means. But *we* won't, Rabbi. The Irish won't. We're an occupied country. We may have been dis- possessed, but we haven't been dislodged. And what's happening here is obscene, Rabbi, obscene. These Black

126

and Tans . . . no one could stand for their savagery. That's the other reason I changed my mind. Did you read what happened in Granard the other day?'

Rabbi Moishe shook his head.

'It's a lovely little village, Granard. Up in County Longford. Inoffensive people – small farmers, peasants really, God-fearing to a man. They burned it down – the Tans did. Not just a simple straightforward burning. Oh, no! There happened to be a wandering violinist in the village at the time – you know, a fiddler who plays a few airs by the side of the road for pennies. Do you know what they did? They set fire to the main street and commanded him to march up and down it playing English songs while they laughed and taunted him. Sure how would a poor beggar like that have English songs! So he played an Irish song, Rabbi. Of course that didn't suit these devils, and just for that they shot him. Yes, they shot him and threw his body and his fiddle into the flames. That's what happened in Granard. I know Granard, Rabbi. It's where I was born, where my parents are buried, Lord have mercy on their souls.'

Rabbi Moishe could find no words to express his horror and sympathy after such an appalling story. He stretched a hand forward and laid it on the priest's. Slowly Father McGiff's hand unclenched and turned to clasp the Rabbi's.

'I'll say it again, Rabbi.' His voice was firm, determined. 'I'll preach the same sermon next Sunday, and the Sunday after, and the Sunday after that, and I'll go on until there's only one side left. And that'll be us, the Irish people in their own land.'

'I understand,' Rabbi Moishe nodded.

'You do, sure I know you do. We can't take up arms, we're men of God. But there are such things as just wars, you know, and my sermons will encourage my people to fight for their home just as your journey to Palestine is the first step in your fight for yours.'

'You know, Father,' the Rabbi said, a smile hovering on his lips, 'if I could, I'd appoint you Rabbi of the Cork Jewish Community after I've gone.'

127

'Would I make a good Rabbi, then? Do you think so?'

'A good Rabbi? There's a saying in the Talmud: "A Rabbi whose people do not want to drive him out of town isn't a Rabbi; and a Rabbi they do drive out isn't a man." I don't think they'd easily drive you out.'

The two holy men sat in silence for a while, the strength of their affection and respect for each other charging the air between them. Then the Rabbi took the pack of cards from the mantelpiece and held it up.

'Father, let us play,' he said.

For a moment the priest did not reply and then, suddenly seeing the joke, he burst into laughter. 'As they say hereabouts, Rabbi, I wouldn't doubtcha' – and, chuckling happily, he placed the tea-tray on the floor while the Rabbi commenced to deal two-handed solo.

Further along Celtic Crescent another card game was in progress – Rev. Levitt's Sunday-night bridge school. The minister was not doing well. Somehow the cards would not run for him and his bidding seemed to have lost its accustomed sureness. Already he was down far more points than he cared to think about. He lit another cigarette, reflecting wryly that this week's supply didn't look like being paid for by his bridge friends. Still, there was the wedding very soon. Just as well, he thought, as he arranged the hand just dealt him and saw that once again it boasted barely a single honour card.

At about the same time a man, dressed in a trench coat and with a cap pulled well down over his eyes, jumped out of a dark gateway on Southern Road, poked a gun into the ribs of a soldier passing by, and ordered him into a horse-drawn cart that had been slowly making its way up the hill behind him. Jumping in beside his captive, he directed: 'You just lie down there now, Captain Simcox, and no harm will come to you at all.'

'Good man yerself, Boxer,' came from the small figure on the driver's seat.

Handing him the gun, Boxer nimbly changed places.

'I'll take the reins now,' he said. 'The horse knows me. You take the gun and keep a good eye on his nibs. It's a pity, though, that Denis Hurley isn't with us. Casting no aspersions on yerself, Shamus. But Denis is all right, he deserves a second chance.'

'What'll happen to him?' the little man asked, keeping the gun dug into Captain Simcox's back.

'God knows. And we'll know soon. HQ are having a meeting about it and they've hauled Hardy up to Dublin. Anyway, we've got a better prize now than the old Jew, so they should be pleased enough.'

He cracked his whip, and the horse, reaching the crest of the hill, picked up speed.

'Attaboy,' Boxer sang. 'Full speed ahead, me flower, full speed ahead.'

9

COLD, PENETRATING RAIN swept the city of Cork on Monday morning, masking from sight its friendly hills – weather altogether too miserable for Judith to walk to her father's store as she usually did. When she had first started working in his office that was no bigger than a hut, they had accompanied each other every morning, but the long silences between them had made these journeys embarrassing and she had soon contrived to be a little slow getting ready most days so that the routine they quickly established – to the relief of both – was for him to precede her.

As she sat in the jangling overcrowded tram being rocked uncomfortably from side to side, she buried her head in the fur collar of her coat and gazed numbly through the rain-pocked windows. Rubbing the condensation from the glass she saw scores of weird creatures scurrying along, headless bodies surmounted by domes of sodden weeping umbrellas. All the familiar early-morning bustle was there, but the rain had transformed it into a blind scramble for the shelter and warmth of the city's shops, offices and factories. There seemed to be more than the usual number of police and soldiers on the streets, their wet capes glistening even in the murky light. A huge dray piled with barrels of the local Beamish

& Crawford stout and pulled by a pair of massive steaming horses trundled past. Their manes were matted to their necks as they strained under the urging of the brown-liveried driver, and their hoofs alternately splashed through the puddled road and then slid and slithered on the treacherous cobbled strips between the tramlines. The aroma of stout wafted in through the open front of the tram, causing many of the male passengers to sniff longingly and look forward already to the end of their day's work.

Halfway across Parnell Bridge the tram came to a sudden halt as the long current-rod on its roof broke away from the overhead electric wire. The driver, a young-looking man with an already grey moustache, gave the golden handle a smart flick so that it whirled around madly until he suddenly locked it in the brake position. Then, taking off his official peaked cap with its gold braid and donning a cloth one which had been resting on the ledge in front of him, he jumped down onto the road, oblivious of the mucky splashes that sullied his trouser ends. Judith turned her head to see him take hold of the rope that was tied to the rear of the tram and try to manoeuvre the contact wheel back onto the wire to restore the current. With the rain driving into his upturned face and the wind making the thin cable sway from side to side, the readjustment was taking longer than usual. While the passengers waited, some unfolded the morning *Cork Examiner*, while others impatiently dug a hand inside their overcoats and pulled out heavy watches, each of which trailed an inch or two of gold chain.

Judith looked down through the bridge's criss-cross of girders at the River Lee, its dark surface whipped by the rain. In summer weather it would have been pleasant to be stranded like this – except that in summer, of course, she would have been walking. Parnell Bridge – known as the Blue Bridge because of its colour – was part of her childhood. From the back bedroom window of her home it was possible to glimpse over the rooftops the tall masts of any ship moving up-river, and the sight had been enough for her to raise the alarm and go scampering hand in hand with Molly round the corner and on to the quays to see policemen, whistles to lips, urging all traffic and pedestrians off the bridge before closing the big iron gates at both ends. Then the two girls would watch in awe as the bridge very slowly swivelled around until the waterway was clear and the ship slid through.

Years later another bridge had been built, not more than a hundred yards further on, to link the main Glanmire Railway to the smaller station at Albert Road. This new one was a contrast in every way: though it also was named after an Irish hero – this time the ancient warrior, High-King Brian Boru, who had driven out Ireland's first invaders, the Danes – it was painted red, so becoming known as the Red Bridge; and instead of gliding gracefully around in a semi-circle when a ship approached it raised itself high into the sky from one end like some prehistoric sea-monster preparing to swallow all the river traffic. This performance was far more spellbinding than that of its companion, though not to Judith and Molly, for by then they were young ladies who no longer found any romance in bridges, so Jacob it was who used to rush to see it in action whenever he got the chance. He was proud of the fact that Cork should have two such movable bridges while Dublin, the capital of the country, had none, and when he started writing poetry they and their operation became the subject of one of his earliest odes.

The recollection amused Judith as she waited for the tram to restart its journey and, though she could not recall any lines from the poem, she did remember its title, 'The Ballet of the Bridges'. She wondered if Jacob was still writing. Perhaps she should have taken more interest in his poetry – and not only in his poetry. She and Molly had never been companions for him – how could they be with the gap in their ages? – and he had no relationship at all with his father. Well, neither had she for that matter; but, then, she had had Molly for so long. Now, with Molly gone, she was alone; when *zeide* went, Jacob would be alone. But at least he was going to university, and he was bound to make new and interesting friends there.

Arriving at the store in Old George's Street, Judith hurried into the office. Her father wasn't there, but his bowler hat and overcoat were hanging up so she looked out of the window to see the tip of his umbrella moving behind a small mountain of scrap in one corner of the yard. The office was warmed by a gas-fire, which she turned up higher, and on her work-table was a single letter. Recognising immediately the blue envelope Molly always used, she hurried to open it. It was mostly questions, hardly anything about herself. Had Judith been at Karlinsky's meeting? Molly asked. When was *zeide* leaving? Would her parents be able to come to Leeds for the birth of her child? If not, would Judith come? She'd much prefer that and, after all, surely with all Solly's family fussing around her she needed at least one of her own to give her moral support. She was sorry she had taken a while to write to their mother (had her letter home arrived safely?) but really she never had anything much to tell her. She had told her she was quite well – which she was, but she was getting impatient, and beginning to be made cranky by little things. She found it hard to go out some days because if the weather was dry – which it had been – the air was heavy with the smell of the yarn being used in the mills and clothing factories and it tended to nauseate her. She had never noticed it before – well, she had, but she hadn't minded....

Judith put the letter down and was taking off her coat when there was a knock on the office door. She opened it to find a man there, his raincoat saturated and drops falling from the peak of his soft cap.

'Yes?' she enquired. 'Come in. You're getting soaked there.'

He stepped over the threshold, taking off his cap to shake it out behind him as he asked: 'Is the boss – Mr Cohen – around?'

Judith was about to say she would get him when Joshua himself appeared, *yarmulkah* on his head and his dark suit smudged with darker stains where the umbrella had not covered him. The man turned at his step, and Joshua

133

gave a start of alarm when he saw it was Denis Hurley. His eyes darted to his daughter, and he half-raised his umbrella as if contemplating whether to do battle with it.

Denis, interpreting his action, hastened to reassure him.

'Eh, just a business call – an ordinary business call, Mr Cohen.'

'Business?' Iron Josh queried, still not ready to take any chances.

'Yes. The money I owe you' – and Denis drew from his raincoat pocket a ten-shilling note and a handful of silver and copper coins.

Joshua stifled his surprise. The less Judith's interest was aroused, the better. He didn't want her asking awkward questions – he didn't want any questions at all if he could avoid them.

'Ah, yes, Mr Hurley,' he answered, gratefully responding to Denis's tact. 'Come out to the shed with me. I have some things there....' And then, seeking to make the situation appear as everyday as possible and to persuade Judith that he had nothing to hide, he added: 'This is my daughter, Judith. Denis Hurley.'

Judith smiled and Denis made an embarrassed nod before following her father.

Cohen led him to the covered part of the yard opposite the office. He knew they would be clearly visible to Judith through the office window, but this shed-like structure was the only shelter they could get from the rain apart from the office itself. Twisted girders, tin drums, boxes of rusted iron rivets, huge nails, some broken horseshoes and heaps of other assorted iron pieces were piled up against the dark walls, and at the mouth of the shed were large cumbersome-looking scales with a tall cone of weights stacked beside them.

Denis still had the money in his hand, and Joshua stepped between him and the office window before taking it.

'I had to get you away from my daughter. She doesn't know about – eh, about last Friday.'

'Ah, that,' Denis said. 'I'm sorry about that, Mr Cohen.'
Then angrily he slapped his rolled-up cap against his
thigh. 'It was all a mistake.'

'A mistake?'

'Well, yes, in a way. It was all Hardy's idea – our
commanding officer. I never liked him. I never trusted
him. He said he had orders from Dublin to kidnap you, but
that was a bloody lie. He was just being smart – thought
he'd show Headquarters how clever he was. But Headquarters are on to him. They've hauled him up for an
enquiry.'

'So you didn't get into trouble over it?'

'Sure wasn't I only obeying orders?' Denis protested.
'Even though he had no authority to give them. But how
was I to know that?'

Iron Josh laughed. 'You weren't obeying them very
well. If you had done, I wouldn't be here now. I don't think
there's much of the soldier in you, Denis. But I said that to
you before, didn't I? Tell me, what do you do when you're
not soldiering? Have you a job?'

'I have indeed. I'm a skilled man – a carpenter. I work
for Twohey's, on Lavitt's Quay.'

'He seems to give you plenty of time off – for other jobs.'

The irony in Joshua's tone was not lost on Denis.

'He's a good man, Mr Twohey. A good man.'

'I understand,' Joshua nodded, a half-smile on his face.

'I suppose I'd better be getting back,' Denis said. 'I don't
like to take too much advantage.'

Joshua stretched out a hand. In some embarrassment
Denis shook it.

'Thank you, Denis,' Joshua Cohen said.

'What for? For bringing back your money? Sure I was
only holding it for you – what else would I do with it? I
couldn't keep it.'

Joshua shrugged. 'The money didn't worry me. I was
thanking you for saving my life. Imagine if someone else
had been sent to kidnap me instead of you.'

'I never thought of it like that,' Denis mused for a
moment. Then he put on his cap and said: 'Goodbye now,
Mr Cohen.'

'Goodbye, Denis, and good luck. Take care, my boy, take care.'

Joshua remained motionless for some time after Denis Hurley had left. He stared out at the rain, his words echoing in his mind. 'Take care, my boy, take care.' He thought of *his* boy, his Jacob. Was he taking care? Jacob, oh, Jacob! Denis Hurley's dilemma was not of his own making, he had been born into it; but if the letter about Jacob was true why was his son being so foolish, why was he running to meet trouble? He had a good Jewish home, a good Jewish upbringing, his *zeide* was a Rabbi, how could he bring such shame on his family? To be going out with a *shiksah*! It was anathema. Yet perhaps it wasn't true. He would have to find out. But how? Could he ask him? What would he say? He would never be able to put such a question to his own son. And if he did, and Jacob denied it, would he be satisfied? Would his mind be at rest? Jacob, oh, Jacob....

'Father. Father.'

Judith was calling him. He suddenly realised that she had been standing at the office door, only yards away, calling and calling, and he hadn't heard her. Her voice now was like an alarm waking him from a nightmare. He hurried over.

'Father, what are you doing standing out there in this weather? I've made a hot cup of tea for you. Has Mr Hurley left?'

'Yes, he had to go back to work.'

'Where does he work?'

'In Twohey's. Lavitt's Quay. He's a carpenter.'

'A carpenter?' Judith said in surprise. 'What did he want with you? I saw him giving you money. Did you sell him something? There's nothing in the day-book.'

Joshua stirred his tea. He did not wish to lie to his daughter. He did not like lies. But sometimes....

'I loaned him some money. He came to pay me back.'

It wasn't quite a lie perhaps – not a big one anyway – but he knew it would not satisfy his daughter.

'Oh,' she said, 'that was nice of him. Where did you meet him?'

And how did you come to lend him money? That would be the next question, unasked, for Joshua Cohen knew that, although his daughter's curiosity had been aroused, she would not pry. He could not tell her where and how he and Denis Hurley had met, but the question would hang between them if he just ignored it.

'Would you believe it – he's in the IRA. A fine boy like that.'

Judith looked at him in amazement, and he realised that in his confusion and anxiety to make little of Hurley's visit he had said the worst possible thing. He had made it a greater mystery than ever. And in a way, too, he had betrayed a confidence.

'How do you know that?'

How do I know? He told me. How else? No more lies.

'He told me. He said so.'

'He told you that! Wasn't that a strange thing to do? I mean, people in the IRA hardly go around admitting it to strangers.'

'Well, we got talking. Perhaps he needed to tell someone. . . .' Joshua felt he was still making matters worse. 'Anyway, am *I* going to tell the police? Are *you*?'

'No, of course not. It's none of our business – not even if it's true. But—'

'Judith. . . .'

'Yes, father.'

'Judith. . . .' His mind was spinning. The drumming on the corrugated roof seemed to fill his ears like a storm, making it impossible for him to think.

'What is it?' Judith asked.

Everything. It is everything. *Mein gansa veldt* – my whole world. What will I do? My old father going away – I'll never see him again. My son . . . my son. . . .

'Judith, I got this letter the other day.'

Almost not knowing what he had said, Joshua took the letter from his pocket and gave it to his daughter. 'Read. You read.'

Alarmed by her father's obvious distress, Judith took the letter from its envelope and read it – once – twice.

137

'But who? What? Who could have sent you this?'

Joshua shook his head.

'What it says – do you know anything about it? Is it true?'

The anguish in his voice shocked his daughter.

'I don't know. How would I know?'

'I thought ... you're his sister ... perhaps he talks to you.'

Joshua looked away. He could not let Judith see the guilt in his eyes.

'It would kill his mother. And his *zeide* ... if he heard. It can't be true. It mustn't be true.'

Joshua's lips were quivering, and his eyes grew moist. Judith had never seen him cry. She had to stop him.

'You want me to ask him?' she said.

Joshua stood up. He took out his handkerchief and dabbed at his face. He nodded, unable even to say yes. Then he turned and went out into the rain.

'Father,' Judith called. 'Come in. You'll catch your death.'

I'll catch my death? Impossible. Look how brave I am. I could face a loaded gun and not flinch, but I couldn't face my son.

Joshua Cohen raised his head to the lowering sky.

'*Gott in himmel*,' he declared bitterly as the rain mingled with his tears. 'I'm a brave man but I can't face my own son.'

Percy Lovitch got off the tram at the top of King Street and picked his steps carefully over the muddy road to the footpath. The Glanmire Station was only two minutes away and he still had some twenty minutes to spare before the train from Dublin was due in – if it arrived at all. And, even if it did arrive, the Carl Rosa Company might have decided not to travel and his journey would have been in vain. Reading the *Examiner* every morning with its accounts of houses and farms burned, people pulled off trains, RIC men kidnapped and shot, Black and Tans terrorising whole villages, Flying Columns ambushing patrols, convoys blown up, hunger strikes, arrests, goodness knows what – yes, it must look quite dangerous to any outsider, especially if that outsider was English and prominent, as the members of the Carl Rosa Opera Company certainly would be. They could hardly be blamed if they decided not to risk it. But Percy Lovitch knew their manager; he had toured with him for many seasons throughout Britain and Europe in earlier days when H. Barrett Brandreth was a young tenor and, although Brandreth would probably see the safety of his company as his primary responsibility, Percy also knew that he liked a challenge. H. Barrett Brandreth was a man who met difficulties with ebullient relish, and as the company had always been very popular in Cork – well, perhaps they'd decide to take whatever risk was involved.

The weather had dried up, so Percy didn't need to hurry the last few yards to the station, and before setting off he examined the photographs in glass cases on the walls of the Coliseum cinema at the corner of the street. There was a Charlie Chaplin comedy showing: *Oh What a Night*. Charlie was a card. And not only in the pictures. Percy had read in the *Examiner* only that morning that his wife had been granted a divorce on the grounds of Charlie's adultery with his latest leading actress. Oh, he was a card all right. Always picked a stunner for his films. Percy wondered if that little contralto, Eunice Stanford, would be with the Carl Rosa this time. She was a stunner, too – and she had been quite a sport on their last visit. Good for a playful hug and peck backstage. Not a bad voice, either. Rich in the middle register where, he felt, so many contraltos seemed to produce a hooting sound. It would be nice if she was there again. Not that Percy any longer was interested in passing flirtations. They had been pleasant diversions when he had been a young music student and later during his years on tour. But they had been only diversions. Opera and his operatic career had been the one important pursuit of his life. Religious observance had become secondary, marriage not even thought about. Now, pushing sixty, with his youth well gone and his voice no longer quite good enough for the big roles he loved, he was left with a future that in its predictability and lack of excitement was indistinguishable from his present. He had his nice little music shop in Tuckey Street; it gave him a comfortable living with no great effort – and with the growing popularity of the gramophone he could see his business expanding very profitably in coming years. So why should he even think about Palestine? Wasn't he too old to start a fresh struggle? Wasn't he happy with the Cork Jewish community? He got on with everybody and he knew that they felt really uplifted whenever he took a synagogue service and transformed the whole ritual with the richness of his voice and the sweetness of his melodies. Yes, granted he was a great improvement on Rev. Levitt, but how often did he get the chance? And in five years' time – maybe less – his voice would have deteriorated even more. What difference would it make to him where he lived if his voice became a croak?

He looked along the whole stretch of King Street, as far as his eye could see, and measured its elegance and variety against Karlinsky's picture of what *Eretz* was like and what living there – trying to live there – would entail. For Percy Lovitch, King Street had the colour, the vivacity, the contrasts of a street in any of the big European cities he had toured with the Company. It had the splendid, almost ornate façade of the Metropole Hotel with its red brick topping all that plate glass and terracotta work. Next door it had the Palace Theatre, Percy's favourite haunt, where every week he went to enjoy a programme of music-hall turns that included the best in the world. How could the cinema with its jerky silent pictures possibly compare with flesh and blood, with the wit, the talent, the appeal and aura of such stars as Harry Lauder, Vesta Tilley, Lupino Lane? And the colour – cinemas were darkened tombs whose insides might be wooden pens for all it mattered and where the person next to you could be *Malach Hamovess*, the Angel of Death himself, for all you could see of him. But the Palace, with its wall decorations of red and gold motifs, its resplendent boxes, its regal stage curtains – to Percy Lovitch that was the sort of air he had breathed for so long, that was something he'd not get in *Eretz*. They'd never have his King Street there – not in his lifetime anyway. Why, only a few doors from where he was standing were the premises of Hadji Bey, where every week before going into the Palace Theatre he bought a box of 'Hadji Bey's World Famous Turkish Delight', soft, powder-dusted sweetmeats that to Percy looked like miniature harem cushions. Not much chance of such delicacies in *Eretz*; he might find a few relatives of Hadji Bey left there since the British took over the area from the Ottomans, but it wouldn't be Turkish Delight they'd give him. If he weren't on his way to the station, he'd buy a box right now, but he didn't want the nuisance of carrying it.

He looked at his watch. Time to go. Percy Lovitch fluffed out his white silk scarf inside his dark overcoat, twirled his rolled-up umbrella and, humming 'Questa o quella' to the pace of his stride, set off. Rabbi Cohen didn't even know yet when they were leaving for *Eretz*, so he had time enough to make up his mind. Monday *Bohème*, Tuesday *Carmen*, Wednesday *Cav* and *Pag*.... The possibility that the Company might not arrive was unthinkable. The best week of the year was in prospect; he wasn't going to worry about anything else until it was all over.

He reached the station five minutes before the train was due and to his amazement found Platform 1, where it would be coming in, thronged with people. His face flushed with alarm at the thought that they had gathered to make trouble, but he was somewhat reassured to see that the platform was well patrolled by RIC men, and on joining the crowd his composure was fully restored by the discovery that, like him, they had come to welcome the Opera. Despite their fears – which he heard voiced on all sides – that the Company might not be on the train, they were all in the best of spirits. As he squeezed through it seemed to him that there were almost as many women as men – and not a few of the women had brought along their children, hoping, he guessed, to give them a memory they could hand down in later years to their own families. For

141

the most part the women looked thoroughly respectable, not to say decorous, in their long coats of conservative hues, and square fur-trimmed hats like cloth boxes pulled down to their ears. Working-class youths who were presumably unemployed or else had given up their dinner hour had pushed themselves to the front, forming a line at the edge of the platform, their rough-and-ready apparel of cloth caps, mufflers and no overcoats despite the inclement weather dissuading anyone else from displacing them. The rest of the men were a mixture of middle-class merchants – distinguished by their Homburgs, heavy overcoats and large moustaches – and raffish would-be Lotharios who offered each other cigarettes from silver cases and were continually brushing specks of soot from their expensive suits.

The noise of conversation, punctuated by much laughter and snatches of song, was deafening, echoing back from the high glass roof and augmented by the repeated clamour of porters trying to make a path for themselves and their clanging barrows. When the crowd realised that the insistence of the porters indicated the imminent arrival of the train, they cleared a way for them to take up positions at the platform's edge where they could assist the passengers with their luggage. Anticipation raised the hubbub to an even higher pitch until suddenly, from one end of the station the cry arose, 'It's comin', whisht there, the train's comin'.' Everyone grew silent. Faces were turned in that direction, eyes pinned to where the gleaming tracks disappeared abruptly into the pitch-black, mile-long tunnel that had been gouged out from under the hills of North Cork to commence every journey to the capital and end every journey from it. Ears were strained to pick up the slightest sound, but some of the crowd, more accustomed, for one reason or another, to meeting the Dublin train, knowingly lifted their chins to catch the first, almost ghostly draught of cold air from the tunnel which would tell them that the huge engine was now a quarter of a mile away, somewhere under St Luke's parish. But it was the experts, the porters, who signalled the first tangible proof of arrival when one of them cocked

142

an eye over the edge of the platform and directed the gaze of those nearby to the polished tracks which had quietly commenced vibrating as if infected with the atmosphere of excitement. Then within seconds all the signs and sounds multiplied to a deafening crescendo as with whistle screeching and steam scorching from its funnel engine number 400 crashed out of the darkness and, couplings clanging together, pulled itself to a noisy stop.

Immediately carriage windows which had been tightly closed against the tunnel's smoke and soot clattered down and heads were thrust out. Percy Lovitch forced a way through the crowd, turning this way and that to scan the faces of as many passengers as possible. 'Barry,' he suddenly shouted. Again 'Barry,' he called, fighting his way forward, almost breathless with excitement as, eyes shining, he appealed to the milling people to make way. 'It's the manager. They've come, the Carl Rosa have come.' He might have given the signal for bedlam. The cry was taken up, cheering and shouting broke out on all sides, and Percy, despite his bulk, was almost swept off his feet as he found himself propelled towards the beaming resplendent figure standing in the open doorway of one of the carriages.

H. Barrett Brandreth affected to be unsurprised by the warmth of his welcome. He raised his silver-topped cane in salute to the crowd, his rubicund face and pointed waxed moustaches glistening as if newly polished.

Percy Lovitch struggled to seize his gloved hand and shake it enthusiastically.

'Percy,' Brandreth greeted, seeming to speak in no more than a conversational tone and yet making himself heard above the din. 'How nice of you to meet us, old man. Are these all your friends?'

'No, Barry,' Percy shouted back, 'they're yours. They've come to welcome you. We thought you mightn't come to Cork this year. We weren't certain.'

H. Barrett Brandreth ran a hand over his wavy pomaded hair, gave a few elegant touches to the dark astrakhan collar of his long brown coat, and stepped down from the carriage, turning to gather the members of his Company in behind him. But the crowd surged around, slapping his back and pumping his hands, and Percy had no time to see what old friends from the cast were still in harness before the cry of 'Rise him, boys, rise him,' was heard and the momentarily startled impresario suddenly erupted into the air to land, cane waving triumphantly, on two pairs of burly shoulders.

Percy Lovitch fought to keep in touch with the smiling Brandreth, who, his poise fully restored despite the precariousness of his situation, was being borne towards the station forecourt. Behind him the other members of the Company were being helped down from the train, the male singers struggling to maintain protective embraces around their women in case any of the young men in the crowd might, in an excess of enthusiasm, try to lift them shoulder high in the wake of their manager.

Eventually the swaying mass emerged from the station exits and Brandreth was deposited on one of two horse-drawn floats that had been brought for the occasion. There were many helping hands to push Percy Lovitch up beside him, and the floats quickly became platforms for the bemused members of the Company as the crowd closed in, still cheering and shouting in acclamation. At length there was nothing for it but for Brandreth to hold up a hand in appeal for silence.

'Speech, speech,' came the call, as if he had not already made his intention clear.

'Good friends and fellow opera-lovers,' he said, his restrained tone expertly projected to the furthest listeners, 'my Company and I have been looking forward to our annual visit to Cork for a long time. We heard there had been certain – ah – difficulties in this part of the world in recent months, and I understand there was some scepticism as to whether we would run the gauntlet of existing troubles and fulfil our engagement. Well, you see the answer before you.' He swept a hand around to include the whole Company, and as the crowds cheered and clapped Percy saw the leading tenor, Louis Dorney, was still with them, as was also Gwynne Davies, the bass, and Alice Austen, the coloratura soprano. The Manager

144

motioned again for silence and continued. 'I made some enquiries before we set out and I believe the Carl Rosa is the first theatrical company to visit Cork for several weeks. We are proud and honoured....' The rest of his words were drowned in a fresh outburst of cheering and then, as if at a signal, bands of young men went to the front of each float, unharnessed the horses and, taking their place between the shafts, pulled the floats in triumph out onto the street towards the Opera House and the theatrical lodgings nearby. Catching the mood of the occasion Louis Dorney pushed himself to the front of his float and started to sing, to be joined immediately by the rest of the Company. As the rousing strains of the Toreador's Song rang out, the crowd responded with a will. All traffic halted and drew aside, pedestrians stood still in wonderment, cheering and clapping, shopkeepers and shoppers thronged in doorways, the whole complement of the Royal Irish Constabulary in King Street Barracks poked their heads out of windows or gathered on the Barracks steps to see the cavalcade pass. As the massive chorus of sound reverberated between the tall buildings, Brandreth put an arm round Percy Lovitch's shoulders, while Percy, his face bright red and perspiration gleaming on his brow, waved his umbrella like a conductor's baton and sang with all his heart, and with all his soul, and with all his might.

10

JACOB WAS GLAD he had only anatomy and physiology lectures on Tuesday morning. As it was, he found it impossible to concentrate and take proper notes after Judith's bombshell the night before. He was tired, too – hadn't slept a wink for worry.

He mounted his bicycle in the quad, drew on his gloves and slung his black, red and white striped college scarf around his neck in the careless fashion he had copied from the other students. He suddenly felt self-conscious about the action and for a moment was annoyed with himself for so thoughtlessly aping others. As he cycled off towards the nearby Mardyke bandstand where Deirdre would meet him when her lectures were over, he wondered why on this particular morning such a harmless affectation should, for the first time, strike him as childish. He knew the answer – there was no evading it now that that damned anonymous letter had opened his eyes. The two gifts he had smugly thought put him on a different plane from other boys of his age had been made irrelevant – his gift of love betrayed, his gift of poetry soured – and what really set him apart was his religion. Bloody religion. And if he hadn't been such a starry-eyed adolescent he'd have seen it long ago.

Shifting sands, that summed it up – shifting sands

146

under which he had buried memories of events, situations, comments that were now pushing up into his thoughts like poisonous weeds. 'Pig's ear, wah, wah,' rang again in his ears, and with its sound he saw once more the gaping nine-year-old, aghast at the band of ragged street urchins bundling up the corners of their threadbare coats into their fists and wagging the simulated pigs' ears at him as they shouted their crazy, almost comical taunt.

Was that his first experience of anti-Semitism, the beginning of it all? If so, he had been neither frightened nor angered, only surprised. Its lack of hostility, its mindlessness, gave him no understanding of the daily deprivation and discrimination he had heard his parents and *zeide* recount of their lives in Lithuania. But he had not long to wait for such insights. Soon afterwards, when the time came for him to commence his secondary education, he had to face the ordeal that followed his mother's refusal to enrol him in the local St Dominic's which the other Jewish boys attended. Was it the best school in Cork? Bertha Cohen asked, in a tone that clearly dared any of her family to say it was. Of course they couldn't. St Dominic's was average, at best adequate. They agreed that there were far better schools in the city. But she knew, didn't she, that they refused to take Jewish students?

'I shall go to Max Klein,' she declared. 'He's the President. Let *him* do something about it. Let him go to the Lord Mayor. Let him go to the Government. That's his duty. What does he think he's President for? Just for the *yichas*? Just for the honour?'

Jacob had recognised the familiar signs of battle in his mother's gestures – the way she flicked a wisp of black hair from her eyes as if to see the enemy more clearly, the way she rubbed her hands up and down her apron like a wrestler positioning for an opening. He wished she wouldn't get such ideas into her head. St Dominic's would have suited him. It was used to Jewish students; he would have companions there, boys he already knew. Joshua, too, was upset, and had thrown his eyes up to heaven in despair at his wife's obstinacy. He was heart-sore in

147

advance for the defeat she was going to suffer, for the bitterness of soul that would be visited on her. She was not one to lose easily. When did she ever give best before? But this time.... If Max Klein couldn't get his own sons into a better school – and everyone knew that Dora had insisted he try – then what chance had he of getting someone else's son in?

'You're wasting your time,' Joshua told his wife.

'We'll see,' was all Bertha Cohen replied.

'You're wasting your time, Mrs Cohen,' the President echoed after all his arguments had failed to move her.

His words only roused her to anger. Why were men such sheep?

'What do you mean? Why should my son not have the best? Isn't our money as good as the Christians'?'

In his impatience Max Klein almost made to grasp the lapel of Bertha Cohen's coat the better to persuade her of her wrong-headedness. But remembering that she was a woman, and a *baaleboosta* into the bargain, he continued to plead.

'Mrs Cohen, I can't help you. *Hub a bissl sechel* – have some sense. Send Jacob to St Dominic's. That's where all the *Yiddisheh* boys go. Why shouldn't he go there like all the others?' Like his own sons, he would have added, if he had thought his visitor wouldn't know of his own unsuccessful efforts to place them elsewhere.

Bertha Cohen gave him a cold look that said *her* son wasn't like all the others. The others' parents might be content with St Dominic's – she refrained from adding that in her opinion the President was a weakling to settle for it – but she had made her mind up. All she wanted was the best for her son, and St Dominic's was not the best.

'Of course it's not,' Max Klein agreed. 'But it's not the worst, either. Take my word for it.'

'The best. Only the best.' Her voice was firm. 'You tell me: *vos iz* the best?'

Max Klein sighed. What could he do with such a blockhead of a woman?

'I don't know which is the best, Mrs Cohen. There are two or three supposed to be very good. They're all run by

148

galuchim – religious Orders. But I told you: you're wasting your time. They just don't take Jews.'

'Two or three! And none of them takes Jews. A *skandale*! What are their names, Mr Klein?'

'Well, there's Presentation Brothers College on the Western Road—'

'Thank you. That will do. Jacob shall go there.'

And there Jacob went.

Seven years had passed since the interview with the Superior, and now as Jacob sat in the bandstand waiting for Deirdre and gazing vacantly on the lonely-looking Mardyke cricket ground he experienced the same trapped feeling. Once again his religion was an issue – not his abilities, his ambitions, his opinions, or even his defects, but something as unasked for and as irreversible as his maleness, and as inexorably deciding so much of his life. He closed his eyes but found that blotting out the leafless elm-trees lining the Mardyke Walk and the backdrop of Sunday's Well's corniched gardens only sharpened the images that had been dormant for so long. He saw again the book-lined study, the mahogany desk impersonally bare of anything but a calendar and an empty letter-tray, the walls with a monster portrait of some imperious clergyman as the centrepiece flanked by rows of scholarship-class photographs and the shelves and glass cases of silver trophies, shields and medals won on the playing-fields. Everything he had encountered on that first visit made him conscious to a greater degree than ever before of his foreignness – from the black-cassocked Brothers he had passed in the college grounds to the Superior himself, a chunky man, at home in a massive carved chair, his face angrily criss-crossed by tiny red veins, eyes peering out from behind gold-rimmed spectacles, and his head crowned with a biretta, a piece of headgear Jacob had never seen before and which reminded him uncomfortably of the hats worn by pirates and highwaymen in his childhood tales.

Mrs Cohen, however, seemed in no way put out by the surroundings or by Brother Connolly's appearance. She matched colour for colour and argument for argument.

149

Almost equally forbidding-looking in a boxy dark hat with a veil, her black fur-trimmed coat buttoned up to the neck, and a muff she wore only on chilly winter burials, she contrived to give the impression that her presence was in the nature of a formality, as if she was there merely to make the acquaintance of the Superior and to provide the usual information he would require when enrolling a new pupil.

Brother Connolly had pointed out that as all the students in the school were Christian a Jewish boy would be bound to feel lonely and unhappy – to which Mrs Cohen replied that Jacob had had plenty of Jewish company in his primary school and what he wanted now was to mix with non-Jewish boys if he was to learn tolerance, as the Jewish religion taught. She was sure the Catholic religion preached tolerance, too?

'Tolerance, Mrs, is not something young boys think about much,' said the Superior. 'They can be quite cruel to anyone who is different from themselves.'

'My son understands that' – and she turned to Jacob as if expecting his endorsement. 'But he will make friends quickly. As long as the teachers. . . .' Bertha Cohen left the rest unsaid.

Brother Connolly had raised an eyebrow and mused for a moment before saying, half to himself: 'Of course, Presentation College hasn't had any Jewish students before. . . .'

Jacob feared this was just the Superior's polite way of telling them that the school's doors were closed to Jews, but his mother seemed to miss the point.

'My son will have a great honour on his head, then. It will be a great distinction for him. He will repay it. I am certain of that. He is a very good scholar.'

To Jacob it seemed that there was a slight tremor in his mother's voice – whether of tension or of determination he was not sure. He glanced quickly at her hands, hidden from the Superior's sight under the desk. They were still tucked inside their muff, but now the muff was alive with movement as if there were some small animal nervously turning this way and that within it.

'Of course he's a good scholar, Mrs Cohen,' Brother Connolly accepted, 'of course he is. I'm sure he's a bright boy.'

In the silence that followed Jacob held his breath almost in an effort to deny his very presence in the room. He felt he himself did not matter. His religion was all that concerned Brother Connolly, and his mother's ambition for him was all that worried her.

'Have you applied to any other school, Mrs Cohen?'

'No. Only here.'

'Why here? There are other very good secondary schools in Cork.'

Bertha Cohen measured her reply. '*You* may call them good schools, but they do not take Jews. How can an Irish school be good if it refuses an Irish pupil? These schools, they are run by men of God. Did God tell them to refuse Jews?' She paused and then added: 'Did God tell anyone to refuse Jews?'

Jacob looked at Brother Connolly, but the Superior showed no inclination to answer for God. Instead he turned to Jacob. 'And why do you want to come to Pres., young man?'

Jacob started. He had not been prepared for such a question, and the use of the shortened name by which the school was known everywhere lulled him into thinking he might be on the brink of admission. He could spoil it all with the wrong answer. In his confusion he glanced at his mother. Her look reminded him.

'Because my mother wants me to,' he said.

'Good boy. Sound man. Honour thy father and thy mother – isn't that right? Do you know what number that Commandment is?'

'It's the fifth Commandment.'

'The fifth?' the Superior repeated questioningly. Then he immediately added: 'Of course, of course. The Jews' Commandments and the Christians' are the same but in a different order. "Honour thy father and thy mother" is our fourth. Sound man, sound man. I think you'll do well here.'

For the first time Bertha Cohen took her hands out of her muff and agitatedly raised one towards the Superior.

151

'Religion, Father. He wouldn't be made to attend any religious classes?'

'Certainly not, Mrs Cohen. A half an hour every day is devoted to religious instruction, but Jacob will be able to put the time to equally good use. And by the way, Mrs Cohen, I'm not a Father, I'm a Brother. Just Brother Connolly. We're all brothers here – in both senses of the word, I think I can say. Never you fear now, I'll take a special interest in this little man. I'll look after him like a father.'

Brother Connolly had been true to his word. Jacob remembered the day the Superior had quietly slipped into their English class. The Shakespeare play for study that year was *The Merchant of Venice* and the teacher, Brother Terence, had assigned the part of Shylock to Jacob. That had appealed to his classmates as a great joke and a few of them had addressed him as 'Shylock' at the lunch-break. But the day after the Superior's visit Brother Terence switched the role to someone else and Jacob was made to read the part of Portia. He had not relished the change; he had felt that reading Portia was sissyish.

Had that been his only reaction? he wondered now. He certainly couldn't remember being upset by that incident – or by any other. The one Jew among hundreds of Catholics, and his Jewishness, instead of making him vulnerable, had in fact been his armour. It was as if he didn't exist outside of Jewtown, as if the Jacob attending Presentation College was some *doppelgänger* sent to suffer the pinpricks of its alien world while the real Jacob remained cocooned in his *Yiddisheh veldt*. But now he was seeing that Jewish world for what it was – an anachronism not only of time but of place, too. As long as one didn't have to move outside it, its defences might hold. But if one had to have any traffic with the outside world, then its age was a fragile protection. Growing up – that's what did it. Growing up meant growing out, and in the religious straitjacket of Celtic Crescent growing out was impossible. Had his mother appreciated what sending him to university might mean? Hadn't she realised that university wasn't a bit like school, that it was very

152

different from Presentation College? University had clubs and societies he could join, activities that would open his mind to a different culture, fellow-students with whom lasting friendships might be formed, and girls – far more girls than the handful of the Jewish community, girls whose very strangeness made them attractive, intriguing, even – like Deirdre – irresistible.

Jacob didn't believe his mother took any of that into account. She was incapable of making allowances. He was lucky that the anonymous letter had been sent to his father rather than to her. *She* would have done something about it – Jacob didn't know what, but she certainly wouldn't have shifted the burden on to anyone else. Yet his father wasn't a weak man. Perhaps the frozen years between them made him recoil from personal contact, made him surrender all moral authority over his son. Was the gap so great? Did his father never want to bridge it? The thought filled Jacob with despair. He was completely alone: Molly was gone, his *zeide* was going, Judith lived in a closed world of her own, his mother cared only that he should 'make something of himself' – as long as the 'something' was what she wanted – and his father seemed beyond his reach. Would any of that be the least bit changed if he stopped seeing Deirdre?

'Penny for them. You look really down in the dumps.'

Jacob had been so wrapped up in his own misery that he hadn't heard Deirdre's approach, and she jingled her bicycle bell shrilly to wake him up.

'I'm not sure if my thoughts are even worth a penny – or whether they're worth far more than you'd be able to pay,' he said.

'Oh my, we *are* in a mood. Conundrums so early in the day. Come on, then, mount thy fiery steed and we can commune with Mother Nature while you tell me all about it.'

In silence they cycled the hundred yards to Fitzgerald Park where, in obedience to the by-laws, they dismounted and wheeled their machines past the elaborate wrought-iron gates.

Inside the park the view was gloomy enough to re-

153

inforce Jacob's depression. The trees were leafless, what during the spring and summer had been banks of swaying dahlias and daffodils were now denuded mounds of freshly turned earth, and where a pool of water used quickly to form beneath the mouth of the pump from the constant attentions of thirsty children was now a dry crusty patch.

'I'm waiting. What's the trouble?' Deirdre prompted.

As they walked slowly through the park, Jacob told her about the letter.

'What did your father say to you?' Deirdre enquired.

'Nothing. He didn't speak to me at all. He told my sister, Judith. She button-holed me last night. Wanted to know if the letter was true.'

'What did you tell her?'

'I told her it was. I wasn't going to deny it,' Jacob declared. 'What's so terrible about it? We see each other, we go to the pictures together, we go out walking or cycling, I help you distribute your paper—'

'Did you tell her that – about the paper, I mean?' Deirdre interrupted.

'Yes. Does it matter?'

Deirdre made no reply, and Jacob looked at her doubtfully. Suddenly he realised what was running through her mind.

'For God's sake, Deirdre,' he exclaimed. 'You can't think she'd inform!'

'No, I suppose not.'

'She certainly wouldn't do a thing like that,' he insisted. 'Besides, if she did, how does she know that you wouldn't drag me into it? It would be bad enough from my family's point of view that I was doing a line with you, but if I were arrested as well....'

'Of course,' Deirdre agreed. 'And, anyway, she doesn't know my name. The letter didn't say, did it?'

Jacob hesitated before admitting: 'No, but I did. Oh, not your full name. Just "Deirdre".'

'Why in the world did you do that? You didn't need to.'

'No, but it just slipped out. I couldn't help it. After all, the whole thing took me by surprise.'

They leaned their bicycles against a bench seat on the

154

grassy river-bank and sat looking across the Lee at the back gardens of Sunday's Well mansions rising precipitately to one of the many hills that formed a basin around the city. It was a part of Fitzgerald Park Jacob had begun to look upon as their favourite daylight haunt. Convenient to the college, quiet, deserted at this time of the year, he found it romantic despite the winter depredations all round. This morning, however, he had none of the feeling of repose the slow-flowing river usually engendered, the grand estates on its other bank failed to conjure up their visions of riches and privilege, even missing was the almost frightening disturbance in his body as he sat with an arm around Deirdre, his fingers probing the rising mound of her breast.

'Well, what are you going to do about it?' she asked at last.

'Nothing. Nothing at all. The only thing I *could* do is stop seeing you and that seems – well, rather extreme. After all, we haven't known each other that long and we're not doing anybody any harm, are we?'

When Deirdre did not reply Jacob looked at her searchingly.

'You're annoyed, aren't you? Annoyed that I told Judith so much.'

Deirdre tossed her head. 'No, I'm not annoyed. What's done is done. I don't believe in crying over spilt milk. But what about your father? What Judith has to tell him will be the opposite of what he wants to hear. What will he do?'

'Probably nothing.'

'Won't he even have it out with you?'

'I doubt it. My father and I talk very little with each other and never about anything personal. Personal questions are my mother's responsibility. She's the blunt one.'

'Supposing your father tells *her*?'

'He won't. At least, I don't think he will.'

'Is he really as weak as you make him sound?'

'Weak?' Jacob turned on her in surprise. 'Anything but. He's as tough as all that scrap metal in his yard. It's just that he's shy.'

Deirdre laughed.

'I know,' Jacob agreed. 'It seems ridiculous. But I know I'm right. I'll tell you something: one day, some years ago, I was walking up Washington Street and my father was coming in the opposite direction. I saw him – he wasn't too far away – and, although he wasn't looking at me at that moment, I knew he had seen me. Then some people came between us, just for a second or two, and when I looked again he was gone.'

'Gone where?'

'Across the road to the other side.'

'But you're surely not suggesting—?'

'Oh, yes. Having to acknowledge or salute me would have been too embarrassing for him. He's that shy.'

'Nonsense. He might have crossed the street for any one of a dozen reasons.'

'I thought that myself. So I hopped into a doorway and watched him. He turned round, took a good look, and then crossed back to the other side again.'

Deirdre shook her head as if unable to credit such bizarre behaviour.

'Well,' she said at length, 'even if he is so shy that he can't discuss things with you, that needn't stop him telling your mother.'

'No, he wouldn't want her to be worried and he might be afraid she'd make such a fuss that my grandfather would find out what it was all about. That would be a lovely farewell present for him – just before he goes off to Palestine.'

'When is he going?'

'Within a few weeks, he says. Certainly before Christmas. He expects to be given the date any day now.'

'Do you wish you were going with him?'

Jacob unlocked his arms from around her and sat up.

'Are you trying to get rid of me? Is it that stupid letter that's worrying you?'

'No, you fool,' she soothed, pulling him back into her embrace. 'I was only teasing. If *you're* not worried by the letter, why should I be?'

'That's better,' Jacob said, putting his cheek against hers and slipping a hand inside her coat.

'Aha, young man,' she laughed, grabbing his wrist, 'too late. School's out.'

'Damn,' Jacob said, looking across at the far bank of the river where a man was untying a rowing boat and helping some children into it to ferry them over to the park. He and Deirdre were by now accustomed to the little band of junior pupils going home from the small St Mary's Shandon school in Sunday's Well – it was usually the signal for them to release each other and pretend they were just taking in the view. This time, however, Jacob tightened his arm around Deirdre and kissed her full on the lips until his breath gave out.

'You bully,' she gasped as soon as she could. 'Such an example to set these kids.'

The ferryman, oblivious of the exhibition behind his back, rowed steadily while the children gazed in silent astonishment.

'That's right,' Jacob called, waving cheerily, 'take it all in. Your turn won't be long coming.'

16 November 1920

Dearest Elizabeth,
I must have written Dearest Elizabeth umpteen times today trying to start this letter to you and not known how to go on. Trouble is I don't know if you will ever get this letter and it's dashed awkward to write a letter you are told will be delivered but you can't be sure of it. I feel I may only be talking to myself, and that's not in the best traditions of a British officer. Feeble joke. Sorry. But when you've been a prisoner for two whole days even two days can feel like two months, and when you aren't sure if the letter you're writing is ever going to reach the person it is written to you sort of rather lose control and ramble on.

I've just read what I've written and I hope it makes sense to you. I've taken it for granted that you know the IRA have kidnapped me. The two men who have been guarding me

157

swear that you know. They say it's been reported in the papers at home and they've shown me the report in the local paper here. So I suppose I can take it that you do know. Anyway, I'm sure the Home Office or whatever will have notified you officially.

I was kidnapped on Sunday night on the way to my rooms, and as you can see from the date of this letter (if you ever get it) I've been here two nights and two days. I wasn't injured in any way and I'm being treated well and I'm A-1 as to health and they say that I can write to you as often as I like and that you can reply. I don't know if they are fooling me or not. That's why it has been so hard to get this letter started. I don't like being made a fool of, and if they are just having a bit of sport with me I'll see them damned first. But the only way I can find out if they are telling the truth is to finish this letter and see if I get a reply from you. If you do get this, please reply immediately. Damn it, let them laugh if they like. I miss you and am very worried about you. If you do get this letter, reply to Redmond Cassidy, c/o Central Sorting Office, GPO, Cork, Ireland. That's very important. Just address the envelope to Redmond Cassidy as above. They say your reply will automatically be brought here to me. I don't know where I am. Somewhere near Cork, I imagine. One more thing, my darling. This is most important. On no account tell anyone about this arrangement. If you do, they'll just cancel it. If it's not a joke on us anyway.

All my love,
From your loving husband
RODDY

PS. Don't worry, just keep well. We don't want anything to happen to the baby.

Captain Simcox screwed the top back on his fountain-pen and laid it aside with an air of resignation. Maybe it was all a game and they would read his letter and have a good laugh. Spider and fly, or something like that. Maybe they wouldn't. They said they weren't interested in what he was writing. Claimed they knew more about his battalion than he did himself.

He put the letter in the envelope they had provided, sealed it and wrote the address. Mrs R. Simcox, Warwick House, Sundrive Road, Colchester, Essex. Would she get it? No reason why she shouldn't. All they had to do was drop it in a letter-box, whether they read it or not. But would he really get a reply? The tough-looking one with the scar who had bundled him into the cart – Boxer he said his name was – he had promised that as long as instructions were followed any reply would reach him. It was ridiculous, of course. But, after all, why not? The Post Office was known to be riddled with IRA supporters. Hadn't there even been an occasion when the Viceroy's mail was delivered to the Viceregal Lodge stamped 'Censored by the IRA'! Their men were everywhere, and Roddy had no doubt that 'Redmond Cassidy, c/o Central Sorting Office, GPO, Cork' *could* be a code sign to their men in the GPO. He prayed it was so.

He didn't know why they had kidnapped him. No one had said. They might want to bargain for the life of some captured IRA man. Or they might be going to shoot him as a reprisal. He mustn't think about it. And he mustn't think about a reply from Elizabeth. He might be here for a long time, and it was no use feeding his hopes. If they were dashed, then it would weaken him. And he was determined to be just as tough as they were, damn them.

The Captain stretched his hands over his head in a massive yawn, so that his greatcoat, which had been draped over his shoulders, fell to the ground. He retrieved it and donned it properly, shivering with the cold. He poured himself some more whiskey from the bottle on the table. Thank God for the whiskey – it was the only source of heat in the room. Boxer had said he'd be kept here for a few days and then they'd move him to a warmer place with better grub. In the meantime all he could offer was 'a drop of the hard stuff' to keep the cold out. Did he take a drink at all? Boxer wanted to know. Did he hell! Could a duck swim? And, lo and behold, a bottle of whiskey had appeared this morning. He laughed aloud at the sudden recollection of a joke from his schooldays: 'What did Euclid say after a hard day's work? If there's a drink in the house, let it be produced.' Pity it wasn't Scotch. He was used to Scotch. This Irish stuff was smoother, but it was stronger, too. The locals called it 'Paddy', and someone in the mess – many of the men were partial to it – had told him it was called that because the traveller who went round the pubs selling it was a Paddy O'Flaherty and he was so well known that the publicans just ordered 'so many cases of Paddy'. 'Irish Whiskey' was all the label said. Surely the correct spelling was W-H-I-S-K-Y. He'd been good at spelling at school. Yes, 'whiskey' with an 'e' was wrong. But, then, of course it was *Irish* whiskey. Trust the Irish to have their own spelling. Well, whiskey or whisky, he was glad of it.

He sipped slowly. Didn't know when they might let him have another bottle. Must ask Boxer. And he'd need the whiskey to keep him warm and help him get some shut-eye. The camp-bed had only one blanket. He'd slept all right the previous night, but that was because he was dog-tired after getting no sleep at all the night of the kidnap. His thoughts hadn't let him sleep then even though his limbs had been aching. Legs especially. He almost groaned aloud at the recollection. First, there had been the journey in the horse and cart until they'd got to the edge of the city and he'd been taken out and marched across a field. In a few minutes they came to a fingerpost, but it was too dark for him to see what it said. Then they were joined by other men – he remembered three or four, it was hard to tell. After that came the first of the gruelling walks – he reckoned about four miles – over fields, tracks, stiles, hills, into cowpats, scratched from brambles. God! What a walk! As cold as the Yorkshire moors. Then into another cart, drawn by a plodding donkey, for at least another two miles. And then the worst of all – out of the cart, blindfolded, and pushed and pulled up a mountain before the blindfold was removed and he found himself in front of what seemed to be a barn – but he couldn't be sure at the time because there was no moon and he was feeling too exhausted to notice. He'd seen nobody since then except Boxer and the young fellow Boxer addressed as Joe. They came only to bring him food, so there must be a farmhouse nearby. It was nerve-racking being locked up all day by yourself in this ghastly dump. It wasn't even a barn; might easily have been some sort of stable once – stone floor, hooks on the walls, and panels of wood that could be the remains of a horse-stall. No furniture apart from the camp-bed, a kitchen table and some kitchen chairs, and candles and matches. That was all. And no possible way of breaking out – he'd made sure of that. The walls were solid, the door was locked and bolted, and there was no window – just a small barred hole high up in one corner. Outside was a wooden hut with a primitive lavatory and a cold tap – facilities he could avail of only when they brought his meals and while Boxer stood by, his gun drawn.

Thank God he'd be moving to better quarters – if the RIC or the Army didn't find him first. They'd be looking for him. No doubt of that. At least, the RIC would be. Not old man Windsor, of course, not his CO. He was too wily a soldier to risk patrols on this sort of search operation. Roddy could just see those thin lips tightening over his cigarette-holder at the slightest suggestion of sending out anyone to look for him. And the left eye fractionally lifting in derision to let the monocle plop out of its hold. 'Ever heard of an ambush?' he might rap out. 'As of now Captain Simcox is missing, so we're a body short. One's enough. No need to lose more men trying to get just one back.' That would be Windsor's philosophy – practical, sensible. The Army wasn't there to recover lost property, even its own. Wasn't trained for that. The RIC were. Their job. Leave it to 'em. Couldn't blame him really. Some of the other men might feel unhappy about the decision, but they'd probably agree with it. Campbell certainly would. He'd be crowing that he always said officers should sleep in barracks. It would be so nice to sleep in barracks tonight. But, no, he mustn't think of that. Take it hour by hour.

He finished the whiskey in his glass and forced himself not to pour out any more.

There was a sound of footsteps on the gravel outside. The bolt was pulled, a key turned, and Boxer entered, gun in hand, with Joe at his back carrying a battered tray on which was a mug of steaming cocoa and a plateful of thick sandwiches.

'Your supper,' Boxer said as he deposited a bag on the floor.

Roddy looked into the mug and waved it away with his hand.

'Cocoa. I don't drink cocoa.'

'But you drank it last night,' Boxer objected.

'There was nothing else,' Roddy explained. 'Tonight I have this – what's left of it.' He tapped the bottle of whiskey.

'We could have brought you tea if you'd said,' Boxer complained in a hurt tone as if his failure to anticipate the Captain's tastes was a black mark against him.

'*I'll* drink it,' Joe put in eagerly.

'Go ahead,' Roddy said, pushing the mug towards him. 'With my compliments.'

Boxer held Joe back. 'Are you sure, Captain?' he asked.

'Quite sure,' Roddy answered, with a little bow. Good to show them he wasn't affected by the deprivation.

'OK, then,' Boxer allowed as he released his grip on Joe's arm. He might have made a mistake bringing cocoa but he was still going to let the Captain and Joe know that he was the boss – even as far as an unwanted mug of cocoa was concerned.

'Maybe Joe would prefer a drop of whiskey,' Captain Simcox suggested. 'Keep the cold out.'

Joe's eyes lit up, but even before he could say anything Boxer snapped out: 'He would not. He's on duty all the time he's here.'

Joe gave a wan smile and took the mug of cocoa, wrapping his hands around it to warm him.

162

'I suppose that means it's no use offering *you* a drink so,' Roddy said to Boxer.

Boxer sat down and did not deign to acknowledge the offer. Instead he said: 'I'm afraid, Captain, I have some bad news for you.'

Roddy's heart jumped, despite himself. Were they going to shoot him? So quickly? They might be – they'd captured and shot Black and Tans, so why not a British army officer?

He poured himself some whiskey and swallowed a mouthful. He'd not let them see any nervousness. Take things steady no matter what his fate was to be. Keep cool.

'I suppose you won't be posting this so,' he said, taking up his letter to Elizabeth.

'What's that?' Boxer asked. 'A letter to your wife? Why wouldn't we post it? I said we would, and our boys keep their promises.'

Fat lot of good that would be, Roddy thought, if I'm lying in a bog with a bullet in the back of my head.

'Well, then, what's the bad news?'

'We won't be able to move you after all. The place is swimming in policemen looking for you, so you'll have to stay where you are. They won't find you here.'

'But for how long?' The prospect of being cooped up in this freezing place for any length of time was decidedly unpleasant.

'Can't tell you that.'

'What's going to happen to me? Are you going to shoot me?'

'Ah sure there's no point in worrying your head about that, Captain,' Boxer replied, his tone almost fatherly. Roddy laughed, but Boxer didn't look as if he had been trying to be funny and Roddy didn't know him well enough yet to decide if his answer was deliberately uncommunicative so as not to alarm him or just the Irish way of looking at things. Like spelling 'whisky' with an *e*.

'Anyway,' Boxer added brightly, 'I've brought you some things to make you more comfortable' – and from the bag at his feet he drew a large blanket, which he unwrapped to reveal another bottle of 'Paddy'.

'There, now,' he said. 'That's for the outside' – giving the Captain the blanket – 'and that's for the inside' – and he handed over the bottle with a proud shake of his head and a laugh at his own humour.

'Ha, ha,' echoed Joe, who had been busy drinking the cocoa and demolishing half of the sandwiches, 'ha, ha. That's a good one, Boxer.'

Joe's laughter, full of youthful spontaneity, almost drew a smile from Captain Simcox, but he was in no mood for Boxer's droll humour. The thought of being locked up in this stable for goodness knows how many more empty days and freezing nights, with no sensible replies to his questions, was making him angry. He might be their prisoner but he was a British officer and he'd act as a British officer should act.

He rose from his chair in intended dismissal of his gaolers.

'Thanks for the whiskey,' he said stiffly. 'And the blanket,' And then, slightly less formally: 'And don't forget to post the letter, like a good man.'

'Never fear,' Boxer said jauntily, oblivious of any change in Captain Simcox's attitude. 'Come on, Joe. We'll see you in the morning, Captain.'

Roddy listened to the key being turned in the door and the bolt being shot. He eyed what was left of the sandwiches and lifted one to examine it. Ham. His stomach rumbled with hunger. Ham and whiskey. Pig and 'Paddy'. There was something about the association that brought a smile to his face – but he doubted if it would strike Joe or Boxer as very funny.

164

11

ALL DAY TUESDAY hardly a word passed between Judith and her father. She had little heart for office work, and the familiar routines it called for were too automatic to distract her thoughts from their preoccupation with Jacob's admission. That her father spent most of the morning in the yard supervising the unloading of two carts of scrap iron at least avoided the tension his presence in the small office would have set up. The strain of that would have been unbearable. She felt she was under enough pressure as it was. Not that her father would have harassed her for news – he was too reticent a man to speak first – but she knew that his silence was only increasing his suffering, while his patience increased hers. Yet what could she do? She couldn't just go up to him and say: 'Yes, the letter is true. Your son is going with a *shiksah*. He told me so himself.' Certainly that was all he had charged her with finding out. But her duty didn't end there. She reasoned it out: if she went to a doctor, not feeling well, she wouldn't be happy to have him merely tell her, 'Yes, you are not well. There is something wrong with you.' She would want him to try to cure whatever was wrong. She would expect him to. The more serious the complaint, the more wholehearted should be his efforts to find a remedy.

But what answer was there to this problem, what possible action could she take? The dangers were awful to contemplate. It wasn't only the disgrace to her family if it became known that Jacob was going with a Catholic girl – that in itself was bad enough, even though at his age he was surely unlikely to form any permanent association and in time the whole thing would probably blow over and be forgotten. Judith might have urged her father not to risk strengthening Jacob's defiance by issuing edicts if that was all that was involved. But the IRA bit – that was frightening. It was madness. How *could* he be so foolish, so irresponsible, so blind? Love, she supposed, was the cause. Love is blind, it was said. Yet he was only a child – what did he know of love? Infatuation, more likely. But it didn't matter what it was called, and it was a waste of time worrying about the nature of his feelings – or about hurting them. Better *he* should be hurt than the whole family – the whole community – if he was caught on one of those paper rounds and arrested. He had laughed off the risk he was running, so it would be pointless to talk to him again. There just wasn't the time to try to persuade him. The matter was too urgent for that. But if she couldn't persuade *him*, perhaps she could make the girl – what was her name? Deirdre? – see the risk she was making Jacob run, or at least allowing him to run. If she was a sensible girl, if she was any way fair-minded, then no matter what her feelings for Jacob surely she would see reason. Indeed, the stronger her feelings, the more she should want not to expose him to any danger. Her own risk was her own concern; it was *her* life and her business if she wanted to get involved with the IRA. After all, she was a university student, so she must have some intelligence – at least, enough to see that Jacob should be protected from himself. What's more, quite apart from the family anguish arrest would cause, what might the effect be on his college career? Might it even lead to expulsion? Could it?

The more Judith thought about it, the more certain she became that the girl was the key. But how in the world would she find her? Deirdre. Deirdre what? And, even if

166

she knew her second name, what help would that be? She thought of waiting near the college gates for Jacob to come out – if he came out with Deirdre, then she'd at least know what the girl looked like. She could follow them and hope to get her on her own. No, that was all ridiculous. She didn't even know what time Jacob was due out of college on any day. And what if he saw her waiting there to spy on him? That idea was certainly out.

By half-past five when she normally finished her day's work, Judith had decided nothing. She was in despair over her failure to think of any plan of action, and having to accept the fact that she really was powerless almost filled her with panic.

She walked home slowly, relishing the crisp dry air, cold though it was, breathing it in deeply. The gas-mantles still burned in the shop windows – there was business to be won up to six o'clock – and they glowed like jewels on the phosphorescent arm of Patrick Street. The sober shadowy Victoria Hotel contrasted with the glassy smile of the Munster Arcade; Cash's and Roche's stores vied with each other to dominate the scene. What would it be like a month from now when they would all be showing off their Christmas decorations and the carol singers would be opening their throats to the full to drown the noise of horses' hoofs and tramcars? Yes, and also, as like as not, policemen stomping along ready to deafen you with their piercing whistles, and strutting Black and Tans, hands on holsters, shouldering pedestrians into the gutter.

Judith shook the image from her mind and turned into Winthrop Street where a billboard outside the Imperial Hotel caught her eye. 'Tuesdays and Thursdays – 6 to 9.30 – Thé Dansant – Tickets 3/6.'

For a moment she wished she was going, but the wish was fleeting. She recognised it immediately as a pointless whim, no more than an outsider's envy of those who would be going there. To be like them – to be one of them – that was the only way she could possibly enjoy such an occasion. Not as Judith Cohen – Judith Cohen would feel awkward at a *goyish* dance, out of place. How fitting the phrase was – out of place. She remembered her only experience of such an event. At seventeen, eager to see what life was like outside their enclosed world, she and Molly had enthusiastically agreed when Hymie Lepidus, one of the young men of the community, had suggested that they should make up a party and go to a 'hop' some Rugby club was running. Of course it all had to be done secretly – parents would never have allowed it – and that meant that the girls of the group had a problem: how could they get out of their houses in their dance dresses without their parents knowing? But Hymie had the answer to that: he knew where his father kept a spare set of keys to his dress shop.

What fun! What an escapade! Judith smiled to herself at the recollection of the more madcap elements of the adventure. Stealing into the dress shop in their ordinary clothes, having their choice of the most attractive dresses in the place – some of which they even took from the dummy figures – and then changing behind the drawn blinds of the window amid giggles and screeches as the boys threatened to come out of the small back office to peep at them.

Then later, after the dance, the whole process in reverse, only this time the boys, excited by the close contacts of the evening, had been more daring. As soon as the girls had taken off their dance frocks and were in their slips and petticoats, the boys had grabbed them, warning them not to scream or shout for fear passers-by in the street might hear them. Not that there had really been anything to scream about – cuddles, kisses, breathless hugs for the most part. The girls' muted protests had been no more than token objections; they knew their men, knew they could be trusted not to take too much advantage of them, knew indeed that their own numbers were sufficient to guarantee their safety and virginity. That feeling of safety in daring had been quite blissful, Judith recalled. To experience – for most of them, including Judith and Molly, for the first time – more intimate sexual thrills than their innocent juvenile party games had given them was intoxicating. Judith

168

remembered how her skin had tingled at the sensation of male hands separated from it by little more than the thickness of a vest, and when one of those hands had for a few seconds formed itself around her breast and tenderly caressed it her whole body had shuddered.

Perhaps their sense of elation, that touch almost of abandon, had been a response to the discomfort of the dance itself, a release after the evening's constrictions. It had been a misguided outing really. They might have been a different colour from the rest of the dancers, so much did they feel themselves to be under scrutiny. It was mostly curiosity, of course, but it was easy to imagine otherwise, and the embarrassment had tended to make some of their escorts behave more assertively than usual, so drawing even more attention on themselves. For much of the time they had felt uncomfortably self-conscious and graceless, and in fact had been glad to leave even before the dance ended. While there they had known themselves to be out of place, but that awareness had been quickly wiped clean by the excitement and thrills of the after-dance frolics. Would she feel the same awkwardness now, Judith wondered, if she were going to the Imperial Hotel's *thé dansant*? It was a fruitless speculation. She wasn't going – and wasn't in the mood for going even if Rudolph Valentino himself were to descend from the skies and offer her his arm. She was on her way home, with nothing more romantic facing her for the night than finding a way to put an end to Jacob's association with his Catholic girlfriend.

Responding once more with a tremor of her body to the memory of that warm hand on her breast, she could easily guess that Jacob must be experiencing similar urges. No doubt even stronger for him – young men of his age, she understood, easily became aroused, and what with his poetic temperament he was probably more romantically inclined than most. All the more reason to bring him back to the fold without delay – even if he had never been taking the added risk of being caught and arrested as an IRA helper.

It wasn't until next morning that the way to go about

getting him back suddenly struck her. She was in her father's office, gazing out the window, unable to work, aware only of time slipping by while she was no nearer a solution, when gradually her unseeing eyes began to focus on the view in front of them. They were looking at the open shed into which her father had stumbled, tears in his eyes, after asking her help two mornings before. That image and the recollection of his anguish had stamped itself so vividly on her mind that it had quite blotted out whatever had preceded it. But now, as if a cloud suddenly lifted, she saw her father again in the shed, but this time it was earlier the same morning and he had a visitor with him, a young man wearing a cap dripping with rain who had come to give him some money. Judith sprang up from her chair, almost shouting with joy, and then angry with herself for not thinking of it before. That man – her father's caller – was in the IRA. He had said it himself. He had told her father. Denis Hurley, that was his name. And he worked in Twohey's on Lavitt's Quay. She remembered it all. Thank goodness she had thought of it. Someone in the IRA – that was the solution, and it had been staring her in the face all the time. She would go to Denis Hurley. She would explain her problem to him and ask him to find out who this Deirdre was, and then either he or she would speak to her. Perhaps he could get the IRA to order her not to take non-members out on official business. Perhaps they would expel her for letting a stranger know what she was doing. They might even court-martial her. And then she'd hardly want to keep going with Jacob once she knew it was his sister who had got her into trouble. Oh, anything was possible. At least there was now something Judith could do, someone she could go to. Immediately. There was no time to lose. Remembering only to leave a note for her father saying that she some messages to do, she put on her coat and rushed out of the yard.

Lavitt's Quay was on the other side of the city, behind Patrick Street, but still no more than fifteen minutes' walk from her father's store. As she neared it Judith realised that she didn't know exactly where Twohey's was, but she did know well the Opera House on Lavitt's

170

Quay, so she would start there and work her way down. As she hurried round the front of the long dun-coloured building, she saw the posters on the wall and in the entrance hall advertising the operas the Carl Rosa Company were performing that week. 'TONIGHT – CAVALLERIA RUSTICANA and PAGLIACCI', the main billboard announced, but Judith did not stop to read the names of the cast or examine the portraits and photographs of the members of the Company. As she hastened along the side of the building, past its many tall ground-floor windows and stage door, she remembered Jacob telling her once that it was nearly seventy years old and had been the largest hall in the country when it was built for Ireland's first National Exhibition. The contrast between the relationship she and Molly had with their brother then – no more than three or four short years ago – when he used to read them his poetry and eagerly relay his latest piece of knowledge about Cork, and the way she felt she had to go behind his back now almost brought tears to her eyes. But she had to do it – for his own sake as much as for everyone else's.

Twohey's, she found, was only a few doors past the Opera House, a lock-up yard with large wooden doors now fully swung open, TWOHEY'S freshly painted in white on one and FURNITURE on the other, and beside it a handsome shop window showing off its manufactures.

Resolutely she entered the shop and approached the counter.

'Yes, miss?' enquired the elderly assistant, eyeing her over his half-spectacles.

'I wonder if I might see Mr Hurley, please. Mr Denis Hurley. I believe he works here. It's important.'

'Denis, is it? Of course. He works in the yard. You could go in, just next door, and ask for him.'

Judith thanked him and was about to follow his instructions when the man restrained her.

'Would it be business, miss, or – a personal matter?'

Hesitantly, not knowing which answer would be less complicating, she said: 'It's – well, more personal, I suppose.'

171

'In that case, miss,' the assistant confided with no hint of innuendo in his voice, 'perhaps you'd prefer to see him in here. More private. And, anyway, the yard is a bit messy, wood and things everywhere. We'd be in a nice stew if you tripped over something in there and hurt yourself. Take a seat there, miss, and I'll fetch Denis.'

Judith thanked him again and sat in a chair he indicated.

'A nice piece, that chair, miss, isn't it? One of our own designs. A great seller, very popular. Take your ease now and I'll have Denis in in a tick' – and he disappeared out the back of the shop.

In a few moments the back door opened and a head was poked round it. Judith didn't immediately recognise the face as that of her father's visitor. The man she had seen in the store had been all buttoned up against the wet weather, drops of rain had clung to his eyelashes, and she remembered that when he had taken off his cap his neatly parted sandy hair had been flattened to his head. Now she saw also a pair of large blue eyes, thin lips, and a square chin that slowly lowered in perplexed surprise as a fierce blush suffused every feature.

Judith rose. 'Mr Hurley?' she murmured tentatively.

Denis pushed the door open wider and took a few steps into the office. The blue of his eyes darkened warily as the blush began to fade.

'I'm Judith Cohen, Mr Hurley. We met the other morning – you called to see my father.'

There was an embarrassing silence as each seemed to wait for the other to say something. Denis held himself stiffly, apprehensive of what might follow, while Judith, faced now with the actual task of making her appeal, couldn't think how to express it. Denis Hurley's obvious confusion compounded her own until he was forced to prompt her with: 'Did you want anything? Is it a message you have from your father?'

'No, Mr Hurley,' she blurted. 'I'm sorry to bother you out of the blue like this – but I had to. I've come to ask your help.'

Denis was nervously wiping his hands on his stained

172

overalls, and it flashed across Judith's mind that he might be embarrassed at being caught by her in his working clothes, spots of varnish mottling his fingers. Perhaps she should have sent a note in to him first.

'Help, Miss Cohen?' she heard him say and then he suddenly seemed to straighten up as he turned to pull the office door firmly shut.

'Yes. You're in the IRA and I need someone—'

Denis started with alarm and roughly interrupted her.

'Who told you that?'

'My father did. He said you said so,' Judith explained hastily, taken aback by Denis's tone.

'What else did he tell you?'

'What else?' Judith repeated in some perplexity. 'Nothing else. He just said....' And then, as comprehension dawned, she blushed at her own tactlessness. 'Oh, I'm very sorry,' she assured him. 'You've no need to worry. We wouldn't put you in any danger. We wouldn't dream of telling anyone. My father probably didn't mean to tell me at all but he was upset at the time. That's why I've come to see you – what he was upset about, I mean.'

'You'd better sit down, Miss Cohen,' Denis said, his composure restored, as he drew up another chair.

Gratefully Judith resumed her seat and explained her errand as coherently as she could, but when Denis heard her say that Jacob's girl was in the IRA he laughed.

'I'm sorry, Miss Cohen, but I think that brother of yours is only leading you up the garden path. There are no women in the IRA. It's for men only.'

'But he told me himself,' Judith insisted, 'and I know he wasn't lying. He told me that he often goes out with her around the countryside to help her distribute the IRA newspaper. That's why I'm so worried.'

'Ah, I understand now. The girl must be a member of Cumann na mBan. It's a women's organisation but it's not officially part of the IRA.'

'I thought Cumann na mBan was a social and cultural society.' Judith was vaguely aware of the organisation; she knew it was highly popular with young Irish women of all classes – the Bernstein sisters had been members

173

before the family moved to Dublin the previous year – but she understood it to be concerned with the revival of the Irish language and other aspects of Irish culture.

'Oh, that's what it is all right, Miss Cohen. But some branches do what they can to help our fight against the British occupation. Distributing the IRA newspaper is a good way of helping. It's easier for them to get away with it and much less dangerous than it would be for one of us.'

'I see, yes,' Judith said. 'But that makes things even worse. If my brother was caught with her, the police would never believe he was innocent. They'd never believe he wasn't in the IRA, and wasn't just using this Deirdre girl.'

'I can't deny that, Miss Cohen. I can't give you any comfort on that score. Once these RIC boys get a hand on you, they don't let go. I'm sorry you have this trouble, miss, but I don't see how I can help.'

'I thought you might be able to find out who this girl is – my brother wouldn't tell me her full name – and where she lives. If I could talk to her, I might be able to persuade her to stop going with Jacob. I can't do anything with him. He's – well, he believes he's in love with her.'

'But he's only a youngster, Miss Cohen. That'll probably come to nothing. Youngsters are always falling in love, aren't they?'

'I know. I suppose the chances are he'll get over it. But if he didn't. . . . I just can't explain to you what it would do to our family. How could I take the risk of letting it go on – even if there was never the IRA bit? And I haven't told my father, so it makes everything more urgent. Couldn't you try to find out? You must know people, you must have contacts. There's no one else I can ask. Please.'

Judith's entreaties embarrassed Denis. He didn't know what he could do, but it was hard to turn her away without any hope.

'Well, I don't know. . . . I'd have to think about it. . . .'

'Please,' Judith repeated.

'Let me think it over, then,' Denis agreed. 'I can't promise, but if I can find out anything for you – what will I do, will I write to you?'

'No, that would take too long. And it would be better if you didn't come to the store. I could call here again tomorrow morning.'

Denis demurred. 'No, not here. And, anyway, tomorrow morning might be too soon. Could we meet outside somewhere?'

'Where? When? Tomorrow? Please make it tomorrow.'

'I don't know if I could find out anything by then. It's not much time.'

'But you might,' Judith insisted.

'Well, it would have to be tomorrow night. Is that awkward for you?'

'No, no. I can be free. Where shall we meet?'

'I suppose somewhere in town is best. Say at the Statue. That way it'll just look as if we're waiting for a tram. At the Statue at eight o'clock. Is that all right, Miss Cohen?'

'Yes. And I'm very grateful.' Judith smiled with relief.

'It doesn't give me much time, you know,' Denis warned. 'Don't be disappointed if—'

'I'll keep my fingers crossed,' Judith interrupted. 'Thank you, Mr Hurley, and please forgive me for putting you to such trouble. But there was no one. . . .'

Her voice trailed off as Denis nodded, an understanding smile on his lips. 'I'll see you tomorrow night, then,' he said as he held the door open for her. 'Goodbye now, Miss Cohen.'

'Goodbye. And thank you again.'

As the door shut behind her Judith drew in a long breath and sighed heavily. The feeling of accomplishment and the hope it brought flooding through her was exhilarating. She had taken some action. She could do no more. For the moment the whole nerve-racking business was out of her hands.

The Wednesday-afternoon post brought a letter to Rabbi Moishe from Berel Karlinsky. It told him that all arrangements were now completed. The Rabbi's party was to make its way to Dublin on Sunday, 12 December, cross to

England in that night's packet, and next day they would embark for Marseilles where another boat would take them to Palestine.

The Rabbi folded the letter, put it back in its envelope, and then recited the blessing on hearing good tidings: 'Blessed art Thou, O Lord our God, King of the Universe, Who is good and causes good to happen.'

He opened his eyes, swaying his head from side to side as if in a trance. He would let those members of the party who were not at the moment travelling in the countryside know immediately, and he would make the official announcement in *Shool* on the sabbath. Then, suddenly bethinking himself, he took out his *Luach*, his pocket Jewish calendar, and swiftly turned the pages. Yes, as he had thought – 12 December was the eve of the last day of Chanukah, the Festival of Lights, commemorating the rededication of the Temple and the hearts of the Jews to God's service after the desecration wreaked when Antiochus Epiphanes had conquered Jerusalem. Rabbi Moishe closed his *Luach* and nodded in satisfaction. It was fitting. It was surely a sign. With the help of God he would fulfil his lifelong dream, he would stand on the holy earth of the Land of Israel and his voice would ring out with the final great blessing: 'Blessed art Thou, O Lord our God, King of the Universe, Who has kept us alive, preserved us, and allowed us to reach this occasion.'

Percy Lovitch couldn't remember the last time he had sat in 'the gods' for an opera; it must have been back in his student days. He had watched Monday night's *Bohème* from the wings, and also Tuesday's *Carmen*, but he would never again be able to bring himself to avail of such a privilege. Not, at least, with the Carl Rosa Opera Company. His memories of all his associations with it, of all the years he had given it and had been proud to be in its ranks – and of the more recent years, too, when, no longer an official member, he nevertheless was made part of it when the Company visited Cork – all that would be too

176

much for him now, too embarrassing if he were to try to mix any more with these wonderful people who had for so long been his friends and colleagues. He wasn't feeling bitter – what right had he to feel bitter? it had been nobody's fault – but he was so sick at heart that he almost didn't care if he never attended a performance of theirs ever again. If it hadn't been for tonight's bill, he'd have stayed at home. He couldn't miss *them* – not *Cav* and *Pag*, especially *Pagliacci*, his favourite in the whole repertoire.

Throughout the performance of *Cavalleria Rusticana* he had managed to lose himself in the story and his spirits were lifted by the enchantment of Mascagni's music; but now, in the interval before *Pagliacci* commenced, his unhappy thoughts returned and began to overwhelm him. He couldn't put out of his mind the recollection of the growing discomfort he had sensed during Monday night's opera; the feeling was there again during Tuesday's rehearsal, and by Tuesday night he was certain there was something amiss. In other years he had always had a chat with Barry Brandreth, the manager, during the opening opera, but this time his old friend seemed to be ignoring him, fussing over tasks he didn't normally undertake. In fact to Percy he appeared simply to be making himself busy in order to avoid their customary talk. Percy had expected to be invited to sing an aria or two in Tuesday's run-through so as to allow the leading tenor to rest his voice; in previous years it had been a regular highlight for him, and the enthusiastic round of applause the Company always gave him after his first solo had been worth the whole year's wait. This time, however, there had been no such invitation, and Barry had not been on hand for Percy to offer to stand in.

During the evening performance Percy had taken his accustomed place in the wings, but his mind hadn't been on the opera. He was waiting for an opportunity to button-hole his friend. It came when the last act had just commenced and he saw the manager making his way towards his office.

When Percy followed him, he found the door open and Brandreth was inside, pouring whiskey into two glasses.

'Percy, old man, come in. I've been expecting you.'

He smiled affably as he held out one of the glasses, but despite the friendliness of the welcome Percy's keen ear immediately discerned the strained timbre of the voice. Its habitual bounce was missing, and now it had a note of tiredness that Percy had never heard before.

He raised his glass. 'Good health,' he said and drank.

'Quite,' Brandreth answered. 'And yours, too,' as he sat down, motioning Percy to take the only other seat in the small office.

'Percy, my friend,' he said, rolling his glass between his fingers, 'I don't like this hole-and-corner business. Any more than you do, I'm sure. We've known each other too long for that. And I'm not one to run away from explanations. You know what I'm talking about.' He fingered his moustaches in a show of the old authority and decisiveness.

'I think I do,' Percy Lovitch nodded. 'So what's the matter?'

Brandreth drained the last of his whiskey and held up the empty glass.

'Like this drink, old boy, I may soon be swallowed up.'

Percy was familiar with his friend's dramatics, but this announcement was so out of character that he knew it was no joke.

'What do you mean? Are you ill?'

'No, not ill – unless *anno domini* is an illness. Just as singers come and go, Percy – as you well know, my friend – managers come and go, too. Managers may last a little longer, of course; but in short, old boy, I am on trial.'

'On trial?' Percy echoed.

'Oh, nothing official, of course. These things are always done discreetly. But I have a rival. I learned it from a well-placed friend, close to the top. There's someone who believes my race has been run and it's time for me to take my final bow and be put out to grass.' Brandreth's florid phrases were at odds with the slight mistiness in his eyes.

'Who? Who's your rival?'

'Oh, someone back at base, old boy. You wouldn't know him. Young blood and all that sort of thing. But the position is, Percy, that, being on trial, I just couldn't use you this year. I have to do things by the book. It's not my style. You know that. I never hesitated to cut corners, take risks, if the stakes were worth it. Like this visit to Cork.'

'I thought the Company wanted to come – to keep up the tradition,' Percy said.

'Yes, most of them did. But behind the scenes there were mutterings about the unrest here; you know the kind of thing – natives running wild, law and order breaking down, ambushes, et cetera, et cetera. We'd never get here – performances would be cancelled – the people wouldn't support a British company; it was all said.'

'But none of that has happened,' Percy pointed out.

'It's early days, Percy. I'm keeping my fingers crossed. If the rest of the week is as good as last night and tonight. . . .'

Brandreth poured another drink for both of them before continuing. 'It was left to me, and I decided to take the risk and come. If anything goes wrong, it'll probably mean the end of me. But if the week is a success, then I think I might just be able to repel boarders, old boy.' He held his glass forward as if in silent toast to both of them. 'So you see, Percy, why I must play by the rules now. I'm sure you understand, old chap.'

Percy understood – of course he understood – but understanding did not make the news any easier to take. He had gone home in a daze; he had passed a sleepless night; and all next day he had sat in his shop, staring glumly at the silent musical instruments, the gramophone records, the stacks of sheet music, while his mind reeled through the highlights of his long career. It was over now, all over; it had been over before, of course, when he had retired, but then there had been farewell performances, newspaper tributes, a party on stage, presents, mementoes, goodbye hugs – the sadness of the occasion had been almost completely buried under the flood of affection and comradeship everyone had displayed. It was their loss, he had been made to feel, rather than his own. And then throughout the years in Cork the contact had been maintained, and the Company's annual visit had always seen him, in one way or another, in harness again. But now he really was on the shelf, the very last link had been broken. He would never again hold a stage, never be picked out by the spotlight, never beguile an audience, never again don motley. Never again don motley. He sat in 'the gods', waiting for the curtain to rise on *Pagliacci*, waiting to see the tragic figure of Tonio the clown, who in a fit of jealousy kills the wife he adores, step forward in his baggy pants, painted face and clown's hat, and sing the heartbreaking prologue, 'On with the Motley'. Percy had sung it himself so many times – but no more. For him now, for the rest of his days, it was off with the motley.

He looked around at the packed wooden benches of 'the gods' and for a moment couldn't quite make out why he was there – miles up above the stage that was no bigger than a postage stamp below him – rather than in the wings where he always went. And then he remembered: he couldn't miss *Pagliacci*; he had to hear it again, he had to experience it – perhaps for the last time – as it should be sung, the live throbbing notes holding a rapt audience in thrall rather than a distant bodiless voice emerging from a gramophone trumpet to die in tinny silence. But not from the wings where the unexpressed pity of his ex-colleagues would have been unbearable, and not from the stalls or circle where the ushers and programme-sellers would know him and would have whispered to each other behind their hands. 'The gods' was the place for him now, up under the towering roof of the Opera House with the men and women who had flocked in their hundreds to welcome the Company to their strife-troubled city, men and women to whom every aria was as familiar as the lullabies they sang their children, who even now all around him were buzzing with a current of anticipation so strong that the very air seemed alive with the charge.

As 'curtain up' got nearer and the hubbub of conversation grew louder, Percy began to feel his heart drumming in his breast and a lump, like a stone, rising in his throat. He blinked his eyes, once, twice, but to no avail, and suddenly all the anguish of the moment broke over him like a wave. In an uncontrollable panic he stumbled to his feet, falling over people in his haste to reach an exit and, with one hand begging support from the cold brick wall and his eyes blinded with tears, he reeled down the endless spiral of the echoing concrete steps. As he descended, the opening bars of the orchestral introduction swam around his ears and then came the first words and notes of 'On with the Motley'. He tried to run faster, to get away from the heart-rending music, but the impetus of going down in circles almost tumbled him headlong. When at last he reached the street and leaned against the door of 'the gods' to quieten his bursting heart, there was no more music to torture him. Instead, in his head he heard the final words of the opera, and for Percy Lovitch their message was as iron in his soul: 'La commedia è finita'.

12

Zvi Lipsky wasn't a superstitious man. Even so, he couldn't dismiss as mere coincidence the fact that that morning four patients had failed to turn up for their appointments. Cancellations and non-arrivals he accepted as part of a dentist's normal business risks, and indeed at his age he welcomed the occasional missed appointment – it gave him a chance to slow down and rest. Nor had he forgotten that for many months now few days passed without one or two country patients being prevented from getting to the city because of the sudden train strikes – the *Cork Examiner* that morning reported that more trains had been stopped on the Cork & Bandon line, all passenger traffic had ceased on the Cork & Macroom line, and the Government had threatened to close the railways altogether unless railwaymen agreed to carry munitions and soldiers. Zvi had no doubt all these stoppages were the main cause of his broken appointments – but four in a row in one day! That was unique. And to have it happen on this particular day when only an hour ago he had heard that Rabbi Moishe's group would be leaving for Palestine within a month.... It had to mean something, it had to have special significance. Surely it was a sign to him not to hesitate any more over the idea he had for getting rid of Arnold Wine but to use the unexpected few hours' break to pay the upstart a visit.

Sign or not, he couldn't waste the opportunity. If he didn't go now, he'd have to go after work when he'd be tired, or in the evening when Wine might not be in, or he'd have to write to him, which was something he could not see himself doing. It was now or not at all. Myra, of course, hadn't shown much interest in his idea – as usual she didn't take Zvi's worries and fears seriously – but if it succeeded it would benefit both of them.

The narrow staircase leading to Wine's consulting-rooms was dingy and drab – very much in need of a clean-up and a coat of paint, Zvi thought. His own premises had a much more attractive entrance; Wine would be better advised to brighten up his staircase instead of spending money putting his picture in the paper.

But inside the waiting-room it was a different story, and Zvi was quite taken aback. The room was large, nicely papered, pictures on the walls, net curtains on the windows, the remains of a good fire still burning in the grate. Zvi counted no less than ten chairs, and the table had three copies of that morning's *Cork Examiner* – all of them showing obvious signs of having been thoroughly read – and even some magazines. Ashtrays, too, which Zvi didn't provide in *his* waiting-room – after all, where was the need when he had a cleaning woman in every day? – nor did he bother with a table and papers, either. Well, no doubt this was all very smart, very showy, typical of the frills and flounces these interlopers indulged in. But what was the use of all this nonsense if you had no patients? And there were none, none at all; the room was completely empty. Nor was there a sound from the adjoining room, which was presumably Wine's surgery. Where, then, was everybody? Was this 'the great increase in my practice' that Wine boasted of in his advertisements and that had made him remove 'to more spacious premises'? Of course, perhaps the train cancellations were hitting his business, too – they must be. Even so, the empty waiting-room brought a smile to Zvi's normally lugubrious features. Things mightn't be at all as good as Wine pretended. He might be more than pleased to consider Zvi's suggestion.

Zvi gave a start as the adjoining door opened suddenly and Arnold Wine entered. His white coat was spotless and his wavy black hair flashed with oil. Recognising his visitor immediately, his eyes widened in surprise.

'Mr Lipsky,' he beamed, coming forward with hand outstretched, 'this *is* an unexpected pleasure. To what do I owe the honour? Not a professional visit, I trust. You're not having some trouble, are you?'

Zvi wasn't impressed with his attempt at humour – these young pups never knew when to show respect – but he was quick to turn the tables.

'No, there's nothing the matter with me, but it looks as if you could do with a patient or two. You don't seem to be very busy.'

'On the contrary, Mr Lipsky, on the contrary,' Wine replied, smiling even more smugly. 'I've had a very busy morning. I'm just finished for the day.'

'Finished?'

'Yes. It's my half-day. You see, I work all day Saturday, so I take a half-day off during the week.'

'You work on Shabbos!' Zvi was unable to keep a note of condemnation, almost of outrage, out of his voice.

'Yes. Why not? I'm not particularly religious. And Saturday is a very busy day. So many people in town,' Wine explained, no whit of shame or apology in his tone.

Zvi nodded deprecatingly, as if he expected no better. 'I wondered – when I saw you at the meeting last Saturday night, I wondered why I had never seen you in *Shool* on Saturday morning.'

'And now you know, Mr Lipsky, and now you know. I went to the meeting because I'm a Zionist. You don't have to be religious to be a Zionist – perhaps you disagree with me?'

Zvi gave a shrug which could have been interpreted either way, but secretly he was pleased to hear Wine express such committed interest in Palestine. Surprised, but pleased. Still, he mustn't rush things.

'Come and see my surgery,' Wine said, taking him by the arm. 'I'm quite proud of it. I think you'll be impressed.'

Impressed Zvi Lipsky certainly was, though he was careful not to give voice to his admiration. He saw that everything was brand new and shining – the foot pedals for the chair and drill showed not the slightest sign of wear, the washbasin taps didn't drip, the spittoon was a special separate unit rather than the plain enamel receptacle which did service for Zvi.

'Well, what do you think, Mr Lipsky?' Wine asked.

Zvi grunted noncommittally. A few perfunctory nods were all he would allow himself in the way of qualified approval. Any word of positive commendation would hardly help his cause.

'I suppose you'd get a few pounds for all of this,' he eventually grudgingly conceded.

'Get a few pounds for it!' Wine laughed. 'But I've only recently bought it. Why should I want to sell?'

Zvi shrugged. 'You're young. You might want to move on – not bury yourself in a small place like Cork.'

Wine looked perplexed for a moment and then the confident smile returned and his eyes twinkled, making Zvi wonder if he had shown his hand too soon. He felt that the conversation had already become a cat-and-mouse affair and he wasn't certain who was the cat and who the mouse.

'Cork is big enough for me,' Wine assured him. 'And, besides, I'm not all that long here. Really, I haven't had a proper chance to settle in yet, business has been so good. So why should I want to move on, as you put it?'

Zvi had no alternative but to keep going, despite his unhappy suspicion that he was getting nowhere.

'Well, if it was made worth your while.... You said you're a Zionist. A young man like you could do a lot in Palestine. You're just the kind of person they need. And there's a chance for you to go there now – with Rabbi Cohen's group. I heard this morning that they are leaving on 12 December.'

Arnold Wine said nothing but raised himself onto a bench from where he dangled his legs and contemplated

185

Zvi Lipsky. Or was he weighing the suggestion? Zvi wondered. Perhaps he was. Perhaps all he needed was a little more encouragement. Zvi drew a breath and plunged.

'Look, I'll buy you out. I'll give you two hundred pounds if you decide to go to Palestine – and you can keep whatever you get for all this fine equipment. It's a lot of money, two hundred pounds.' Zvi blinked, then took off his spectacles and busied himself polishing them. He wished he had handled it all more slowly, worked around to it a bit less obviously – but it was out now and he felt a little easier.

Wine drummed his fingers on his knee and smiled innocently. But he made no reply.

'Two fifty?' Zvi suggested. 'I wish someone had offered me two hundred and fifty pounds when I was starting out.'

Wine burst into loud laughter, and Zvi, in the act of replacing his spectacles, fumbled and almost dropped them with shock.

'Life is strange, Mr Lipsky,' Wine commented, 'life is strange. You know, I was going to make *you* an offer. Oh, not just yet. Later on; next year, I thought. And of course I wasn't thinking of offering you two hundred pounds, or two hundred and fifty pounds, or anything at all in fact.'

'*Vos?* What?' Zvi spluttered. 'What are you talking about? What offer?'

'Well, Mr Lipsky, since you set the ball rolling, I'll tell you what I had in mind. I thought we might go into partnership together.'

Zvi went pale. Was he hearing aright? Was this pup making fun of him? He couldn't possibly be serious.

'Are you mad?' he managed to say. He could think of nothing else.

Wine got off the bench and took Zvi by the arm.

'Come with me,' he said, in the tone of a father taking pains to help his son with a difficult problem. He led Zvi back into the waiting-room and propelled him to a chair by the fire.

'Would you like a cup of tea?' he asked. 'I could make one. No trouble.'

186

Zvi waved the offer aside, and Wine took a seat opposite him.

'Look, Mr Lipsky, I'll tell you what I had in mind. You tell me I'm young. So I am – not thirty yet. But I have a difficulty: I like money. I want to be – rich? Well, very comfortable, let's say. The only way I can make as much money as I'd like is to work hard. Which I do. But, on the other hand, I also like living. I want to enjoy myself. I want not to have to work so hard that I haven't the time or the energy to enjoy life.'

Zvi felt pinned to his chair by Wine's words. He took off his hat and mopped his balding head, wishing he had accepted the offer of a cup of tea.

'Now, you, Mr Lipsky,' Wine went on, 'are no longer a young man. No offence intended, you understand. You've been here a very long time. I know about your reputation, your career, the hours you put in travelling around the country, building up your practice. You didn't have it easy, Mr Lipsky, I know that. What you've got, you worked for.'

Wine paused, and Zvi, while mollified by his praise, told himself that Wine didn't know the half of it. He was about to expand on the trials and tribulations he had suffered to get where he was, when Wine resumed, stunning him completely with 'Don't you think it's time you took a rest, Mr Lipsky?'

Zvi held his breath in amazement.

'What do you mean?' he finally managed to say, his eyes watering as they always did in moments of great stress or emotion.

'I'll explain,' Wine replied. 'You work five days a week. Yes?'

Zvi nodded.

'It's hard work, physical, tiring. Fillings, extractions, you're on your feet all the time. It takes it out of you. You don't have to tell me how hard it is. I know – because I don't work five days a week, I work five and a half days a week. Until seven or eight most days. Of course I haven't been at it that long – four years only. While you. . . .'

'Over forty years,' Zvi boasted.

187

'Over forty! My, my, a record to be proud of. I don't know how you did it.'

Zvi wished Wine would get to the point. As if reading his thoughts, Wine said: 'Here's what I suggest. We become partners, keep our separate rooms, but you work only four days a week and I work only four days a week, and we share the proceeds. We could arrange our days to suit ourselves. Maybe you'd work Monday to Thursday, that way you'd have *Erev Shabbos* off as well as the Sabbath itself; and I could work Wednesday to Saturday. We would raise our fees, of course. We're not charging enough as it is, and anyway people have to get their teeth seen to. We'd make at least as much money as we're making now – probably more – but we wouldn't have to work so hard for it. What do you say to that, Mr Lipsky?'

Zvi opened and shut his mouth a few times, then took off his spectacles to dab at his eyes.

'I think you're *meshuggah*! I don't want a partner,' he protested. 'I have a good practice. I don't mind working hard. I'm used to it.'

'You think *I'm meshuggah*? Is it mad to want to make one's life as easy as possible? By doing that you prolong your life. Do you want to die in harness? Do you want to work yourself into your grave?' Wine pressed.

'Oi, *tzirifooeh!*' Zvi ejaculated, spontaneously spitting into the fire in the traditional action of expelling an evil thought.

'How long do you think you can continue practising dentistry, Mr Lipsky?'

'What sort of a question is that?' Zvi said.

'Well, what about the possible changes you may have to face soon?'

'Changes? What changes? I haven't heard of any changes.'

'No,' said Wine quietly, 'I don't suppose you have. You'd have to be a qualified dentist, a member of the Dental Association, to know what's happening. And you're not a qualified dentist, are you, Mr Lipsky?'

'What do you mean?' Zvi bridled. 'I'm as good as any

188

qualified dentist in this city. I have more experience than any of them.'

Wine waved a pacifying gesture. 'It's nothing to be ashamed of. It's the way the profession has developed – never subject to government legislation. There are hundreds of unregistered, unqualified dentists in Ireland and Britain. Very many of them are unscrupulous. Dangerous charlatans. On the other hand, some of them are highly competent. From all I hear, I know that *you* are one of the highly competent ones. But the fact is that you are not qualified.'

'What of it?' Zvi demanded. How come this upstart to question *his* credentials? What gave him the right to sneer? The kettle calling the pot black.

'Well, Mr Lipsky, the difference between us is that I *am* a qualified dentist.'

Zvi stiffened in his chair and his jaw fell.

'Yes,' Wine assured him. 'There's my certificate – a graduate of the London School of Dentistry.' He pointed to the wall just inside the waiting-room door – the wall Zvi had had his back to when he entered. He turned to look at it now and saw a framed certificate hanging there. He tried to say something, to think of something, but all he could feel was a massive incomprehension. He was aggrieved that Fate could have dealt him such a blow, could have so betrayed him.

'At this moment, Mr Lipsky, there is a British government departmental committee considering the whole situation of the dental profession in Ireland and Britain,' Wine said quietly. 'You didn't know that?'

Zvi remained silent. How would he know such a thing? If it was in the newspaper, he hadn't seen it, and he didn't mix with other dentists – qualified or unqualified. He did his work; he did it well, he cared about it; he minded his own business.

'And I'll tell you something else you don't know: the Irish branch of the British Dental Association has made recommendations to that committee which would very much concern you.'

'Me?' Zvi echoed, his voice almost dying in his throat.

'Yes. They are recommending that there should be a way of distinguishing between qualified and unqualified dentists. That the unqualified ones should not be allowed to call themselves dentists. And the suggestion is that they should have to pass an examination before being allowed to continue practising as dentists.'

Zvi's face, naturally pale, went white. His hands began to tremble.

'Of course,' Wine added, seeing Zvi's agitated state, 'we don't know whether the committee will accept these recommendations. They might; they might not. But the decision will be made quite soon. How would you feel about doing an examination, Mr Lipsky?'

Zvi's heart began to pound and his breath was coming in big gasps. How could he possibly face such an ordeal at his age? And if he failed....

'Well, it might not come to that,' Wine said easily, affecting to dismiss the magnitude of the threat to Zvi's whole life and livelihood. 'But, even if it did, we could probably get round it.'

Zvi's wet eyes opened wide in enquiry.

'Well, if we were partners – with our own private agreement – and if there were some rule about examinations for unqualified dentists, I'm sure there would be exceptions made, allowances for special cases. Perhaps approval by a qualified dentist would be enough – or even if the unqualified dentist was acting as the assistant of the qualified one. Only nominally assistant of course, Mr Lipsky – just as a possible way of satisfying the requirements. But I'm only speculating. We don't know yet. Still, as you can see, a partnership between us might be to your advantage more than just financially. Of course you'll want to think about it. Discuss it with Mrs Lipsky.'

Zvi nodded. He felt as if all his strength had drained away. He didn't know if he'd be able to rise from his chair.

'I must go,' he muttered.

'Let me take you to lunch,' Wine suggested, helping him up. 'They do a nice three-course in the Victoria Hotel.'

Zvi's look was a mixture of perplexity and affront. What was lunch? At one o'clock in the day he had his dinner –

always. And eat in a hotel, where nothing was kosher!

He shook his head savagely and made his way to the door, trying not to look at the certificate which, in its thin black frame, was like a mourning-card marking the burial of his career, the end of his life.

'Let me see you down the stairs,' Wine said, 'they're a bit dark' – and as he would with an aged patient who had just endured a difficult painful extraction, he took Zvi's hand and, step by step, led him to the street.

'Think about it, Mr Lipsky,' he advised in farewell, 'and let me know your answer.'

It was as if Zvi heard nothing. He took a few steps in the wrong direction, paused, turned, looked past Arnold Wine, and then slowly shuffled away.

The rain was falling steadily – it had been for some hours – and the sky was so dark that Judith saw no hope of any improvement in the weather for the rest of the evening. Her umbrella had already become soaked in the few minutes she was waiting for the tram – she had to hold it away from her knees during the journey into town – and now large drops were chasing one another along its ribs to splash down onto the pavement at her feet. There would be mud stains on the bottom of her coat, she knew – even though she had only stepped off the tram at the Statue and hurried over the road, she hadn't been able to avoid treading through puddles. She was early of course – Mangan's tall street-clock showed ten to eight, so Denis Hurley wasn't due for another ten minutes. If he was on time. If he turned up at all! The thought alarmed her. It hadn't occurred to her before, but she quickly dismissed it. He had seemed an honest sincere man; she couldn't believe he would deliberately let her down.

She closed her umbrella and stepped into the doorway of Gilbert's Print Shop for shelter but within moments she was pushed to the back of the entrance by people trying to keep under cover until their tram arrived at the terminus.

191

Unable to see over their shoulders into the street and completely hidden from the view of anyone who might be looking for her, she had to squeeze her way out on to the pavement again despite the downpour. She looked towards Patrick's Bridge – she had no idea from which direction Denis Hurley would be coming – but it was hopeless for her to imagine that she might recognise his figure among the few pedestrians hurrying across it. The rain and the darkness together almost veiled the bridge and, indeed, part of Castle Street and the towering Patrick's Hill beyond it were completely obscured. Really, the Statue was not the most sensible place to have arranged to meet. With the screeching and bustle of trams constantly reaching and leaving the terminus and with so many people getting off and getting on, it would be the simplest thing in the world to miss or be missed by the person you were expecting. Just as she was upbraiding herself for not thinking of this sooner, there was a touch on her arm and she turned to find Denis Hurley at her side.

'Oh, Mr Hurley, I'm so glad you came.'

'I'm not late, am I?'

'No, I'm afraid I was early. I've been so anxious. . . .'

Her words trailed off as she saw how wet he was. With his saturated mackintosh and dripping cap, he was again the figure she had first seen when he had knocked at the door of her father's office on Monday morning. She felt guilty, as if this time it was she who was responsible for his almost bedraggled state, and she raised her umbrella higher to bring him under its shelter. Her action almost whipped the cap off his head and he drew back sharply.

'Oh, I'm so sorry,' she apologised.

'Better let me hold this, Miss Cohen, and we can both get under it then,' he said, grasping the handle and for a moment imprisoning her hand in his.

Involuntarily she pulled her hand away, covering her embarrassment with 'Did you get the girl's name, Mr Hurley?'

'I'm sorry, Miss Cohen,' Denis interjected, 'but I haven't any news for you. The person I wanted to see is away and I haven't had enough time to find anyone else who might be able to give me information.'

'Oh,' Judith exclaimed, unable to keep the disappointment out of her voice.

'I'm sorry to disappoint you, but I did say, didn't I—?'

'You did, Mr Hurley. You did warn me. But the person you want to see – when will he be back?'

'Maybe tomorrow. I'm not sure. People don't like to give out much information.'

'No. I suppose you can't blame them.'

Judith saw now that from the moment Denis Hurley had promised to help her she had allowed herself to live in a fool's paradise, taking it for granted that because he was in the IRA he would easily be able to find out Deirdre's second name. The sudden realisation of her naïvety was chilling after the near-euphoria of believing that her problem was about to be resolved. She felt isolated again, and the horrible weather on top of the clanging of the trams' bells and the screeching of their iron wheels was adding a real measure of physical discomfort and annoyance to all the miseries and doubts that once more began to grip her.

'You won't give up. You'll keep trying for me.'

Denis Hurley was still her only hope, and the urgency of her plea added to his efforts to keep them both protected by her small umbrella made their bodies press closely together. With his free hand he grasped her arm and squeezed it reassuringly.

'Of course, Miss Cohen, I'll do my level best. Honest I will. But – well, I can't promise.'

'I know. I realise that now. When will we meet again? I can't see you tomorrow night or Saturday because it's the Jewish Sabbath.'

'That's just as well,' Denis replied. 'It gives me more time. Would Sunday suit you?'

'Yes, please, Sunday, if you're free. The afternoon would be best. But could we meet somewhere else?' Judith was thinking that if by chance anyone who knew her saw them together in Patrick Street on a Sunday afternoon it would be bound to start gossip.

193

'Afternoon, yes,' Denis agreed. 'Say, three o'clock. We could meet at the Marina. If it's not wet, it's a nice place to walk and talk.'

'No, not the Marina.' The Marina was far too near Celtic Crescent for Judith's liking. 'Could we possibly make it somewhere on the other side of the city?'

Denis thought for a moment. 'The other side.... Well, how about outside the College? It'll be closed on Sunday, so there's no fear of your brother being there to see you, and it's on a tram route.'

'Yes, that's a good idea. I'm very grateful, Mr Hurley. Three o'clock on Sunday outside the University. I'll see you then.'

'Are you off now?' Denis asked.

'Yes. I'll get the tram,' Judith replied, reclaiming her umbrella.

'I'll see you home. I'm not doing anything else.' Denis thought he should make up for not being able to bring Judith any news. The least he could do was give her some company home after her fruitless journey. He also had a vague feeling of regret that their meeting was so brief. He'd have liked to talk more with her, but he had no idea how to detain her. There was a restaurant – O'Riordan's City Hotel and Restaurant – next door to Gilbert's right behind them where they could have a cup of tea and still be out well before curfew time, but he had never been in a restaurant and he didn't want to make a fool of himself.

Judith, however, was already saying goodbye. 'There's no need to come with me, Mr Hurley, really. I'll be home in ten minutes and I don't want to bring you out of your way.'

'Ah sure it's no trouble,' Denis assured her.

'No, I couldn't let you,' Judith insisted, fearful of being seen with him near home. 'Look, there's my tram. I'll just catch it. And I'll see you on Sunday at three. 'Bye now' – and before Denis could even accompany her across the road she had lowered her umbrella, scampered between the trams and was lost to sight.

* * *

194

The sound of the rain drumming on the tin roof of the hen-coop in the yard reminded Joshua Cohen of his childhood days in Akmeyon. The shed next to their small home, where the horses his brothers bought and sold were stabled, also had a tin roof, and during heavy showers the noise made the horses neigh wildly. Other memories of that long-ago drifted back to him. Where, he wondered, was his boyhood friend, Chaim Kilkoff, with whom at first light on winter mornings he used to steal out to gape at the younger men of the village rolling naked in the snow? Why should he remember that now? He hadn't thought of Chaim Kilkoff, or of the horse-shed, for years. He must be getting old. Yes, that was it. It wasn't that his mind wasn't willing to face reality and was fleeing to its childhood recollections so as to escape its present worries. It was just that he was getting old and his mind tired easily, and when an old mind tired it liked to think back to the distant past.

He shook his head, as if the action could disperse the memories, and concentrated once more on the *Cork Examiner* in his hands. He sensed his wife's eyes staring through the paper from the other side of the kitchen table.

'An RIC sergeant has been shot dead at Tuckey Street barracks,' he read out in an effort to divert her attention.

Bertha grunted. 'That's news?' she questioned. 'It's the same every day in the paper. Shoot, shoot, shoot! Shoot, shoot, shoot! Don't annoy me with it.'

Joshua lowered the *Examiner* to see what his wife was doing. Writing a letter – it would be to Molly.

He put the newspaper up between them again so as he could think about his daughter while still pretending to read. She was carrying his grandchild – his first grand-child. The prospect was the only thing about his whole future that warmed his blood. He remembered how his own father used to dote on Jacob when he was a boy. '*Yankele, Yankele, geb tzu zein zeide a bonkelah.*' He had felt at the time that it wasn't manly to drool so over a boy-child, yet now he wouldn't trust himself not to want to be just as sentimental with Molly's child, be it boy or girl. Oh, yes, he was certainly getting old. He would need that grandchild. In three weeks he would have no father himself – he was sure it would be like having no father when Rabbi Moishe was so far away. And his son, Jacob – *he* might as well be a strange lodger in the house. But at least he wasn't out with his *shiksah* tonight; he was in the front room studying his medical books; and Judith.... Judith *was* out – Joshua didn't know where, he never knew where – she never told him, he never asked. He cringed inwardly at the recollection of how he had broken down before her and showed her the letter about Jacob. Had she found out if it was true? He had to know, but he couldn't tell which was worse: waiting for the news or the embarrassment of having eventually to hear it. It was all too much to bear. He took his *Sidur* from the mantelshelf and opened it at the 'Prayers Before Going to Bed'.

Bertha Cohen continued her letter to Molly, writing easily and swiftly. She had determinedly mastered English within a year after her arrival in Cork and, though her speech might still fall into the idioms of the Yiddish language that had been her first tongue, her writing was carefully correct. In Akmeyon she had never needed to put pen to paper – who in their ghetto-*shtetl* did? – and so writing a letter was an accomplishment that only officials and people of a high social class practised. It was for something important, something permanent. Notepaper could survive, the words on it remain legible, eyes other than those it was intended for might come across it – they must be able to recognise the superior ability behind the hand that guided the pen.

In his room Rabbi Moishe was also writing, but not a letter. He was making notes for the sermon he would give in the synagogue on Shabbos. It wouldn't be strictly a sermon – more a talk to accompany his announcement of the date of their departure for Palestine. *Vayyetze* was the portion of the Law to be read on the coming Saturday. *And Jacob went out*, the story of Jacob's going forth to Haran. Rabbi Moishe nodded his head and stroked his beard. *Vayyetze* was a good text – a fitting text for such an occasion.

Jacob's medical textbooks lay open on the table in the front room, but Jacob had given them little of his attention. He was standing at the window, gazing out into the shadowed street at the rain beating on the pavement. Were it not for the rain he would have been out with Deirdre, but at college that morning she had felt a cold coming on and said she would stay at home in the evening if the weather was bad. Jacob was not too disappointed – not that he wanted time for his studies; he had something much more important to write, much more interesting, more exciting: a poem to Deirdre.

Ada Neumann had gone to bed early. She always did in the winter – it saved fuel and she liked to lie in bed and remember Harry, her husband. Though she had grown used to the space beside her and had stopped grieving long ago, she thought about Harry every night. Remembering him helped her to get to sleep. Tonight, however, sleep did not come too easily, for Abie Klugman was also on her mind. She would miss him. He was a child; he needed care, to be cared for, and she had given him that care. Who would give it to him in Palestine? She turned over on her side and tried not to dwell on her fears. Better for her to be looking out for someone to take his place – the money came in useful, not that she was too badly off with her little shop doing steady trade. But God is good – someone would come along – her reputation as a *baaleboosta* was known to the whole community – and maybe she would get a man who would be able to handle Mickey Aronson. *Ai, ai*, he was a joker, that boy, but a cruel joker. Boy? Mickey Aronson a boy? Ada smiled to herself at the ridiculous thought. Well, she could be a joker, too.

Sam Spiro was also thinking of his dear departed. Since his wife's death he had been alone, but because her grave was only a few miles away in the Cork Jewish burial-ground outside the city he felt near to her spiritually. It was her physical presence he missed. It would surely be different thousands of miles away in Palestine. He had

197

thought that at the end of his life he would be lying beside her. She would be waiting for him. But now that would not happen. Would she understand? Would her spirit forgive him? He would have to visit the graveyard before his departure. It was something he knew he had to do. He would say goodbye to his beloved.

Rev. Levitt was also concerned about the departure of so many of his flock to Palestine. It would mean less money for him in extra earnings but, on the other hand, with Rabbi Cohen gone, too, the community would be making a great saving in wages and so they should be able to give him a rise. He would talk to the President about it.

Max Klein, however, had a different view of Rabbi Moishe's departure. The Torah taught that the departure of any righteous man from a community diminished those who were left. If that was so in the case of just a righteous man, then how much more seriously would the Cork Jewish community be diminished by the loss of its Rabbi? Gone would be their status, their spiritual centre, their very rock. It was the President's duty to do something about it. He would raise the matter at the next Committee meeting. He would get agreement that they should contact the Beth Din in London and put out a call for a new Rabbi. The new Rabbi might not be another Rabbi Moishe – who could be? – but a good man, a holy man, a *galernta mensh* he would be, and the community would have a spiritual leader again.

Neither Zvi Lipsky nor Miriam Levy was thinking about Palestine. Zvi had still not got over his visit to Arnold Wine and the shock of what Wine had told him. His mind was still too frozen, too paralysed, even to approach the possibility of losing his livelihood. Had Wine just been trying to frighten him into the partnership he wanted? Zvi drummed his fingers on the arms of his chair and watched Myra knit. He was troubled ... he felt troubled ... he knew he must look troubled – yet she saw nothing. Her hands, moving automatically, rhythmically, hooked his

198

eyes and held them until his head began to nod and gradually sink to his chest in sleep.

Miriam Levy sat in her bedroom, gazing at her reflection in the dressing-table mirror, imagining herself in her wedding-dress. Only seventeen more days to go – sixteen if she didn't count 5 December, the wedding-day itself. She took up the oil-lamp and held it closer to the mirror to examine a spot on her chin. Even if it did come up, it would surely be gone in seventeen days. The dress would be ready for a final fit in a week, Mrs Burns had promised faithfully. That would leave plenty of time for any alterations she might need. If she went to bed now and could fall asleep quickly, she'd wake up that much nearer the day.

Only as she was dropping off did she at last remember that a week after the wedding she and Reuben, her husband, would be leaving for Palestine. But the prospect of the wedding was too momentous to allow the departure any room at all in her thoughts at this stage. Except for one small worry that had not occurred to her before – what if she got a lot of bulky presents, how would she take them with her? Oh, it wasn't likely. The community knew she'd not want to be too burdened. And, anyway, that would be Reuben's problem. She stretched out in her bed and soon sleep came, its misty arms engulfing her with images of her bridegroom – of the two of them under the marriage-canopy – together – husband and wife – husband and wife – and later, later, children. . . .

Percy Lovitch was not at home – not yet anyway. When he closed his shop at six o'clock, the rain had been so heavy that he decided to wait a while. He retreated to his little office at the back, made himself some tea, took out a tin of biscuits he always had at hand, and brooded. The Carl Rosa would be giving *Tales of Hoffmann* tonight. He wouldn't go. Even if the night had been warm and fine, he wouldn't have gone. Never again. Why should he, any-way? He didn't need to. He wound up his demonstration phonograph and put on the records of the opera. Percy had never sung in it – the main role was for a baritone – but the music never failed to take him out of himself. It had everything. 'The Mozart of the Champs-Elysées' Rossini had called Offenbach. *Tales of Hoffmann* was his greatest triumph, but the poor man hadn't even lived to see its first performance. What an irony! Typical of life! And as the music drew to a close Percy remembered something else about Offenbach: he had been a Jew. Was that another piece of irony? Never mind. The knowledge stirred Percy Lovitch with pride and banished his gloom. He pushed shut the office door, stood up, closed his eyes, and with full voice sang all the baritone's arias. They sounded even better in the tenor register. 'Tch, tch, Offenbach,' he murmured with a smile. He'd have expected more *chachma*, more box-office awareness from a Jew. After all, who wanted to hear a baritone when a tenor was around?

13

Friday, 20 November 1920

Darling Elizabeth,
Your letter was brought to me this morning. I
don't know what to say. The whole thing is
quite crazy. Here I am, a prisoner in a shed
somewhere in Ireland, kidnapped by the IRA,
and there you are in England, and we're able
to write to each other. It doesn't make sense,
but here's hoping it goes on like this for as long
as I'm here.

You can't possibly know what a difference
it's made to me hearing from you and knowing
that you are keeping well and keeping your
chin up. I didn't really believe that my letter
would reach you, I certainly didn't believe
that, if it did, I'd get a reply from you. I thought
they must be playing some cruel joke on me.
But they were telling the truth after all. And,
as far as I can see, your letter wasn't opened by
them. It was brought to me first thing this
morning by Joe. He's the young fellow with
Boxer who kidnapped me. Boxer seems to be
the boss, at least he's the one who does the

talking and brings me the food every day. And the local paper. Hotel service, you might say, though the quarters could be better. Joe is only a youngster – nineteen or twenty, I'd say. Boxer doesn't let him talk when they're together, and he didn't say much this morning. Only that Boxer sent him with the letter so as I could have a reply ready to give them tonight, when they bring my supper. I don't understand them. I don't understand what's going on. They won't tell me why I'm being held prisoner, but I suppose they don't know, only following orders. And they're straightforward simple blokes really. Though I suppose they can be cruel b-----s when they want. Some of the atrocities they've done – but you don't need to worry about that, my love. It's not the Army they're after, it's the Tans. And I don't blame them. The Tans aren't human. All the men in the 16th are ashamed of the reputation they are giving us. You should have heard what the Old Man, Colonel Windsor, thinks of them. I don't suppose the British public has much idea what's going on. But they should know now, after Asquith's speech at the National Liberal Club yesterday. It's reported in the *Cork Examiner*, the local paper that Joe brought me this morning. So I suppose it must be in the British papers, too. I hope it is. Someone – Boxer, I suppose – put a big red circle around it to make sure I'd see it probably. I don't suppose you read it. Asquith said that things were being done in Ireland by the Government that would take fitting place in the blackest annals of the lowest despotism of the European world. Those were his words. He said that what was happening was opposed to the fundamental principles of Christianity. He should know. I don't know where it will all end. I've been here nearly five days now with nothing to do and nothing to read but the newspaper every day, so I've had a lot of time to think. I think a lot about us of course and the wonderful life we will have together (plus the little stranger) when I finish soldiering. I have decided that as soon as I get out of here I'm going to get out of the Army, too. Buy myself out some way or other. When? Immediately this caper is over. I'm sure it will be soon, my love. I know the RIC is out in force looking for me. Boxer told me that. He had promised to move me to more comfortable quarters the day after I got here but he said they had to drop that plan because there was too much police activity in the area. So I'm keeping my fingers crossed.

The worst thing is the boredom. I sleep most of the time, doze really. I read every word in the newspaper – cattle reports, auctions, advertisements, sport. I pass the time trying to pick the winners of the horse-race meetings. I go by names just. But when I get the results next day I seldom have a winner. Just as well. I might get a taste for it otherwise, and that wouldn't do. I was never a gambler. The Irish are great horsey men, I'm told. I read an amusing thing in the paper this morning. A woman in Paris broke the world record with a high jump of four feet eight inches. Doesn't sound very high to me, but I think the women probably wear bulky bloomers even while doing the high jump. You could probably do more than four feet eight inches yourself, but better not try it in your present state!

Well, I've been rambling on, but there isn't much of importance to tell you, and just to be able to write to you and know you'll get the letter is – well, I can't tell you how wonderful it is.

Write to me immediately you get this letter, my darling, and remember the instructions

203

about the address. Take good care of yourself and keep your chin up.

I'll close now with all my love and kisses.

RODDY

Captain Simcox read over his letter and wondered if he should have mentioned anything about atrocities. No point in alarming Elizabeth. But she wasn't a milk-and-water girl. She was tough, and a realist. She'd have no illusions about the danger he was in even if his letter was nothing but jokes. Better to be frank with her – well, fairly frank anyway. Anything else would only make her suspicious, make her think he knew something that he wasn't telling her. But he knew nothing – nothing more than he said. The most likely thing was that the IRA were holding him as a hostage for some of their own men who had been captured by the RIC. But in that case why not take an RIC man hostage rather than an army captain? Roddy had no answer to that – and there was no point in brooding over it all the time. His life was in danger – yes, but worrying about it wouldn't help. He didn't really believe that the RIC would find him – though he'd keep hoping. They hadn't been able to find Lucas when he was kidnapped a few months ago – and they'd had troops searching as well. And even an aeroplane! But, then, Lucas was a brigadier. Fat chance they'd send an aeroplane for only a captain. No, escape was the only way out, impossible though it seemed. The door was always locked and bolted from the outside, the walls of his prison were too thick, and that grille high up in the wall was hardly wide enough for his head to go through, never mind his body – even if he could reach it.

He folded the letter, sealed in it an envelope, and lay down on his bunk to reread Elizabeth's letter. At least he was no longer cold – Boxer had brought him enough blankets, and a new bottle of whiskey always accompanied his breakfast. Crazy. The whole business was quite crazy.

14

THERE WAS NOBODY in the assembled congregation at the Shabbos-morning service who didn't already know the date Rabbi Moishe would be leaving for Palestine, yet when he faced them and announced that his group would be departing on 12 December people turned to each other with raised eyebrows, confirmatory nods, grunts of satisfaction – as if all the earlier information might have been only rumour but now was clearly official and true. It was, at last, beginning to happen. Those who were already intended members of the party were the recipients of encouraging smiles, good wishes, blessings, even some handclasps, so that embarrassment momentarily shrouded the mixture of elation and apprehension that was their common reaction. Except for Abie Klugman. Sitting in his usual seat at the back of the synagogue, he felt only bliss and gratitude. His eyes were closed tight to keep in his tears, and his two arms were wrapped across his chest to contain the surge of ecstasy that pushed like a tide through his body.

Rabbi Moishe leaned on his pulpit, the Ark enfolding the Scrolls of the Law behind him, and contemplated his congregation.

'My friends,' he said, his eyes twinkling, 'you have only another three weeks to bear with me and with my sermons. Normally I would not be giving a sermon today, but as I had to make the announcement I have just made and would be on my feet anyway....'

He smiled through his beard and nodded happily at the chuckles with which the congregation responded to his note of levity.

'Today's *Sedra*,' he continued, his voice now serious, 'the Portion of the Law we have just read, tells us about Jacob going forth from Beer-Sheba to Haran and of the dream he had when he rested on the way. In that dream the Lord spoke to him, saying! "I am the Lord, God of Abraham thy father, and the God of Isaac. The land whereon thou liest, to thee will I give it, and to thy seed. And thy seed shall be as the dust of the earth, and thou shalt spread abroad to the west, and to the east, and to the north, and to the south. And in thee and in thy seed shall all the families of the earth be blessed. And, behold, I am with thee, and will keep thee whithersoever thou goest, and will bring thee back into this land; for I will not leave thee, until I have done that which I have spoken to thee of."'

Rabbi Moishe paused, ran his tongue over his lips, and repeated, leaning his voice on the words: ' "... I am with thee, and will keep thee whithersoever thou goest, and will bring thee back into this land...." That was the Lord's promise made to Jacob, and through Jacob to all his seed – to you, to me, to our parents, grandparents and ancestors. Two promises, my friends, a double promise: to keep us, and to bring us back to the Holy Land. The first promise the Lord has kept. Despite all our trials and persecutions, the Children of Israel have survived. We are here safe and well in body and spirit, in a land where we are free to move about, practise our religion, earn a living. Very soon some of us will no longer be here, in Ireland, but on a journey, in boats, trains, a journey to the Land of Israel. Those of us on that journey will be doubly blessed, for not only are we already part of the fulfilment of the Lord's first promise to Jacob, but we will also be part of the fulfilment of His second promise. The Lord will be bringing us back to the land whereon Jacob laid down his head and dreamed his wondrous dream. To those of you who will not be with us physically on that journey I say: you are not left behind, for we take you with us in our hearts, and your seed, too, will in its turn be brought back to the Land of Israel. As the Lord promised, as the Torah records, so it will be.'

Rabbi Moishe hitched up the shoulders of his *Talith*, the voluminous praying shawl that was wrapped around his body, its fringes almost sweeping the ground. The congregation, recognising the familiar signal, rose for his blessing, many of them turning to each other in surprise at what seemed to be a sudden ending to his sermon.

'May the Lord bless you and keep you; may the Lord cause His countenance to shine upon you and preserve you; may the Lord lift up His face unto you and grant you peace – ay, everlasting peace. Amen.'

The answering amens broke from every mouth, and as the Rabbi descended from the raised platform of the Ark and walked slowly down the aisle each man bowed when he passed. Rabbi Moishe, however, stared fixedly in front of him, refraining from his customary inclination of the head to each side in acknowledgement of their bows. It was an omission that none could fail to notice, but his light blue eyes, blinking and tearful, were an eloquent explanation of the brevity of his sermon as they begged forgiveness for his inability to trust himself, at that moment, to look upon the faces of his people.

15

SUNDAY MORNING found Ada Neumann's shop busier than usual. The extra custom was provided by those who had come to purchase the special box of Chanukah candles for the approaching Feast of Lights, the only secular celebration in the Jewish calendar and one of the few that were joyous. The occasion seemed already to cast a pre-festival glow over the main topic of conversation – the departure to Palestine – for the sense of sadness and regret at the impending loss of Rabbi Moishe and his party was replaced by expressions of wonder and rightness at the coincidence of the two events. The journey to Palestine would be commencing on the last day of Chanukah: it was agreed that this was a sign almost biblical in its implication, for just as Chanukah commemorated the rededication of the Jewish Temple after three years of desecration, wasn't Rabbi Moishe and his followers' mission that of rededicating the Land of Israel after two thousand years of exile?

It was Benny Katz who had drawn the parallel, and Max Klein, having collected his candles, his bag of *bagels* and other titbits, paused on his way out to joke: 'Spoken like a true Rabbi, Benny. A pity you're going off with them – we'll be looking for a new *Ruv*.'

The men stood at the door to watch the President drive

away and then whistled and cheered in good-humoured greeting as Mrs Burns appeared, basin hat wedged firmly on her head and the fur collar of her coat drawn tight under her chin.

'He did it again.'

There was pride in her voice, mixed with the satisfaction of having news that would make her the centre of attraction as she hurried into the shop. The customers jollied her to the counter, glad to have a fresh source of diversion – she was a gossip, certainly, but a pleasant and harmless one, and her enjoyment of their banter was of a piece with the unbuttoned feeling of relaxation they displayed in making the best of the one day in the week they didn't have to go to work or to synagogue.

'He did it again,' Mrs Burns repeated. 'Isn't he terrible altogether, God bless him!'

'Who did it again?' asked Mickey Aronson, fussing behind the counter. He never lost an opportunity of helping Ada Neumann when the shop was very busy – the touch of authority that the position gave him and the chance to rag every customer put him on his mettle.

'The priest, of course. Father McGiff,' Mrs Burns replied indignantly, as if it must have been clear to everyone except Mickey Aronson whom she was talking about.

Mickey, unable to resist a coarse innuendo but anxious to avoid general condemnation for indulging in loose talk in front of Ada, leaned over the counter and whispered to Percy Lovitch: 'I thought priests weren't supposed to do it at all.' Then turning to Mrs Burns he enquired, with a wink to the customers: 'And what was it the holy man did that made you so excited?'

'He preached another sermon about the Tans and the IRA. Only worse than last week. Much worse.'

'How do you mean worse?' Sam Spiro asked.

'He was angry, Mr Spiro. He was that angry. Lord above, I never heard such strong words from the pulpit.'

'But what did he say? Why was he angry?' someone enquired.

'Sure haven't you been reading the paper at all?' Mrs

209

Burns asked in a tone that clearly condemned such ignorance. 'It's wild them Tans are going. Like beasts in the jungle. Didn't they burn down Granard last week, Father McGiff's own village! And it's attacking the clergy they are now. That poor priest up in Meath – the one that was missing for three days – his body was found.' Mrs Burns paused. 'In a bog,' she announced, her voice pitched high in outrage. Then she paused again, looking around to hold her listeners before revealing in a whisper: 'And a bullet-hole in his head.' The fur collar at her mouth quailed before her horrified breath. 'A bullet-hole in his head!' she repeated, eyes popping with incredulity and horror.

'*De urimah nishuma*,' Ada Neumann declared, lifting her hands in sympathy, 'the poor soul.'

'Oh, he was that angry, missis,' Mrs Burns continued. 'Father McGiff said it wasn't a matter of patriotism any more. He said we had a pack of wild dogs in the land and it was the duty of every able-bodied man to stand up and be counted. "Stand up and be counted." Them were his very words.'

'And did you stand up, Mrs Burns?' Mickey Aronson joked, but Mrs Burns ignored him.

'What's going to happen to us at all? Where will it all end?' She pulled her fur more tightly about her body and shivered theatrically.

'Don't upset yourself, my dear woman,' Percy Lovitch urged her, but there was a hint of reprimand beneath the sympathy in his voice. It was as if he recognised a fellow-performer but would have preferred such unpleasant tidings to be conveyed with more restraint.

'It's all right for you. Sure couldn't you go off to Palestine with the Rabbi if you want,' Mrs Burns complained. 'But we have to stay here.'

'Percy in Palestine,' laughed Reuben Jackson. 'What would he do there?'

'Don't joke,' Percy admonished. The suggestion that he was on the shelf was as salt in his wounds. 'Funnier things have happened. I'm not an old fogey yet.'

'You're not serious, Mr Lovitch?' Reuben asked, trying

to make amends. 'You're not thinking of coming with us?'

'No, I couldn't leave that quickly. But I might join you later. You never know. It's not impossible.'

'At least you won't find any Tans there,' Mrs Burns said. 'Not like here. We could be murdered in our beds any night and no one would do anything to stop them.'

'Too true, Mrs Burns, too true,' Mickey Aronson interposed, mischief twinkling in his eyes. 'You wouldn't know from one moment to another when you wouldn't be hurled into maternity.'

'Shush, shush,' Ada Neumann stilled the men's guffaws as she turned to comfort Mrs Burns. 'It's not that bad, my dear.'

'I don't know about that,' Benny Katz suggested. 'I was on a train last week when some Black and Tans came in at Kilmallock and dragged off a young lad. He was screaming and shouting, but they just carted him away. And they weren't gentle about it.'

'There you are now,' Mrs Burns crowed, 'didn't I tell you? Ah, Ruby, you're a lucky fellow to be off to Palestine, you and Miriam. You're a wise boy.'

'It's not Palestine he's thinking of now,' put in Mickey Aronson, reluctant to yield the limelight. 'He has much more important duties before that.'

'Go 'way with you,' Mrs Burns winked. 'Don't be embarrassing the boy.' And then, turning to Reuben, her voice descending almost to a confidential whisper, she told him: 'Just wait till you see Miriam in her wedding-dress. She's having the last fit this week. She'll be a vision, Ruby, a vision. Simply gorgeous. Oh, you're the lucky boy altogether.'

'Where's the honeymoon going to be?' Percy Lovitch asked. 'Or maybe you're making the journey to Palestine your honeymoon.'

'No, we'll have a few days in Dublin first.'

'A few days only,' Mrs Burns protested. 'That's not much of a honeymoon.'

'It's all we have time for,' Reuben explained. 'With the wedding only a week before we're due to leave for Palestine, we can't be away long.'

211

'So why don't you spend the whole week in Dublin,' Benny Katz suggested, 'and wait for the rest of us there? We'll be going through Dublin on our way to Palestine.'

'Yes, we thought of that,' Reuben replied, 'but we decided we'd prefer to be with everyone when we leave Cork finally. We don't want to miss any part of the excitement.'

'Ah sure God love them,' Mrs Burns commended. 'Isn't it great to be young!'

'And in love,' Percy added lugubriously. 'Don't forget that – and in love.'

'Watch out for him,' Mickey Aronson advised. 'A bachelor of his age – you can't be too careful.'

'At least he's got some flesh on him anyway. He's not a scrawny thrawneen like you.'

The laughter that greeted the sally momentarily silenced Mickey Aronson. Percy Lovitch bowed to Mrs Burns in mock gratitude, doffed his hat to the company and turned from the shop.

'You know,' remarked Ada, 'I didn't think Mr Lovitch was himself today. He looked upset. I hope he's not ill.'

Percy Lovitch wasn't ill, but he *was* upset. It took a great effort of will on his part to turn in the direction of his home. All his inclinations, all his memories, the whole tapestry of his life made him yearn to be at Glanmire Station where the members of the Carl Rosa Opera Company would be arriving in a few minutes to board the train for their departure. But Percy Lovitch wouldn't be there. Not this time. And not ever again – in greeting or in farewell.

'I'm the one who's early this time,' Denis said, coming forward from the entrance to the University as Judith stepped off the tram.

'Oh, I'm glad. I mean I'm glad I wasn't late myself.'

Judith felt an unexpected embarrassment as she faced Denis. She immediately noted that instead of the raincoat he had on when she had met him before he now wore a belted brown overcoat and a scarf, and he had left his peaked cap at home. Perhaps the outfit was his Sunday 'best' and he would have been wearing it anyway, but she thought there was an air about him that suggested the effort had been made for her. He might almost have been her 'date', not merely a very slight acquaintance who was meeting her more for business rather than for personal reasons. It was as if she was seeing him properly for the first time – which, it struck her, she was, because she couldn't count the time he came, all wet and bundled up, to her father's store, or the time she had called on him in Twohey's when she was too upset even to notice his looks, or their meeting at the Statue on Thursday night when it had been wet yet again and very dark. But now, in November's clear afternoon light, she did notice his looks. They were such a contrast to those of the Jewish young men she knew – ruddier, trimmer, less worldly.

'Have you any news for me?' she asked eagerly. 'Did you get the girl's name and address?'

'No, Miss Cohen, not yet. But I have a little news – just a little. I managed to see the man I was waiting for and he'll try to find out what you want to know.'

'Oh,' Judith exclaimed in obvious disappointment.

'I'm sorry I couldn't do any more than that,' Denis said.

'Of course. I know. I'm putting you to a lot of trouble and you really are very kind, Mr Hurley. But do you think this man will be able—?'

'Well, his mother is in Cumann na mBan. She's an officer of one of the Cork sections, so we couldn't have a better contact.'

'That's something at any rate.'

Judith hesitated. Their business virtually concluded for the present, there seemed to be nothing more to say, but she was completely unprepared for the feeling of anticlimax that overtook her. She knew it would look churlish, at the least ungrateful, to arrange another meeting just like that, say 'Thank you,' turn her back on him and go off home.

'When . . . ?' she asked doubtfully.

'Better give him a few days,' Denis replied; and then,

213

when neither of them seemed to know what to say next, he filled the silence with 'What is your brother studying in college?'

'Jacob? Oh, he's doing medicine.'

'Oh, yes, you told me that. He must be very clever.'

No, not really,' Judith said. 'At least, I think he's clever enough but I don't think he's all that keen on being a doctor. Not yet anyway. He's more interested in poetry – he writes a lot of it. And local history – I suppose that's what you'd call it. I mean Cork – he's very fond of the city and knows a lot about it.'

'We have something in common so. I'm a city boy born and bred myself and I wouldn't want to live anywhere else in the whole country. What about yourself, Miss Cohen, are you fond of Cork, too?'

'I never thought about it,' Judith replied, glad to keep the conversation going. 'I've never been out of Cork and I've never really seen much of the city except for around the part where I live – and town of course. This district, for instance, the Western Road – would you believe I've never been here before!'

Denis took a step back in mock amazement.

'You've never been here before! Sure this is one of the nicest parts of Cork. The Park and the Lee Fields. Don't you ever go out walking, in the summertime like?'

'Yes, often. But we always go along the Marina or out Blackrock.'

'Well, now's your chance to see another part of Cork. Come out a bit of the road with me. I could show you the Lee Fields. There's nothing special about them – just fields and countryside – but at least you could say you've seen them. It's not very far. We'd reach there in no time.'

Judith hesitated – not because of any inclination to reject his invitation but because the start of pleasure that shot through her took her completely by surprise. Denis, thinking she was about to refuse him, pressed her.

'It's a grand day for a walk and what would you need to be going back early on a Sunday afternoon for? We could be out there and back before it's dark. Will you come, Miss Cohen?'

The unfamiliarity of the surroundings and their distance from the Jewish area removed from Judith any fear of being seen out strolling with a *goy*. What harm could there be in taking a short walk with him?

'All right, then. On one condition – that you stop calling me Miss Cohen. It makes me feel awkward. My name is Judith. Will you call me Judith?'

Denis smiled, and it seemed to her it was the first natural smile she had seen on his face.

'That's a bargain, then. My name is Denis.' He put out his hand and, as if they were strangers who hadn't known each other before, Judith took it in hers and shook it. As their eyes met they broke into laughter at the recognition of their own awkwardness.

For a few hundred yards on its northern side the Western Road boasted large solid-looking houses, their Victorian façades and front gardens – well kept even at the height of winter – contrasting in Judith's mind with the pinched pokiness of Celtic Crescent. These were the sort of abode that as yet few in the Jewish community aspired to. It was not only, she reflected, the money cost that would be beyond them. What about the spiritual cost of separating themselves from the close-knit streets and familial web that were both their sustenance and their protection? All their lives they had been imprisoned in their ghettos, but how bad a prison was it when you could be yourself? Was the Western Road freedom?

'I think I'd like to live in one of those houses,' she said suddenly.

Denis was surprised. She was surprised herself.

'Where do you live now?' he asked.

'In Celtic Crescent.'

'I know the place. Jewtown.'

Judith felt hurt by the designation but she knew it was not meant insultingly. It was what Celtic Crescent was called by most people in Cork.

'Yes, Jewtown. It's where nearly all the Jews live. Most of us came from the same district in Russia and when we – I mean the older people – first arrived in Cork, naturally they stuck together.'

215

'Russia,' Denis mused.

'Well, a little country called Lithuania in fact, but Russia ruled it.'

'And that's where your father comes from. He's a fine man. A brave man.'

The word had slipped out before Denis could stop himself. He looked sharply at Judith.

'A brave man?' she repeated. 'Why do you say that? I never thought of my father as particularly brave.'

Denis remained silent. Judith sensed his discomfort, and it suddenly revived her own curiosity about their acquaintanceship.

'I was wondering how you met him,' she said. 'My father is seldom anywhere apart from the store and our home.'

'Oh, we just sort of bumped into each other,' Denis mumbled.

'I must say, you're very vague about it,' Judith laughed. 'But I can't blame you. I suppose you feel embarrassed about the money he lent you.'

'The money he lent me?'

The uncertainty in Denis's voice was too obvious for Judith to miss.

'Yes. He told me you came to the store last Monday to pay him back.'

'Is that what he said?'

Denis, apprehensive at the trend of the conversation, involuntarily quickened his pace.

'You're walking too fast for me,' Judith protested.

'Oh, I'm very sorry, Miss Cohen,' Denis apologised, stopping to turn towards her. 'I mean Judith.' His expression was distant, harassed, and Judith knew the change had something to do with her father.

'Look, Denis, I can see you're hiding something. What is it?'

When he didn't reply, Judith said: 'You may as well tell me now because I won't stop asking you till you do. And, what's more, I won't go any further with you.'

Denis turned to face her but found himself unable to meet the look in her eyes.

'It's nothing you need know. Honest.'

216

'But I want to know. Please.' Judith put a hand on his arm. The deliberate note of feminine appeal in her voice was a wile she had never used before but, even so, she was immediately aware of the sense of power it gave her. 'Please tell me.'

Denis continued to stare fixedly ahead. 'You won't thank me for it if I do. You'll be very angry. And it won't give you a very good opinion of me.'

They had reached the last of the houses, and now both sides of the road were flanked by uncultivated fields marked off by rough stone walls.

'Are these the Lee Fields?' Judith asked.

'No, not yet. This place is Jail Cross. That's the Cork jail over there.'

Judith saw, across the road and back from the railway line that ran along it, a squat forbidding-looking building, its stone portico supported by four naked columns like sentinels guarding the iron-studded door and the grilled windows. Some policemen were standing around, appearing at ease but keeping a sharp watch on the approach to the prison.

'Ugly, isn't it?' Judith said as she walked on, Denis following almost reluctantly behind her. 'Come on, I'm not letting you off. Tell me about yourself and my father.'

'I first met him last Friday week,' Denis eventually said, but when this admission was followed by a silence Judith nudged him and insisted: 'Where?'

'In your store.'

'Ah, I don't go in on Fridays. I usually do the weekend shopping then. What brought you there?'

She had to shake his arm again to make him continue.

'Go on. Answer me.'

He drew a deep breath. 'When I went to your store last Friday week, there was someone else with me from the IRA. I had a gun and my orders were to kidnap your father.'

Judith laughed and then became stern.

'Look, Denis, I want the truth. Stop your joking and tell me.'

217

'That *is* the truth.' And in a rush he poured out the story of the kidnap and of Iron Josh's defiance.

Judith listened in silence, her astonishment increasing with each revelation. It was all so totally unbelievable, yet it had to be true, as Denis had said. Why should he make it up? And then she thought of his return visit on Monday – that hadn't been explained.

'But what was that money you gave him when you called last Monday? What was that all about?'

'I had to go over again – because of the money. I couldn't keep it. You see, it was his money I was giving back to him. When we were returning to the city in the cart, he made me leave him off before we got there in case we'd be stopped by the police or the Tans. He said he'd walk the rest of the way and he asked me to take what money he had. He wasn't supposed to carry money on the Jews' Sabbath – but you'd know that – and he said he wouldn't get home before the Sabbath started.'

'I remember,' Judith nodded. 'He was late home that day and he missed synagogue. He never missed synagogue on Friday night before, but he didn't tell us what delayed him. It worried my mother.'

'Now that you know, are you angry with me? You should be.'

Judith shook her head. It was difficult to take in such a story – it was still quite incredible. But the fact that it was over and done with, and that nothing had happened – nothing bad anyway – stunned the sense of shock she should have felt.

'I don't know whether I'm angry or amused,' she said. 'Angry, I suppose, in a way. You might have killed my father.'

'No, Judith, honest, I couldn't have. He knew that. That's why he defied me. But it took a lot of courage. I couldn't get over him. So calm he was. He even gave me some of his lunch – Jewish-bread sandwiches.'

Judith burst out laughing. 'I can just imagine the two of you munching your sandwiches. If my mother knew who was eating her bread, she'd have had a fit. What a sight it must have been!'

218

'It doesn't seem funny to me. I'll never forget it. I'll always be ashamed of what I did.'

'But you had to. You were ordered to, weren't you?'

'Yes, that's what your father said. He said it was lucky it wasn't someone else instead of me, someone who wouldn't have thought twice about shooting him.'

Judith fell silent, and Denis was relieved that she had taken his story so calmly. They had come to the end of Western Road and before them lay a vista of open fields as far as the eye could see. Southwards flowed the River Lee, and beyond that the hilly wooded land had been planted with some strange, almost Gothic buildings.

'Well, there's the Lee Fields for you,' Denis said.

'I can see what you meant when you said they were just fields. But what are these circusy buildings over there with the tall chimney?'

'Circusy is right,' Denis laughed. 'That's all the different-coloured stone that's been used – there's a lot of it in Cork. The building is the waterworks. I know it well. I used to go swimming there when I was a lad.'

'In the river?'

'Yes. It's not the same as the sea of course – no waves, no salt, not as buoyant – but I enjoyed it.'

'And what's that huge monstrosity at the top of the hill behind it?'

Judith's 'monstrosity' was a long, seemingly unending building of grey stone, scored by countless windows that were contrasted with the succession of turrets, minarets and gables that surmounted them.

'That', said Denis, straight-faced, 'is the madhouse.'

'Goodness,' Judith exclaimed. 'I never realised there were so many lunatics around.'

'Its official name is the Eglinton Asylum. Ask your brother about it – he probably knows how it got that name.'

'Do you know? Tell me.'

'Well, it was the Lord Lieutenant, Lord Eglinton, who insisted on having it built against the wishes of the local authorities, so when it was finished and they came to name it they called it after him.'

'Serves him right.'

'Do you want to turn back now?' Denis asked.

'Yes, I suppose I might as well – now that I've seen the Lee Fields.'

'I'm sorry if you're disappointed. But they're very popular with Cork people.'

'Yes, they must be. They do give you a feeling of freedom – away from city buildings. And of course there's the swimming. But I suppose that's mainly in the summer – and only for men and boys.'

'Oh, the Lee Fields are popular with girls, too – in the summer. It's a favourite spot for courting couples.'

Judith threw him a sharp look.

'Have you ever been out here with a girl?' she asked half-jocularly. Denis blushed, and Judith laughed at his embarrassment.

'Well, have you?' she insisted.

As the colour rose in his cheeks, he looked full at her. 'Today's my first time,' he replied.

It was Judith's turn to blush.

'We'd better get back,' she said. Everything about Denis suddenly seemed to disconcert her. He had kidnapped her father, threatened to shoot him, and now here she was out walking with him – a *goy* – and – was she even flirting? She knew she could have if she wanted to, if she could allow herself to.

'All right, then. And you're not angry with me over your father?' Denis said.

'I'll let you know,' Judith teased. 'Next time we meet. Of course I can't be, can I, if I want you to help me?'

'Oh, I'd help you anyway,' Denis insisted loudly. 'I promised.'

Judith was surprised at how seriously he had taken her. In a spontaneous gesture of reassurance she put an arm through his. 'I know, Denis. I was only having you on. You're easily stirred up, aren't you?'

'Depends,' Denis replied laconically as they began the walk back.

'I do hope your friend can find out the name of Jacob's girl. Though even if he does I may be unable to do anything about it. And it means so much to my father.'

'Don't cross your bridges till you come to them,' Denis advised.

That was all very well, Judith thought, but how could she stop worrying? And, even though her father appeared to have been unaffected by the kidnapping, that might only be an act he was putting on so as not to upset anyone before her *zeide* went to Palestine. He was being brave. Yes, as Denis said, he must be a brave man. Only a really brave man could go through such a frightening ordeal and bottle it up in himself as if nothing had happened. No wonder he had broken down over the letter about Jacob. He must be at his wits' end. She'd have to help him – she'd have to, somehow.

'Well, when might you have word for me?' she asked.

'Let's say Tuesday,' Denis suggested as they reached a tram-stop. 'And keep your fingers crossed that it won't be raining.'

'Where will we meet? Not at the Statue – it's too busy there.'

Denis hesitated.

'Hurry up,' Judith urged him. 'My tram is coming.'

'Look,' Denis said in a rush. 'Meet me outside the Pavilion Cinema at eight. We can go up to the restaurant and have tea or something. Will you do that? Please?'

The screech of the tram wheels almost drowned the appeal in his voice, but it was not lost on Judith.

'I'd love that, Denis. No one has ever invited me to a restaurant before. Thank you very much.'

As the tram drew to a halt Denis handed her up onto the step. Neither of them said goodbye. It was suddenly as if there was something they both found disagreeable about the word, something that didn't any longer suit their relationship. Judith waved once and then turned and disappeared into the tram. When she had gone out of his sight, Denis raised a hand almost in a restraining gesture, but the tram's twinkling lights sped on into the now fast-falling darkness.

* * *

The darkness would not be long delayed, but there was still enough light for Jacob and Deirdre to be confident of reaching the city before having to use their bicycle lamps. The end of another Sunday round distributing the IRA newspaper with Deirdre always filled Jacob with a sense of elation. It was not due to any feeling of relief that with all the papers delivered there was now no fear of being stopped by the RIC and arrested – that was something he had never been able to believe would happen to them. Partly it was the exhilaration of speeding along the open road, skin tingling, warmth coursing through his limbs and the prospect of a long evening almost just around the corner. On this occasion, however, it was mostly the knowledge that with Deirdre's assignment once more successfully completed she would not be under any pressure. She would be free of obligations. Free of constraints, and therefore free to give him her full attention. Her responses would depend on him alone, on his initiative, for he could hardly expect her to make the running. And today he would convince her of the serious-ness of his love; in his pocket was the poem he had been writing for her, finished at last. Once they reached Blackpool, there was a bench by the riverside which as Deirdre said, 'had their name on it'. There they would stop – as they had always stopped before – and rest and court. Above it was a gas-lamp that bathed it in soft light, sufficient for Jacob to read his poem. Not that he'd need any light – he knew the poem by heart – but Deirdre would if she preferred to read it herself. His excite-ment at the thrill of what was ahead made him sing aloud.

'Good job there's no one around,' Deirdre jibed. 'Your screech would deafen the crows.'

They were approaching Dan Mulcahy's cottage. It had been the first house on their list on the way out and now was the last milestone before reaching home. Mulcahy was an old bachelor who lived almost exclusively in the kitchen at the back of his cottage, so they were surprised to see a glow flickering in both the front and side windows. As they drew level, the front door suddenly

222

opened and in the clear splash of light a policeman emerged, holding a paper in his hand. He looked up quickly as Deirdre and Jacob sped past.

'My God,' Deirdre exclaimed, 'that's Armstrong and he's got a copy of *An tÓglach*. It must be the one we just brought to Dan. Oh my God!'

'Who's Armstrong?' Jacob asked.

'RIC. He's been in our district. He searched our house once but found nothing. We'd better hurry – he's probably following us now.'

'Nonsense,' Jacob said. 'He'd never have recognised you in the dark.' He turned his head to see whether Armstrong was in pursuit and was just in time to catch sight of him running to his bicycle which lay against the side of the cottage, and mounting it hastily.

'Did you see anything?' Deirdre asked anxiously. 'Is he coming?'

'He's behind us all right. But isn't it better for us not to try to give him the slip? You have no more papers left, so you have nothing to worry about.'

'No, we'd better hurry,' Deirdre gasped. 'I'm certain that was *An tÓglach* he had and I think he had a clear look at me. I know he suspects me. Come on, we have a good start on him. We can beat him home.'

'OK,' Jacob grunted, not wishing to put Deirdre in bad humour by arguing.

They both pedalled at their fastest, their legs working like pistons, backs arched forward and fists clenched tightly on the handlebars. Trees and hedges swam up on either side and then became dark blurs that were roughly whipped past the corners of their eyes. There was no traffic to hinder them, but frequent stones and potholes, invisible in the darkness, were spine-jolting hazards. Jacob, urging his body up and down with each leg-stroke, was reminded of the ritual swaying that accompanied Hebrew prayers, when he suddenly realised that Deirdre was no longer beside him. He looked back to see her bicycle careering wildly from side to side and a grimace of frozen terror on her face. He braked madly, swung his own bicycle around in the same action, and as he sped

223

back Deirdre's machine crashed into a bank, hurling her off with sickening force.

'Are you all right, Deirdre? Are you hurt?' he called, running to help her.

'My chain came off. Oh Jesus, Armstrong will catch me. What'll we do?'

Her voice was breathless and frightened, but Jacob was relieved to see that she had gathered her wits together quickly and didn't appear to be badly hurt.

'No, he won't. Can you climb the bank? We can hide in the field behind it. Hurry. I'll help you.'

'What about the bikes?' she said, as Jacob half-pushed, half-lifted her over the top. Then, manhandling the bicycles, he swung them one after the other onto the bank, jumped up himself and pulled them down into the ditch after him. He was just in time to duck his head out of sight when he heard the creak of Armstrong's machine and the swish of its wheels as it raced past.

'He's gone,' he said.

'Thanks be,' Deirdre groaned.

'Are you hurt?'

'My hands and knees are skinned, and I'll be all bruises tomorrow,' Deirdre complained. 'And my coat's ruined.'

'If that's all, then you'll have little to worry about – as long as I can fix this chain,' Jacob said.

'What a time for it to happen! I thought Armstrong had us. I hope Dan Mulcahy told him nothing. But you never know. He's an old man, and Armstrong could probably talk rings around him.'

Jacob grunted as he worked at the chain. The darkness made it difficult to fit it back, and his hands were soon slippery with grease.

'Now,' he said after a moment, 'I think I'm getting it. Yes, it's back on. And it should stay there as long as we don't have to go on another mad dash like the one we just did.'

'Thanks, Jake, you're great,' Deirdre said. She had recovered her composure, and as she got to her feet she gave Jacob a peck on the cheek.

He swung the bicycles back onto the top of the bank and put an arm round Deirdre to help her over it.

'Oh, that hurts now,' she groaned as she got a grip on the grassy top and pulled herself up.

'Can you ride?' he asked anxiously. 'I could take your bike back to Dan's and give you a crossbar home.'

'No, I'll cycle,' Deirdre replied. 'My shoulder is beginning to pain, but I want to get back.'

'OK, then, but take it easy,' Jacob warned as they resumed their journey. The chase and accident had killed all his feeling of anticipation but, anyway, he reflected ruefully, it had also put paid to his little plan. There'd be no stop in Blackpool now; Deirdre certainly wouldn't be in any mood for poetry and she'd need to get home quickly and rest after her fall. He felt desperately disappointed, but it couldn't be helped. Patience – there'd be another opportunity when everything would be just right. He wasn't going to have his great moment spoiled. For tonight he'd have to be satisfied with that peck on the cheek.

Rabbi Moishe greeted the priest warmly and eyed the bulky parcel under his arm.

'It's too big to hide from you,' Father McGiff joked, noting his curiosity. 'I thought I'd better bring it tonight. I've heard the news that you're off today three weeks, and in case you'd be too busy for the next few Sunday nights and I wouldn't get a chance. . . . Well, here, take it. It's for you.'

The priest gave an embarrassed shrug as he pushed the parcel into the Rabbi's hands.

'What is it?' Rabbi Moishe asked.

'Open it and see. It's not much. Just a little going-away gift.'

Rabbi Moishe sat back in his chair while the priest stood over him watching the long white fingers methodically open the knots in the string and then unwrap the brown paper. Inside was a rug, and the Rabbi had to stand up again to shake it out to its full size.

225

'It's just a travelling-rug,' Father McGiff explained. 'You may not have much use for it in the Holy Land – I imagine the weather is fairly warm there. But there may be some cold nights – and, anyway, it'll come in handy on the journey. It's a long trip, and you'd want something thick and heavy around your shoulders, wouldn't you?'

The priest took one corner of the rug while Rabbi Moishe held another so that the specially woven pattern became properly visible. Set in the centre of a soft-green woollen field was a white Star of David and in the centre of that had been stitched a small three-masted ship, riding on a sea of wavy blue lines between two castle turrets.

'They're the Cork arms, the symbol of the city,' said Father McGiff.

'I know,' the Rabbi answered. 'My grandson, Jacob, told me about it some years ago. I remember there was some Latin sentence, too.'

'That's right, but I didn't bother with that. If I'd have known the Hebrew for it, I'd have put it in,' the priest joked. 'Anyway, the castle is enough. It'll remind you of Cork. I preferred it to a harp or a shamrock. They'd do for any Irishman but, damn it, it's a Corkman you are.'

Rabbi Moishe was shaking his head in wonderment at the splendour of the present.

'To do so much for me ...,' he mumbled, '... specially made ... and the Jewish colours, too, the white star and the blue sea. You know they are the Jewish colours?'

'Oh, yes, I looked it up. Wouldn't I be a great *amadán* if I got that wrong?'

The Rabbi was still slowly shaking his head from side to side, and then he suddenly stopped, paused, and began now to nod back and forth rhythmically as he intoned a Hebrew blessing. When he finished, he embraced the priest, hugging him briefly to his chest.

'That was the special blessing we say on getting something new. And now, Father, I have a present for you, too. I'm sorry it isn't wrapped up as yours was, because I was expecting to see you again before I leave, but it is here, waiting for you.'

226

Rabbi Moishe went to the mantelpiece, at each end of which stood a silver *menorah*. He took one and handed it to the priest.

'You know what that is?'

'An eight-branched candlestick,' Father McGiff said.

'Yes. It is called a *menorah* and it is used only for the Festival of Chanukah, the Feast of Lights. That will be in two weeks' time. It lasts eight days, so it will be ending just when I'm leaving for Palestine.'

'Handsome. Elegant. It's a beautiful piece, Rabbi, but it's too much for me, really,' Father McGiff protested, and as Rabbi Moishe demurred he held the *menorah* out in front of him the better to admire it.

'What is its significance? Tell me about the Feast of Lights – a lovely name.'

'We celebrate it', Rabbi Moishe explained, 'in remembrance of the rededication of the Holy Temple. It had been taken and defiled by the Greeks, but after three years' war Judah the Maccabee recaptured it. There is a legend that when he re-entered the Temple he found sufficient holy oil for only one night, but the Lord worked a miracle so that it lasted eight nights until fresh oil could be got. So now we light candles for eight days, one on the first evening and adding one each evening.'

'But I see there are nine holders on this *menorah*,' Father McGiff said. 'I always thought it was known as an eight-branched candelabrum.'

'Yes, the ninth holder is for the *shammas*, the servant. That's the one we light first each night and it is used to light all the others. They are allowed to burn out, but the servant is not – not until the last night.'

'The "servant" you call that one.'

'Yes. It shows that one can give light to others without losing any of one's own brightness.'

'Like us, Rabbi, I hope,' Father McGiff laughed.

'Like us, my friend,' Rabbi Moishe repeated as the two men sat in their usual chairs.

'You don't sound convinced about that – or am I wrong, Rabbi?'

'No, I'm not convinced,' Rabbi Moishe replied, worrying his fingers through his beard. 'The nearer I get to leaving here, the more I wonder.'

'Do you mean about what the future holds for you?'

The Rabbi smiled. 'Not for me. I have little time left. No, I'm thinking of a more distant future. If this new Zionism – this return to Palestine – grows, what will it mean for the Jews who are left, the Jews in all the other countries all over the world who decide not to go back to Palestine?'

'But surely it will be a good thing for them, Rabbi. If their fellow-Jews are back in the Holy Land, in a land of their own, think of the comfort it will be to them.'

'Comfort – or refuge?' Rabbi Moishe pondered.

'What do you mean? What are you getting at?'

'If Palestine ever does become a National Home for the Jews – which is the object of the Zionist movement—'

'And what the Balfour Declaration aims at, too,' Father McGiff interjected.

'Yes, but will that put an end to persecution? It might make it worse. It might make other rulers more ready to attack their own Jews, make scapegoats of them if they feel the need. They could say: "Get out. You have a country of your own now. You're not wanted here."'

'That's a very pessimistic view, Rabbi. Not like you at all. Where's your faith in human nature, man alive?'

Rabbi Moishe smiled at the priest and stretched out a hand to touch his companion's knee.

'You reprimand me, Father. And quite right, too. If I lose my faith in human nature, where, then, is my belief in God?'

'That's more like it. Sure everyone needs a home – peoples as well as persons. The Jews have been orphans long enough. It's time for them to fight back. Like that Judah Maccabee you told me about. He fought the Greeks, you say, and got back your Temple. Take it from me, Rabbi, a home of your own is worth fighting for. That's something I should have realised long ago.'

'That's what your people, the Irish, are doing, yes?'

'Yes. And more power to them.'

'You also, Father. I believe you preached – ah, a strong sermon again this morning.'

228

'As strong as I could,' Father McGiff declared defiantly. 'And I'll continue to until Ireland is ruled by the Irish.'

'You're a brave man, my friend, a brave man.'

'Yerra, what is it?' the priest replied in a dismissive tone. 'Only words. They're cheap. What about the lads putting their lives at stake? That's denied to me.'

'Nevertheless,' Rabbi Moishe said, 'you *are* a brave man. The only way a holy man can be brave is with words.'

'Sometimes with deeds, too, Rabbi. Oh, I don't mean taking up arms, I mean something like giving active example to your people. As you're doing by going to Palestine.'

Rabbi Moishe took up the pack of cards from the mantelshelf.

'Enough of this discussion,' he said, extracting the pack from the box. 'We must not let these last evenings together be burdened with worries about the future. Let us play our usual game, Father, My turn, I think, to deal first. You dealt first last Sunday night, yes?'

'Right as usual, Rabbi. Your memory is as sharp as ever. But I notice you haven't mentioned that *I* won last Sunday's round. You didn't forget that now, did you?'

'Ah, my good friend,' Rabbi Cohen laughed as he dealt, 'it's the future that's important, not the past.'

16

THE NEWS in Monday morning's *Cork Examiner* shocked the whole city.

'APPALLING WEEKEND,' the headlines proclaimed. 'MANY DUBLIN OFFICERS KILLED – DREADFUL SEQUEL – FOOTBALL CROWD FIRED ON – SEVERAL DEAD – DUBLIN ISOLATED – EXTENDED CURFEW.'

Grimly men read the report as they went to work, many unable even to move from their newsagent's doorway until they had taken in the full details. On the trams passengers ignored the discomfort and difficulty of trying to hold their papers steady in the swaying vehicle while any who hadn't an *Examiner* of his own leaned over his neighbour's shoulder to read the story.

> Dreadful events happened in Dublin yesterday.
>
> Shortly after nine o'clock in the morning, the official report says, simultaneous attacks were made on military officers and ex-officers in their lodgings in various parts of Dublin. Fourteen appear to have been killed and six injured. In one case, auxiliary police captured three persons. Two auxiliaries, despatched for reinforcements, were killed on the way. The dead included two court-martial officers.

During the day a shocking sequel happened at a Gaelic football match in Dublin. A crowd of 15,000 people was fired on. A wild panic followed. About ten are dead and numbers wounded.

The effect of these events on the atmosphere in Cork was immediately noticeable. The south of Ireland had long been the most difficult part of the country for the Government to hold down. A pedestrian might find himself stopped and searched by soldiers or police as much as half a dozen times a day; a knock on the door at night followed by the command to open up could mean a visit from the Black and Tans, a military search party, an IRA man on the run or a gang of robbers; a private motorist might have his car commandeered by the military on Monday, the RIC on Tuesday, the Black and Tans on Wednesday, the IRA on Thursday, or armed robbers on Friday. The daily shootings, burnings, ambushes, kidnappings, strikes, curfews, and in more recent months the activities of the IRA's Flying Columns had made many areas of the province of Munster almost ungovernable, and the policy of fighting fire with fire through the virtual free hand given the Black and Tans had so far led only to a worsening of the situation. As yet, however, that policy was still in favour, and in the streets of Cork that Monday morning it was being implemented with little restraint. Houses were raided, police stopped vehicles at random, subjecting them to meticulous searches and their drivers and passengers to detailed questioning. Vagueness of reply, or any hesitation at all, frequently meant being hauled off to the nearest barracks. Many roads were patrolled by Crossley tenders with a full complement of soldiers, arms at the ready, and on the pavements the hated Black and Tans swaggered threateningly, young and old who did not immediately give way to them being roughly pushed aside.

At the end of early Mass in the church, Father McGiff moved among the worshippers, comforting the frightened, encouraging the faint-hearted, admonishing all to

231

stand firm, to keep their pride and dignity, to remember that they were Irish and descended from heroes.

In his isolated prison Roddy Simcox read the news and wondered whether it made his situation more hopeless than it already seemed. Boxer had brought him the day's supplies – breakfast, fruit, a bottle of whiskey, and a letter from Elizabeth – earlier than usual, and had triumphantly thrown down the *Cork Examiner* onto the table.

'Read that, Captain,' he said, 'read that. You're on the run, me lad. That right, Joe?'

Behind him Joe stood at the door. He didn't answer, but Boxer, taking his agreement for granted, had turned back to Roddy.

'The Tans are all over the place this morning. All excited they are. Suits us. Get them out in the open – they're no match for our boys there.'

Roddy skimmed through the newspaper report. He looked up at Boxer.

'How long are you going to keep me here? What are you holding me for?' He asked the questions coolly, allowing no trace of apprehension to show in his voice, as if asking what the weather was like outside.

'We'll see, Captain, we'll see. I'm waiting for orders. Whatever it is, I hope it's soon. I don't want to miss all the action.'

When he and Joe had gone, Roddy read Elizabeth's letter but didn't start replying to it immediately. He was disturbed by the Dublin killings and for the first time deeply apprehensive about his chances of survival. Massacres in this sort of struggle always led to a spate of reprisal killings, and at such a time a prisoner could expect scant consideration from his captors. He couldn't tell Elizabeth that, of course – he wouldn't dare even hint it to her – but on the other hand he wasn't feeling at all up to adopting his usual light-hearted unconcerned tone. Later, perhaps tonight, but not just now. He poured himself some whiskey from the new bottle and set about getting through another long, boring, uncomfortable day.

'Ah well,' he consoled himself aloud – he had found that listening to his own voice was better than smothering in a

232

blanket of silence – 'I won't be complaining if I get through it without a bullet in the back of my head. Here's to myself, then.' He took a mouthful of whiskey, held it a moment before swallowing and then raised the glass again. 'And here's to tonight.' And, throwing his head back, he drained what was left.

In contrast to the native inhabitants of the city, the *Cork Examiner* report made little impact on the Jewish community. Most of them had left on their weekly trip to the country before any copy of the newspaper reached Celtic Crescent, and the first to hear the news were some of those who, planning to journey by rail, arrived at the station and found their train cancelled as a result of a protest strike by the drivers and guards. That the strike was a spontaneous gesture rather than the usual fomented stoppage arising from the deliberate boarding of the train by soldiers made no difference. The result was as usual – hurried efforts to arrange other means of transport or revise plans to take advantage of whatever lines might still be running. Those with their own conveyance of horse and trap did not learn of the Dublin carnage until they reached their first customers in the countryside – by then the news had spread everywhere and was the only topic of conversation. Business, they found, was difficult to conduct. They were asked what they thought, whether they knew any more than the paper reported – travellers might be expected to pick up fresh information on the road – what was the reaction in the places they had passed through, were there a lot of soldiers and police where they had been? They answered as best they could – which meant that they had nothing to tell and so, in the interests of getting their business done, collecting their weekly payments, moving on to the next village, they were careful to agree in general terms with whatever opinion was expressed.

The exception was Abie Klugman. Nothing was ever discussed with Abie, his views were never canvassed – he was recognised as removed by God's hand from involvement in everyday social or political commerce. Besides, this week Abie had news of his own for his many

233

customers. This week he would take no money from them, he would pay their dues out of his own pocket – that would be his going-away present in return for their business and their kindness throughout the years. The idea of some sort of present had been forming in his mind for some time, and now that the date of departure for Palestine had been made definite, he had worked out what the present was to be. He could not buy a gift for each customer – he did not know what they might like or what might suit them, and he might make the mistake of seeming to favour some over others – but to forego each one's weekly instalment, that was fair to all and he knew it would be welcomed by everyone. And then he thought that instead of waiting until the last week before departure he would do it this week, and give himself a present of a holiday from work for the final few weeks of his life in Cork. He had never had a holiday before. He did not know what he would do with the time; he had nothing in mind beyond resting from his labours and trying to imagine himself in *Eretz Yisroel*, the Land of Israel.

Preparing to set out on that Monday morning he performed each part of his ritual more slowly than usual. Just as a man about to be released from long captivity takes stock of those small, hitherto unconscious actions which, threading moment to moment, had sustained his seemingly endless days, so Abie Klugman gave thanks after his own fashion. Filling his cases and packs with his stock-in-trade he examined each article, fondling the jewellery, feeling the softness of the sheets and blankets, even admiring the colours of the holy pictures. As he placed his old rifle under his seat he rubbed a hand along its stock in acknowledgement of its ever-readiness to protect him from the evil ones, the pursuers who would still, even at this almost final hour, be searching for him, to drag him back under their sway. Soon he would have no need of it; it would be part of his past. And as he harnessed the horse and slipped the bridle over its head he rested his own head for a moment against its neck. The animal rolled its eyes and shook itself. It might have been aware of what was in Abie's mind.

To Jacob Cohen the weekend's events in Dublin meant only that his Monday-morning lectures took place in an atmosphere of heady distracting excitement. He had heard the news from his fellow-students immediately he arrived at the college and, though he could not feel any personal involvement in its implications, he looked forward to hearing Deirdre's reactions. But when his lectures were over and he went to meet her he found that she had not attended college that morning. He wasn't really surprised. After the bruises she had collected on the previous evening, no doubt she needed a day's rest in bed.

17

It was the next day before Captain Simcox wrote to his wife. He had spent all Monday trying to ignore the feeling of despair that seemed to take root in him as the day wore on, but he knew it was unrealistic to deny the increased threat to his life that the Dublin massacre would bring in its train. Yet, if the threat was now greater, what was the point of continuing just to sit on his bum and do nothing about it? What was the point of telling himself that there was nothing he *could* do? Maybe there wasn't, but now his policy of refusing to dwell on the thought of being free and accepting without question that escape would be impossible seemed stupid. If he wasn't going to be found by the RIC, and if he wasn't going to be released by his captors, then his eventual fate was obvious. And damned if he was going to go like a lamb to the slaughter.

The long day had passed with him either at his table, glass in hand, one blanket over his shoulders and the other around his legs, or lying on his bed with both blankets piled on top of him, as he tried desperately to think of some plan. Idea after idea was examined, each one more impractical than the one before, and as each idea was in turn dismissed the level of the whiskey in the bottle dropped lower and lower. In the end everything came down to the same couple of hard implacable facts:

there were two of them and only one of him; *he* was unarmed, *they* had a gun. He was certain there was no way of forcibly breaking out of his prison and it would be sheer lunacy for him to try singlehanded to tackle Boxer and Joe together. As a last resort, yes, but it would really have to be the very last resort; if it was certain that he was to go down, then it would be better, and easier, to go down fighting.

The long bout of fruitless concentration left him completely exhausted by night-time and in no mood or condition to write to Elizabeth. He decided to get up early the next morning, write to her immediately while his mind was fresh, and have the letter ready to give to Boxer or Joe when they brought his breakfast.

His head was quite clear when he awoke on Tuesday, and he lay on for a while savouring the realisation that he had after all lived through another day and night without getting a bullet in the back of his skull. That much was something to be grateful for, but his relief was instantly forgotten when he saw the empty whiskey bottle. He cursed himself for not leaving the usual tot in it – he had grown accustomed to relying on a sweetener to set him up for breakfast – but then he remembered his unwritten letter and was quickly on his feet and at the table.

Preparing to write, he rubbed thoughtfully at his chin. The action awakened all his physical discomfort, which had been increasing daily until now it was almost a constant irritant. He wished he had a mirror to see what he looked like with well over a week's beard. Presumably it would be red, like his hair; but it wasn't long enough yet for him to see it, no matter how hard he gazed down his nose. In another few days maybe. . . . He pulled himself up at the thought, suddenly recalling his new determination to concentrate on being free rather than just accepting his situation.

He yawned and scratched himself mightily. God, these clothes must be crawling by now. Once or twice he had almost asked Boxer if there was a chance of some clean underwear, but a mixture of reluctance to let Boxer see that his condition was getting him down, fastidiousness at the idea of wearing someone else's discards, and a grave doubt that IRA hospitality would extend to the purchase of new winter woollies for a captured British officer had held him back. The thing was to try to forget corporeal discomforts and indignities, to stop scratching, to keep busy. Keep busy – not exactly much to occupy him, Roddy reflected, but for the moment there was, at least, the letter to Elizabeth.

What could he say? She'd probably have read about the Dublin events, but his best bet was to make little of it or even not to refer to it at all. After all, it had happened almost two hundred miles away; if he ignored it, it might not occur to her that it could possibly affect his fate. OK, then, the recipe was chat, optimism (just a touch of), health enquiries of course, and buckets of light-heartedness about anything and everything that would just make her feel almost as if he was writing from the officers' mess rather than from an IRA hideout.

He pulled out of his greatcoat pocket a handful of pieces of paper he had torn from past *Cork Examiners* – items of an unusual, even bizarre, nature that he thought he might be able to use to lengthen his letters and that might at the same time be entertaining. God knows he hadn't any news of his own to tell. Most of the items were already crossed through – these, the best of the bunch, he had used before and he could hardly use them again. There wasn't much left. He remembered he hadn't marked anything on the previous day's paper – the report from Dublin had distracted him. He opened it now and ran his eyes down the columns. Auctions – they'd be no use; Corporation meetings – no – except that the Cork Corporation wanted the street-lamps lit throughout curfew hours over Christmas, but the authorities had refused. Might use it; a reminder of local conditions might not be the best topic to pitch on but, after all, Elizabeth knew there was a curfew in Cork. He read on. Nothing much in the sports columns. Kid Lewis had knocked out Johnny Basham in the nineteenth round for the welter-weight championship of Great Britain – she'd hardly be interested in that. Cricket? The MCC team in Australia

238

had suffered their first defeat. Some girls followed cricket. Did Elizabeth? Roddy didn't know; he'd never asked her. Damn it, he just hadn't had anything like enough time with her to find out much about her interests.

His glance roved on to scan the entertainments section. The Leeside Players were doing *The Lovers Arms* in the Opera House. *The Lovers Arms.* He had no idea what the play was about, but the title sent a shiver of nostalgia through his body. He took up his pen and wrote:

My dearest, darling Elizabeth. . . .

After lectures on Tuesday morning Jacob wheeled his bicycle over to the Arts building to meet Deirdre. He searched among the students emerging, but she wasn't with them. Jacob was disappointed and worried. He had brought his poem along to give her, and now it looked as if he was going to be frustrated again. That damned poem, would she ever see it? And her absence for a second day made him fear she had been more seriously hurt than he had thought.

One of her classmates approached him.

'You're Cohen, aren't you?'

'Yes,' Jacob replied.

'You looking for Deirdre Buckley?' came the almost hesitant enquiry.

'Yes. Did she miss the lecture?'

'Don't you know? She's been picked up.'

'Picked up?' Jacob repeated, wondering what he meant.

'Yes. Arrested.'

Jacob was speechless for a moment.

'Are you kidding?' he asked, though he could tell from the student's tone that it wasn't a joke.

'No. Honest. The police arrested her. Jack Murphy lives near her. He told us. Ask him if you like.'

'When?' Jacob's heart was suddenly pounding.

'Last night, I believe. I thought you'd know. You're doing a line with her, aren't you?'

'Where have they taken her?' Jacob enquired. It was no surprise that her classmates knew he was her boyfriend.

'Don't know. The Bridewell, I suppose.'

Almost dazed with fear and shock, Jacob jumped on his bicycle and raced off, pedalling madly up Western Road towards the Grand Parade. Armstrong must have recognised her on Sunday – she was certain he had and she must have been right after all. But why had they arrested her? On suspicion? Or had old Dan Mulcahy given her away? He might have; he was an old man, tough all right, but if the RIC had beaten him up, perhaps. . . .

The Bridewell police station was a squat dun-coloured building within a stone's throw of the Coal Quay market. Busy though it always was, the constant slamming of doors, the rough voices and loud laughter of the policemen, the clatter of their heavy boots on the wooden floors could never – during daytime anyway – drown the raucous cacophony of the black-shawled women of the market shouting their wares. Neither group took any notice of the other, and at least the women's voices were a link with the world of freedom for the suspects being held in the cells for questioning or charging.

Jacob rested his bicycle against the barracks wall and hurried in. He found himself in a long hall and entered the first open door he saw. The room was bustling with activity, the air thick with cigarette smoke, the hum of conversation frequently punctuated by calls and instructions that seemed to echo through the building. In one wall a huge fire burned but, despite the heat, only a few policemen had opened even the top button of their tunic collars.

Jacob approached the counter and looked for some attention.

'Yes?' a young policeman said peremptorily, his face glistening with perspiration and the gun in his holster slapping against his hip.

'I'd like to see someone who was arrested yesterday. I was told you're holding her here.' He spoke with as little show of nervousness as possible.

'Name?'

'My name is—'

'Name of the suspect,' the policeman interrupted sharply.

'Oh – Deirdre Buckley.'

'Are you related to the suspect?'

'No. My name is Cohen. Jacob Cohen,' he volunteered, and when the blank face in front of him remained passive he added, 'I'm a friend of hers – a fellow-student. In college.'

The policeman eyed him for a moment, repeated 'Jacob Cohen,' and then went to consult an older-looking colleague sitting behind a small table at the back of the room. The two whispered together, and Jacob heard the unmistakable scything sound of 'Jew' before the older policeman lowered his spectacles to the end of his nose and peered over them at Jacob. After a few more words his interrogator turned and said, in what seemed to Jacob a more kindly tone: 'Just a moment, son. Take a seat there while you're waiting.'

The policeman disappeared, and Jacob sat down on a bench along the wall, staring vacantly at the various notices and posters pinned up, oblivious of their messages, his eye held only by the large picture of King George V gazing back at him unsmilingly like a stern sea-captain warning with his withering glance a recalcitrant member of his crew.

It was some minutes before the policeman returned, and Jacob sprang to the counter to meet him.

'You say you're a friend of the girl,' the policeman stated.

'Yes. I told you. I'm in college with her.'

'Well, she says she doesn't know you and doesn't want to see you.' The policeman slapped shut a ledger with a loud bang. 'Sorry, son,' he added.

'But of course she knows me,' Jacob insisted, certain there had been some mistake. 'Miss Buckley – Deirdre Buckley. Are you sure you asked the right girl? And my name is Jacob Cohen.'

'I know your name, Mr Cohen,' the policeman patiently replied. 'And I did ask the right girl. But she was quite

241

certain she didn't know you. Now, if you'll take my advice, young man, you'll not press the matter. Maybe she does know you, maybe she doesn't, but I can do no more.'

'But I'm her boyfriend,' Jacob protested in a half-strangled voice that he barely managed to force out of his throat. Had Deirdre gone mad? Or was it some insane conspiracy to keep them apart? His mind was so stunned that he couldn't think straight.

'Best get home, son,' the policeman whispered sympathetically.

Jacob thought of giving him the envelope with the poem to pass on to Deirdre, but how could he be sure it would reach her?

'But – but . . . ,' he spluttered, and as the policeman went to attend to another caller he rushed out of the building and jumped onto his bicycle.

What was happening? What was she up to? Why, why, why? Almost blind to the pedestrians and the traffic, he cycled wildly through the city, tears springing to his eyes.

The Pavilion Cinema and Restaurant was positioned almost halfway along Patrick Street, its very wide entrance hall with billboards and 'stills' from the film on show making it look like a vulgar-mouthed interloper in the line of staid shop-fronts on either side.

In the restaurant upstairs diners were so few that Denis and Judith were able to choose their table. In the winter, lunches and evening meals were normally the main business; afternoon tea had a steady clientele, but as yet the young men of the city had not adopted the practice of taking evening tea or coffee with their girlfriends, while the imposition of a curfew had discouraged late diners. For Denis and Judith this first visit to a restaurant was inhibiting and they both felt glad they were able to find a corner table that was protected – indeed, partly concealed – by a tall potted plant. Denis had removed his cap on entering, but they hesitated to take their coats off, each waiting for the other to give a lead, and the prompt appearance of a waiter was of more immediate concern.

'Tea?' Denis queried, the ruddiness of his cheeks spreading with embarrassment down to his neck.

Judith nodded. Denis's discomfiture seemed to affect her, for she bent to place her handbag on the floor by her side, keeping her head down as if looking for something in the bag until she felt she had safely discouraged her rising blushes.

Conversation, anyway, would not be a problem, not initially in any event, and immediately the waiter disappeared she said: 'Did you find out the girl's name?'

'Yes,' Denis replied. 'I did. At least, my friend did – yesterday. Her name is Deirdre Buckley.'

'Where does she live?'

'Casimir Street. Number 2. It's on the north side. You probably wouldn't know it. You don't know that part of the city, do you?'

'No, but I'll find it.'

'Look, Judith,' Denis suggested, 'wouldn't it be better to let me handle this?'

'Oh, no, you've done enough already. It's not your responsibility.'

'But...,' Denis commenced, and then they both fell silent while the waiter brought their order.

'It's not a matter of responsibility,' Denis resumed immediately they were alone again. 'It's just that there may be no need for you to trouble yourself.'

'What do you mean?' Judith asked as she poured the tea.

'Well, it might be best if something was said to her on an official basis like. I mean, her own organisation wouldn't be pleased if they knew she was taking a non-member out with her on an official assignment. Not that your brother would tell the police of course. But her people wouldn't know that. So if one of our boys had a word with them and they spoke to her....'

'But how long would all that take?' Judith asked.

'Oh, not long at all. The boys are always very sharp when it comes to security.'

'I don't know,' Judith said doubtfully.

243

'Look, don't decide now. You can be thinking about it and make your mind up before the night is out.'

Judith said nothing. She was gazing at the plate of cakes the waiter had brought.

Denis pushed them towards her. 'Have one,' he said.

'No, I don't think so.'

'Ah, watching your figure, like all the young ladies.'

Judith smiled, but it was not her figure that concerned her. She was thinking that the cakes might have been made with margarine and so would not be kosher. She had never eaten anything but kosher food, and to break a lifelong rule just for a cake struck her as almost wicked. And yet....

Impulsively she took one and bit into it.

'That was a quick change of mind,' Denis said. 'They're nice cakes.' And then, looking around: 'Not very busy, is it?'

'No. And it's evidently too early for the orchestra.' She gestured towards the platform along the wall behind Denis, where chairs and music-stands waited emptily behind a closed grand piano. She wished there were music – it would have lightened the gloomy atmosphere and helped fill the awkward silence threatening to engulf them.

'That was terrible in Dublin last Sunday,' she said, to make conversation.

'Yes,' Denis replied.

Judith sensed his reluctance. 'Perhaps you'd rather not talk about it. About the IRA, I mean.'

Denis shrugged. 'There's nothing much to talk about. I'm not exactly an important member.'

'But you must be if they sent you to kidnap my father. That sounds important enough to me.'

Denis hesitated before saying: 'If you must know, the truth is that I was given that assignment as a test.'

'How do you mean?'

'Well, my commanding officer at the time didn't trust me. He wanted to test my loyalty.' Denis paused, crushing some crumbs into his plate and dropping his voice, so that Judith had to lean forward to hear him. 'You see, my father was in the RIC. He volunteered for army service during the war and was killed in France. But that's not an ideal pedigree for a member of the IRA, so to see if I could prove myself I was given the job of kidnapping your father and getting money out of him or shooting him if he didn't pay up. I was told that Headquarters in Dublin had ordered it, but that was a lie. In fact it was all the local commanding officer's idea.'

'But if the order didn't come from Dublin, then they must have been glad you didn't kill my father,' Judith said.

Denis shook his head. 'It's not as simple as that. Oh, they were glad of course, but the point is that I didn't know at the time that Dublin hadn't ordered it, so I failed the test – I didn't get any money and I didn't shoot your father. So, you see, I hadn't proved my loyalty. And signs on, I've been ignored since then.'

'Well, do you mind – really mind? You're safer out of it.'

'That's easy for you to say,' Denis declared, 'but I don't want to be out of it. If I had wanted to be out of it, I wouldn't have joined the IRA. I'm an Irishman and I'm ready to help free my country. You don't get freedom without taking risks. Even if it means losing your life.'

'I can't make out how grown men can talk so easily about losing their lives. Does it mean so little to you? And it isn't as if you have a chance of winning. Why risk your life when you haven't? It's such a waste.'

'That's what your father thinks, too,' Denis told her.

'Did he say that?'

'He did.'

'And what was your answer?' Judith asked.

'I asked him if he thought Palestine was worth fighting for.'

Judith laughed.

'Palestine! What a hope!'

'Well, there's one thing certain. The Irish won't get Ireland and the Jews won't get Palestine without a fight. You must see that.'

Judith stared across the table at Denis. Into her mind flashed an image of him lying in some dark street, his eyes

245

closed, his face white, and a pool of blood at his head. She shuddered and looked away through the windows down onto the still busy Patrick Street, the shimmering gas-lamps, the bright shop-fronts, the jarveys outside the Victoria Hotel, and also the many policemen, some standing in doorways scrutinising the passers-by, some walking briskly, their authority and menace setting awry the whole scene. She shuddered again.

'Are you cold?' Denis asked.

'No, it's warm in here.' Judith paused and then added: 'I was just thinking of you out there with a gun, perhaps shot. If you must know.'

Denis laughed.

'It's not something *I* think about.'

'I wish you would,' she answered, hearing herself say words that seemed to come unbidden to her lips.

'Why? Would you be sorry if I was shot?' he asked, light-hearted still.

'I'm sorry to see anyone shot,' Judith replied, but she knew that was not what she was thinking.

All the way home, as Denis walked at her side, she felt confused and worried. She could no longer pretend to herself that she had no interest in Denis Hurley beyond her need of his help to find Jacob's girl. The walk to the Lee Fields with him on Sunday had left an aftertaste of sweetness that was more than just the excitement of physical attraction. What had been special – although this had not occurred to her until afterwards – was the unique experience of spending time with a young unmarried man and not having to feel that she was under inspection as a possible wife. Previous encounters with strange Jewish males had always been arranged by her mother, and Judith had never been a very co-operative participant. The question of marriage didn't arise when she was in the company of the boys she had grown up with in Celtic Crescent – there weren't all that many of them and, anyway, marriage between members of the community tended to be the natural and expected outcome of lengthy teenage pairings, like Reuben and Miriam – but visits by young eligible Jews from England to relations in

246

Cork, for a holiday, were recognised by everyone as a time-honoured step in the marriage-making process. Indeed, wasn't that how her own sister, Molly, had found a husband? Judith recalled. Molly had been ready for marriage of course. She had wanted a husband because a husband would mean her own home and children, and Molly feared the thought of never achieving such blessings, of being left a lonely spinster. There had been no love involved – not at the start anyway – and love was not a word Molly had ever used in her letters to Judith when writing of married life. But acceptance, yes; contentment, yes; perhaps love was growing, would grow. And now that Molly was starting a family she had what she wanted. But that wasn't what Judith wanted. It never had been. So her feeling of being attracted to Denis could be indulged with safety. Offering no marital prospect, it held no danger. Even if Denis felt attracted to her – and some instinct told her he did – there was really no need to run away from such involvement. The religious gap between them – the very factor which should have made her keep her distance – was, to Judith's way of thinking, her safeguard. Why, then, deny herself? Why deny him?

Nearing Celtic Crescent she linked arms with him for a few steps and then casually stopped in the dark shadow of a large factory doorway.

'You'd better not come any further,' she said.

'Why not?'

'Well, you know – if anyone from the Crescent saw us together like this, it might cause talk.'

'You mean because I'm not a Jew?'

'Yes,' Judith admitted.

'Would that worry you?' Denis asked.

'It doesn't worry *me* that you're not my religion. If it did, I wouldn't be standing here like this with you. But I don't want it to get me into trouble or arguments at home. After all, look how upset my father got when he heard Jacob was going with a Catholic girl.'

'Yes, but *we're* not going together, are we?' Denis pointed out.

'No, but if we were seen together people might think

247

we were. And I do have to see you again, don't I?'

'Does that mean that you've decided to let me look after Miss Buckley for you?'

'I suppose it would be better if you did,' Judith conceded. 'But how long would it take? My poor father must be out of his mind waiting for news.'

'Not more than a few days at the most. And I could always get any news to you if you don't want to see me again.'

Judith hesitated. In the quarter-light she could see a smile at the corner of Denis's mouth. Her heart leaped at the realisation that he was looking for something – a hint as to her feelings? Encouragement for his own? She did not balk her reply.

'But I do want to see you again, news or no news.'

'Sure?' he asked her quietly.

'Yes. That's if you want to see *me*.'

Denis did not answer, but in the darkness his hands briefly found her arms to draw her closer.

'Tomorrow night?' she said.

'Where? What time?'

'How about half-seven? Outside the GPO. That should be safe enough. We could go for a walk if it's not raining. Does that suit you?'

'Yes,' he said, and with a swift movement he touched her lips with his.

She held him for a moment. Then 'I'd better get home,' she whispered before running off towards Celtic Crescent. Already her thoughts, outpacing her hurrying steps, raced towards the next evening. She felt she was beginning an adventure, each phase of which promised not only excitement of a sort she had never experienced before but also a warmth of anticipation that would help to smother the doubts and pricks of conscience she knew would trouble her. She would make it a brief fling. She would allow herself that much. After all, she was no giddy adolescent; she was old enough to be able to control it as well as herself. And why not? How was she to know if she'd ever have another chance of tasting some of the joys of—? She stifled the word before it could form in her mind.

She wasn't going to be silly and imagine this was the beginning of a grand passion. She didn't want a grand passion – certainly not with a *goy*; that would be madness. But the sensation of Denis's arms around her, of his lips on hers, still tingled, arousing urges too clamorous to suppress. As she turned the corner into Celtic Crescent and saw house after cramped house within which she and all the other Jews had for years led lives of unchanging toil and narrow pleasures, the prospect of a romance with Denis Hurley – yes, that was it, just a romance, sweet, swift and, surely, harmless – was irresistible.

Her elation was short-lived. No sooner was she in the door of her home than Jacob, clearly distraught, emerged from the kitchen and drew her into the front room.

'What's the matter?' she asked.

'Judy,' he appealed, appearing close to tears, 'it's Deirdre. She's been arrested.'

'My God! When?'

'This morning, I think, or last night. I'm not sure.'

'How do you know? Are you certain?'

'Yes, yes. A classmate told me. She's in the Bridewell. I went to see her—'

His voice choked, and he slid into a chair. Judith put an arm around his shoulder.

'She'll be all right, don't worry. She's only a young girl. They won't harm her. Keep calm now and tell me how it happened.' She sat down beside him and held his hand. Never since he had been a child had she had to comfort him for any reason. She had a pang of guilt at the thought that there must have been times since then when he had needed comfort but she had never been interested enough to notice or find out.

'What happened?' she repeated.

'On Sunday – we were out together – she was distributing the paper – you know – and we were seen by an RIC man who knows her.'

'You were both seen?'

'Yes, but it was nearly dark and he wouldn't have known me. I'm not worried about being arrested, if that's what you're thinking.'

'No, of course not. You're worried about Deirdre, aren't you?'

A tide of sympathy and fellow-feeling encompassed Judith as she took her brother into her arms and hugged him. She remembered the stab of anguish that had cut through her at the vision of Denis lying shot in a dark street. How much worse would she feel if the vision became reality? Now her brother's girl was in prison – her life might not be in danger, but being arrested and held by the RIC could not be pleasant. She could see that it had really shaken Jacob, and her heart went out to him. His infatuation, or love, or whatever it was, might be an awkward fact for her and their father, but for him fact was feeling and that was what mattered now.

'She'll be all right,' Judith tried to reassure him. 'I'm sure she'll be released quickly. They'll hardly prosecute a young girl for distributing an illegal paper. She'll be all right, you'll see.'

Jacob shook his head.

'Yes, but it's not that. I went to the Bridewell to see her – as soon as I heard about it. She wouldn't see me. She told the policeman she didn't know me.'

'Well, of course she did. She didn't want you involved – to be arrested, too. Surely you can see that. I think she was being very noble.'

Jacob lifted his head, his eyes still misting.

'I thought of that. But – but I'm not. . . . Judy, will you go to see her – for me? Find out why she won't see me. Please.'

Judith's initial reaction was to try to talk Jacob out of such a suggestion, and it was only his acute distress that made her hesitate. And then she saw the irony of the situation, how what she had sought all along – the opportunity of a meeting with her brother's Catholic girlfriend – had suddenly come about without her own intervention or Denis's or that of his friends.

'All right, Jacob, if that's what you really want. I'll go first thing in the morning.'

'Thanks, Judy, thanks,' Jacob said. And then, drawing an envelope from his pocket, he handed it to his sister.

'Would you give her this, please?'

'A letter?' Judith remarked, almost envying him the complete lack of caution that allowed him to write what she presumed was a love-letter to his non-Jewish girlfriend.

'No,' Jacob said, turning away his face shyly. 'It's a poem I was writing for her. I'd like her to have it.'

Judith took the envelope and saw that Jacob had written 'Deirdre Buckley' on it.

'I'll see she gets it,' she smiled. 'Now, you go to bed and sleep. There's no point in staying up moping.'

Jacob nodded. 'Thanks, Judy,' he said again as she squeezed his hand.

When he had gone, she sank back into her chair and yawned in sudden weariness. She'd slip off to bed herself. What a night, she thought, her mind in a whirl. What a wonderful, sad, crazy night!

18

BERTHA COHEN stood back and assessed her progress. Just one wall whitewashed and half the morning gone – she had never been as slow as this. Perhaps she had been foolish to start it. It wasn't as if the kitchen needed whitewashing. Barely three months since she had last done it – for Rosh Hashanah, the New Year – and in not much more than another three months she'd be doing it again, this time for Passover. The biannual task was as fixed a part of her domestic routine as the festivals themselves. From time to time in the past Jacob, and Molly and Judith, too, had offered to help her and had taken up a brush, but she preferred to do it herself. That way she was certain it would be done properly – the way she wanted it – no streaks, no hairs stuck on the wall, no drops of whitewash staining the linoleum.

She never minded all the heavy work entailed – pushing the table and chairs, and the dresser, into the middle of the floor, washing the linoleum, black-leading the range and picking out the lines of the red brick surrounds in gleaming white paint. She always found it relaxing. Her limbs and muscles did everything, no planning was required, no close attention was needed, her mind was released to roam freely, or to reflect on some small domestic detail, or to remain just vacant; or very occasionally to face up to a real family problem – which was why she had suddenly decided that morning to wind a scarf around her head, fill the bucket with water and lime, and give the kitchen this additional going-over.

She needed to think. Her life seemed to have become, almost overnight, a succession of worries. One after another they had settled on her – it was like the rain of plagues the Lord had visited on the Egyptians. At least the Egyptians knew what they were dealing with – when frogs invaded their homes, when clouds of locusts descended on their fields, when darkness covered the land, when the water turned to blood – whatever the plague, it was something they could see, hear, touch, feel – it was a physical abomination. And to be rid of it, all Pharaoh had to do was let the Israelites go. But her worries were intangible – worse than intangible. Was there one member of her family who at that moment wasn't facing some crisis, some new experience in which she would have no part, or wasn't being crushed by some secret from which she was excluded? Not one – not even one. Rabbi Moishe's imminent departure, the birth of Molly's child – these were ordeals she could face up to. She knew what they involved and she knew they could not be avoided. The Rabbi would go to Palestine and she would never see him again, the cornerstone of the Cohen household would be removed, the world of Celtic Crescent changed for ever – it was not a pleasant prospect, but at least she could get some satisfaction from the knowledge that Rabbi Moishe's life-dream would have been fulfilled; as for Molly – all being well, and with God's help, she would have her baby, and that at least *was* something to look forward to. Molly's latest letter, delivered that morning, had been a comfort to read – her daughter was well, the doctor was pleased with her, there was nothing to fear. First babies were often late, so it might happen that the birth would not take place until after Rabbi Moishe had left, and then Bertha and her husband could be with their daughter for the blessed event. It was up to the Lord, it was in His hands and, if He decreed otherwise, their visit would still be made after Christmas.

253

But the others – Joshua, Jacob, Judith – *oi vey*, what was it with them...?

Her arm began to feel heavy, and she realised that the brush-strokes had slowed down. She stood back a pace for an overall view. If she couldn't be quick, she could at least make sure that what she had done was perfect. Really, there was little or no difference between the freshly whitewashed wall and the others – none that she could see anyway, and if *she* couldn't see any difference no one else was likely to. Maybe it would be sufficient to wash down the other walls, or perhaps whitewash just one of them – the smaller one looking onto the yard – and wash the other two.

She moved the bucket to a more convenient point, rubbed down the next wall with a cloth, and resumed the automatic movements – up, down, up, down – while she thought about her husband, Joshua. He it was who disturbed her most. For nearly two weeks he had been a changed man. She had said nothing about it to the family, they had said nothing to her. Maybe they hadn't noticed anything; it wouldn't have surprised her, for they appeared to have their own distractions. Then, again, even if they had thought him to be out of sorts, they would hardly have found anything untoward in that. A grown man about to be separated for the rest of his days from the father he had spent all his life with – you wouldn't expect him to be dancing a *hora* or going about the house smiling like a *meshuggeneh*, and so they would probably think that was all that was on his mind. But not Bertha; she wished that *was* the explanation but she wasn't going to delude herself. She knew her husband; she should do – thirty years since they had arrived in Cork, a newly married couple, and in all those years she had never known him to be really upset by anything. No matter how bad the times were or how long their struggle. Indeed, it wasn't until the War that business had begun to pick up. Yes, her husband had had to suffer and strive to get where he was, Bertha nodded to herself in affirmation. But through it all he had never changed; he had remained calm, strong, confident, good-humoured – better than

254

good-humoured, for hadn't he always been able to laugh at adversity? Just like his own father, the old Rabbi. On such occasions Bertha would snort and comment, '*A bitterah galechter,*' but, bitter or not, laughter had been his answer. Yet for the past fortnight his good humour had deserted him. He was like a man who, having seen what was round the next corner and been struck dumb by the sight, was powerless either to change his direction or go back. How could she help? What could she do?

Bertha Cohen changed the brush from her right to her left hand to get at a difficult corner and made her mind up: she'd say nothing before Shabbos – let him get over the weekend – but if there was no improvement by then she'd ask him outright what the matter was. And she'd insist on being told. Strong he was, yes, and obstinate, yes; so was she. She could be just as obstinate when she wanted, as he well knew. And this time she wanted.

'*Oi vey,*' she muttered wearily as she tucked a straying wisp of grey hair back under the headscarf. It was a phrase Bertha Cohen rarely, if ever, used. She didn't approve of it – it was too much an admission of defeat, a gasp of surrender, almost a cry for help. 'Skitch, skitch,' she shouted as she angrily waved a hand at the hen that had squawked across from the coop in the yard and jumped up on the window-ledge. When it stared back at her with a piercing eye she was galvanised into action. Rushing out, she caught the offending bird and stuffed it back behind the wire netting. Then she returned to the kitchen and her other two worries – her son and her unmarried daughter.

Jacob she already thought of as 'the doctor', but she was realistic enough to realise that at this stage her ambitions for him were no more than a dream. Still, the dream was one which gave her a new interest in life and compensated to some extent for her disappointment with Judith. But a dream you live with through every waking moment was very different from a night dream that could be forgotten or shrugged off when you woke up. She smiled to herself at the recollection of how every morning when she was young the first thing she and her mother –

may her peace be everlasting – would do was exchange dreams. As they prepared the day's tasks each would recount her own strange tale of where she had visited when asleep, the people she had met – living or ghosts – what she had seen, whether it was sad or funny or silly or frightening. They would laugh at each other or hold their hands up in horror or try to suggest meanings or associations. Then after a while they would bustle about, throwing themselves seriously into the housework and dismissing their speculations as nonsense. But Bertha's dream for Jacob was not something she could dislodge from her mind, and already she was learning how unwilling she was to alter it even in the slightest detail, no matter what early discouragement she was feeling. Why was it that Jacob seemed to do so little studying? Why did he spend so much time out of the house? Even Sundays. He said it was all connected with college, there were so many societies, so many new activities. No doubt there were. She supposed the first few months at university could be especially busy, getting settled in, absorbing, adjusting, meeting new people, making new friends. But there was more to it than that – a mother can tell immediately a child of her womb is harbouring some secret. She might have no idea what it could be but Bertha Cohen was certain there *was* something. How could she find out? Not by asking – that would only serve to lock it away more securely from her. She would have to get at it by some other roundabout approach. Through Judith? But that one also had been acting strangely in the last few days. She, too, had suddenly become a problem. No, first Joshua. Her husband was her biggest worry. When she had drawn his trouble out of him it would be time enough to deal with the children.

Bertha Cohen attacked her task with renewed vigour. It was a relief already to have come to some decision. Perhaps she would whitewash all the walls after all. '*Oi vey!*' was far from her mind.

* * *

To Judith, Casimir Street looked even more working-class than Celtic Crescent. She was standing at one end of it, gazing down the long vista of identical houses which seemed to be devoid of any privacy with their doors opening straight onto the footpath and their narrow front windows like a row of spy-holes. But she knew better than to judge by appearances; after all, if a stranger were to take Celtic Crescent at face value, he'd never guess that any family there could send a son to university, so why shouldn't someone from Casimir Street be able to go to college, too? At least the houses were real two-storey buildings, not like Jewtown's one storey and an attic.

From the door numbers Judith realised that number 2 would be at the other end and she steeled herself to make the long walk towards it. This was a mission she didn't relish; she almost wished Deirdre Buckley wouldn't be in. The policeman at the Bridewell had said she was released early that morning and that her father had collected her. Presumably she had gone straight home. But that was hours ago; she might no longer be there – she might even have gone to the university. But there was no point in such wishful thinking – better for all concerned that the girl should be in so that they could have a heart-to-heart talk.

A little way down the street doors were open and some of the housewives had gathered on the footpath in conversation. Despite the cold air they had not put on any coats or shawls over their aprons, and Judith felt embarrassingly conspicuous as she walked towards them. She was wearing her best coat with its thick fur collar, and her gloved hands were awkwardly trying to cover up a shiny new handbag. The women hid their curiosity as she approached, but she could feel their eyes following her right to the door of number 2.

She lifted the knocker, almost recoiling at the noise it made, its leaden echo reverberating in the silent street. There was the sound of steps from inside the house, and she quickly pulled off her gloves and stuffed them into her bag. The door was opened by a dark-haired girl.

'I'm looking for Deirdre Buckley,' Judith offered tentatively, attempting a friendly smile.

'I'm Deirdre Buckley,' the girl answered, her hand still on the door-latch.

'Oh. My name is Judith Cohen. I'm Jacob's sister.'

Deirdre looked puzzled for a moment, saying nothing, waiting for Judith to speak again.

'I'm sorry to trouble you. Jacob asked me. . . . I went to the Bridewell, but they told me you had been released.'

'You'd better come in,' Deirdre invited, opening the door wide.

Judith stepped into the cramped hall and immediately her nose picked up the unusual odour. She recognised it particularly from Mrs Burns's, the only other non-Jewish house she had ever been inside, and there was usually more than a trace of it in Mr Watson's butcher shop when she went to buy the meat on Friday mornings. Warm, heavy, slightly choking, she had always taken it to be the smell of pig and she felt it would make her sick if she had to endure it for long, but fortunately it disappeared completely when Deirdre showed her into the front room and closed the door.

'I went to the Bridewell. Jacob asked me to. He told me you refused to see him,' Judith said.

'That's right,' Deirdre replied a little defensively. 'I suppose he was upset.'

'Very upset. He couldn't understand it.'

Deirdre smiled and then nodded. 'Poor Jacob – he's so serious.'

'He – he thinks a lot of you,' Judith said, and looking at Deirdre she could see what her brother found so attractive – the shoulder-length black hair, the lively green eyes, and particularly the blooming, rosy complexion, its clear texture so different from the sallowness of the Jewish girls he would have encountered.

'I'm very fond of Jacob, too.'

'I think *his* feelings for *you* are stronger than that,' Judith suggested.

'I know.' There was a note of unhappiness in Deirdre's voice, as if the knowledge afforded her no satisfaction.

258

'Had that anything to do with why you wouldn't see him? Or was it because you didn't want him to be involved in your arrest?'

Judith opened the top button of her coat – although there was no fire in the room, she was beginning to feel uncomfortably warm.

'I'm so sorry, Miss Cohen, I'm forgetting my manners,' Deirdre immediately said. 'Won't you take your coat off and sit down?'

'I won't take it off. I'll only be staying a minute,' Judith answered with a smile as she sat in the chair that Deirdre pushed towards her. The room, though very different from their own front room, had the same unlived-in feeling, and she knew that for the Buckleys, just as for the Cohens, it was a room used for special occasions only and that home was the kitchen. There was no bookcase, but there was a side-table with sepia photographs, a potted plant in the window, a closed upright piano, a sofa, uncomfortable-looking chairs, and two small scenic pictures on the walls. Over the fireplace was a wooden cross with the figure of Jesus, and above that a very large coloured print of a stern-faced man in resplendent white robes and a skull-cap – Judith guessed it must be the Pope.

'I'm afraid I've made a bit of a mess of things,' Deirdre said, sitting to face her visitor.

'In what way?'

'I like your brother, Miss Cohen, I like him a lot. But I don't feel about him the way he feels about me.'

Judith felt a surge of relief at Deirdre's disclosure.

'I didn't mean him to get so involved,' Deirdre continued. 'I would have stopped seeing him when he told me about the letter your father got, but he wouldn't hear of it. But when I was arrested that changed everything for me.'

'It must have been very frightening,' Judith said.

'Frightening?' Deirdre queried, as if she was surprised at the suggestion. 'No, not frightening. It made me stop and think, of course – a thing like that – but it doesn't frighten me. Not that I hadn't thought about it before – being caught, I mean – but it's different when it actually

259

happens.' Deirdre turned her head towards the window, adding, as if to herself: 'Beforehand, you don't realise ... you just can't imagine how being caught might change you, change your attitude to things.'

Judith remained silent until Deirdre turned back to her.

'It made me see how silly it was to keep leading Jacob on. Silly, and unfair, too. I decided to tell him immediately I'd be released. I didn't expect him to come to the Bridewell. The police knew someone had been with me on Sunday, they tried to make me say who he was, but I wouldn't. When they told me Jacob wanted to see me, I said I didn't know him. I didn't want him involved. I didn't want them to think he might have been with me. If they had questioned him, I think Jacob would have admitted he had been there.'

'So it *was* to protect my brother that you said you didn't know him.'

'Yes, of course,' Deirdre said. 'But I can't deny I'm glad it happened like this. I'm hoping it might put an end to our ... our relationship – that it might save me having to tell him myself. I don't know if I'd have the courage to do that.'

Judith laughed. 'That's a surprise. I mean, you do things that could get you into a lot of trouble, danger even, things that take courage, yet....'

'It's not the same,' Deirdre interrupted. 'It was great fun being with Jacob. He's so interesting, so different. We really got on well and enjoyed being together. I don't mind hurting people I hate, like the police and the Tans – it doesn't take courage to hurt *them*. But to hurt someone you like....' Deirdre lowered her eyes.

'I tried to convince Jacob that the reason you didn't see him was because you didn't want to involve him,' Judith said. 'I don't know if he believed me. He was very upset. He'll be even more upset when he knows that you don't want to see him again. But it's best for everyone that way.'

'I hope so,' Deirdre agreed. 'He'll soon forget me. I know he's sensitive and I don't want to sound callous but...

well, he's very young' – and then, as if suddenly realising how patronising this might seem, she quickly added: 'I'm only a year older than him, admittedly, but it's different for me. I'm a woman and I'm – I'm involved in something that's very serious. I know he told you about it. It doesn't concern him, and it's stupid to continue taking the chance of getting him mixed up in it.'

Judith felt as if a burden had been lifted from her. It was heartless of her, she knew, to rejoice – even inwardly – at what would seem to Jacob like the end of the world, but he would get over it in time. For him there would be other worlds, other interests, surely other loves, too. Deirdre Buckley was right about that. But, if the affair had continued, goodness knows what it might have led to. The end of his father's world certainly – and his mother's – and without doubt that would be something they would never have got over.

'You do understand, Miss Cohen, don't you?' Deirdre asked, uncertain as to the implication of Judith's silence.

'Oh, yes, yes, I do,' Judith answered her. 'I'm sure you were right. A clean break is best in the end.'

She stood up, anxious to get away from the house. Only out in the open air would she find the freedom to savour the feeling of exultation at how well it had all turned out. But there was still Jacob's poem.

'This is for you,' she said, taking the envelope from her handbag. 'Jacob asked me to give it to you.'

'A letter?' Deirdre said doubtfully.

'No, it's not a letter. It's a poem, in fact. I think he's been secretly writing it for you.'

Deirdre took the envelope, fingered it for a moment and then handed it back to Judith.

'I'm flattered,' she said, 'and burning with curiosity. But, as you said yourself, a clean break is best.'

'Yes,' Judith agreed sadly, putting the poem back in her bag. 'I suppose this is one time we have to be cruel to be kind. It will make Jacob realise it really *is* all over.'

'A pity,' Deirdre said wistfully. 'I don't suppose anyone else will ever write a poem to me.'

'You never know,' Judith remarked as she rose to go.

'You're certainly worth one. And that's not flattery – I do mean it.'

There was a moment of indecision at the front door, and then instinctively Judith leaned forward and put her cheek to the other girl's. It was more than a gesture of farewell; it was a recognition of the sisterhood between them that no words could encompass.

19

As JUDITH HURRIED into South Mall on her way to meet Denis, excitement and anticipation made her impervious to the gloom of the black sky, the shorn leafless trees, the austere stone-faced buildings. She couldn't recall when she had last felt so happy. But the past did not concern her – it was the present, this night and its promise, that bore her along now.

She could imagine how surprised Denis would be at the news of her visit to Deirdre Buckley – and especially at how well it had turned out. Not for poor Jacob, of course; it hadn't turned out well for him. And for her, too, telling him had been painful. She had found him in his room when she returned from Casimir Street. He hadn't gone to college that morning, pleading a tummy upset and saying he'd wait at home until she came back.

'Did you see her?' he asked eagerly, jumping up from his bed.

'She wasn't in the Bridewell. They released her this morning,' Judith replied, quickly adding when she saw the disappointment in his face, 'but I went to her home.'

'You went to her home? How did you know where she lived?'

'They told me at the Bridewell,' Judith lied.

The silence that followed, though only momentary, was

almost as unbearable for Judith as she knew it must be for her brother. She looked away from the mixture of anxiety and hope in his eyes – and the fear, too, as he sensed her hesitation and what it meant. He lowered himself slowly back onto his bed. Instinctively Judith went and sat beside him.

'I'm so sorry, Jacob, I'm so sorry,' she whispered, putting an arm round his shoulders. He turned his head away, saying only, 'What ... what did she ... ?' before his voice caught.

'It isn't that she isn't fond of you – very fond. She said so.' The truth stuck in her throat. How could she tell him? How could she bring herself to shatter his young dreams? But she had to.

'Then, why?'

'Oh, Jakey, Jakey, you know why. You must know. There just wasn't any sense in going on; she saw that as soon as she was arrested and began to think about it. What could you look forward to? You'd have to part in the end – and it would be much harder on you the longer you stayed together.'

Jacob shook his head from side to side as if trying to regain full consciousness after some stunning blow. He stood up and went over to the small chest of drawers on which the ewer and basin had been moved to one side to make room for his medical books. He looked down at the books, then slowly traced with his finger the scored and dented edge of the chest's surface.

'She doesn't....' He hesitated. 'She doesn't love me. That's it, isn't it?'

Judith's first instinct was to tell him that what he felt for Deirdre couldn't be love, either, not really love, only infatuation. At his age, his first involvement, what else could it be? But she realised that to say that now would only be turning the knife in the wound. Later on perhaps. In time he'd probably recognise it for himself.

'Well, that's it, isn't it? She just doesn't love me,' he repeated.

'That's part of it,' Judith agreed, trying to soften the blow. 'But it isn't only that. It's what she's doing – what

264

she's involved in. I said so to you last night, didn't I? I said she probably didn't want to take any more risk of getting you into trouble – it's enough *she* was arrested without *you* being caught, too. She doesn't want you dragged into it. It's not your fight; it doesn't concern you. And she knows that.'

Jacob shrugged his shoulders but did not turn to face his sister. His silence forced her to continue.

'It's something you can't understand, Jacob, and neither can I – this dedication of hers to fighting for Ireland. It's something we can't experience. But at the moment it means everything to her and she can't let anything else – or anyone else – get in its way.'

Judith went over to her brother and took his hand. In the mirror above the chest of drawers she saw his face – the long sensitive features, the high forehead, the full lips – his mother's stamp. His eyes were brimming. If only, she thought, he had more of his mother's hardness.

'Did you give her the poem?' he asked sharply, almost angrily, pulling his hand away from her grasp.

Judith took the envelope from her pocket.

'She thought it would be better not to read it. It would make it easier for her – for both of you – to forget.'

Jacob nodded, took the envelope and put it down among his books.

'Thank you,' he murmured, though whether it was for the return of his poem or for all she had done Judith couldn't tell. She had an urge to take him in her arms and soothe the worst of his anguish out of him, but he turned away to his bed and lay down on it, staring up at the ceiling.

'Will you come down to dinner?' she asked, and when he did not reply she said: 'I'll tell them your stomach is still upset. You might have something later.'

Outside his door she paused, suddenly aware of a tightness like a band around her chest. She leaned against the wall and breathed in huge sighs of relief. What an ordeal! Thank God it was over at last. All the way home from the store, having to be the bearer of such news had weighed her down, blotting out the recollection

265

of her father's joy when she had told him that, though it was true his son was friendly with a girl from college, there was no danger in it and certainly no need for him to worry about it any more.

'After all,' she had said, 'what can you expect? He's meeting a lot of new people, all of them are Christian and some of them are girls. And he's a young man now, growing up. He's not a schoolboy any more. Is he not supposed to make friends with any of them? Or only with the boys?'

Iron Josh had looked at her, his eyes glowing, his head hopping up and down in quick bounces as if mounted on a spring. He asked her no questions. She could see that all he wanted was her assurance. He seemed almost contrite, as if it was he who had been at fault for ever believing that a son of his could be guilty of what the letter had implied. He was so ready to believe what she was saying, so willing to agree unhesitatingly with her explanation, that she felt pity for him flood through her.

'*Gott tzu danken*,' he kept repeating. '*Gott tzu danken.*'

The fervour in his voice startled Judith. As she caught his glance she saw that there was much more than gratitude in his eyes, much more than mere relief at the avoidance of family disgrace and communal scorn. There was love shining there, love, lighting up his face, warming all his stolid features into twitches and puckers of emotion. She was shocked at the realisation. It was so totally unexpected. He was not, after all, the cold unfeeling father he had always seemed to be. For the first time she knew that he loved his son. Whatever inhibitions had prevented its expression, whatever psychological barriers had smothered even a show of affection, there was no doubt in her mind of that love.

The sudden intuition stirred in her a recollection of the feeling she had experienced for Denis as they had stood embracing each other in the shadows on the previous night. It wasn't the same sort of love, of course – it couldn't be. Could it even be love at all – so quickly, so soon? Judith didn't know. But there was no denying the new emotion in her life, the strange turbulence that had

266

invaded her, almost like an electric current charging the secret parts of her body. And the excitement was not only physical. She wanted to talk about Denis; for one moment with her father that morning she even had a mad urge to tell him how Denis had helped her contact Jacob's girl. She could so easily, so naturally have slipped it into the conversation.

She was glad now, as she hurried towards the GPO, that she had restrained herself. She was determined to stick to her resolution not to let anything serious develop between her and Denis. An interlude – short and sweet – was all she had promised herself, and it would have been utterly foolish to have said anything to her father which might have made him worry. He had had enough worry over Jacob.

As she turned off the South Mall and crossed the road to be on the GPO side of the street, she came abreast of the Imperial Hotel. The entrance and foyer were brightly lit, and a porter was just removing a large sign from outside the door. It was the sign advertising Miss Miller's Dance. Judith smiled to herself. What a difference from the time she had last seen it. It was hard to believe that so much could have happened to her in barely a week – that what had then seemed a hopeless world could now hold such joy, such passion. She could see, ahead of her, a man who looked as if he might be Denis. He was standing by the street-lamp outside Corrigan's, the newsagent's, across the road from the Post Office. His back was to her as he studied the books and papers in the window, and when he turned she saw that it was indeed Denis. She almost broke into a run to meet him, but her sense of propriety asserted itself and held her back. Instead she raised a hand to wave a greeting, and as she did so the whole street suddenly exploded.

The wall of cold air that hit Judith almost knocked her off her feet. A moment of eerie silence followed the explosion, and through the clouds of dust dark sky became visible above the newsagent's shop where before had been all brick and tall windows. Screams lanced through the rumble of falling masonry, and Judith found herself rushing forward to where she had seen Denis hurled to the ground.

As she reached him two men had already run to his aid and were bending over his inert body. Some of the people who had been waiting outside the Post Office had immediately begun to hurry away, fearing more explosions, while others, shocked into silence or numb terror, seemed incapable of movement. A girl's hysterical sobs rose above the clamour, but Judith, oblivious of the pandemonium, had fallen to her knees beside Denis. He was lying on his side, facing the shop's shattered window. Books and papers littered the path and roadway, and among them was his cap, blown off by the force of the explosion.

'Better move him onto the road,' one of the men said. 'The rest of that wall might come down on us any moment' – peering up at the gapped and broken façade.

'No, don't move him, don't touch him,' Judith urged. 'He may have some broken bones.'

The nearby gas-lamp had been extinguished, and the combination of darkness and dust made it impossible for them to see if Denis was even breathing.

'Are you a nurse, miss?' the man asked as others now began to gather round.

'Someone's gone for an ambulance,' a voice assured them.

Groaning, Denis opened his eyes and turned over on his back. Judith gasped as she saw that one side of his face was covered with blood and there was a dark red pool where his head had been lying. A hand reached forward over her shoulder, and gratefully she took the proffered handkerchief. As she started to wipe the blood away she heard someone murmur solicitously: 'Easy there, miss, there may be some glass in the wound.'

'I'm all right,' Denis said, taking the handkerchief and continuing to dab at his cuts. 'I'll be all right. I'm not hurt.'

'Are you sure, Denis, are you sure? Better wait for an ambulance,' Judith urged as she put an arm under his head to support him.

Suddenly piercing blasts of a police whistle reached their ears. Denis immediately sat up and tried to get to his feet. Willing hands helped him rise. 'I'm all right,' he repeated, 'I'm all right. I'm only cut.'

The handkerchief he was holding to his face was by now soaked with blood, and he took out his own to staunch the flow. As the sound of the whistles came nearer he turned to Judith.

'I must get away from here or I'll be picked up. You go home.'

'No, I'm going with you,' she insisted, holding on to his arm as he tried to push his way through the knot of men surrounding him.

'Hurry up, lad, if you're going,' one helper urged. 'We'll keep them busy a while.'

With Judith slapping at his mackintosh to shake off the dust, he picked his way over scattered bricks, glass crumbling under his feet like spilled sugar.

'Go home, Judith, for God's sake,' he pleaded.

She did not reply but hurried to keep pace with him as he strode off down Maylor Street, one hand to his face, away from the sound of the police whistles and an ambulance's clanging bell.

'This is no place for you,' he threw at her over his shoulder. 'Please go home. I'll get in touch with you tomorrow.'

'No, I won't go home. You'll need help. Your face is still bleeding.'

'I won't die of it, girl. It's nearly stopped anyway.'

'Where are you going?' Judith gasped, her breath beginning to shorten as his stride quickened.

'The bottom of this street – a friend – one of the lads. I hope to God he's in.'

'Let's run, then. I'll keep up with you.'

'No, don't run. That'll only draw attention if there's any police or Tans around. Don't talk any more. Save your breath till we get there.'

Denis put his free arm around Judith's waist, as much to help her match his pace as to give the impression that he was just a young man out with his girl. The action sent a warm thrill of pleasure through her, but she froze abruptly when she saw an RIC man running in their direction, summoned by the continuing shrill blasts of the police whistles behind them. Impulsively she pulled Denis into a doorway, threw her arms around his neck and kissed him lingeringly, turning the injured side of his face away from sight.

'Great girl,' Denis whispered as soon as the danger had passed. 'Let's get on in case there'd be any more following him.' Fortunately Maylor Street, comprised mostly only of depots and warehouses for the big Patrick Street stores, was deserted and Denis was able to keep the handkerchief against his cut face without fear of being seen.

'Is it still bleeding?' Judith asked.

'I don't know.'

'Sore?'

'Not much. We're nearly there now anyway.'

But what if his friend wasn't in? Judith thought. Where would he get help then? Beyond Maylor Street was Warren's Place – and anywhere less safe for an injured IRA man on the run she couldn't imagine. It was an open busy thoroughfare, linking the South Mall to the docks, with a few small houses, a few huckster shops, but mostly pubs. Judith knew that the whole area was a favourite target for police or Black and Tan raids, searching for members of the IRA, or for information, or more often than not just on wild drinking orgies. Lurid, sometimes frightening stories of the almost nightly disturbances were familiar to the women of the Jewish community, for Fanny Rubin and her husband lived in one of the houses and there was seldom a Friday morning in the butcher's shop that Fanny didn't horrify everyone with her catalogue of the week's outrages. Even allowing for her love of exaggeration, for the uninhibited zest with which she made the raids and arrests sound like spectacular shows put on for her enjoyment, no one doubted that Warren's Place was somewhere to be avoided once darkness fell. Judith couldn't imagine herself living under such constant threat; and the thought that she and Denis might have to make their way through the area, where the police were bound to be patrolling, sent shivers through her.

They had reached almost the end of Maylor Street when Denis stopped at a door above which three golden balls gleamed in the darkness.

'This is Sean's,' he said. 'Say a prayer that he's in.'

He knocked softly with his knuckles.

'He'll never hear that,' Judith said. 'Knock harder.'

'If he's in, he'll hear it. If I knock harder, he might think it's a raid and he'd just escape out the back.'

Judith squeezed Denis's arm.

'Knock again anyway.'

Denis did. They waited in trepidation, Judith staring fixedly into Denis's eyes, her body rigid with tension.

Denis put his ear to the door.

'Not a sound. He's not there, then.'

'My God, what'll we do? Let me see your face.'

Denis took the handkerchief from his cheek, and Judith saw that it was still bleeding.

'You'll have to get that seen to quickly. We could go to the Victoria Hospital – it's not too far away.'

'No hospitals for me, thank you. And we're not going anywhere together, Judith. You're going home – it won't take you ten minutes and you'll be safe enough.'

'And where will you go?'

'I'll go home, too, and I'll get cleaned up there.'

'I'm going with you, then,' Judith insisted, stifling Denis's protestations. 'You'll have a much better chance of getting through Warren's Place if we're together – there's bound to be some police or military there.'

'And if we're stopped – what then? I'm not having you get into any trouble. Isn't it bad enough that your brother is taking risks like this?'

'That's all over with. I spoke to Deirdre Buckley this morning. I'll tell you about it later. If we're stopped, we can say that you fell and cut your face. Leave it to me.' To dispel Denis's doubts she added: 'Once we're over the river I'll go to the Statue and get a tram home. I promise, Denis. Now, stop arguing. You *have* to get that cut seen to as soon as possible.'

271

'Wait. I'll try Sean once more,' Denis said. 'He may just have been out in the back last time.'

He knocked again, a little harder on this occasion, but still there was no answer.

'He's not there; we're only wasting time,' Judith urged. 'Put your arm round me again.'

As they covered the last hundred yards of Maylor Street, Judith wished she could think of something to say that would calm her nerves and give her the confidence to feel she could act naturally if anyone stopped them. She was anything but as assured as she had pretended to Denis. Her legs shivered so much that she knew she would have sunk to the ground if his arm hadn't been around her. Fear gripped her heart, so that it hammered frantically against her chest as step after step brought her nearer to the nightmare tumbling through her mind – confrontation by the Tans, arrest, Denis captured, and her association with him revealed to her family and the whole community – all the shame and sorrow that Jacob's affair had threatened revived now by her. But this would be far worse, for she was older than Jacob, supposed to be a mature adult, and she was a girl. Bad enough a Jewish boy disgracing his family and his religion; that would be a tragedy of course, a desecration, but it was not unknown – boys became men, and men.... But for a Jewish girl....

She felt almost a sense of relief when they reached the end of Maylor Street – at least Warren's Place wouldn't be dark and silent, there would be people about, and she could forget her pangs of conscience in the face of more pressing threats. With luck – with a lot of luck – she might even get Denis across the river safely.

Luck, however, was not on her side in Warren's Place – she saw that immediately. Just as they entered one end, a covered truck roared in from the docks end, not fifty yards away, and a company of Black and Tans jumped out, some stopping all pedestrians in their path while others, rifles held menacingly, burst into Mackey's public house, the first building on the corner.

Denis cursed under his breath, and immediately Judith

272

made to turn their steps in the other direction.

'That's no use,' Denis said, holding her back. 'They'll seal that off, too. We're trapped, girl. We'll have to brazen it out, but fat chance we have with this face of mine.'

Judith pressed against his side, her heart pounding rapidly. It was up to her to get them out of their predicament. 'Leave it to me,' she had said foolhardily. How easy it had been to display such bravado in the silent darkness of Maylor Street, with his arm around her and not a soldier or policeman in sight. Words had been cheap then, but she feared in her heart that Denis was right: words wouldn't be enough to get them out of this.

'Trapped, damn it,' she heard him say again.

She looked straight ahead to the other side of the broad street. They couldn't go left and they couldn't go right, but straight in front of her was the Rubins' little house. It was their only hope.

'Come on. Come with me.' She pulled at Denis's arm.

'Where to, for God's sake?'

'That house just across the road. The Rubins live there. They're Jews. We can stay in there till the Tans pass.'

'You're mad, Judith,' Denis exclaimed. 'You can't expect strangers to take such a risk.'

'Fanny Rubin is no stranger. I know her well. She'll help me. Come on, you're wasting time,' Judith protested, already starting to cross the road.

Reluctantly Denis followed her. Around them pedestrians were hurrying to get off the street, though a few jarveys waiting on their side-cars for any stray drinkers needing a conveyance home and still with enough money left to pay their way sat on, cigarettes smoking between their fingers, as unconcerned as their patient horses.

Judith knocked on Mrs Rubin's door, praying there'd be someone in. She didn't dare contemplate their prospects if there wasn't. Mr Rubin, she knew, would be in the country at this time of the week, and Fanny had the reputation in the community of being anything but a stay-at-home, never mind that she'd never see fifty, or even fifty-five, again. She had plenty of Christian cronies, and displayed an uncurbed zest for the kind of company and amusements she had developed a taste for during many years spent travelling the province with her husband. Tough and bluff, and open-hearted, Cork might have been her natural home, so easily had she picked up its style, its sayings, even its very accent. If Fanny Rubin was at home, she'd not turn anyone away, especially anyone in distress.

As Judith was about to knock a second time the door was flung open and Fanny peered out, her red hair almost aglow in the light thrown by the street-lamps. She had a coat draped loosely over her shoulders, and a bright yellow scarf, fluffed cravat-like, set off her oversize beaky nose. To Denis she had the appearance of some exotic jungle bird.

'Judith Cohen! Lord above, girl, what brings you here at this time? And who's yer fella?'

'He's a friend of mine, Mrs Rubin. I'm sorry to bother you, but he's cut his face and it's bleeding a lot. If he could just wash it. . . .'

'Of course he could and welcome! Come in quickly there out of the night and don't be bringing attention on yerselves. It's soon enough the boyos will be paying me a visit.'

She drew them in and half-closed the door. 'I'll leave it open. Saves them hurting their boots kicking it in.' She gave a throaty laugh at her own joke, but Denis was alarmed at the precaution.

'You'll have no warning if you leave the door open, ma'm,' he protested.

'And what about it? Sure what use is a warning? They'll be in anyway – as soon as they finish in the pubs. Come on now, Judith. Bring that young man in here to the kitchen till we have a look at him.'

Leading them through the tiny hallway into a small kitchen where a fire glowed in the range, she lit the gas-lamp hanging from the low ceiling, and as its light rose Denis saw the gleam of a polished table in the centre of the linoleum-covered floor, a well-stocked dresser and a horsehair sofa against one wall.

'Sit down there, let ye. I'll get some warm water and

274

we'll cure your trouble in no time.' As she threw her coat on to the sofa she said casually, 'What brought ye this way at all?' and when there was only a mumbled reply from Judith she gave a cackle of laughter, adding: 'Ask me no questions and I'll tell you no lies.' Then to their relief she bustled off into the scullery, from where they heard a tap running.

'You had your coat on, Mrs Rubin. Were you on your way out?' Judith called.

'Yerra, only a few doors up the road to Mrs Barrett,' Fanny called back. 'She's a widow, you know, and these raids always put the heart across her, so I keep her company if I'm here. Sure it's company for me, too. Not that these boyos frighten me. But she's eighty, the poor soul, and it's hard on her.' Denis and Judith exchanged glances as she chattered on. In the light of the kitchen he dabbed at his face, which by now had almost stopped bleeding. He looked around, his eye immediately alighting on two large, ornately framed pictures hanging above the mantel – photographs of King George V and Queen Mary. Before he could voice his surprise, Fanny Rubin emerged from the scullery, a basin of steaming water between her hands and a towel flung over her shoulder.

'What's yer man's name, Judith?' she asked, setting the basin on the table.

'Denis,' Denis replied quickly before Judith could speak.

'A nice honest name. Very popular in the country. Dinnys and Din Joes all over the place. And tell me, Denis, how did you get these cuts at all?'

'Ah, 'tis only a scrape,' Denis replied evasively.

'Ask me no questions and I'll tell you no lies,' Fanny said for the second time, in no way put out that her curiosity was not being satisfied. She winked at Denis. 'It wasn't that her ladyship has been paring her nails on your cheek, was it? Sure what matter? That'd only be passion and an encouragement to a fine man like yerself.'

Judith laughed awkwardly; Denis, his chin held firmly by Mrs Rubin while she washed the blood from his face, was glad he didn't need to make any reply.

'They're more than scrapes anyway,' she told him. 'And there's still a doosheen bit of bleeding. I'll put some lint on it.' She went to the dresser and rummaged in a drawer.

'I see you have His Majesty up on the wall, Mrs,' Denis said, at last able to put the question that had been troubling him.

Fanny Rubin gave her throaty laugh. 'Don't be sayin' a word against Georgie boy; he's my protector.'

'King George!'

'He's the one. I got my husband to put him up there on the wall, and his missis to keep an eye on him in case he'd turn out to be like his oul' fella. So when the police or the Tans come bargin' in while my man is away in the country they see their Majesties up there and they say to themselves: "Now isn't this a fine, upstanding, loyal establishment!"' She winked broadly at Denis. Then turning to Judith she said: 'Go out there to the door, love, and see how far these blackguards have got. Don't show yourself too much, just take a good look.'

As Judith went out of the kitchen, Mrs Rubin bent to attend again to Denis's face.

'You know I don't want them to find me here,' he told her, guessing that frankness was his best card.

'No more do I,' she replied jauntily.

'Have you somewhere to hide me?'

'I have indeed.'

'Where?'

'Where but where they'd never look.'

'Where's that?'

'Under their noses,' Fanny laughed as Judith returned.

'The Tans are across the road,' she said, 'and some of them are on this side, about five doors down.'

'Ah sure that'll be time enough for us.'

Mrs Rubin took the basin and towel to the scullery, and they heard her open the back door to throw out the water.

'Now, come with me, the pair of ye,' she directed as she returned.

They followed her out of the kitchen and into one of the rooms off the hall. Seeing it was a bedroom they paused on the threshold. Inside, she lit a candle that stood in its holder beside a double bed. 'Yerra come in and shut the door,' she ordered. 'And, Dinny, take off your coat and jacket. Hurry up, we haven't all night,' as she saw Denis hesitate. When he handed her the two coats, she said: 'Better take the shirt off as well.'

'What for?' he asked, his face colouring.

'Because my husband never went to bed with a shirt on under his pyjamas,' she explained.

Denis looked in consternation at Judith.

'It's not embarrassed you are, is it?' Fanny Rubin cajoled. 'Sure wouldn't she see as much on the sands at Youghal or Crosshaven! Come on, now, if you want to get home safely tonight.'

Denis nodded and took off his shirt.

'Shoes as well. Under the bed with them,' ordered Mrs Rubin as she threw the shirt over a chair. She put the two coats in a wardrobe from which she brought out a pair of men's trousers which she draped conspicuously over Denis's shirt. Judith and Denis watched her preparations.

'Now,' she said, taking a pyjama jacket from a drawer, 'put that on and button it up, and when that's done sit down on the bed till I finish the job off with this.'

'This' was a long woollen scarf which she proceeded to tie under his chin and over his head until little of his face could be seen. Judith burst out laughing at the sight, and Fanny smiled. 'It mightn't be very elegant but it'll hide the plaster on his cheek. Now, Dinny, what you'll do is get into the bed there, turn your face to the wall and pull the covers well up, and let there not be a move out of you no matter what happens. And you, Judith, go into the kitchen, hang up your coat, and put on the kettle for a cup of tea. And when you hear the Tans at the door go out and meet them and tell them that your mother and father are in bed because your father isn't well – he has a terrible toothache.'

'And where will you be, Mrs Rubin?' Judith asked.

'Haven't I just told you, girl! I'll be in bed with Dinny here. Yerra, don't worry yourself, I won't steal his virginity. I suppose I can trust him, can I?'

277

She turned to Denis, who was sitting up in the bed, a look almost of horror on his face.

'Would you do as I tell you, Dinny,' she ordered. 'Turn your face to the wall there and no peeping while I get ready to join you. Go on, now, if you don't want us all to be caught like this and it's not only the Tans I'd have to answer to, but my husband as well.'

She gave Judith another of her knowing winks, and as Denis pulled the bedclothes around his head and curled up with his back to the two women Fanny quickly took off her blouse and skirt. She draped them over the chair next to her 'husband's' clothes and added to them a petticoat and a pair of voluminous pink bloomers which she took from a drawer. Then, taking her nightdress from under her pillow, she smartly put it on and got into the bed beside Denis.

'Now, Judith, close the door behind you. You know what to say, girl – just that your mammy and daddy are in bed because your daddy had some teeth out today and they're still bleeding and he's not well. They'll want to come in and see for themselves, so don't try to stop them. Don't worry, now, I'm used to these boys. I know how to handle them.'

Judith turned, her heart pounding with fear at the audacity of Fanny Rubin's plan.

'And don't forget to boil the kettle,' Fanny called to her as she closed the door. Boil the kettle! How *could* the woman worry about tea at such a time!

Judith found, however, that busying herself in the kitchen was at least better than just waiting for something to happen. She hung up her coat on a nail behind the door and put on an apron she found there to help make her look a more convincing daughter of the house. At the side of the range the kettle was already full, and she moved it over the burning coals. Then she went to the dresser for cups and saucers. Spoons were a problem as two of the drawers contained cutlery and there was no knowing which set was for meat dishes and which for milk. In her own home the dietary laws rule was meat delph and ware to the right, milk to the left, but how could she

278

tell which was which in Mrs Rubin's kitchen?

A loud bang on the front door and the noise of it being roughly thrown open banished the problem from her mind. Controlling her alarm she went to the hall where two Black and Tans stood, one of them about to enter the bedroom. Judith held her ground, hoping to draw them into the kitchen so that they might see the portraits of the King and Queen. Through the wide-open street-door behind them she saw other police and Tans rushing past, brandishing guns and calling on someone to halt.

'What's your name?' one of the Tans in the hall shouted at her while the other turned and ran out to join his comrades.

'Rubin,' Judith replied, glad she had remembered not to give her real name.

'Wotcher mean Reuben? That's a bloke's name.'

'Rubin is my last name. Judith Rubin. We're Jews,' she blurted out, hoping he'd be surprised enough to take their non-involvement for granted and leave them alone.

'Blimey! Kikes! You live here?'

'Yes.'

'Who else? Anyone else in the house?'

He opened the door opposite the bedroom and peered in as Judith answered.

'Only my father and mother. They're in the other room – in bed – my father isn't well.'

'What's wrong wiv him?'

'He had some teeth out today and they won't stop bleeding.'

The Tan said nothing but pushed open the bedroom door. In the dim candlelight he saw Fanny Rubin sit up sharply, ostensibly guarding her modesty with the bed-sheet held high under her capacious bosom but also effectively blocking Denis from view.

'Sh! Sh!' she warned.

'What's the matter wiv you, missis?'

'It's my poor husband, Sergeant. Didn't my girl tell you? He got some teeth out today and the poor craytur has had a terrible time with them. I've only just got him off to sleep, so don't be creating, Sergeant, or you'll wake him

279

up. Go into the kitchen there and I'll get up and make you a cup of tea.'

The torrent of words combined with the threat of tea seemed too much for the Tan.

'Jesus!' he exploded as he turned and ran out of the house. Judith rushed to shut the front door behind him and then hurried back to the bedroom.

'They're gone, Mrs Rubin; it worked.'

'Of course it worked, girl. Sure it's drink and a fight those ones are after, not the likes of us. Though it's a good job he didn't get a proper look at Dinny here.'

'Why so?' Denis asked, sitting up now and smiling with relief.

'Why so! If he saw your carrot head alongside my red hair, he might have wondered how we produced that black-haired one there. Now, young man, turn your face back to the wall again until I get dressed. And no peeping, mind! Is the kettle on, Judith?'

'Oh,' Judith exclaimed, hurrying out of the bedroom. 'It'll have boiled over by now.'

She had hardly reached the kitchen when Fanny Rubin followed her, fully dressed again in coat and scarf.

'I think I'll pop up to Mrs Barrett and see if she's all right. Never mind about tea for me; I'll have a cup with her.' At the door she turned to add: 'Let you take a cup in to your young man while you're waiting for the street to clear. He'll need it after the fright he got. I might be a while with Mrs Barrett, so close the front door after you when you leave.'

'Mrs Rubin...,' Judith said, then hesitated in embarrassment.

'It's not a chaperon you need, is it, girl? You wouldn't want me to play gooseberry now, would you? Sure that young man is a gentleman. I can tell, you know. I'm never wrong about people.'

Judith felt her cheeks burning. 'I just wanted to thank you—'

Fanny Rubin cut her short. 'No need, Judith, no need. I couldn't let him get arrested, could I? And maybe you with him. Sure wasn't it a great bit of excitement? It made the day for me, so don't you worry. I'll be off, then.'

Her footsteps sounded down the hall, and immediately the front door had closed Judith heard Denis call from the bedroom.

He was sitting up in the bed, his pyjama coat discarded, grappling with the scarf tied around his head.

'Where's Mrs Rubin gone? She made such a knot in this that I can't get it open and it has me nearly choked.'

'Let me,' Judith said, kneeling behind him to get at the knot. 'It's in an awkward place when you can't see what you're doing. There, now.'

The scarf dropped from Denis's neck, and Judith rested her hands on his shoulders, her mouth nuzzling the back of his head. He took her hands in his and pulled them down onto his bare chest. His skin felt cool to her touch.

'You're cold,' she said.

'Reaction, most likely, after the fright we got.'

'Were you afraid?'

'Not afraid. A bit nervous.'

'*I* was afraid,' Judith whispered, hugging him closer to her.

Denis half-turned his head, then let his body sink back onto the pillow, drawing Judith down with him.

'I'd never have known it. Anyway, you're all right now. You were very brave.' He placed his lips against her forehead. In contrast to his body, they felt warm and vibrant against her skin.

'You're all right, too, my love,' she said. 'We're both safe, thank goodness.'

'And thanks to Mrs Rubin, too. Where is she? I heard her go out.'

'She's gone to see after the old lady up the road. She said she'd be gone a while.'

'She must trust us, then,' Denis said lightly.

'She does. She told me you were a gentleman.'

'She might change her mind if she saw us now.'

'What of it?' Judith whispered. 'I don't care.'

She could feel the beat of his heart against her breast. Or was it her own heart? She really didn't care. She had never experienced passion before, never before been aware of a bodily hunger such as this. There was nothing sinful in having these sensations – there couldn't be – they were natural. Why should she deny them? She was old enough to own such feelings and to enjoy them.

In the flickering candlelight she lifted her head and looked into Denis's eyes. As his arms encircled her, the hardness of his body, all along hers, answered desire with desire. She saw his lips open in a smile. They seemed to be the only part of him that no part of her was touching. Eyes closed, she plunged her mouth onto his.

Suddenly she was flung into the air as, in a single movement, Denis swung them both over so that she was lying on her back on the bed, spreadeagled under him. Neither of them paid heed to the noises still coming from the street outside the bedroom window – the throbbing of engines as the armoured cars rumbled up and down, the clatter of the Black and Tans' boots on the pavement, the raucous shouts, the police whistles. Judith was conscious only of the gathering torrent inside her, drowning all care in its violent current. Her hands scrabbled frantically up and down the bare skin of Denis's back, nails digging into his writhing flesh in fierce clutchings – now of encouragement, now of restraint, she knew not which. The candle by the bedside had somehow become extinguished, the brute noises from the street had receded and died, the house was at peace and the room still as inside her the storm at last broke.

20

COLONEL WINDSOR allowed his monocle to fall from his eye as he placed his cigarette-holder with its half-smoked cigarette against the already full ashtray on his desk. Outside the window the sky was so grey and lack-lustre that it was impossible to imagine it had ever been sunny, or ever would be again. Not the kind of weather for a soldier on patrol – poor visibility, the damp seeping into your bones, the cold stiffening your fingers and making the gun in your hand seem like a bar of ice. All your responses became about as sharp as a slug's, so that you hardly cared what might be around the next corner. Oh, it was good not to have to be out there picking your steps through muddy treacherous lanes and boreens. Except that there *were* men out there, and they were his men, and he was responsible for them.

The Colonel leaned his head back and closed his eyes. It wasn't exactly that he was tired of it all, or even angry about what was happening – and he certainly wasn't getting fed up with army life and its strains. He just felt – helpless. That was rare for him, and he didn't much like it. Helplessness was a dangerous feeling for a soldier. It tested so many qualities at once – nerve, self-control, sense of discipline, powers of reasoning. Found wanting in any one of these and a soldier might be tempted into some rash unplanned action. Worse still, he might suffer an attack of the jitters; worst of all, even physical and mental breakdown.

Eric Windsor couldn't visualise himself succumbing to such a fate – though, God knows, one shouldn't look on oneself as invulnerable. After all, it had happened to Tubby Walters, and Tubby and he were close enough in age, experience and record. Nevertheless, as events had proved, there must have been some fundamental psychological or temperamental difference between them. He hadn't thought there was but, then, he hadn't ever thought about it at all really. Poor old Tubby. Had he resigned from the Tans? the Colonel wondered. He hoped so. For Tubby's own sake it was the only course to take. A blind man could see that the situation was getting worse day by day, and once it began to get you down – as it had Tubby – a chap really had little chance of recovering.

Colonel Windsor snapped his eyes open and jerked back to attention in his chair. He took up his monocle, briskly polished it, re-affixed it in his eye and lit a fresh cigarette. No matter how bad things might be, they weren't going to get *him* down. He had his job to do – to help the civil authorities to maintain law and order. That was it – official version. The Colonel's snort expelled two thin jets of smoke from his nostrils as if to sum up what he thought of *that* idea. The civil authorities! Law and order! It was the very civil authorities – the RIC and the Black and Tans – who were the greatest abusers of law and order. Oh, yes, there was the IRA; there was always the IRA. But the Army wasn't at war with the IRA, whereas by being cast in a supporting role to the Tans and the RIC in their war the Army was being tarred with the same brush and was increasingly becoming a target for IRA attacks. If it wasn't an ambush – like the one that got young Byford – it was something equally sudden and almost unavoidable, like the kidnapping of Captain Simcox.

Colonel Windsor didn't give much for Simcox's chances of survival, and even less for the chances of the police ever finding him – unless it would be his body they'd stumble on. But there was nothing – not a damn thing –

the Colonel could do about it. Or anyone else for that matter. Oh, yes, when Lucas had been kidnapped the Government had authorised an all-out search for him. But Lucas had been a brigadier. And that had been in June, when conditions had been favourable to a large-scale search – fine weather, bright evenings, bright enough to send even an aeroplane scouring the country-side for him until ten o'clock, though how an aeroplane could find him the Colonel was dashed if he knew. Now, with bad weather, dark evenings, and the country boiling over, an army search for Simcox was out of the question. The poor bastard would just have to stew – and pray. Colonel Windsor knew there had been mutterings among the men about his inactivity, but he knew, too, that they were only letting off steam. At least he had rescinded the Order allowing officers to sleep out of barracks. But a fat lot of good that would do at this stage – locking the stable door after the horse had gone!

The Colonel pulled open a drawer in his desk and took out a large folder. He'd have to start a second folder soon, so bulky was this one getting. Now there were three more reports of Black and Tan capers in Cork to add to it. It had all been so predictable. What had the Government ex-pected of such men? Churchill had claimed that they were selected 'on account of their intelligence, their character, and their records in the war'. Colonel Windsor snorted again. Typical Churchillian persiflage! They had been selected 'to face a rough and dangerous task' – as he understood the first recruiting posters in Glasgow and Liverpool had put it – and to face it in a rough and dangerous way. These were men who had returned from the war only to find that they had no jobs to go to. Now, in the Tans, they were getting ten shillings a day and all found – a king's ransom when many of their ex-comrades were walking the streets not knowing where their next meal was coming from. It was hardly surprising that they very quickly kicked over the traces. Their morale was low enough to start with, but then suddenly finding them-selves back in uniform, in a strange country, not subject to the authority of the RIC officers, having to fear no

285

military discipline or to worry about a pension, and as much drink as they could lower by merely cocking a gun – well, what else would you expect them to do but run amok? Colonel Windsor had no doubt that was what they had been sent over for in the first place.

And the IRA had been on to them from the start. The very first item in the Colonel's file was a copy of the proclamation that had been posted all over the south of Ireland only five days after the Black and Tans had landed.

> Whereas the spies and traitors known as the Royal Irish Constabulary are holding this country for the enemy, and whereas said spies and bloodhounds are conspiring with the enemy to bomb and bayonet and otherwise outrage a peaceful, law-abiding and liberty-loving people:
>
> Wherefore we do hereby proclaim and suppress such spies and traitors and do hereby solemnly warn prospective recruits that they join the RIC at their peril. All nations are agreed as to the fate of traitors. It has the sanction of God and man.
>
> By order of the GOC
> IRISH REPUBLICAN ARMY

Colonel Windsor always smiled at the phraseology of that notice, but there was no joke in its message. It had promised trouble and, by God, trouble was what followed – more and more, and worse and worse. Something new every day to add to the pile. The Colonel read the three reports of the previous night's incidents – a bomb outside the GPO; Shandon Street Hall, a Sinn Fein meeting-place, destroyed by fire; and the Pipers' Club boardroom in Hardwick Street burned down. That would mean goodness knows what mayhem tonight when the IRA was sure to seek revenge. It was all so monstrous, so useless, so misguided. And only the British Government could put an

286

end to it. Did they not realise what was happening? Did they not know? Of course they did. And if they didn't appreciate the stupidity of their policy they had to be made to see it before it was too late and the whole country blew up. But how? One was so helpless. How could a mere army colonel influence them – even one with his record and on-the-spot knowledge? If he told them, would they listen? Probably not. Yet wasn't it his duty to try? Perhaps a despatch to Greenwood, the Secretary for Ireland? Perhaps. . . .

Colonel Windsor closed the file, returned it to its drawer, and sat back. If he wrote to Greenwood, mightn't that be just the sort of rash unplanned action that a helpless soldier should avoid? He'd think about it some more. But not for long. Time, he felt certain, was running out.

Roddy Simcox drew the greatcoat around his shoulders and shivered. A brass monkey of a night without a doubt, definitely the coldest yet. How long would he have to endure caged in this icebox? Supposing it got colder, what then? It could do. He glanced at the date on that day's *Cork Examiner*: 25 November. Another month and it would be Christmas. Oh Christ! Surely he wouldn't be held that long. Surely he'd be free by then. Or dead, more likely.

'No, no, no, no, you stupid bugger,' he told himself. He wasn't to think like that. Here and now was all that existed, all that could exist for him. And here and now was bloody cold. That was all he was to worry about. If it did get any worse, he'd have to insist on being moved – or at least being provided with some heat. Insist? How could he insist?

'Now, look here, you chaps, a joke is a joke but this is going too far. No way to treat a British officer, you know. What are you trying to do – freeze me to death so as to save yourself a bullet? Another few nights like this and. . . .'

Suddenly realising he was letting his fears get the

better of him again, the Captain stopped talking to himself. He wasn't being funny enough to cheer himself up. And anyway it wasn't something to joke about – a man could easily catch pneumonia out of this. Why, look at Boxer! Even though he'd have had a warm bed to sleep in and plenty of heat throughout the day, the weather had still got him. The bold Boxer hadn't been at all himself that morning – nor had he been any better at midday. A streaming nose, bloodshot eyes, and his face had gone so pale that the scar on his cheek stood out like a livid streak. 'Poor bugger,' Roddy had commiserated, 'you're nothing to write home about'; but Boxer hadn't even the spirit to attempt a reply, and young Joe, standing at the door, gun in hand, had smiled wryly behind Boxer's back.

Captain Simcox shivered again. Even to catch a cold in his present situation would be hell. Supposing he did get ill, really ill? If he was bad enough, he might need medical attention and presumably his captors wouldn't want to go to such trouble. No doubt they'd have plenty of sympathetic doctors, of course, supporters of their cause. Even so, bringing a doctor could prove risky.

'Stop it!' Roddy shouted, crashing a fist down on the table in angry self-recrimination. He rose from his chair, determined to switch his mind to something else. But the only 'something else' was a letter to Elizabeth, and he groaned aloud at the difficulty that presented. What had *he* to write home about? Sweet Fanny Adams! A great big nothing. It was sheer mental torture trying to find things to say time after time when absolutely nothing was happening. How the hell could he be light-hearted and gay – and hopeful – when he was almost two weeks in captivity and no wiser now about his fate than the first moment he had been taken prisoner?

He stared malevolently at the table on which was spread every piece of news he had torn out of that morning's paper, every story that by any stretch of the imagination he could use in his letter. What rubbish! How could Elizabeth possibly be interested in any of that? She'd be thinking only of one thing, worried sick about it

288

probably – his safety – and no amount of chit-chat was going to make her feel any better, or give her any hope, or fool her into imagining that he wasn't worried sick about it, too.

Suddenly he scooped up all the cuttings, rolled them into a ball and flung them violently at the door. His chest heaved with frustration. But the flash of anger passed in a second. 'Silly bastard!' he muttered. What had he to complain about compared with Elizabeth? If she could suffer all that she must be suffering and still write him letters full of encouragement and love, then the least *he* could do was to sit tight and not lose his head. He was a soldier, a British officer.

He pulled himself to attention, clicked his heels, saluted, and loudly recited: 'You are Captain Rodney Willoughby Simcox, 16th Infantry Division, stationed in Cork. You have seen service in the trenches, you have been under fire, you have had to live on your nerves for long periods. This is just another nerve-test. Imagine you're a prisoner-of-war in Germany.' He paused a moment, then continued: 'No, don't imagine that. You're not a prisoner-of-war in Germany. A prisoner-of-war in Germany would be in a camp, with other prisoners, and probably better living conditions. This is Ireland, 1920, and you're being held by the IRA, not by the Hun. Keep calm. Keep alert. Don't crack. You're a trained soldier....'

His voice trailed off as he heard footsteps approaching. That would be Boxer and Joe with his supper. Thank goodness! Someone to see, perhaps have a chat with, something to do, something to take his mind off himself. With a sigh he relaxed back onto his chair.

To his surprise it was Joe who entered, and no Boxer. He had the supper-tray in one hand and his gun in the other. Kicking the door shut behind him, he put the tray on the table.

'Boxer has the flu,' he announced in a tone that almost suggested some satisfaction at Boxer's misfortune.

'I might have expected it,' Roddy replied. 'He looked properly washed out today. Has he gone to bed?'

289

'Had to. He couldn't stand up. Shiverin' like a leaf he was.'

Joe backed a few paces from the table so as to slip a bag from off his shoulder onto the floor while still keeping his prisoner covered with his gun. Roddy guessed that Boxer would have warned him to take no chances.

'So you have to act nursemaid to Boxer, eh, Joe?' Roddy asked.

'Nursemaid be damned,' Joe replied tersely, but without rancour. 'Until Boxer is back on his feet, I'm boss.' A small smile of embarrassed pride at his new authority flitted over his face, and Captain Simcox observed him sharply. The hand holding the gun was steady, the voice was normal, there was absolutely no sign of nervousness. That suited Roddy – a nervous man would be difficult to handle. He'd much prefer to deal with a self-confident Joe – self-confidence, especially when it wasn't based on experience and maturity, could easily turn into overconfidence. And Joe was only a youngster; he couldn't possibly have any maturity, and Roddy doubted that he had any experience, either.

Joe lifted a bundle from the bag and held it out.

'Another blanket!' Roddy exclaimed. 'I could do with that.'

'Well, it's the coldest night yet, so you'll need it. Careful,' he warned as Roddy took the bundle, 'there's a bottle of "Paddy" inside it.'

That was even more unexpected. The fresh bottle Boxer had brought that morning was still on the table and still a quarter full. Roddy had grown expert at regulating his intake to his supply. But another bottle was more than welcome – especially with the temperature so freezing.

'That's jolly decent of Boxer. You must thank him for me. Unless', he added, a thought occurring to him, 'this is tomorrow's bottle I'm getting.'

'Indeed an' it's not,' Joe declared, somewhat hurt by the Captain's suggestion. 'And it's not from Boxer, either. It's from me. Boxer knows nothin' about it.'

'From you? Oh, of course, I see. You're in command while Boxer is *hors de combat*.'

Roddy put the bottle on the table and took up the opened one and his empty glass. His mind was racing. Careful now, easy – every move, every word was vital. The slightest miscalculation and whatever opportunity the new development offered could be squandered.

He poured some whiskey into the glass and turned to Joe, who was standing, gun in hand, a self-satisfied smile on his face.

'You must let me drink your health, Joe. If I have to be a prisoner, at least it's a consolation to have someone as thoughtful as yourself guarding me. Not that Boxer hasn't been kind. But he's a bit strict, isn't he? A bit of a stickler for the rules.' And then, as if the idea had suddenly come to him, he held the glass out and said: 'Here, why don't you have a drink with me? There's plenty, now that you've brought me a new bottle.'

Joe's eyes flickered momentarily, but he shook his head. 'Oh, no, I couldn't.'

'You do take a drink, don't you? You're not a teetotaller? You're not wearing a badge anyway. I've seen a lot of Irishmen wearing it. What's that it is?'

'You mean a Pioneer pin. Total abstinence. No, I'm not one of them. Sure there's no harm in a drop now and again.'

'My sentiments exactly, Joe,' Roddy assured him. 'So will you change your mind and join me?'

'No, thanks, I'd better not,' Joe answered. 'I'm on duty, you know.'

Captain Simcox thought he detected a change in Joe's tone, a hint of regret, perhaps, at having to resist temptation. He guessed that going through Joe's mind must be the echo of Boxer's orders; with luck that echo would be struggling with Joe's desire to exert his new-found authority and show he wasn't under Boxer's thumb. Roddy would have to bank on that.

'As you wish, Joe, as you wish. I just thought that as you're the boss now you could make your own rules.... And, as you said yourself, a drop now and again never did anyone any harm.'

Roddy paused, the glass halfway to his lips. Joe said nothing.

'Are you sure, old man? There's still some left in this,' Roddy added lightly, taking up the not yet empty bottle from the table and again offering his glass to Joe. 'You're hardly likely to get drunk on this little tot. I can pour some for myself in my cup. It'd be a pleasure for me to have someone to drink with after drinking alone for so long. And with Boxer in bed with the flu *you* won't have any company when you go back.'

He held his breath, praying he had measured his man correctly. Joe was eyeing the glass now almost under his nose. Suddenly he ran his tongue over his lips.

'Sure it's a cold oul' night out. A drop would warm me up,' he allowed.

'Good man,' Roddy encouraged, topping up the measure.

Joe took a step forward and stretched out his hand. Roddy tightened his grip on the nearly empty whiskey bottle and his innocent smile lasted just until Joe's fingers were almost on the glass. Then with a lightning thrust he dashed its contents into his face and swept the bottle down in a savage blow on the hand holding the gun.

'Jesus!' Joe shrieked.

Gun and pieces of shattered glass went flying as Joe involuntarily brought his hands up to his drenched and smarting eyes, oblivious of the blood spurting from his knuckles. Roddy flung himself on the gun, and before Joe realised what was happening the weapon had been turned on him and he was being pushed back into the chair.

'Blast yeh,' he gasped. 'I thought you could be trusted.'

'In war, Joe, it's every man for himself. Never trust anyone if you want to survive.'

Swiftly Roddy stepped behind the chair and dealt Joe a crushing blow with the gun on the back of the skull. With only a grunt, almost as of a man turning over in sleep, Joe's head slumped forward onto his chest.

'Sorry, young lad,' Captain Simcox murmured as he feverishly buttoned his coat and slipped the fresh bottle of whiskey into one of its deep pockets. 'I might need that,'

292

he muttered to himself. He dropped the gun into the other pocket, grabbed a few sandwiches from his supper-tray and cautiously opened the door. The adjoining farmhouse was bathed in moonlight, and there was no sign of any movement. He locked the door, flung the key as far from him as he could, and sidled along the wall, away from the farmhouse. Then, crouching low, he ran to the boundary fence, turning only to look back at the shed from which he had just escaped. There was still no sound from it.

The air was freezing, but Roddy was too excited to feel its cold. On the other side of the fence empty fields fell steeply down into the darkness. Out there was freedom, but he'd have to get as far away as possible, and quickly, quickly. He climbed over the fence, the bottle of whiskey slapping against one thigh as he threw his legs over, the gun slapping against the other. At least he had food and drink and a weapon, so he'd be able to keep going for quite a while and defend himself if necessary. All he had to do was find a main road, hide in a ditch until dawn, and wait for some transport to come along – any sort of transport, perhaps even a police or army patrol if he was lucky.

He jumped off the fence and started to run.

21

JUDITH AWOKE, wondering what time it was. Drowsily she moved her legs until they made contact with the stone hot-water bottle. Still warm, so there was quite a while to go yet before morning.

She turned in the bed, not quite settling back into sleep. Some thought at the bottom of her mind was struggling to push its way into her consciousness, some idea which, though she couldn't quite pin it down, gave her a feeling more blissful than the prospect of further sleep, more gladdening even than the realisation that when she woke up again it would be Friday – her favourite day. She snuggled into the blankets, hugging them closer to her, and suddenly what her mind had been trying to grasp formed itself into an image and a name that sent a quiver of ecstasy through her. Denis! Of course, Denis!

Since Wednesday night she had been unable to think of anything else but the joy of his body with hers. The terror of the bomb explosion and the ordeal of their escape from the Black and Tans might never have taken place, so completely had they been subsumed into the passion of what had followed.

She didn't want to sleep now; she just wanted to lie and dream about Denis. She would be seeing him again on Sunday. Before they parted on Wednesday he had wanted them to meet again the very next night, but she had put him off. She didn't know why she hadn't agreed – she couldn't have given him any reason, she had acted merely on impulse. But now she was glad – she saw that the break would help her regain her composure. Her composure? No, her control. It would be madness to let their affair get out of hand; she knew the dangers – they must never be lost sight of – and perhaps, without realising it at the time, that had been the reason for her reluctance. What had grown between her and Denis had been so swift, so overwhelming. She needed a few days to catch her breath.

And to savour it all.

She turned over once more in the bed, drew up the hot-water bottle until it was cradled against her thighs, and began to float back into sleep, in her reverie repeating the magical litany: 'Friday – then Shabbos – and then Denis again.'

A few doors further along Celtic Crescent Miriam Levy also lay in bed and dreamed between waking and sleeping. Her wedding dress was finished and hanging in the wardrobe. It fitted her perfectly – Mrs Burns was a jewel of a dressmaker – not a single alteration would be needed. Little more than a week and she would be married – Mrs Jackson – a new life – a husband – a man to live with and lie beside. She was excited, happy, and nervous, too....

Zvi Lipsky was more than nervous; he was almost sick with worry thinking about what Wine had told him. He couldn't go to bed; there was no point in tossing and turning beside Myra and having her kick at him every time he disturbed her. She'd be asleep by now – it was hours since she had last knocked on the floor to summon him. But he'd have to go up sometime; he couldn't sit there until morning, hunched before an almost dead fire. It was a freezing night, and the room was fast losing its heat.

Zvi yawned, and the yawn made tears of aggravation and self-pity spill down his cheeks. What could he do? He was afraid to try to find out if what Wine had said was true. It must be true. Why else would he have said it? After all his years of work – a lifetime – was it now to be destroyed, go for nothing? But Wine had made him an offer that might save him. Should he accept it? '*Oi vey*,' he wept, '*oi vey!*' If only someone would tell him what to do. But there was no one, and Myra couldn't be made to realise that there was anything seriously worth worrying about.

He struggled up out of the chair, his head aching, his bones creaking, his eyes grimy with tiredness. He felt too old for such a problem. If only he could get some sleep, at least that would be a little relief.

Slowly, almost painfully, he hobbled up the stairs, pausing to look out the landing window as if somewhere in the broad heavens the answer lay. God was out there – he believed that. But he couldn't see God, he couldn't talk to Him, he couldn't expect God to tell him what to do. All he could see was the darkness, the cold glow of the stars, and frost already riming the window.

Miles away, in the countryside around the city of Cork, the same stars that had given Zvi Lipsky no comfort sparkled from every corner of a cloudless sky and the moonlight lay like silver over field, track and tree. Families were abed, animals in their barns or lairs, birds in their nests – nothing could be seen to move except a single horse clip-clopping steadily along a narrow hedge-lined road, pulling a trap that carried a bulky triangular-shaped object from the middle of which the reins dangled loosely. The object was Abie Klugman, completely enveloped in a blanket held tightly under his chin like a nun's cowl and exposing only his two moist eyes, his roly-poly nose and the red balloons of his cheeks. But the tears in his eyes were not caused by the cold air. They were tears of joy, which every now and again he brushed away while his glowing cheeks puffed into smiles of delight and wonder at his good fortune. Abie Klugman was finished with being a *viklehnik*; he was leaving his weekly country round for the very last time.

He had made his final calls, as he did every week, in the town of Bandon, and now he was going home. No, not home – that was before, in the past; Bandon to Cork was the last road home then. Not any longer, though. Now Bandon to Cork was the first road home to *Eretz*. Abie Klugman threw off the blanket, stood up, and with arms raised to the sky drummed his feet in a wild dance on the floor of the cart. The cart bucked and swayed, making the horse toss its head and momentarily lose its rhythm as the shafts jerked against its sides, until Abie collapsed back onto his seat. Chuckling and gurgling to himself like a baby being tickled, he gathered up the blanket and draped it once more over him.

All the customers on his list had received Abie's going-away present. He had held every weekly-payment book under its owner's nose as he slowly wrote the date on a fresh line, followed by a heavy unmistakable tick in blue pencil to show that the payment due had been made. Then he had taken a fistful of coins from his pocket, extracted the amount of the particular customer's regular payment and before their very eyes deposited the coins in the black purse they were familiar with. On the preceding Sunday he had carefully calculated how much he would require; he had collected all his savings from the tin box locked in his bedside cupboard and had slowly moved a podgy finger from name to name in his tally-book, each time putting aside the necessary amount. What was left of his money would still be more than sufficient to pay for the rest of his needs in Cork, and this he returned to its box to be locked securely back in the cupboard.

As the cart approached the outskirts of the village of Ballinhassig, Abie pulled a fob-watch from a waistcoat pocket. He peered at it closely before striking a match to confirm his reading of the time. Not yet four o'clock. Some hours to go to dawn. Any other week he would have halted at that point to let his horse rest and have some food himself. But this week he wanted to get on, get back to Cork, to Shabbos, to the beginning of his fortnight's holiday, to the beginning of his journey to *Eretz*. He pulled on the reins a little to slow the horse to a walk – *he* might be in a hurry, but the animal wasn't going to *Eretz* and it was entitled to some relief; at dawn he would feed it. He felt around the floor of the trap and found the apple one of his customers, Mrs McCarthy, had given him for the journey. As he bit into it, recollections of his last farewells warmed his thoughts.

'A real Christian,' Mrs McCarthy had called him. But he wouldn't tell anyone about that. If he did, it would be bound to get back to Mickey Aronson's ears and he would make a big joke of it and laugh at him; and even though Abie had only two more weeks of his fellow-lodger to endure he didn't want them to be spoilt by any more than the normal aggravation.

He let out a bellow of laughter and slapped his fat thigh. 'A real Christian' – Abie Klugman a Christian! Well, it was a Christian country, a Christian world. How different it would be in Palestine, the Land of Israel. A Jewish world! He looked up at the star-studded sky. It was the same sky that now, at this very moment, stretched thousands of miles over *Eretz*. He was here, *Eretz* was there, the same sky was above them both. Soon he would be no longer here, but in *Eretz*, yet still under the same sky. The thought overwhelmed him and he lay back in the trap, full length, hands crossed under his head to ponder the enormity of its miracle.

Eretz – what would it be like? The question defeated his imagination. Berel Karlinsky had told them the *kibbutzim* were often in the desert or on stony soil. He pictured sand and rocks – Youghal or Crosshaven, which he had often visited on his rounds, had sand and rocks. Was that what *Eretz* would be like? No, that was not the kind of sand Mr Karlinsky had meant. Youghal and Crosshaven were seaside places; the sand there was called a beach. Still, sand was sand. How could things grow in sand? How could houses be built on sand? That was something he would learn, something he would soon see for himself.

Abie sat up and took the reins again to urge his horse back into a trot. As he did so, he saw a figure some yards ahead climb over the low roadside wall and run out into his path. In the darkness he could not be sure, but it seemed to be wearing a uniform. A policeman? A soldier? He stiffened in his seat. This was real, it wasn't his imagination. The figure was waving its arms over its head. It wanted him to stop. The Tsar's guards! They had found him. At last they had tracked him down. They had come to take him back. He would not go. Not now. Not when his new life, his new world, his *Eretz* was waiting for him, beckoning him to its bosom. Abie saw it all swim before his eyes – not sand but lush green fields with neat houses and palm-trees, not rocks but soft silent seas with warm currents and abundant fish, not guards and police-men, but men, women and children with sunburned skins and loose robes – and all Yiddin, all his own Jewish brothers and sisters, his family. He had suffered, worked and waited for this miracle. It had been promised to him. It was his reward. He would not lose it now. No one was going to take it from him – no guards, no soldiers, no policemen, no ruler, no king, no tsar.

As the trap drew nearer, the figure still waved its arms wildly.

'Halt!'

The shout was clear, real and sharp. Abie heard it. There was no doubt. It was not in his imagination.

He bent and felt for his old rifle under the seat. Dropping the reins, he threw the sacking off the weapon and awkwardly raised it to his shoulder.

A shot rang out.

The horse neighed in fright and reared up, throwing Abie back into the well of the trap as the rifle flew from his grasp. The man in the roadway rushed forward, grabbed the horse's head and quickly calmed it. Then, gun still in hand and ready to fire again, he went and peered into the trap.

One look was all Captain Simcox needed. He had seen enough corpses on the Western Front to know at a glance that the man in the trap had gone to his reward.

22

THE FUNERAL of Abie Klugman took place on Sunday. A few miles into the countryside beyond the walls of the old city, the Jewish burial-ground was a hilly plot with good drainage but no shelter from the frequent rain-bearing Atlantic winds. Intermittent showers had harassed the cortège as it faced away from Celtic Crescent towards its bleak destination, and the little knot of Christian neighbours who had gathered from the surrounding streets to accompany the coffin for a short distance clung together under shared umbrellas. Mrs Bürns was not among them – she, and Father McGiff, too, would do no less than be present at the graveside itself and they now sat together in one of the horse-drawn carriages, consoling as best they could a still numb Ada Neumann and a wet-eyed, strangely silent Mickey Aronson.

The news of Abie's death had spread quickly among the Jewish community on the Sabbath eve. The travellers returning from their country 'weeklies' had come home light-hearted at the prospect of a rest from their labours and eager once more to embrace their families and greet 'the bride of the Sabbath', but the world they found froze the blood in their veins. 'It's not true!' they said. '*Sversach?* Do you swear it?' And on being promised that it *was* true all they could utter was 'Abie Klugman dead! When?

What happened?' There were rumours – he had been ambushed and had tried to escape, the Black and Tans had shot him – accounts so wild, so incredible, as to make many refuse to have any truck at all even with the report that he was dead. So Abie had not come home early for Shabbos as he always did? So he had been delayed. His horse had got sick. At worst he had had an accident and been taken to hospital. But when in the afternoon Max Klein arrived at Celtic Crescent from the city morgue, having been summoned there by the police to identify the body, and when not ten minutes later a hearse appeared and Ada Neumann's back room was hastily made ready to receive Abie's remains, those who had doubted and hoped at last accepted the truth; and, accepting, the more devout of them recited the blessing on hearing bad news: 'Blessed art Thou, O Lord our God, King of the Universe, the True Judge.'

The men of the Burial Society came to wash the body and dress it. Zvi Lipsky hurried there to place on the mantelpiece the framed message of consolation that was always displayed in a house of death: 'May God comfort you among all the other mourners of Zion and Jerusalem.' Then he nervously rushed around, arranging for watchers to sit with Abie. He had to find one for Friday night, somebody to relieve that one at dawn, and others to sit through Saturday and Saturday night, for no burial could take place on the Sabbath. His task was made easier by Mickey Aronson, who declared that he would sit through both nights. Lipsky was doubtful – two nights was too much for the same person – but Mickey quietly insisted; and when Ada Neumann put a hand on Zvi's arm and said, '*Luz em*, Mr Lipsky, let him. It's what he wants,' he did not argue. Then the mirrors in the house were covered, the curtains drawn, and a tall candle was lit beside Abie's head. With these preparations completed, Mickey Aronson took his seat on one of the hard low stools that had been provided for the mourners and those who would call to pay their respects. In his crouched posture and with his hands still trembling with shock he seemed like a small wounded animal, unable to tear his

301

eyes away from the body of the man who for so long had
endured his jokes and gibes, and who was now beyond his
pity, beyond his regret – beyond even his love.

On Saturday the *Examiner* reported Abie's death in a
brief news item, describing it as 'a tragic accident' and
Abie as 'a respected member of the local Jewish community and the first of that little band to fall victim in the
present unrest'. What was in the hearts of the community
Rabbi Cohen gave voice to at the Sabbath-morning
service, in an oration which would have been delivered at
the graveside were it not that as a descendant of the
Kohanim, the priestly sect that had ministered in the
Temple, he was not allowed to approach a dead body.

The synagogue was packed for the tribute, and they
heard Rabbi Cohen speak of Abie's goodness, his humil-
ity, his holiness. 'No one,' he said, 'could be more
innocent of sin in God's eyes, for he honoured God's word
and in the Almighty all his trust rested.' He reminded
them of Abie's determination to go to *Eretz Yisroel*; how
he believed – as they knew – that *Eretz* would be his
haven, his protection, the only place in the world he could
feel safe and at home. He also reminded them – and this
they also knew – how much this dream had meant to him,
though they might not have realised the depth of Abie's
fears that it was a dream which at the last moment would
not come true and that for the second time in his life his
world would be destroyed and his hopes mocked. 'I know
what *Eretz* meant to Mr Klugman,' he said. 'I saw with my
own eyes, I heard with my own ears, how strong these
fears were the last time I spoke with him' – and Rabbi
Moishe started to tell the congregation of Abie's visit to
him the previous Sunday and his dread that it would be
decided there was no place for someone like him in *Eretz
Yisroel*. And here the Rabbi faltered.

The people looked at each other in puzzled surprise as
Rabbi Cohen seemed to lose the thread of what he had
been saying, and when his sudden silence continued for
much longer than the space of a normal pause a whisper of
alarm swept through them. Max Klein, from his seat in
front of the minister's central platform, half got to his

302

feet, thinking that the Rabbi was perhaps having a bad turn and upbraiding himself for not insisting that a glass of water should always be by Rabbi Moishe's hand whenever he was addressing the congregation – a man of his age, every comfort should be provided, every precaution taken. Then, quietly, the Rabbi resumed – so quietly, indeed, that at the back of the synagogue they had to strain to hear him, but his listeners felt able to relax again, satisfied that there was nothing the matter with their beloved Rabbi and that he had only been momentarily overcome by the emotion of the occasion.

At the funeral on Sunday, as soon as the coffin had been placed in the hearse Ada Neumann poured some water over the flagstones outside her front door to prevent Abie's soul from being trapped in her home – for it was known that spirits could not pass over water – and then Rabbi Cohen sat in the President's new Ford with the other officers of the community. It was the only motor-car in the cortège – ahead of it was the hearse drawn by a pair of black horses and behind it some half-dozen funeral carriages – and the noise of its engine was all but drowned by the commotion of the horses' harness and the rattle of their hoofs on the hard road. As they passed through the city streets people stopped to raise their hats and make the sign of the cross, and some reversed their steps to observe the custom of walking a short distance alongside the coffin. There were those, too, who, recognising it as a Jewish funeral, turned to inform other onlookers that 'It must be the Jewman who was killed the other day. Didn't you read about it in the paper?' – and they shook their heads as if in disbelief that the country's troubles could claim such an innocent and uninvolved victim.

Once the cortège reached the outskirts of the city the horses were allowed to go a little faster so that the last few miles to the burial-ground were soon covered. Max Klein welcomed the increased pace – the atmosphere in the car was too sombre for him, and the presence of the Rabbi among his passengers discouraged all but much-repeated comments deploring the tragedy that had taken place.

After prayers had been recited in the small prayer-house just inside the cemetery gates, Abie Klugman's coffin was carried out to the grave that had been made ready to receive it. The mourners were relieved that the shower of rain they had heard drumming on the corrugated-iron roof while they were praying had passed, for it was cold enough and windy enough out on the open slopes without having to bear with rain as well.

Rabbi Cohen, his son Joshua, and Joshua's son Jacob stood apart, some distance away from the graveside, along with the handful of others who traced their descent from the priestly sect of *Kohanim*. The wind, veering from point to point, whipped around them, sometimes carrying clearly to their ears Rev. Levitt's voice as it intoned the graveside prayers, at other times scooping his words away so that they seemed to be coming from one or other of the distant fields.

Prayers over, everyone at the graveside took his turn to cast three shovelfuls of clay down onto the coffin, the regular thuds of the earth sounding like the beats of a muffled drum. When the last mourner had plunged the shovel back into the bank of clay, the gravediggers took over and the congregation turned away from the rush of noise as the grave was rapidly filled. Rabbi Cohen and his family, followed by most of the others, started to return to the prayer-house, bending their heads into the rising wind that roughly pushed them back, as if in protest at their abandoning Abie Klugman almost before he could have had time to settle into his last resting-place. But some of the mourners – those who had kith and kin buried nearby – looked around first to get their bearings, and then struck out towards the plots where their own loved ones lay.

Sam Spiro's wife was buried in a far corner, and as he made his way in that direction he glanced from side to side to read the inscriptions on some of the tombstones, pausing whenever he came on a name that kindled special memories. Much as the bond he still felt for his beloved Rachel forced him on, he did not hurry, a feeling of guilt that his departure to *Eretz* would leave her to lie there alone for ever making him drag his steps. For weeks he had planned – he had promised himself and in promising himself had promised her, too – that he would make a special journey to the cemetery at the last moment to explain and to say goodbye. It was to be his final act before leaving Cork. But he knew now that he could not face a second pilgrimage. By the time he reached his wife's grave the whole agony of his dilemma had become too much for him and he stood numbly, the people waiting in the prayer-house forgotten, the pitiless weather unheeded. Through brimming eyes he saw the words on the tombstone he had put at her head a year after she had been buried, when his period of deep mourning was supposed to have been over. But, though the religious sanctions that had bound him to almost a hermit's existence throughout that period had fallen away, his mourning had not ended, would not end.

'Rachel Spiro, 1870–1913,' the stone read. He needed no reminding. They had married in Cork when she was twenty, he twenty-five. Twenty-three years of love and companionship, the absence of children their only misfortune; and that misfortune, being shared, was lightened. Then, when they had quite given up hope, Rachel had become pregnant – only to lose the baby within a few months. From that moment on she had begun to slip away from him into a depression that became an illness that became a disease. No doctor could cure her, no amount of love or comfort that Sammy could give her did anything to arrest her decline. She knew she would not conceive again and, while childlessness before had drawn them together, now Rachel looked on it as her offence alone, one for which there could be no forgiveness.

As Sam Spiro stood by his wife's grave the wind stung his eyes, drawing from them the tears of grief he had been striving to restrain. His heart spoke to the beauty he saw under the dumb earth, asking it why it had gone, telling it that it need not have left him – that he had accepted their childlessness as God's will, that once he had her he had all. Now he had nothing. His lips kept forming his wife's name, but the words tumbling through his mind counted out the miseries of his loneliness without her, a loneliness

305

that had eaten into his soul, warping the person he had been. He was not an old man – not yet – only fifty-five, but he felt he had already entered death's anteroom, for with Rachel gone all point and purpose had departed his life. Except that his body still woke and slept and pained and became weary – always so weary; and his longings and memories gave his mind no rest at all. If he stayed in Cork, how long more before he joined his wife under the earth? If he went to *Eretz*. . . .

'I have not forgotten you, *Rucheleh, meine liebe*. You have been with me every moment since . . . since. . . . And you will still be with me – even in *Eretz*. No matter what happens to me there – no matter who I meet. *Rucheleh, Rucheleh*, why did you die, why did you leave me alone?'

He stumbled away. What was he doing talking to a seven-year-old grave? His wife was not there. Only dead bones were there. He shuddered. He was right to go to *Eretz*, for there Rachel would still be in his heart, a part of him he could never lose, never want to lose, no matter what, for ever.

He rejoined the other mourners, some still in the prayer-house, others already in their carriages, and now one less they quickly began their journey back to the city.

The funeral over, Bertha Cohen was glad to regain the warmth of her home, and once she had the lamps lit and the fire in the range blazing again she didn't give a care for the early darkness and the rattle of the wintry showers on the windows. Usually a visit to the cemetery would leave her silent and subdued until at least the next morning, but this time it had little effect on her, for was she not still feeling restored by the return of her husband's good humour? Wednesday it was that the change had suddenly come over Joshua. She noticed it immediately he came home for dinner. His step had been lighter, his look clearer, and for the first time in a few weeks as he opened the front door he called out from the hallway, '*Nu?*' She had been upstairs when she heard his voice, and at that word she had given a start of delight. '*Nu*' – so meaningless, really only a sound, a gesture, yet used by Jews all over the world to convey almost any emotion, and for Bertha it stirred the well of memory.

In the early years of their marriage it had been Joshua's habitual greeting when he returned home from the 'weekly' that was his living in those days, its message to Bertha being that her man was back safely, and the way he said it telling of his need. When she heard him say it again on Wednesday she knew that whatever worry had been on his mind had been resolved; it was gone and forgotten. There were still other anxieties, of course, but they were not as grave. Abie Klugman's death, for instance. That had shocked him – as it had shocked her – it had cast the dark shadow of God's hand over them all; but that was over now, Abie had been laid to rest and they could take up their lives again. Jacob? Yes, her son was still a problem – he seemed to have become morose and sullen, more silent than ever. What was it with him? Whatever it might be, it couldn't possibly be serious; he would grow out of it, he would settle down. And the Rabbi? People had asked her what happened to him in *Shool* when he had been talking about Abie. Why had he suddenly stopped? And for so long. Had she noticed? Of course she had noticed. Everyone had, why not she? But did she know the reason? Could she explain it? What was there to explain? Remember, Abie Klugman was to go to *Eretz* with the Rabbi, so why should anyone be surprised that the death, such a terrible death, of one of his followers even before they could leave Cork should overcome him for a moment? What else could it be?

No, it could be nothing else, Bertha Cohen assured herself. Everything would be all right. In a fortnight, yes, this day two weeks, the Rabbi would be on his way to *Eretz*, on his way to the realisation of his life's dream; soon, too, they would surely have news of Malka and her baby, good news, God willing, great news. So what was there to worry about? Judith? *Ach*, she'd find a husband some day. Why not? If only she wasn't so choosy.... But she'd see sense in time. Meanwhile they were all together, safe, secure, comfortable – God was good. She'd make some tea; it would take the graveyard cold out of their bones.

'Judith, you'll take a cup up to your *zeide*. And a *bissle* sponge cake. He'll want something warm.'

As Judith placed the tea-tray on his bedside table, the Rabbi looked up at her from his chair, his face serious, his glance distracted, almost apprehensive. 'I have something to say to you, *mein kinde. Zech sich anider*. Sit with me a while.'

Judith's heart jolted with fear. What could her *zeide* want with her? Surely he couldn't possibly know about Denis. All the weekend she had been worried about not being able to keep her appointment with him that afternoon, but there was simply no way she could send him a message. She kept telling herself that he was bound to have read of Mr Klugman's death and so would probably have guessed she had to go to the funeral, but there was still the problem of how to contact him to arrange another meeting. She had to see him again – she could think of nothing else.

Anxiously she sat on the edge of the Rabbi's bed as he concentrated on the slice of lemon in his black tea, pressing a spoon into it again and again to release its juices. Supposing he *had* heard about Wednesday night and her visit with Denis to Fanny Rubin? Fanny wouldn't have said anything, but she might have told her husband and perhaps he. . . . Judith tried to calm her nerves, to look composed. To her the Rabbi seemed to be waiting a long time before speaking, as if trying to find the right words for what he had to say.

'What is it, *zeide*?' she asked, now fearing the worst.

Rabbi Moishe took a piece of lump sugar from his plate, put it in his mouth and sipped his tea until the sugar had melted. Then he replaced the cup and, turning to his grand-daughter, shrugged his shoulders. It seemed a gesture of weariness.

'One less, *mein kinde*,' he said.

'One less?' Judith echoed, utterly confounded.

'Mr Klugman. One less for *Eretz*.'

'Oh, yes ... yes.' Judith was as sorry for Abie Klugman as anyone was, but what was the point of dwelling on it? There was nothing more to be done. She wished her *zeide* would say what he had to say and not keep her in suspense. If it was that difficult for him, then almost certainly it was what she feared.

'You know he came to see me last Sunday?'

'Yes, I knew that. And you said so when you spoke about him in *Shool* yesterday.'

'I did, *mein kinde*, I did.' Rabbi Cohen paused and looked away. It reminded her of the hesitation everyone had noticed in the synagogue, and the stunned look was the same, too.

'He was so afraid that he would not be allowed to go to *Eretz* – that even at the last moment someone would say, "*Nein*, Mr Klugman, *Eretz* is not for you".'

'But that was silly. Who would stop him?'

'Nobody would stop him. He would have been as welcome in *Eretz* as any other Yid. Silly? Yes, but you know the kind of man Mr Klugman was....'

Judith nodded, still wondering what her *zeide* was leading up to. 'He was very nice, very good. A bit soft in the head, as the people here would say.'

'Yes, a bit *tzumist*,' the Rabbi echoed sympathetically, 'a bit mixed-up.'

'But he had already been accepted for *Eretz*, hadn't he? Didn't he know that?'

'Of course he knew it. But' – and the Rabbi shook his head – 'it made no difference. He was not convinced.'

'*Zeide*,' Judith interrupted, 'you've forgotten your tea. It'll be ice-cold.'

Rabbi Cohen broke off a piece of sponge cake but did not put it in his mouth. He stared at it, his fingers kneading it into golden crumbs, his head moving slowly, sorrowfully, from side to side.

'Do you mean he left you still believing he wasn't wanted in *Eretz*?'

'*Nein, mein kinde, nein*. He was a happy man when he left me. I convinced him in the end.'

'Oh, I'm so glad,' Judith smiled. 'How did you manage that?'

'I said to him,' Rabbi Cohen whispered, speaking almost into his beard, '"Mr Klugman," I said, "if *you* don't go, *I* don't go." That's how I convinced him.'

Rabbi Moishe pushed away his half-finished tea and uneaten cake in a gesture of resignation.

'So?' Judith queried.

'Don't you see, *mein kinde*? Mr Klugman is dead – he will not be going to *Eretz*. And I promised him' – the Rabbi passed a hand wearily across his forehead and then adjusted his *yarmulkah* – 'I made a promise ... a promise.'

'But he's dead, *zeide*. Abie Klugman is dead,' Judith protested. 'He can't go. It wasn't your fault. And a promise to a dead man – that sort of promise – you're not bound by it. Surely....'

Rabbi Moishe was shaking his head slowly from side to side, his eyes solemn as he reached out a hand to touch Judith's fingers.

'Never in my life have I broken a promise. Should I start now?'

'*Zeide*, is this what you wanted to tell me about?' Judith said, her hopes rising. 'Is this why you asked me to sit with you?' – and when she heard the Rabbi answer 'What else? Is it not important?' her heart leaped with relief and she was able to feel an almost maternal sympathy for her so conscientious, so pious grandfather.

'But, *zeide*,' she argued, 'what are you saying? Surely you're not thinking of changing your mind? You *have* to go to *Eretz*. It's what you have lived for, isn't it?'

Rabbi Moishe considered her words for what seemed to be a long time while Judith sat contentedly, still light-hearted at her own deliverance. At last he spoke.

'*Mein kinde*, I made a promise to Mr Klugman. *Nu*, Mr Klugman is dead. I do not want to change my mind, but a promise to man is a promise to God, too.' He spoke the last words pleadingly, as if begging for Judith's under-standing.

She stood up beside him and, placing her hands on

his shoulders, bent to lean her head against his.

He looked up into her eyes.

'If anything should happen to me....' His face hardened, and he pulled Judith around in front of him again. '*Zitz*,' he urged her.

She sat down. Rabbi Moishe leaned towards her.

'I want you to promise me something.'

'Of course,' Judith responded happily. 'Of course, *zeide*. Just tell me what.'

He wagged his head at her, a smile of gentle reprimand on his lips.

'You make a promise before you learn what it is you promise! *Ai, ai*, and I thought you were a sensible girl.'

Judith smiled back at him, and the Rabbi's face became serious once more. He took her hands and held them in his.

'I want you to promise that if anything happens to me *you* will go to *Eretz* in my place.'

'I!' Judith exclaimed. 'Go to *Eretz*!'

'Yes, you. Listen, *mein kinde*. Why do I want to go there? For myself?' He waved a hand in dismissal of the suggestion. 'I am old. How long more can I live? A few years perhaps. Yes, I would be happy to end my days in *Eretz*, but that is no longer so important. It is not for myself I go. You are listening?'

Judith nodded.

'*Eretz Yisroel*, the Land of Israel. The Promised Land, *mein kinde*, the Promised Land. Promised by God to our people. We have spoken of promises. They must be kept. So God will keep His promise – when we show him we are ready. And how will we show him? We must go there, to Palestine, how else? Not just in tens, not just in hundreds, but in thousands and tens of thousands. For too long our people have had no home of their own. Wherever we have lived, we have lived there on sufferance.'

'But we're not on sufferance here in Ireland,' Judith objected.

Rabbi Moishe raised an eyebrow.

'No, not here, not now. I hope never. But who knows? Look at the Irish – even in their own country they are on

311

sufferance, having to fight for what should be theirs. A time might come when the Jewish people will need a home of their own. Not tomorrow, not next year, but perhaps sooner than you think. Now is the time to ask the Almighty to fulfil His promise to our ancestors and to us and to our children. Before it is too late. That is why our little group *must* go from Cork to settle in *Eretz*. Already we have lost one. Without me—'

Judith tried to protest, but the Rabbi motioned her to be silent.

'The Almighty will find a way to help me keep my promise,' he insisted. 'But, if *I* don't go, who else might decide to drop out then? In the end would there be any left? So you, *mein kinde*, would have to take my place. If you go instead of me, then they will understand, and go, too. They will know it is my wish.'

Judith was overwhelmed by her *zeide*'s request. Her mind was in a turmoil at the idea.

'But what about Jacob?' she blurted out. 'He'd be much better.'

'A young boy? No, no!' Rabbi Cohen insisted. 'And he has a career to make yet. He will be a doctor. Maybe then he will go to *Eretz*. Especially if you are there. And if you go, and he goes, then perhaps your mother and father, too, no? Why not? By then you could be married there, with a family....'

Judith laughed.

'Married!'

'Of course. You will marry some day. Why not in *Eretz*? Is there a better place to find a husband?'

He paused a moment. Then 'Will you promise me, *mein kinde*? If I can't go, you will take my place?'

Judith looked at her grandfather. She could see how troubled he was, but really it was hard to take his request seriously. She knew she had to, of course – out of respect and love if for no other reason. Still, there was no harm in saying yes to him – after all, what could happen in such a short time? But what really worried her was that when nothing did happen might he refuse to go to *Eretz* just so as to keep a promise to a dead man?

'All right, *zeide*,' she said almost gaily. 'I'll promise – on one condition.'

'Condition? What condition?'

'On condition that, if nothing happens to you, you *will* go to *Eretz*.'

Rabbi Moishe pursed his lips and tugged at his beard, an unhappy look in his eyes.

'But I promised Mr—'

'Mr Klugman is dead,' Judith interrupted. 'Your promise to him meant only that if someone stopped him from going, then *you* wouldn't go – not if God stopped him. You weren't thinking of Mr Klugman dying when you made the promise, were you? So, if nothing happens to you, that will mean God isn't stopping you. It will be His way of telling you He wants you to go.'

The Rabbi tilted his head as if weighing Judith's words.

'And anyway', she added, 'you say that if anything happens to you, and I don't go instead of you, others might drop out. But what if nothing happens to you and you still don't go – how sure can you really be that they will understand? They may all stay at home. And could you blame them if they did!'

She almost laughed with pleasure at having bested her grandfather, for she saw by his eyes that her solution of his dilemma had given him hope again.

'*Ai, ai, ai*,' he sang, smacking one of Judith's hands between his palms. 'So you have some sense after all. Almost as much as your old *zeide*, eh?' Then he fell serious again. 'So, *mein kinde*, I agree to your condition. It is a promise – you to me and I to you.'

Judith stood up, elated at the outcome of their talk and especially that after all it had had nothing to do with Denis. She'd get in touch with him somehow and, though she might not be able to spend much time with him in the next few weeks, once her grandfather had left for Palestine the excitement would be over and they would be able to see much more of each other.

She bent and kissed her *zeide* on his forehead.

'Some more tea?' she asked.

'*Ga nug, mein kinde*,' he answered as he squeezed her

313

arm. 'No more tonight. I can sleep now. I'll lie down for a while.'

'Happy dreams,' she whispered, taking the tray and softly closing the door.

23

MAX KLEIN stiffened in surprise as the knocker on the front door beat out a sharp aggressive summons. Half-past seven on a grey Monday morning – who could want him at such an hour? And for what? It sounded serious. *Gott in himmel*, not more bad news!

The knocking was repeated, even more impatiently. Max Klein kissed the phylacteries he had just taken off after his morning prayers and tucked them neatly into their blue velvet bag with its gold-braided Star of David. Such noise! It would surely wake Myra and the boys. As he hurried from the kitchen, not waiting even to button his waistcoat or don his jacket, Myra was already calling to him from the top of the stairs. She was crouched down, her baggy nightdress hiding her body completely, ready to dart back to the bedroom if the caller was someone she wouldn't want to be seen by in such an unprepared state.

'Who is it, Max? Who's there?'

'Go back to bed!' His gravelly voice, rough with annoyance at the stupidity of the question, rasped back at her as the tattoo continued. Such a woman! Could he see through solid wood?

'All right, all right, I'm coming,' he shouted, rushing to answer the summons. On the doorstep was a soldier, but Max looked past him, his attention being immediately

315

caught by the army car, its lights piercing the morning darkness, drawn up on the roadside beside his own gleaming Ford. In the passenger seat a British officer sat stolidly, but seeing Max he alighted, regimental stick in hand, and strode smartly up the garden path.

'Mr Klein?' he enquired, his tone clipped and his accent sounding the name as 'Clayne'.

'I am Max Klein,' Max replied, emphasising the correct pronunciation, but the hint was ignored as the officer continued: 'You are the President of the Cork Hebrew Congregation?'

'Yes,' Max agreed, refraining from making a second correction – 'Cork Hebrew Congregation' was a title over which he had had many arguments with traditionalists and diehards who vociferously opposed his insistence on jettisoning it in favour of the much less pompous, more modern 'Cork Jewish Community'.

The officer gave a sharp nod and slapped his stick against his gloved palm, satisfied with the attainment of his first objective. He dismissed his adjutant, took up the monocle which hung from his collar, fixed it in his eye, and then introduced himself.

'I am Colonel Windsor, Colonel-in-Chief of the 16th Infantry Division. May I come in, Mr Clayne?'

'Yes. Yes, of course. Come in, Colonel.'

Puzzled, Max showed the Colonel into the front parlour, hastening to draw the curtains and open the shutters.

'Take a seat, Colonel,' he said as he lit the gas-mantle against the morning gloom. 'I'm afraid the room is a bit cold,' he added, casting an eye towards the empty fire-grate.

The Colonel sat down. As if to demonstrate his indifference to the temperature he pulled off his gloves, let the monocle drop out of his eye and took from his pocket a silver cigarette-case and a holder. Unhurriedly he went through a careful ritual of tapping a cigarette three times firmly on the case, then affixing it in the holder before lighting it. Smoke and speech issued simultaneously from his mouth.

'I've descended on you rather suddenly,' he said, flicking his stick at Max's arms, the left one of which had its shirtsleeve rolled up as far as it would go. It had been bared for the winding of one of the phylacteries seven times around the limb nearest the heart. 'Perhaps you'd like to finish dressing before we proceed to the business of my visit.'

'Yes,' Max agreed, taking advantage of the Colonel's offer to escape into the kitchen and put on his jacket. He threw a quick glance at the looking-glass over the mantelpiece, straightened his *yarmulkah* on his head and tightened the knot in his tie. Whatever Colonel Windsor had come about, it did not seem to be in any way threatening; the Colonel was quite civil. It might have been different if it had been the Black and Tans, or even the RIC – though Max was on good terms with the local inspector and would not expect any difficulty from that quarter. Business perhaps? Hardly. The colonel of the regiment wouldn't come himself on business – and certainly not to Max Klein's home at seven-thirty in the morning.

He buttoned his jacket and strode back into the parlour.

'Now, Colonel,' he announced, briskly rubbing his hands together in a show of confidence. 'I'm ready. What can I do for you?'

The Colonel had risen from his seat and was standing at the fireplace, examining through his monocle the array of photographs filling the whole length of the mantelshelf.

'You're quite a family man, Mr Clayne,' he said, turning to Max. 'Are *all* these your relatives?'

'Yes, all, mine and my wife's,' was the proud reply. 'They're scattered everywhere – Dublin, England, America, Russia....'

'Russia?' Colonel Windsor repeated in surprise.

Max took one of the photographs in his hand. It showed a sallow-featured middle-aged couple, with on each side of them three or four other men and women against a nondescript empty background. All had clearly dressed

317

up for the occasion and they stared unsmilingly into the camera.

'That's one of my wife's aunts and her husband and their family. They lived in a little village called Kursan, in Russia. We tried to get them out and bring them here, but....'

Max made a grimace that summed up the failure of his efforts. 'That was before the war; we haven't heard from them since then.'

'But this is obviously a studio photograph. Would there have been a professional photographer in a little Russian village?'

'No, not in Kursan. I sent them money to go to the nearest town and get this picture taken. Many of the Jewish families here did that with the relatives they left behind.'

'Strange,' the Colonel murmured, 'fascinating and strange.' Then, placing his stick and gloves neatly on the tasselled red velvet cloth that covered the dining-table, he turned and resumed his seat.

'My visit is an official one, Mr Clayne. Official, but – ah – man-to-man, so to speak. Which is why I've come to your residence at this hour to make sure of finding you in. I believe you people are accustomed to making an early start.'

Max nodded.

'It's about that unfortunate accident last Friday morning when one of your people was shot by one of my officers.'

'Abie Klugman, yes.'

'Ah, yes, Mr Klugman. A very sad business. You know how it happened, I take it?'

'Yes, the police gave me the details.'

'Quite. Most regrettable. But there really was no alternative for Captain Simcox. A fine officer, Simcox. It was dark at the time, of course, and Mr – ah – Klugman did raise his rifle to shoot at my officer. Self-defence on Simcox's part, y'know.'

Max Klein gave a small sympathetic laugh. 'Abie's rifle – people made fun of him about it, Colonel. It was from the time he was conscripted into the Russian army.'

318

'Indeed? I wondered where he got it.'

'He was only a youngster then. He deserted – the Tsar's army wasn't a pleasant place for Jewish conscripts – and he took the rifle with him for protection. It was the only thing he had when he escaped from Russia, and he always kept it with him in case the Russians followed him and tried to take him back. He wasn't all there of course, poor Abie, a bit soft in the head. Probably thought your officer was a Russian.'

Colonel Windsor shook his head. 'Ironic! It was too old, of course. The rifle. Rusted inside. It couldn't shoot.'

Max Klein sat down heavily.

'I didn't know that.'

'Yes, we examined it afterwards. Useless.'

'All for nothing,' Max lamented. 'So he lost his life for nothing.'

'Ah, yes, Mr Clayne, I'm afraid so. For nothing. Like so many lives being lost today, one might add.'

The Colonel rose smartly. He took his cigarette out of its holder and threw it into the fire-grate.

'I've come to offer my regiment's condolences, and my own of course, to – to your people. Mr Klugman, I understand, left no kin.'

Max Klein rose, too, impressed by the importance of the occasion and anxious to match authority with authority.

'Thank you, Colonel,' he said. 'I'll convey your condolences to my committee and to the community.'

'They do understand, I take it, that it was an accident, that no blame attaches to anyone. As an officer of His Majesty's Forces it is my duty to maintain good relations with all friendly sections of the population.'

'Of course, Colonel, of course,' Max Klein assured him. 'Of course it was an accident. A very sad accident – especially as Mr Klugman would have been gone in a few weeks.'

'Oh, was he planning to leave Cork?'

'Yes. He was due to go to Palestine.'

'Palestine?' the Colonel repeated in surprise, raising his eyebrows sharply so that the monocle fell and danced against his chest.

'There's a group emigrating to Palestine next Sunday week,' Max explained. 'Our Rabbi is leading them. About a dozen people.'

'But what do they expect to do in Palestine, Mr Clayne?'

'They'll set up a settlement, cultivate the land....'

'In Palestine? But it's all desert there surely.'

'Even deserts can be changed, Colonel. It was once a land flowing with milk and honey, you know.'

'Ah, yes, of course,' the Colonel smiled thinly. Then, as if recalling something long forgotten, he added: 'The Promised Land, you mean? And was Mr Klugman going to work on the land, be a farmer? How extraordinary!'

There was a moment's silence before he took up his stick and gloves.

'Well, then, Mr Clayne, you will convey to your people how much we regret what happened.'

Colonel Windsor shook hands and turned to leave.

'If there is anything I can do....'

Max's eyes suddenly lit up. 'There is, Colonel. There *is* something you can do.'

'There is?' Colonel Windsor was surprised.

'Yes. The group leaving on Sunday week – they'll be taking the noon train to Dublin and then crossing to England on Sunday night to board a boat for Marseilles. If they miss the connection, it would make things very difficult for them. So if Sunday's train should happen to be stopped by a strike....'

'You mean as a result of any military boarding it?'

'That's it, Colonel. Can you make sure that doesn't happen?'

Colonel Windsor nodded briskly. 'I can and I will, Mr Clayne. Rest assured on that. Glad to be of help. Noon train to Dublin, Sunday week?'

'December 12th.' Max was smiling broadly as he thought of the credit he could claim for his quickness of mind. 'Thank you, Colonel. Your help will be appreciated by the whole community.'

At the front door the two men shook hands again, and as the Colonel marched down the path towards his car, stick rammed under his armpit, Max saw his adjutant quickly douse a cigarette, come to attention and salute smartly. Colonel Windsor took his seat, and Max stood on his doorstep to watch the car until it was out of sight. Then, highly satisfied with himself, he shut his front door and was returning to the kitchen to have his breakfast when Myra's voice assailed him again from the landing.

'What did he want?' she called.

'Later, later,' Max grumbled. 'I'll tell you later.' His information was too weighty a story to be wasted in a rushed reply. He entered the kitchen, rubbing his hands, but the smile on his face froze when he suddenly realised that he had left his egg boiling on the range. It would be like a stone – just the way he hated it. *Ai, ai,* could a *mensh* think of everything?

24

FATHER MCGIFF sat at his desk, staring blankly into the dark window, seeing nothing but a dull glow. The glow was reflected from the low flame of the oil-lamp before him, which also threw him in monster silhouette onto the wall at his back. His figure in the chair seemed to be merely a projection of the shadow, a motionless captive held in its brooding embrace. There was no sound in the room, no sound from anywhere in the house, although Father McGiff knew that down in the kitchen his housekeeper, Mrs Roche, would be preparing his tea.

Food ... what use was food to him? What use was he making of the energy it gave him? He was like an engine shunting up and down the same siding, going nowhere, drawing no load, just puffing and blowing windily. Had he done anything that day, or the days before, or the weeks before, that could possibly be of any practical value to his people? Comfort he had given them, consolation, encouragement – incitement even. But what was all that except hollow words, blunted by repetition? Sure any man could say them. He felt so powerless, so ineffectual. Things were getting worse day by day and here he was, locked into his comfortable chair, spiritless and exhausted – from doing nothing. Even the most piffling of parish duties, along with anything important, he was leaving to his assistant, for he had less and less mind for work, less and less mind for anything but self-recrimination.

He gazed down at the pale fragile-looking hands resting on his black cassock. Here and there small brown stains mottled the skin. Yet he didn't feel old. Frustrated, depressed, angry, despairing. But not old. He wished those hands were able to hold more than just a prayer-book. What use was a man of God these days when the violence was reaching out to blight more and more families, more and more innocent people. Poor Mr Klugman! If ever there had been a devout, simple, inoffensive soul, it was Mr Klugman. Father McGiff had never exchanged a word with him, but he knew his type. Similarly afflicted mortals were not rare in the Irish countryside. He had often come across them, men and women who either from birth or as the result of a particularly shocking trauma at some later stage were only half in this world, the other half of their minds living in some secret twilit place of their own. *Duine le Dia* such a person was known as in Gaelic, literally 'a person with God', a holy person, one who has been touched by God's finger. That was Abie Klugman all right, and now the poor man was mouldering in the grave, a victim of the bestiality that had gripped the country.

Before Father McGiff had attended Abie's funeral on Sunday he had given his most impassioned sermon yet. Gone were any lingering doubts about the morality of a priest openly preaching violence. Turn the other cheek, yes, but in God's order there were some causes that had to be defended by force of arms if necessary. More exalted clerics than he – princes of the Church indeed – had publicly supported the IRA's struggle. If he, in the very thick of it, were to appear less than total in his commitment to their bravery and sacrifice, he would be failing his people – and himself. He had to make that clear to his parishioners. And that Sunday morning he had certainly made it clear. His previous sermons seemed to him now to have been merely preparations for his ultimate ringing message: 'It is every Irishman's bounden duty to play an active role in his country's fight for freedom. Anyone who holds back is no better than a traitor. The duty to take up arms is a sacred one and has God's blessing. Banish all fear. He who lays down his life for Ireland will find a reward both on earth and in heaven – for on earth he will have contributed to the freedom his countrymen are determined to win, and in heaven he will have a place on God's right hand.'

His words had had an exhilarating effect on himself as well as on his congregation. For a while their echo had coursed through his veins like strong drink, giving him a sense of achievement that rendered him light-headed. In his temporary euphoria it was as if each word had been a bullet in the heart of the enemy, and the exhortations he hurled from his pulpit the practical deeds his body had begun to crave.

But the feeling of feverish elation had been swept away like a puff of smoke before the winter wind when he approached Rabbi Cohen before Abie Klugman's funeral to express his sympathy. He had taken the Rabbi's hands, pressing them together in his own in silent communion, but he could feel no answering life in them, no effort to grip his own fingers in an understanding response. Rabbi Cohen murmured some words of thanks, but his blue eyes seemed unfocused, his manner absent. Only when the priest, anxious to leave his friend to his private mourning, said, 'I won't delay you, Rabbi. But I'll see you again before your departure,' did Rabbi Cohen seem to recollect himself.

'Yes, Father,' he replied, 'I hope so. But not next Sunday. Today we have a burial ... next Sunday we have a wedding....' And he shook his head as if the contrast and clash of two such events was too bizarre for him to absorb.

'Ah, isn't that life, Rabbi? The Lord giveth and the Lord taketh away....' He paused before adding: '... and then the Lord giveth again.'

'Amen,' had come from Rabbi Cohen's lips, quietly, submissively, and Father McGiff had heard in the whisper the holy man's age-old acknowledgement of the Inscrutable.

324

The encounter had served to bring the priest down to earth again, to remind him of the cloth he wore, of the collar round his neck. Since then he had had to fight the urge to regard the collar as a halter. Now he lifted his hands before his eyes and regarded them coldly. They would never hold a gun, never strike a blow for his country. They were hands that had raised the Host, had held the body and blood of Christ, had performed all these holy acts, part of the role he had chosen for himself. *He* had chosen? No, the Lord had chosen, the Lord had called him, his role was his vocation. His mind, his spirit, his body were all dedicated to the service of the Lord. There was no higher service. He must cease yearning for other involvement, other glories. The Rabbi had accepted God's will. 'Amen,' he had said. 'Amen,' Father McGiff repeated to himself, letting his hands fall back in acceptance of the bitter fact that there was no role for them in the people's struggle.

There was a sudden thunderous hammering on the front door, as if some poor soul's distress was so urgent that he thought kicking in the door rather than using the knocker would bring him swifter relief. Father McGiff was about to hurry down himself when he heard Mrs Roche bustling along the hall, her normally homely voice squeaking angrily at the impatient caller. As she opened the door, the priest heard his name shouted roughly, heavy boots banged up the stairs, the door of his study flew open and three Black and Tans burst into his room.

Father McGiff rose to his feet to protest at the uncouth invasion, but the leading Tan pushed him back into his chair. While another stood grinning at the door, the third one started to pick books at random from the wall-shelves and hurl them to the ground.

Father McGiff looked up at the figure towering above him. In the half-light of the room the black and tan uniform was one dark mass blotting out the outside world, and the menace of the rough unshaven face above it clutched icily at the priest's heart. A revolver prodded him hard in the chest, causing him to flinch with pain.

'McGiff,' the Tan growled, and the priest, smelling the

drink on his breath, made no answer. The Tan bent forward threateningly, his mouth wide open as if to bite off the priest's trembling head.

'McGiff,' he bawled. 'Answer to your name, you papist bastard.'

The insult stunned the priest. Anger swelled in him, its sudden heat burning up his earlier fear. Deliberately he pressed forward against the revolver's mouth, pushing it back with his body and refusing to let his face reveal how much it was hurting him.

'I am Father McGiff,' he said, and then with barely held indignation added: 'What right have you to break into my house like this? And what have you done with my housekeeper?'

'The old biddy, is it? I think she's gone and locked herself in the lavatory.'

The other Tans laughed raucously, and the one scattering the priest's books called out: 'Oi, Bill, give us a bit of light, will yah? It's dark over here.'

Father McGiff noted the familiar form of address. Not 'Captain' or even 'Sergeant'. He feared the worst. They were just three loutish Tans who had filled themselves with drink and decided to have some sport. They were capable of killing him. The image of a black-garbed body in a bog flashed before his eyes, and his mind began to recite an Act of Contrition. The Tan standing over him motioned towards the oil-lamp with his gun. Slowly Father McGiff raised the wick, hating his hands that, no matter how hard he fought them, had started to shake. The sudden brightness made him blink, and he looked around the study. Already the floor was littered with his books, and now the third Tan had joined in the rape of his shelves. Of Mrs Roche there was neither sight nor sound. God grant she was not hurt. Father McGiff mastered the tremor in his hands and rested them on the desk.

'That's better,' said the voice beside him. 'Naw, then' – and the Tan's head was lowered until his mouth was against the priest's ear – 'a little birdie told me you was a naughty boy.'

The smell of drink engulfed Father McGiff, making him

almost dizzy with its fumes. He turned his face away to avoid them, and the Tan roughly grasped his chin and pulled it round.

'You bin giving bad advice, eh? You bin preaching revolution? That's treason, that is.'

Father McGiff stared at his tormentor, not deigning to reply.

''Ere, Colly boy, I think we may have the wrong man, y'know.'

Colly, the Tan who had led the ransacking of the bookshelves, unslung his rifle from his shoulder and went over to the desk.

'How d'ya make that out, Bill?'

'We heard, didn't we, as how this fine papist was telling people to join the IRA? We heard that, didn't we, Colly? But will yah look at him. He's struck dumb. A blighter who loses his voice like that couldn't be much of a preacher, could he?'

'Lost 'is voice, Bill? Never!' Colly replied, affecting a tone of ridicule. And then, with a movement so swift that Father McGiff had no chance of avoiding it, he brought the butt of his rifle down with crushing force on one of the priest's hands. Father McGiff could not suppress a scream of agony. The pain was paralysing; he knew some of his fingers must have been broken.

'What did ya do that for, Colly?' Bill asked in mock concern.

'A fly. A bleedin' fly.'

'In November, Colly? I never 'eard of a fly in November. Summer insects, ain't they? It's the heat what brings 'em out.'

'Not Irish flies, Bill,' Colly replied, taking his companion's cue as Father McGiff moaned softly. 'Y'see, over 'ere they don't have no summers. Not worth talkin' about anyway. So they has to breed winter flies.'

'Well, did you get him?'

'Naw, I missed him. But at least I got somethin' out of his Eminence here. So he ain't dumb, is he?'

'Best make sure,' Bill said, and matching Colly's swiftness and ferocity he crashed his revolver down on the priest's uninjured hand. No sound came from Father McGiff, but his whole frame was squeezed rigid as if an electric shock had shot through him. His already pale face went chalk white, his eyelids closed tight like a stitched wound and his mouth formed a slow yawn of agony.

'I think you got 'im that time, Bill.'

'Got somethin' anyways. Didn't I, *Father*?' The Tan bent until his face was almost touching the priest's. 'You understand, don't you, *Father*? You be a good boy and don't preach any more of your silly sermons or we'll be back. And next time it won't be your 'ands, it'll be your tongue we'll cut out. Savvy?'

With a jerk of his head to his companions Bill turned and made for the door, kicking books out of the way as he went. Father McGiff hadn't moved in his chair, his broken hands still resting on the desk. He heard their shouting and laughter as they clattered down the stairs, followed by the sharp bang of a revolver shot. He prayed they had not been firing at Mrs Roche. If she had been shot, how could he help her with his broken hands? He wouldn't even be able to open the front door to call a neighbour or raise a window to shout for help. He felt his heart pumping madly – he could hear its beat in the sudden silence. His body was trembling violently, and as he prayed for enough strength to lift himself out of his chair and search for his housekeeper he heard her footsteps emerging from the kitchen and rushing up the stairs to him.

'Thank God,' he breathed. He turned his face towards the door as she appeared. 'Thank God you're safe, Mrs Roche. Did these savages molest you?'

Mrs Roche stood in stunned horror, appalled at the chaos of the study. Strands of her thin white hair straggled down over one ear, and her eyes, already red-rimmed from years of hanging over hot ranges and peering into steaming saucepans, blinked in disbelief.

'Jesus be praised,' she gasped. 'I thought they'd killed you, Father. You're not hurt, are you?'

Painfully Father McGiff lifted his arms off the desk. As

328

he held them out to Mrs Roche, she could see his hands trembling, their fingers either hanging limply or splayed out at grotesque angles.

'They broke my hands, Mrs Roche. With their guns.'

'Jesus, Mary and Joseph!' Mrs Roche made the sign of the cross as she hurried over to the desk. 'Oh, Father, you poor man! You poor, poor man!'

Reaching the priest's side she recoiled in horror at what she saw. 'God above!' she breathed, certain Father McGiff's mind had been deranged by his experience. He had raised his mashed hands up, stretching them out in a gesture of dedication, and on his face was a glowing smile of pride, satisfaction and triumphant joy.

25

'I FEEL IT'S ALL very near now,' Molly's letter to Judith
said. 'I haven't had any pains yet, but I know it won't be
too much longer. Solly wants a boy of course, but I don't
mind – boy or girl, what's the difference? One thing I've
made my mind up on: my child will not be brought up the
way we were. Being girls meant we couldn't satisfy
Father and we weren't the kind of girls to satisfy Mother.
Oh, I suppose we haven't turned out too badly, and I
shouldn't complain, but have you ever thought what it
might have been like if we hadn't had each other?'

Judith folded the letter and put it in her bag. Yes, she
had thought what it would have been like. Indeed, she
knew what it was like – had Molly forgotten that for over
a year now Judith had had no one while Molly had had
her husband? Did *she* never wonder what being left alone
was like? Probably not – she had no reason to. Not that
Judith herself had worried greatly about it for that
matter. At least, not until now. For it was now that she
was really feeling the slow pain of loneliness. A week
since she had last seen Denis, and no word from him.
Could it be that he hadn't heard or read about Mr
Klugman's death and so didn't know why she hadn't kept
their appointment on Sunday? Of course, even if he *had*
guessed the reason she didn't turn up, how could he have

got in touch with her anyway? He didn't know where she lived – at least, not the exact address. And he obviously wouldn't want to come to the store and take the risk of bumping into her father. So it was really up to her. There was no risk involved in her going to Twohey's where he worked and asking to see him. Then, why hadn't she? The longer she delayed, the more likely it was that he'd think she had changed her mind – that she was having regrets over what had happened in Fanny Rubin's. And was she?

Wearily she closed her eyes and tried to answer herself. Regrets? No, not regrets. How could she regret such ecstasy? But worries, yes; and the longer the delay in seeing Denis again, with time dragging like a heavy chain through each day and night, the more chance there was for her to worry. If only she could have seen Denis even once, if only she could have been with him just for a while, she wouldn't be questioning herself like this. But waiting and wondering – the cruelty of it all. And doubting. And not knowing what to do. Should she call to Twohey's? Hunger for Denis said yes, but the same hunger made her fear that if she gave in to her desire again she would have lost completely the control over herself she had been so confident of over a week ago. And, if that happened, where would it all end? Goodness knows what she might get herself into. There seemed to be no solution to her dilemma, no one to turn to, and only heartache before her, early or late.

Captain Simcox also received a letter that Wednesday – from Elizabeth. He had written her a crazy note immediately he had got back to barracks on Saturday to tell her he was free and fit and well, and now her reply was full of joy and relief. She had heard of his release – the Home Office had sent a special messenger to tell her – and she guessed he would write first thing. Now Roddy had more good news for her: he was getting some compassionate leave and would be with her again very soon. In view of what he had gone through it would be a lengthy furlough.

Certainly it was unlikely he'd be recalled before the baby was born, so he'd have a chance to see about buying himself out of the Army and find a more normal way of life. There was to be a party for him in the mess that night, to celebrate his escape – provided the IRA didn't put on a special party of their own that would keep them all busy. He wondered about Boxer and Joe. Boxer would probably not get into any trouble – after all, the poor blighter had been in bed with the flu, so there wasn't much he could do about the escape. But Joe. . . . Roddy was sorry for Joe. He was only a youngster, couldn't have had enough preparation for the unexpected responsibility. Still, the experience would certainly have made a better soldier out of him – if his IRA bosses had the sense to give him a second chance.

Now that Roddy was free, with the ordeal behind him, one thing he regretted was that his beard hadn't, after all, grown quite enough to be retained and encouraged. Even if his first sight of his own face in two weeks hadn't quite convinced him – he had begun rather to fancy the idea of a royal-looking bushy growth – his fellow-officers' derisive comments soon shamed him and 'By-the-book' Campbell's tart advice summed it up. 'Better get cleaned up quickly, mon,' he had said. 'The way ye are now, ye're like a fox cub with ringworm.' That did it for Roddy!

Colonel Windsor carefully cut the piece out of that morning's *Cork Examiner*, fixed his monocle in his eye, and read it once more.

IMPORTANT NOTICE

We, the undersigned, do now give the male sex of Cork City notice 'which must be obeyed forthwith' that any person of the said sex who is seen or found loitering at street corners or on pathways without reasonable cause why he should be there, or any man or boy found to be standing or walking with one or both hands in his pockets will, if he does not adhere to this Order, suffer the consequences which will no doubt ensue.

(Signed)
Secretary of Death or Victory League

God Save the King
and
Frustrate His Enemies

To the Colonel the appearance of such a notice in a newspaper was almost incredible, and a flash of outrage at such audacity made the monocle plop from his eye. Of course he didn't – couldn't – blame the *Examiner* for printing it. They had no alternative if they didn't want their premises bombed or burned down.

Was he being foolish to think of sending the cutting to the Secretary for Ireland? Greenwood must surely already know the full details of the horror that was engulfing Ireland. And threatening to spread to England, too. Why, only on Monday the *Examiner* had reported the burning of Liverpool warehouses by Sinn Fein. Yesterday he had read that the public galleries in the Commons had been closed and Downing Street barricaded at both ends. And right beside that abominable notice in this morning's paper there was the news of an explosion at London Bridge. So whom did Greenwood think he was fooling with his glib denials, his refusal to acknowledge that the situation was going from bad to worse? Of course it was government policy to pretend that everything was under control. They were clearly intent on turning a blind eye to the daily atrocities. What fools! Didn't they realise that their policy of terror had already failed? That if they persevered with it they would lose all honour and blacken for ever their country's name? Somehow they must be made to see how stupid and obstinate their attitude was. That notice in the *Examiner* was a perfect illustration of the kind of barbarism it had produced. It would help to bring home to Greenwood the depths to which the Tans

333

were ready to sink. And in the name of the King, into the bargain.

Colonel Windsor clipped the cutting to his letter and sealed it in an envelope. What he was doing was his clear duty. The powers that be might not like it. He knew that. Well, let them not. He'd take the consequences. He'd faced worse in his time.

Abie Klugman's death was the first the community had suffered for some years, and Zvi Lipsky found himself more affected than he had ever been before by the loss of one of their number. Not because it was Abie Klugman who had gone. Not because it was Abie? No, Zvi was certain it wasn't that. 'Well, what is it, then?' his wife, Myra, had nagged. 'You haven't said a word to me for three days.' Zvi snorted, thinking that whenever he did speak to her she didn't listen anyway. But he hadn't made any retort apart from a grunt, a shoulder shrug, and a muttered '*Nu*, I suppose I must be getting old'. It had been Myra's turn to snort at that, for she didn't think her husband's explanation was any excuse for his moroseness – and, anyway, he had never complained about his age before.

But there was truth both in Zvi's quietly spoken suggestion and in Myra's reason for doubting it. Concern at the passage of the years had not previously much disturbed Zvi Lipsky's preoccupation with his work and his communal duties, but now it had begun to grip him with the suddenness and ice-cold terror of a pain in the heart.

And all because of Arnold Wine.

Zvi took off his spectacles, cleaned them with his handkerchief and then dabbed at the moistness in his eyes. He pushed away his dinner-plate, the meat only half-eaten, an abandoned potato growing cold and dry in its curdling pool of gravy. Myra shrugged and removed the plate. She had cooked his dinner – if he didn't want it, it was his own worry. What more could she do?

Zvi replaced his spectacles and scratched moodily at the tablecloth. Before coming up from the surgery he had looked at his appointments-book. There were five more patients to be seen that afternoon – if they all turned up. Four of them were from the country, so he'd have to be prepared for some disappointments. Wasn't it only last week or the week before that four country patients hadn't arrived? Was it possible that that could happen again? How long more could such a state of affairs continue? Zvi guessed that Wine didn't have such a problem to contend with because of course Wine was an interloper who hadn't laboured for years to build up a country connection as Zvi had. So Wine's clientele would be virtually all city-based. *Oi vey, a missa meshuna off em* – may his hair fall out and he suffer an unfortunate death! He had everything in his favour – good looks, youth, a more up-to-date surgery, and to cap it all only city patients to worry about. And wasn't there something else, too? Of course, of course, there was Wine's dental degree. Zvi didn't want to think about that – the most cruel twist of the knife. What chance did he have against such odds? So should he join up with such a man? If he didn't, and if some law was passed to stop him practising, what would he do? But with Wine as his insurance policy ... and no premium to pay for it into the bargain.... Shouldn't he perhaps consider it, find out a bit more? It mightn't be such a bad idea. Maybe Zvi had been hasty in condemning Wine – after all, even if Shabbos meant nothing to him he was at least a Zionist, so there must be some good in him! And Zvi wasn't getting any younger. So ask already, enquire, get more details, see what he has to say. You don't have to talk to him – not yet anyway. Or meet him face to face. Write him a letter. Keep him at a distance until he has put all his cards on the table.

Zvi rose from his chair, muttered a shortened Grace After Meals, tucked his *yarmulkah* back into his pocket, and slowly made his way downstairs again to his surgery. There was no point in thinking about it any more, no point in putting off a decision. He promised himself that if one of his afternoon patients failed to keep his

335

appointment he'd use the time to compose a letter to Wine. If a second patient didn't turn up, he'd write it. And if a third one let him down he'd go straight out and post it.

But what if the fourth country patient didn't appear, either, what would he do then? 'Then,' Zvi Lipsky muttered to himself, deriving little solace from his bitter humour, 'then I'd better pray that Wine hasn't changed his mind.'

When Percy Lovitch closed his shop and went home that evening the first thing he did was to put a match to the fire. The chill and damp seemed to have somehow got indoors with him, and he needed a good fire to cheer him up. As he bent down to blow the flames to life, something at the back of the coals suddenly burst alight before quickly curling and crackling into little black shards. It was the one-page letter Percy had received that morning from Barry Brandreth, telling him how sorry he had been not to have had a chance to say goodbye to Percy before he had left Cork and how he and the whole of the Carl Rosa looked forward to seeing him again on their visit next year. 'If I'm still with the Company,' Barry had added. 'A lot I care,' Percy had sullenly replied before tearing up the letter and throwing the pieces into the grate. At that moment he had doubted whether, even after a year, he would want to have anything to do with Barry Brandreth or the Carl Rosa Opera Company. Now, however, with the flames glowing on his face and the heat beginning to warm his blood, his mood softened. 'Your old, good friend, Barry,' the letter had been signed. Barry *was* an old friend, *and* a good one – and what had happened hadn't been his fault. What's more, if Barry was still the Carl Rosa's manager when next they came to Cork, that would surely mean that his position was secure and then perhaps their old relationship – and routine – would be re-established. Why not?

Percy rose heavily from his crouched posture and gazed into the brightening coals. Since he had retired from the stage, the Carl Rosa visit had been the high point of every year. He had looked forward to it for months beforehand. If he was going to stay in Cork, what else had he to look forward to? Please God, Barry would win through. In a few months' time Percy would drop him a line and ask how he was getting on. Barry would know what he meant. Barry would tell him. In the meantime, it was fingers crossed and hope for the best. He didn't want his dreams to go up in smoke just like Barry's letter. With luck they wouldn't.

Humming Beethoven's 'Ode to Joy' – he wished he had been able to sing it in public, but the opportunity had never come – Percy set the table and considered what he'd cook for his supper.

Denis Hurley had read about Abie Klugman's death and thought that the funeral might have been what had kept Judith from meeting him on Sunday. But, then, why hadn't she got in touch with him since then? After all, she knew where he worked. He couldn't suppress the idea that perhaps what had happened between them had led to her silence. He had never gone that far with a girl before and he was still feeling stunned by the suddenness of his passion, the way it had come on him like a monster wave, engulfing him, blotting out everything but the force of his desire and the mad pull of her body. No thought of consequences. No thought of guilt, either. That was a worry. Did Judith blame him for it? He wanted to know. He needed to know.

He thought of sending a note to her at her father's store, but how could he be sure that Iron Josh wouldn't see it and wonder who it was from? He didn't want to take the risk of getting Judith into trouble. Besides, he didn't want, either, to get on the wrong side of old Cohen. Things were happening in the movement that Denis felt could give him a real chance to establish himself, and he had a fair idea that he and Iron Josh hadn't seen the last of each other yet. Not, anyway, if his plan worked.

*   *   *

Jacob, too, had formed a plan, but he was frightened by its boldness and by the prospect of the fight he'd have on his hands to carry it out. It had come to him suddenly, yet it seemed so obvious that he was amazed he hadn't thought of it before. Perhaps if he hadn't been so wrapped up in himself over Deirdre, if he hadn't been so absorbed in tending his wounded self-esteem, he might have been able to come to his senses before this. He had spent night after night wondering if he should write Deirdre a letter, trying to convince himself that there must be some way he could persuade her to continue their relationship. But deep down he knew he was only fooling himself; if she hadn't even wanted to read his poem to her, how could he expect her to pay any attention to a letter? No, she was out of his life. And now he had to get her out of his mind. He was certain his plan would do just that – it would wipe out all his unhappiness and give him a fresh start. But he mustn't forget the difficulties it presented. There was no use rushing at it bald-headed. His arguments would have to be mighty persuasive. He'd need to think them out carefully. Not in the house, however – the atmosphere there was too overpowering for him to scent the breath of freedom, the expectations too ordered for him to shake them from his mind. Outside – abroad in the streets of the city he had made his own – that was where he'd go to find himself.

Through those streets he cycled, coatless, capless, the spokes of his wheels flashing in the light of the gas-lamps. He made for the north bank of the Lee, away from the University, away from Fitzgerald's Park, away from all his poignant memories. He made for what he had always felt to be the heart of Cork: Shandon with its goldfish weathervane gleaming against the leaden sky, its north and east sides of limestone, its south and west of sandstone because the two contractors who built it each had his own quarry; and its four clock faces, no two of which ever showed the same time so that it was called 'The Four-Faced Liar'. He waited there for the hour to strike, waited to hear its carillon playing out over the city, and as he cycled on he recited to himself the poem he had learned at school, a poem with all a lonely exile's longing:

> With deep affection and recollection
> I often think of those Shandon bells,
> Whose sounds so wild would
> In days of childhood
> Fling round my cradle their magic spells.
>
> ... 'Tis the bells of Shandon
> That sound so grand on
> The pleasant waters of the River Lee.

On to Blackpool he travelled, the swish of his wheels against the wet surfaces of its narrow lanes and alleyways sounding like an exchange of whispered secrets. He imagined himself back in earlier centuries, when Blackpool and its Butter Market were the centre of the world's butter trade, when farmers drove their cattle in from miles around to meet the slaughterers' knives and have the beef exported to distant lands, when traders bought and sold their wares and went home counting their profit not in pence alone but in the pride and satisfaction of having to answer to none but themselves. On then into the hills of Montenotte where many of the wealthy merchants of Cork resided, their mansions flanking the broad river, and as he went Jacob reflected on the irony of the area's Irish name, Baile na Bocht, the Town of the Poor. At the estuary mouth he stopped to follow the dance of the street-lights jigging and winking on the surface of the water until pattern after pattern bumped and broke against the dark mass of Blackrock Castle on the far bank.

Then he turned and cycled back, thinking now of the men whose lives and labour had given him this city. But they had given him more than a city, more than mute streets and buildings: they had given him an example. For they had not allowed themselves to be trapped in any conventional mould or forced to wait on fortune and opportunity. They had made their own lives, their own

339

freedoms. As *he* must. As he would. He realised now that his long ride had not been through dumb streets and past tongueless buildings. There was a message there to be heard, courage to be sucked from stones and bricks, resolution to be learned from the heritage of pioneers.

And win it he had – he was certain now of his purpose, confident of his determination. As soon as he reached home he would tell them: he was leaving college and going to Palestine with his *zeide*. He'd be a man – his own man.

But when he got back to Celtic Crescent and wheeled his bicycle in the door his family had just heard the news of the attack on Father McGiff, and all was confusion and shock. His distraught *zeide* was being consoled by his parents, Judith was busy getting cups of tea, and Jacob could see there was no part for him in that drama. They hardly even noticed his return. Certainly they would have no mind for *his* news. Not for the moment anyway.

Disconsolately, angrily, he trudged up to his room. It seemed that, whichever way he turned, Fate conspired against him.

26

NEITHER THE NUNS at the Mercy Hospital nor the surgeon who had set Father McGiff's broken fingers could persuade the priest to stay even overnight. The Matron, Sister Cecelia, had told him that he'd need proper attention and couldn't possibly get that at home, but Father McGiff had refused to flinch from her rasping tongue. He didn't care to leave poor Mrs Roche in the presbytery by herself after the shock she had had, and the Matron's implied insult to his housekeeper's devotion and competence stiffened his opposition. The surgeon had murmured something about possible complications if there wasn't adequate supervision, but his warning had been so unemphatic that Father McGiff felt safe in discounting it as obligatory subservience to Sister Cecelia's wishes. He guessed that, like himself, the surgeon had frequent cause to feel surprised at the Lord's sufferance of bossy nuns.

But, however bossy Sister Cecelia might be, Father McGiff wasn't about to capitulate. 'Yerra, what complications?' he had said, affecting a more bluff, garrulous manner than normal. 'Sure if it was my legs were broken I'd be as well in bed here as at home, but once I can get around what matter where I eat and sleep? Mrs Roche, God bless her, is used to my ways, and I have a curate who

341

can take care of all my duties. Not my Sunday sermon, of course – you wouldn't want me to miss that, Sister, would you?' And when the Matron opened her mouth with every sign of being ready to disabuse him the priest scotched her intentions with a cajoling 'Sure of course you wouldn't', as if to perish the thought that a holy nun would even dream of suggesting he should neglect such an important priestly duty. 'Besides,' he added, 'I'll not have these devils think they've silenced me. They'll have to work much harder to do that. Since the Lord has left me the use of my legs, it can be for no other reason than to get me to my church where I can use my tongue to give thanks to Him and the back of it to anyone evil enough to attack one of His servants.'

Sister Cecelia threw up her hands and followed them with a heavenward raising of her eyebrows as if trying to tread the flood of Father McGiff's arguments, the while the surgeon allowed himself a little smile and a quick wink of encouragement. Suppressing any show of satisfaction, Father McGiff solemnised the closing of the matter with his most sacerdotal cough.

So it was in his study chair rather than in a hospital bed that he greeted Rabbi Cohen when his old friend came to visit him on Thursday afternoon. Mrs Roche, almost mesmerised by the magnificence of the Rabbi's beard and aghast at the snaking white side-whiskers that curled from under his hat to below his ear-lobes, stole frequent glances behind her as she led him up the stairs, and when he entered the study Father McGiff jumped to his feet to greet him.

'No, no, you must not get up,' the Rabbi pleaded, but the reply was a hearty laugh.

'Sure there's nothing wrong with my legs – as I told the fussy Matron they have over at the hospital. It's the other extremities that suffered' – and he held up his bound and bandaged hands as if he were raising battle trophies. Rabbi Cohen recoiled at the sight, and his lips trembled in silent horror and sympathy.

'Mrs Roche, pull up a chair for the Rabbi – and bring us some tea if you would,' Father McGiff directed.

Rabbi Cohen waved away the suggestion. 'No, nothing, thank you. Nothing.'

'But you must, Rabbi, you must take something. This is the first opportunity I've had to return the many years' hospitality you've given me in your home. Sure you wouldn't deny me, would you now?'

Mrs Roche was already at the door to carry out the priest's instructions, but the Rabbi persisted in his refusal.

'Please, Father,' he almost implored. 'I mean no insult but I cannot. You see, I can partake of food or drink only in a kosher house.'

'Ah, of course, of course, I should have known,' Father McGiff replied apologetically as he nodded his permission to his housekeeper to leave.

Rabbi Cohen sat down, unable to take his eyes from the priest's fingers.

'*Ach*, it's not as bad as it looks,' Father McGiff assured him. 'It won't be long before they're as good as new.' Then he laughed as he corrected himself. 'Well, maybe not new, for they weren't very new before. But they'll do me, they'll do me.'

'But how could such a thing happen to a man of God?' The Rabbi's tone was one of complete incredulity at the scale of the sacrilege involved. His blue eyes widened in mystification.

'Ah, it could have been far worse, my friend. I was lucky.'

'Have these people no respect at all?'

'Divil a bit, Rabbi, divil a bit. But, then, they had drink taken, you know. Not that I'm trying to excuse them. Though I suppose I must find the grace to forgive them.'

Rabbi Cohen put his head on one side, and with only a small sigh of reluctance nodded his agreement.

'If you can say that, Father, then you already have forgiven them.'

'Ah, I wouldn't be worthy of the cloth I wear if I couldn't muster that much charity. Not that it'll make any difference to my attitude to what they represent. Hate the sin but love the sinner.'

343

Behind the priest's vehemence was a note of exhilaration, and Rabbi Cohen looked at him in some surprise.

'You have had a terrible experience, yet you seem even happy – happier than I've seen you for some time. Could that be? I must be wrong.'

'You're not wrong; indeed, you're not. For months past, Rabbi, it has all been boiling up inside me. You know yourself how disturbed I've been.'

'Yes, I do know. It was not something you could hide from an old friend. All the fighting, all the killing, it was worrying you – I think even more than you pretended.'

'Even more than I pretended – that's about the size of it. And that's what made me start preaching my – I suppose you'd call them my political sermons. But the more I preached, the more thwarted I felt. Words, words – what good were words? I kept asking myself. I wanted action. My blood was up, Rabbi. I wanted to get into the fight.'

'But look what your words have got you,' Rabbi Cohen protested, his body almost visibly shrivelling in self-defence at the thought of what his friend had suffered.

'Exactly what I wanted: *that's* what they got me. Oh, I'm not saying these are very pleasant' – and he held up his hands – 'but they're not that bad; some fingers broken – the thumbs are all right and the knuckles, too, thanks be – but they show me that my sermons haven't been wasted breath after all. They've been more than just a release for my own frustrations.'

Rabbi Cohen shook himself as if some faint pollution still hanging in the very air of the room had suddenly made his skin crawl.

'It was here it happened?'

He looked around unhappily. Were it the Holy Temple that had been violated rather than his friend's sanctum, he would have been little less affected.

'In this room,' Father McGiff agreed. 'Sitting in this chair, at this desk. Bad enough that they were brutal savages, but they were three vandals as well.' He gestured at his shelves, which now bore long wounds where they had been denuded of their books to expose the bare flesh of the walls. Mrs Roche had already picked up the scattered volumes, meticulously dusted off each one and stacked them in neat piles against the walls, to be put back in their places by Father McGiff as soon as he was able.

As the Rabbi's gaze ranged around, his look of outrage gradually melted into admiration for the study's airy homeliness. He felt no envy of his friend's surroundings, but his mind could not refrain from comparisons.

Instinctively Father McGiff guessed what he was thinking.

'Yes, I suppose it does seem a bit large, but you know that where I come from I was used to fields and open countryside – though that wasn't today or yesterday. So I like to stretch my legs a bit when I'm working, without losing touch with my desk so to speak, and I've space enough for that here.'

The Rabbi made no answer. In his mind's eye he was seeing his own room in Celtic Crescent – could he call it a room? – and it seemed to him that it would neatly fit into just a corner of the priest's study. But, although he was as happy there as the priest was here, he suddenly had a vision, a glimpse into another era, that almost dazzled his senses. He saw a room such as this, a study just as commodious, with as many bookshelves as this had, its floor also covered in rugs and its furniture warm and inviting, but on the walls the pictures were not of Jesus, on the mantels were no crosses or holy statues, on the shelves the books were not in English, and the figure in the chair before him was no bare-headed black-cassocked priest but an old Jew wearing a skull-cap and a praying-shawl. And outside the window the sun was bright, the sky was blue, and the land flowed with milk and honey. This was the Zion of the future, the new Israel, where the people were his people, speaking the language of their ancestors, making their own laws, living by their own customs and traditions. As quickly as it had come, the vision faded, leaving him not the ache of despair that might possess a desert wanderer as his chimera escapes his embrace, but a surge of exhaltation at the certainty that he had been vouchsafed a divine foresight, and not even the knowledge that what he had seen was too far in

345

the future ever to include him in its pattern could dim the glow in his soul.

Finding himself once more back in Father McGiff's study he realised that he had not heard a word of what the priest had been saying.

'Forgive me, my friend,' he apologised. 'My mind strayed for a moment.'

'Ah, Rabbi, I thought I caught a faraway look in your eyes. Was there something troubling you?'

'No. I was thinking of Palestine. Not Palestine as it is now, but as it may become some day – a Jewish land, a Jewish country, for the Jewish people.'

'That's the spirit,' Father McGiff snapped back. 'That's the talk I like to hear. I know exactly what you mean. I have the same sort of dream. I dream of *this* land becoming an Irish land, an Irish country, for the Irish people.'

'But your dream, Father, is much nearer reality than mine. Yours could come true tomorrow, or next month or next year. At least in your lifetime.' Rabbi Cohen's voice dropped. 'I will not live to see mine come true.'

'Ah, now,' the priest admonished, 'you mustn't be despondent. The Lord works in mysterious ways – I don't have to tell *you* that.'

Rabbi Cohen did not answer, but a deep sigh escaped his lips.

The priest tried to put a hand out to comfort him but stopped short when he remembered his injuries. He leaned forward, as if by getting closer to his friend he could take on some of his burden.

'Perhaps I know what's troubling you, Rabbi. I haven't spent all those years listening to people's confessions without having a fair idea of what's in their mind. Not, of course, that you would have any transgression on your conscience, but' – and he paused before continuing – 'would I be far wrong in thinking that you're still grieving for Mr Klugman, that you still haven't got over his death?'

Rabbi Cohen's immediate willingness to talk about Abie Klugman confirmed the priest's instinct.

'How can I get over it? Do you know, Father, I think he

346

was the one among us who most needed to go to Palestine.'

'Rabbi, Rabbi, who can measure a man's needs except the good Lord?'

'None can, none. I do not question God's will, but....' And Rabbi Cohen's voice trailed off.

'But what? You sound almost as if you felt a responsibility for his death, as if in some way you'd have to pay for it.'

It was a shot in the dark, an intuition that struck home.

Rabbi Cohen looked into his friend's eyes and quietly, almost fearfully, said: 'If the Lord saw fit to take him of most need, what certainty has any of the rest of us?'

'Nonsense, sheer nonsense,' Father McGiff rejoined sharply. 'Do you know what you remind me of, Rabbi? You remind me of a little boy looking forward to his birthday party, and looking forward so intensely that he makes himself ill before the day arrives. Nerves, it's all nerves – and aren't you old enough now to have got over that, eh?'

Rabbi Cohen smiled but in his mind he dismissed the priest's suggestion. He was tempted to reveal his promise to Abie Klugman, to show what real cause there was for his misgivings, but he knew that if he did he would be chastised for being childish. Was he being childish? Was his old age really akin to a second childhood, so that, like the boy with the birthday, the strain of looking forward was too much for him?

'I'll tell you what you'll do, Rabbi,' Father McGiff broke in, his warm voice like balm to the Rabbi's troubled thoughts. 'I'll tell you what you'll do. Just take it day by day – day by day of the future, not of the past. Forget Mr Klugman, get him out of your mind, don't let the past prey on you. You have only another ten days in Cork and on Sunday you have a wedding in your community. Rejoice in that, Rabbi. Celebrate that. Think of that. And the happy couple will be going out to Palestine with you. What could be more perfect? Look at that now for the Lord's design. It's as if you were bringing seed with you to plant in the Holy Land.'

347

Rabbi Cohen's eyes lit up, enlivened by the felicity of the priest's inspiration. He was right. It was so. The Rabbi himself was an old man, and all the others going to Palestine were middle-aged or elderly, but Miriam Levy and Reuben Jackson were young. They were the future – the most important of the emigrants. Even if no one else was going except them, it would still be a golden day for the community, a golden day for *Eretz*. And on Sunday they would be wed, so that they would set foot in the land of Israel as man and wife, and there, as the Bible enjoined, they would be fruitful and multiply and their seed would cover the earth.

Rabbi Cohen stood up and, placing his hands on the priest's shoulders, he looked into his eyes.

'Thank you, Father,' he said. 'You are a wise and good friend. I came to you today to sympathise with you over your broken fingers and instead I rejoice in your unbroken spirit. I brought you my own broken spirit, and you have made it whole. I came with a heavy heart, and you made me see that what I was carrying was a weight of selfishness, that I was too concerned with myself instead of with my people. We may not meet again, but we part as we first met, so long ago, with hope in our hearts and faith in our God. My friend, I will leave you now. Do not get up, but grant me one last favour: accept the blessing of an old and now a wiser Rabbi.'

He gripped the priest's shoulders, and as he did so Father McGiff raised his broken hands, rested them on Rabbi Cohen's wrists and gazed into his eyes.

'*Yevurechichah Adonai v'yishmerechah*,' Rabbi Cohen intoned. 'May the Lord bless you and keep you.'

He paused, then bent and touched the priest's forehead with his lips before turning and walking slowly from the room. Behind him Father McGiff's eyes filled with tears.

27

ON FRIDAY MORNING Denis Hurley decided that he couldn't wait any longer. Time was already short, and to let the weekend pass before talking to Iron Josh might be cutting things too fine altogether. He had delayed as long as he could in the hope of seeing Judith and getting her agreement – perhaps even her help. But there was still no word from her.

He was confused and upset by her silence – didn't know what to make of it. But he did know that he had to put his own feelings aside. Presumably she must have looked on their relationship as just a passing flirtation – he hadn't thought that was how she regarded it at the beginning, and it certainly had seemed to mean much more than that to her at the end – if, indeed, it *was* over. He was probably attaching too much significance to what had happened on Wednesday night. After all, given all the circumstances – the relief and euphoria after their escape from the Tans and the two of them finding themselves alone in Fanny Rubin's bedroom with him almost half-naked – well, given all that on top of their mutual attraction, it wasn't so surprising that they had allowed their passions to get the better of them. And the attraction certainly had been there – on his side anyway – there was no denying that. But perhaps it was just as well if Judith wasn't really as serious about him as she had seemed. And if she wasn't, then with the business about her brother taken care of there was no occasion for her to see him again. Anyway, even in the best of times what sort of future would they have to look forward to together? And these certainly weren't the best of times.

As he made his way from Twohey's down the narrow Academy Street and along by the side of the *Cork Examiner* into Patrick Street, he noted that there were more RIC men than usual on patrol. Patrick Street itself displayed its usual Friday morning bustle, and he guessed the jarveys on their stand outside the Victoria Hotel wouldn't want for custom. Christmas decorations were already up in many of the shops, but what hope was there for a peace-and-goodwill festival in this year of Our Lord, one thousand nine hundred and twenty? Precious little with army lorries passing through every hour, with swaggering Tans making everyone give way to them, and with policemen on every corner stopping people at random, demanding identification and sometimes hauling them off to the station. Peace and goodwill? No, sir, not from them, and neither – for that matter – from the IRA.

He crossed Patrick Street, careful to give the military and the RIC a wide berth. Now that he had made up his mind to pay Iron Josh a visit, he didn't want anything to hold him up and force him to postpone it. He knew Judith didn't go to work on Fridays, so there was no danger of seeing her, and the way things seemed to be between them that suited him down to the ground.

At the open gates of Joshua Cohen's scrapyard Denis suddenly recalled his first visit. That had been on a Friday morning, too, and so nervous was he that if Boxer Sullivan hadn't been striding purposefully beside him he would almost have turned tail. He had had a gun that time also, not that it had been much good to him. The recollection of his ineptness with it – and especially of Joshua Cohen picking it up off the ground and handing it back to him just before they had started back to the city – still made him blush to his toes. Well, it had been a stupid idea anyway to try to hold a man like Iron Josh to ransom, and he was glad it wasn't his. Even if he had been ready to use the gun, it wouldn't have made any difference. He wasn't carrying a gun today but he didn't need one – today's plan was his own.

As he stepped into the front yard he stopped and looked apprehensively at the window of the small hut that served as Iron Josh's office. He wasn't expecting to see Judith there, but one never knew; if by any chance she had changed her routine and come in, that would certainly complicate matters. The hut, however, was in darkness and the door was locked. Clearly Judith wasn't at work, but instead of relief Denis felt his heart lurch with a cold gust of disappointment. He hesitated – confused and almost lost. What was he doing? Had he concocted his plan just to give himself an excuse to visit the yard so as to see Judith and then disguised its true object from himself by choosing a Friday morning to put it into operation? No, that didn't make sense. He might be that smitten but he wasn't that mad. He took off his cap and wiped his brow. The plan – that really *was* why he had come. It was far more important than his love for Judith Cohen.

He walked over to the covered shed opposite the hut and peered into its darkness. There was no sign of Judith's father there, either, so Denis turned towards the extensive yard behind it.

It was full of every sort of scrap metal he could possibly have imagined. Brass bedsteads there were by the score, so many that he wondered what their former occupants were sleeping on now. There was a pile of broken zinc baths, reminding him of his childhood days when his mother would bath him in one in front of a roaring fire. Nearby were lengths of iron rails that must have come from some disused country line, and beside them, stretching as far as the narrow metal gate at the back of the yard, was a mountain of copper and lead. Denis couldn't imagine from where Iron Josh had got so much scrap, or where he would get rid of it all. Presumably he still sent it to Britain where no doubt he had built up his market during the Great War when it would all have been used

351

for making munitions. There must have been a pot of money in it – thousands of pounds – and even if the prices might not be as high as they had been there was still a small fortune in what Denis could see. And despite the masses of material the yard presented an orderly appearance. Trust Joshua Cohen! Denis guessed that if he were asked to find one particular discarded object he'd be able to tell you exactly where it was. That sort of man obviously had a logical methodical mind. It should be possible to persuade him with a convincing argument.

But where was he? He had to be somewhere around; he'd hardly have left the yard open and unattended.

'Mr Cohen,' Denis called, 'Mr Cohen. Are you there, Mr Cohen?'

Immediately there was the noise of clanging metal, and Iron Josh, an old coat over his shoulders and bowler hat on his head, appeared from behind a mound of copper so high that he had been completely obscured.

He looked across the yard at Denis, took a step before recognising him, and then stopped short.

'Good morning, Mr Cohen,' Denis called, walking towards him, hand outstretched.

Reassured, Joshua went to greet him.

'Denis Hurley! A surprise visitor. Good morning, good morning.'

The two men shook hands. 'You want to see me about something?' Joshua asked, and when Denis nodded he added: 'Come into the office. It's too cold to talk out here.'

'You've got a powerful lot of stuff here, Mr Cohen,' Denis commented as the two men made their way back across the yard.

'Progress,' Joshua Cohen answered cryptically.

'Progress?'

'Things get old. They're no longer any use. Their owners throw the old away and buy something new. Wouldn't you call that progress, Denis?'

They reached the hut. Joshua unlocked the door and led Denis in.

'Sit down, my boy, sit down.' He motioned Denis into an ancient armchair that filled one corner. It was the only

352

piece of furniture there apart from a table in front of the window with a hard-bottomed chair where Denis presumed Judith sat. The table was neat and shelves around the walls held many old ledgers as well as a conglomeration of tool-boxes, tins, weights and measures, scales and a calendar. In another corner was a gas-ring on which stood a battered old kettle which looked as if it might have come from one of the piles in the yard. Iron Josh's overcoat hung on a nail, and on another nail beside it he placed the old coat he had been wearing. Then he took off his bowler hat, revealing the skull-cap on the back of his head, and settled it carefully over his good coat. That done, he turned and looked quizzically at Denis.

'If you have something you want to talk to me about, then this isn't a social visit, eh? Business?'

Denis, with vivid memories of how frustrating word-fencing with Iron Josh could be, smiled nervously.

'Well, Mr Cohen, I suppose you could call it business, in a way. It's friendly anyway.'

'In that case....' Joshua Cohen replied, holding up a hand to stop Denis from saying any more at that stage. He went to the gas-ring, shook the kettle to satisfy himself that there was sufficient water in it and then lit the gas. Denis watched him impatiently as he lifted two cups from a shelf and put them on the table. From a tin box on the floor he extracted a bag of tea, a bag of sugar and a corked bottle with some old label on it but which was now half-full of milk. As he prepared the tea he hummed to himself, and Denis wondered if this uncommunicative method was his natural way or deliberately adopted to make him nervous. You could never be up to Iron Josh – he was as cute as a bag of foxes. Then, just as Denis was deciding to match his silence, Joshua Cohen came to life again.

'Sugar?' he said.

'Two – please.'

'Two for you,' Joshua sang as he put two spoons into each of the cups, 'and two for me.' And then with a twinkle he turned to add: 'This time, my boy, at least we start equal, eh – not like the first time we met.' His laughter discounted any malice in the remark, and Denis, confused

353

now by his sudden volubility, had no reply. Feeling he was allowing too much initiative to Iron Josh, he jumped up, turned off the gas under the boiling kettle and poured the steaming water into the cups.

'Thank you, Denis,' Joshua said as he pulled the cork from the bottle of milk and put a nose to the contents.

'It's not today's but it's not sour. Not in this weather. My daughter brings fresh milk with her but she doesn't come in on Fridays.'

He stirred the two cups and handed one to Denis, motioning him back to the armchair.

'No,' Denis said. 'I'll sit here. I'm sure the soft chair is yours, Mr Cohen.'

'It's not all that more comfortable,' Joshua laughed, 'but to my older bones it is perhaps a bit kinder. And now, before we get to your business' – and he went to his overcoat.

Denis guessed what was coming, and he was right. Iron Josh pulled from the overcoat pocket his brown-paper parcel of sandwiches, opened them and placed them on the table.

'Jewish brown bread – you liked it the last time, I think – and cheese. You'll have one?'

'No, really, Mr Cohen,' Denis protested. 'I can't be taking your lunch.'

'Nonsense, my boy. It's Friday, and I don't eat much on Fridays until the evening. A special meal we have then, a Sabbath meal. And there's too much here for me anyway. My wife always makes more than enough. You will help me. Eat, eat.'

Denis gave in; it was better to do what his host suggested if he wanted to keep on his right side. And he did like the Jewish bread.

As Denis bit into a sandwich, Iron Josh's lips moved in a brief prayer. Then he sank into the armchair, took a sip of tea and munched away happily.

Denis, however, was far from happy, now that his moment had come. He reflected that the cup he was drinking from was probably the one Judith used, the chair he was sitting on was certainly hers, and waiting to hear

354

his proposition was her father. The whole situation was too bizarre. The atmosphere was friendly enough, but in view of how his relationship with Joshua Cohen had commenced Denis suddenly saw what he had in mind in a new light and he thought he must be stone mad to imagine that Joshua Cohen would not either explode in anger or collapse in derisive laughter at his request.

'Well, Denis Hurley,' Iron Josh said encouragingly, 'to business. You have something to sell me?' He put his cup down on the floor beside him and swallowed the last of his sandwich as if a business proposition was something to which he always gave full attention.

'Something to sell you? Well, I suppose I have, in a way. An idea.'

Denis put down his own cup – he wanted to appear just as serious and responsible as Iron Josh – and waited for a reaction. Joshua inclined his head to one side and smiled.

'An idea, my boy? I should pay money for an idea?'

His voice was mild, but Denis could detect the backing of scepticism, perhaps even of ridicule. He told himself that he should have known it was wrong to show so much of his hand so quickly to someone like Joshua Cohen – it allowed him get his bearings in advance and be a step ahead of developments. Denis's misgivings seemed to be confirmed when Iron Josh stretched for another sandwich and lifted his cup from the floor. Evidently he didn't think that this particular business discussion need interrupt his lunch after all.

'No,' Denis quickly responded, 'there's no money involved. I'm not looking for money this time.'

'Ah, then, this visit has nothing to do with the IRA.'

Denis's lips tightened in frustration. It seemed that, however he tried to make his request, it was the wrong way. Was he really stupid or was it simply that Iron Josh easily had his measure?

'You know, Mr Cohen,' he laughed, 'you're a very hard man to do business with.' And then, in response to Joshua's raised eyebrows, he quickly added: 'I mean you're far too clever for me.'

'Have you any experience as a businessman, Denis?'

'No, not a bit.'

'Not a bit. And I've been a businessman all my life. I've had to be. So don't be surprised that I know more about it than you do. Or upset. But I'll help you. What you've come about does concern the IRA, doesn't it?'

'Yes,' Denis admitted.

'You said you haven't come for money, so you must want some other kind of help, yes?'

'Yes, again.'

'But you know what I think of the IRA and their chances. You know I think they're wasting their time – killing people, and themselves, needlessly.'

'How can you talk like that?' Denis shot back, almost angrily. He was on firmer ground now. 'Ireland is our land, our home; that's what they're fighting for. Sure aren't some of your own people going out to Palestine soon to fight for *their* land?'

'How do you know that?' Joshua asked in surprise.

'Ah, it's not a secret,' Denis answered quickly, blushing at what had almost been a gaffe. 'News gets around. Cork isn't that big.' He was relieved to see that his explanation wasn't questioned.

'But,' Iron Josh pointed out, 'the Jews going to Palestine are not going out there to fight. They're going to settle in the country. They're not soldiers.'

There was a note of triumph in Denis's voice as he pounced on Joshua's words. 'But what will happen if the Arabs attack them and try to put them out? Won't they have to fight then? You told me yourself that you wouldn't fight for Ireland but you *would* fight to protect your home and your family if you had to. If the Jews in Palestine regard that country as their home, wouldn't they be right to fight for it if they were attacked? Wouldn't they?'

Denis's enthusiasm and his evident delight in the logic of his argument made Joshua smile. It was a sympathetic, almost an affectionate smile.

'So? And if you are right?' he queried.

'I *am* right. And you know I'm right, Mr Cohen,' Denis insisted.

356

'So. You are right,' Joshua conceded. 'If they were forced to fight, they'd have to fight.'

'Aha, and with what? What would they do for arms?'

Iron Josh threw up his hands.

'But that's what I told you, my boy. It would all be just self-sacrifice. What hope have the IRA with the little arms you have? Isn't that why you tried to make me give you money, to buy arms? You could never have enough to beat the British Army.'

'But we don't need to match them gun for gun. We could do with more than we have, of course. But we have enough to make things so uncomfortable for them that in the end they'll just give up and get out.'

Joshua Cohen snorted in derision.

'Anyway,' Denis persisted, 'would you help us if you could? Not with money. And there'd be no danger involved.'

Iron Josh put his empty cup on the table and gestured to Denis to take another sandwich.

'No, thanks,' Denis said, anxious to make his request but by now having learned enough about his adversary to know it would be foolish to force the pace. Then, realising it might be good tactics to hide his anxiety and to preserve the friendly atmosphere, he changed his mind. 'Maybe I'll have another one after all. They're very tasty.'

'Good, good,' Joshua encouraged, but immediately Denis bit into the sandwich and had his mouth full the question came at him.

'So how can I help the IRA? What do you want from me?'

Denis swallowed quickly and put down the remains of the sandwich.

'Well, I'll tell you,' he commenced. 'It's not so much helping the IRA – though of course it's that, too. I mean it's as much to help me as to help the IRA.'

Joshua leaned his head back and closed his eyes. Denis felt disconcerted. He had a momentary crazy fear that Iron Josh might fall asleep while he was talking.

'I'm listening, my boy.'

It was almost a whisper but it was encouragement enough.

357

'Well, it's like this, Mr Cohen. What arms we have are very precious to us, so we have to find places to hide them – safe houses, places like that. But that's getting harder and harder, and the Tans and the Army are stepping up their raids every day.'

Denis paused, but his listener said nothing. Could he be asleep after all? Denis remembered how, indeed, he *had* fallen asleep, even with a gun at his head, the day they had kidnapped him and their mission had ended in total failure. Oh Jesus, he thought, he's going to turn me down again.

He plunged on, almost in desperation.

'Our unit is planning a certain action very soon against the Tans. We have the arms and ammunition ready for it but we need a safe place to hide them until the time, a place no one would ever think of looking. I thought you might let me hide them here.'

Iron Josh's eyes sprung open.

'Here!'

'Yes. In the yard. It's ideal. Just inside that gate at the back – under some scrap. There's only a lane on the other side of the wall. I've been there a few times to examine it and there never seems to be anyone else there. I could climb over the wall easily and hide the arms and ammunition just inside the gate. There's plenty of stuff to cover them with. No one would see me – you could be certain of that. And it wouldn't be for long. I can't tell you when the action is to be but I promise you it wouldn't be for long.'

Joshua Cohen stared at Denis, but the look in his eyes revealed nothing of his thoughts. Denis hoped he might at least be considering his suggestion, that he wouldn't just dismiss it out of hand. At last he spoke.

'And how safe do you think your hiding-place would be with all the men in your unit knowing it?'

'Oh, no,' Denis replied quickly, glad that there was something on which he could offer Iron Josh some reassurance. 'No one knows about it – not even our O.C. You see, it's my own idea, and I wouldn't tell him unless you gave me the go-ahead. And also I would tell him where the hiding-place was only on condition that no one

358

else was told and that he would allow me to put the arms and ammunition there on my own – and get them back, too, on my own as soon as we need them. He'd have to promise me that. I swear to you, I'd make certain there'd be no danger of anyone finding out and no chance that you could get into trouble. Please, Mr Cohen. Don't say no. I need your help.'

In the silence that followed, the intensity of his own appeal made him blush with embarrassment. Joshua turned his head away and looked around the hut. Denis waited tensely until he felt forced to make his final point.

'You see,' he added, almost apologetically, 'I'm not exactly in favour after the kidnap mess-up, and if you agree to this it would put me back in their good books. And, besides, I didn't have to come and ask you, did I? I could just have hidden the arms and ammunition in the yard and you'd have been none the wiser.'

Iron Josh smiled, and his eyes twinkled.

'And supposing I just happened to find them? I'd have to tell the police and you'd lose everything. No, my boy, you had to ask me so as to be sure that couldn't happen, eh?'

Denis coloured again. It was best to say no more until he had some idea of what sort of answer he was going to get.

'So really, Denis Hurley, you're asking me to do this for *you* – to help *you*.'

'Yes.' Denis could see that his only chance lay in putting his fate in Joshua Cohen's hands, as once Joshua's fate had been in his.

'But why should I put myself in danger? You say there is none, but who knows for certain? If you are wrong, and the arms are found, I could be arrested, I could lose my licence and my livelihood. For what should I put so much at risk?'

'Look, Mr Cohen,' Denis pressed. 'Why should the police, or anyone else, find the arms and ammunition here? Even *you* wouldn't know when I'm going to bring them. And I give you my word it would only be for a matter of days. So even if they *were* found – they wouldn't be, but even if they were – you could honestly say you knew

359

nothing about them. You'd be believed. The police would never think you were helping the IRA. So there's no danger. And anyway....'

He hesitated.

'Yes?' Joshua encouraged.

'Well,' Denis replied haltingly, 'you said I saved your life – that if anyone else had kidnapped you they might have shot you.'

'So I owe you a favour in return, is that it?'

Denis looked away sheepishly, unable to admit that that was his trump card and embarrassed that Iron Josh had put in bald terms what amounted to moral blackmail on his part. But he was surprised to hear a hearty laugh, and when he looked around to find its cause Iron Josh had stood up and was rummaging in a corner of one of the shelves.

At last he found what he was looking for and quietly placed a large, slightly rusty iron key on the table.

He put a hand on Denis's shoulder and squeezed. Then he took his bowler hat off its nail, fitted it on to his head and stepped to the door of the hut. Turning, he said: 'I have to get back to the yard, my boy. It's a lot of work keeping such a big yard tidy, you know.' He smiled. 'I might be a while, so if you have to get back to work don't wait for me.'

Denis sat stiffly, looking at Iron Josh, too amazed at what was happening to move or speak.

'Goodbye, Denis,' Joshua said. 'And good luck to you.'

He strode away.

'Thanks. Thanks, Mr Cohen,' Denis suddenly called, but he didn't know if Iron Josh had even heard him.

When the Friday night meal was over and Grace had been sung, Jacob felt the time had come for him to announce that he had decided to leave university and go to Palestine. The family was still gathered around the table – except for Judith, who was in and out clearing the dishes into the kitchen, but she would have no say, anyway, in this. He had already gone over and over in his mind countless ways of breaking the news and he had the chosen words just about off by heart. But actually finding the courage – finding the very breath in his lungs – to say those words was far harder than he had expected. And then, before he could speak, his *zeide* said: '*Kinder*, I'll go up to my room. Perhaps I'll go to bed early tonight.'

Joshua nodded, and Bertha Cohen encouraged him with '*Gei, gei*. Have a *shluff*. You need it.'

Rabbi Moishe didn't usually leave the table so soon on Friday nights, but they had seen that this evening he had not been himself. He was still talking about his visit to Father McGiff, still thinking about it, still not recovered from the shock it had given him.

As he bade them *guten nacht* and went upstairs, Jacob squeezed his fists in chagrin. What more could go wrong? Anger at the totally unexpected change of routine surged through him, throwing him completely off balance so that he forgot his nervousness and blurted out his speech. It wasn't the speech he had prepared – his anger had made him forget that, too – but once he had told them his decision it didn't matter how he had scrambled over the hurdle. The important thing was that he *had* got over it and was on the other side.

His announcement was greeted with a stunned silence. Then his mother and father found their tongues simultaneously.

'This is a joke?' Joshua suggested, eyes wide.

'What did you say?' Bertha asked harshly, starkly disbelieving.

Jacob found that saying it again was even more difficult than the first time, but in as steady a voice as possible he ground through it.

'I don't want to be a doctor. I don't want to go to college. I want to go to Palestine with *zeide*.'

Joshua closed his eyes and leaned back in his chair. What was it with the boy? One thing after another. But the other trouble had been taken care of – *he* had seen that through. This was his wife's affair.

Bertha Cohen was about to ridicule her son's idea when Judith returned from the kitchen.

'You know about this?' she asked her daughter aggressively. 'You've heard his *mishegoss*?'

'Know about what?'

'He says he wants to leave college and go to *Eretz*. Is he mad?'

Judith collapsed in surprise into a chair.

'No, Jacob, no.' It was a message of sympathy and understanding as much as a plea, for she alone knew what must have prompted her brother's desire.

'Why not?' Jacob responded truculently. 'I don't want—'

But before he could say any more his mother screamed: '*You* don't want. *You* don't want. What about me? What about your parents? Is this what we've worked our fingers to the bone for? Is this what we educated you for? Sent you to Presentation Brothers. Paid big fees for you. To make something of yourself. Is this how you repay us?'

Bertha Cohen's normally pale face was flushed with passion, and Jacob almost visibly wilted under the onslaught.

'Wait,' Judith interrupted. 'Wait. Go easy, Momma. Don't upset yourself. Let Jacob go and ask *zeide*. *Zeide* will know the right thing to do. Believe me, Momma, let *zeide* decide.'

Judith could be confident that her grandfather would not take Jacob with him. Hadn't he already dismissed the idea that her brother should go instead of him if anyone had to deputise for him? Yes, she remembered that her *zeide* wanted Jacob to qualify as a doctor first; then, if he wanted, he could go to *Eretz*. So let Jacob ask him. Refusal was certain, but her *zeide* would show Jacob much more sympathy than her mother would.

'This time, Momma,' she said, laying a hand on her mother's arm, 'listen to me. Let *zeide* decide.'

Bertha Cohen threw up her head angrily.

'He can ask his *zeide* if he wants. But it doesn't matter what the answer is; he's not leaving college.'

Jacob was trembling with anxiety at the storm of opposition he had aroused.

'Go on, then,' his mother barked at him. 'What are you

362

waiting for? Go and tell your *zeide* your *mishegoss*. He won't be in bed yet.'

Slowly, as if pushing against unseen hands pressing him to the chair, Jacob got up and left the room. His father stared after him, his heart heavy with sorrow. The question – the question – no one had asked Jacob the question: *why* did he want to leave college and go to *Eretz*? No one had asked him that. His eyes squeezed tight in anguish at the knowledge that he hadn't asked it himself, that he hadn't been able to take his son into a corner and in a quiet voice say: 'Jacob, my boy, what's the matter? Why are you unhappy?'

Rabbi Cohen didn't ask his grandson the question, either, but it wasn't from embarrassment or lack of courage. He didn't need to ask it. Quietly he sat Jacob beside him on his bed, held his hands, and talked.

'*Yankeleh*,' he said, 'you are how old – seventeen? Four years ago you were thirteen and you celebrated your bar mitzvah and people all around said to you what is always said to a bar mitzvah boy: "Today you are a man." Remember?'

Jacob nodded.

'Tell me, *Yankeleh*' – and the Rabbi moved his hand around his grandson's shoulders – 'did you feel like a man that day? Did you look at your father, who runs a big store, and at the other men in the *Shool* who go out to business every week to earn money and feed and clothe their families – did you look at them and say to yourself: "Today I am a man like them"?'

Jacob shook his head.

'No, you didn't. Why? Because that day you became a man only in the religious sense. At thirteen you were old enough for all the religious rights and obligations of a Jewish male. But were you ready then to go out and make a living? How could you be? You hadn't even finished school. And when you did finish school this year, and you went to college to become a doctor, did you feel a man then, *Yankeleh*?'

'Well, yes,' Jacob answered. 'I did, in a way.'

'*Goot, goot*,' Rabbi Moishe enthused. '"In a way" – that

363

was it. In a way you were a man then – you were beginning to become a man – not a man for the religious world, *that* you were already – but a man for the other world, the world that surrounds our Jewish world. That's a very different world, *Yankeleh*. You are beginning to find that out, yes?'

'Yes.' Jacob's admission was brief, and his *zeide* did not miss the bitterness in its tone.

'Yes, *mein kinde*, yes, a very different world from our Jewish world of Shabbos and *Shool* and festivals and laws and customs. It is different, *Yankeleh*, because it can hurt.'

Jacob looked at his grandfather and then turned away, but Rabbi Moishe's hand felt its way around his grandson's head and pressed it for a moment against his own.

'I know, *Yankeleh*, I know. It has hurt you already. I don't know how, but that does not matter. It has hurt you before you were ready – long before you were ready, before you were a man. You see, *mein kinde*, you can't become a man in one night – a boy one day, a man the next – no, not possible. It takes time. For some a short time, for others a long time – maybe even never. But a man does not run away when the world hurts him. A boy might – yes, a boy might; but if he does, then how does he become a man, eh, *mein kinde*?'

Rabbi Moishe paused and then asked quietly: 'You want to go to *Eretz*?'

When Jacob made no reply, his *zeide* continued.

'I could say to you: what will you do in *Eretz*? Be a farmer? Be a labourer? You would like that, eh? There's nothing else there yet. That's the sort of work all the men have to do in the settlements. Some day, some time in the future, *Eretz* will need more than farmers and labourers. It will need scientists and businessmen and lawyers and manufacturers and artists – and doctors. You could be a doctor in *Eretz* some day – if you want to be. Or a doctor here. Or anywhere in the world. I could say all that to you, *Yankeleh*, but it's not a question of being a doctor or not being a doctor, is it? It's a question of being a man – first.

364

And if you go to *Eretz* now it will not be as a man, but as a boy – a boy who has run away from his first battle as a man. *Du fur steisht, mein kinde*, you understand?'

Jacob nodded and rose from the bed.

'If you want to go to *Eretz, Yankeleh*, I will help you. If you're sure you want to go. But you must be sure.'

Jacob stood for a full minute with his back to his *zeide*. At last he turned and shook his head.

'No,' he murmured. 'I'll stay.'

Rabbi Moishe smiled. He closed his eyes, and his old head went up and down as if in prayer. Then he looked at his grandson and said: 'Your mother and father will be pleased. They will understand. You would like me to tell them?'

'No, I'll tell them myself,' Jacob said as he went to leave the bedroom.

'*Goot*,' Rabbi Moishe encouraged, '*goot*. It is your decision. You tell them.'

At the door Jacob turned and went back to his grandfather.

'Thank you, *zeide*,' he whispered.

Rabbi Moishe took his hands again and put them to his mouth.

'Remember, *Yankeleh*, when you were a boy, remember, "*Yankeleh, Yankeleh, geb tzu zein zeide a bonkeleh*". Remember that? But now that you're a man of course. . . .'

Rabbi Moishe's eyes twinkled with joy and love. Jacob threw his arms around his neck and kissed him. The Rabbi held him for a moment and then said: 'You know, Jacob, a boy of your age wouldn't have been able to kiss his *zeide*. Now go; your parents will be anxious.'

When his grandson had gone, Rabbi Moishe cried for a while and then took up a prayer-book and opened it.

28

THE WEDDING of Miriam Levy and Reuben Jackson on Sunday was an especially welcome event – marriages in the community were infrequent enough for the members to be uplifted by one for weeks ahead – but this particular wedding was not without a melancholy undertone. It was the last celebration their beloved Rabbi would be present to share with them, and without him things would never be the same.

By now the signs were clear: sooner rather than later authority was going to change hands in Ireland. What might such a change mean to a tiny alien group such as theirs, most of whom had neither roots nor an independent stake in the land? The prospect of finding themselves before long in a different Ireland was daunting enough; to have to face it without their spiritual leader filled them with apprehension. The savagery of the struggle going on around them and the increasing harassment and brutality had already invaded their daily lives. Just trying to earn a living had for many become especially arduous, and death itself had struck down one of their favourites. Their own history, their race-memories, made them sympathise in their hearts with the cause of their Irish friends and neighbours, but where would it all end and how would they fare if Britain did abandon the country? They had no reason to expect disfavour or intolerance under native rule, but could anyone tell? The devil you know. . . . Yet that devil was the same one that had declared to the world its intention of providing a home for the Jewish people, their people, in Palestine, but more than three years later seemed to have done little or nothing to fulfil its promise. Was it likely, then, that it would lightly release its grip on a country it had held for centuries, one it considered vital to its interests? If it didn't, the situation must surely become even worse. Worse? How *could* it get any worse?

There were many answers and no answer – discussion would usually end in a shoulder shrug or a deliberate change of subject.

On Sunday, however, no such preoccupation clouded the thoughts of those who came together in the synagogue to witness the wedding rituals of Miriam and Reuben and then to celebrate the union with them and their families in the communal rooms. Man, woman and child, they were bent on enjoyment – the children being uniquely privileged on this occasion, for it was also the eve of Chanukah, and once the marriage ceremony was over they would be allowed to run among the adults, wearing around their necks the little cotton bags their mothers had specially sewn for them and into which the grown-ups would drop coins in keeping with the age-old custom of giving the young gifts of Chanukah-money.

For Miriam the excitement was too much to take in, almost too much to bear. It was as if the weeks of preparation and anticipation had been experienced by someone else, so much more intense was the brightness of this day which, like a firework, those weeks had at last succeeded in igniting. That the enchantment would last only a few hours, and would never be repeated, in no way dimmed its glow.

She and her father had been driven to the synagogue in a carriage drawn by a gaily festooned pair of greys with the coachman wearing a tall hat and livery and carrying a white whip. And, although the shortness of the journey and the emptiness of the Sunday morning streets meant that there were few pedestrians to remark her progress, she nevertheless imagined that a princess parading through her domain could hardly have felt happier or more fortunate. Even her father beside her was not the tubby jocular father she knew but a dignified, quietly perspiring figure in made-to-measure morning coat, grey waistcoat and striped pants, hands encased in chamois gloves, spats setting off the high polish of his boots, and gleaming top hat resting on the seat where, with a grunt of relief, he had deposited it.

Soon afterwards, as she slowly walked up the synagogue aisle on his arm, she was hardly conscious of the sighs of admiration that rose from the onlookers, aware of them only as a caressing tide floating her towards the *chuppah*. There, under the red velvet canopy stretched across four slender mahogany pillars specially set up before the Ark of the Law, waited the man whom within a matter of minutes the magic would transform into her husband.

She had already seen Reuben that morning, for an hour earlier he had come to her home, and in the company of her family and all her female friends who had gathered to see her off to *Shool* he had performed the traditional ceremony of covering her face with her veil. As she looked into his eyes her desire for his embrace stormed through her blood, and when, attaching the veil to her headdress he had cheekily pulled the lobe of her ear, she had barely succeeded in suppressing an urge to pull his head down to hers and kiss him. It was his broad back to which she pinned her gaze as, step by careful step, she neared the *chuppah*, and like a magnet it held her steady and true until she reached his side. She stood there, quietly trembling, while the words of the marriage ceremony – those holy words which Rev. Levitt intoned to bind her to Reuben for the rest of her life – swam about her ears, and it wasn't until she heard the crunching of the wine-glass under Reuben's heel, the noise of which was believed to frighten away evil spirits, that she knew the ceremony was over and she was married. Her husband just had time to lift her veil and touch her lips with his before they were surrounded by relatives and friends smothering her with embraces, shaking hands with Reuben and calling '*Mazeltov, mazeltov*' all the way to the central dais to sign the marriage register. As she wrote her name 'Miriam Levy', Reuben whispered into her ear: 'That's the last time you'll use that name, Mrs Jackson.' His words startled her. For days she had secretly practised writing 'Miriam Jackson' and it had given her a strange uncomfortable feeling which she had put down to the fact that she was still single. Now, writing her maiden name when she really *was* Mrs Miriam Jackson brought on the same sensation. She was surprised, not expecting to *feel* married so quickly. But perhaps it was just nerves.

There was no time to ponder over the thought, for immediately they were bustled into an ante-room where the photographer was waiting to take the wedding pictures. Mrs Burns suddenly appeared out of the crowd and began to fuss around her, smoothing out creases in the white satin dress and straightening the long net veil with its silk-embroidered corners. 'You look gorgeous, love, a picture,' she kept repeating as she gave a hoist to Miriam's hand holding the shower bouquet of white flowers, and only when she was satisfied that every detail was as she wanted it did she allow the photographer to proceed. Then it was up the stairs to the communal rooms where all morning family and friends had been dressing the long lunch-table and bringing in seemingly endless supplies of crockery, cutlery, glasses and bottles, and the varied dishes that had been cooked for the wedding feast.

As she sat beside Reuben, only picking at her food despite his urging that she should eat well because they wouldn't get another meal until the evening when they arrived at their hotel in Dublin, her head rang with the din of conversation and laughter. Every time she raised her eyes and saw all the people she knew and loved, the people with whom she had grown up, she was assailed by the realisation that this was what she was leaving for a strange land and a much harder life than what she had been used to. For the first time since she had agreed with Reuben that they should go to Palestine, the consequences of that decision began to be made real. The familiarity, the comfort, the security, the shared enjoyment, the long years' memories – everything that contributed to her image of home and that was implicit in this celebration in her honour came together with such force and clarity that the risk she was taking in leaving it all behind sent a wave of fear blowing through the heat and smoke and jollity of the wedding feast. She was aware of Rabbi Cohen and her father and Reuben's father rising to make speeches and she almost wished she could have stopped her ears, so affecting were their words. She listened closely only to the final speaker – her husband, Reuben, thanking everyone and using the occasion as an opportunity, on his behalf and on hers, to say farewell to the community before their departure to Palestine.

Then Rabbi Cohen led the blessings and Grace After Meals, and gratefully she joined the mixed voices in the responses. The familiar tunes were a haven to her, and she sang them with fervour. The knowledge that they at least would be the same in *Eretz* made them more precious, and Percy Lovitch's dominating tenor, harmonising each cadence, infused them with a poignancy they had never had before. She squeezed her eyes closed, as much to lock in her mind the picture before her as to hide from those around her the tears she could not hold back.

When she opened them again it was to catch the gaze of Judith Cohen, and the two girls smiled at each other in sisterly encouragement. Miriam's smile was meant to say 'Some day it will be your turn – may that day be soon' and behind the smile Miriam experienced a thrill of gratitude that such a day had dawned for her and that she would never, from now on, have to face life alone; Judith's smile was to say 'Bless you, all you wish yourself I wish you, too, and may God grant it,' but behind *her* smile Judith felt only her own unhappiness. Was it just the occasion that moved her – the romance, the sentiment? She felt no envy of Miriam, yet did she now want something she had never wanted before? Did she now see herself under the *chuppah*, wearing a white satin wedding dress – a bride? And with whom? Denis? Nonsense. Fantasy. Never in this world. So what was it she had begun to miss? If not a husband, then a man? Denis? Yes, yes, yes. She didn't dare close her eyes because she well knew that whenever she closed them now the image of her and Denis on Fanny Rubin's bed blazed like a fire in the darkness of her mind. She let her voice join, full-throated, the chorus of the guests around her, as if sound might by its very force make the picture fade. But the louder she sang, the more vivid her recollection grew, until at last she broke under her want, vowing to herself to wait no longer but call on Denis the next morning.

As soon as Grace was finished the newlyweds got up to leave – first they would go to their homes to change and then to the station to catch the afternoon train to Dublin. Slowly they negotiated their way to the door, for virtually everyone in the room had to be thanked and said goodbye to, but eventually they broke away, and with the best man and a girlfriend of Miriam's they went out to a waiting car. Parents and relations followed them into the street to prolong the farewells and see them off, while many of the guests crowded the windows with a final wave and shouts of 'Good luck' and 'God speed'. When the car had vanished from view they turned from the windows almost with regret, the older couples filled with nostalgia, the younger with a dream of their own. Very quickly, however, the moment of melancholy vanished as more drinks were poured and the returning parents urged everyone to enjoy themselves, have a good time and continue to share with them their day of happiness.

With the lunch finished and the bride and groom gone, the festivities were taken over by the young people. Tables and chairs were pushed to the wall so that a space could be cleared for dancing, while the older guests gathered in groups, discussing the wedding, communal affairs, the state of the country and the impending departure to Palestine. Many could not forbear to compare this Sunday afternoon with the last one when in the cold and wet of the cemetery they had buried Abie Klugman. The women sitting with Ada Neumann would not have mentioned it, for they knew how much she had cared for Abie, but the tragedy was too fresh in her mind and the contrast too stark for Ada herself not to give voice to her sorrow. 'That such a thing should happen,' she kept repeating until someone, in an effort to turn her thoughts, pressed her to look to the future and think of getting another lodger. No one could really take Abie's place of course – they knew that – but.... Yes, she had agreed that no one could take Abie Klugman's place in her memories and then, being the woman she was, she expressed even more concern for the effect of Abie's death on Mickey Aronson than on herself. 'He sits there *shtum*,' she said, 'not a word out of him. No talk, no jokes. Who would have thought ...?'

The proof of her statement was there for any to see, and her companions surreptitiously turned their heads to where Mickey sat in a corner. But their attempts to conceal their curiosity were unnecessary, for he seemed oblivious of the noise and activity around him. He took no interest in any of the gossiping groups he would normally have joined with his barbs and sallies, but now crouched forward on his seat, hands joined between his knees, staring emptily at the dancing couples. Max Klein tried to engage him in conversation, but the response was so lacklustre that he soon had to give up and rejoin Rabbi Moishe and the other leaders of the community with whom he had been talking. The Rabbi, noting the President's failure to get any reaction from Mickey Aronson, approached him himself and spoke to him, but Mickey's monosyllabic replies soon persuaded him that even *his* efforts were an intrusion and that, for the moment anyway, Mickey Aronson was best left to get over his grief himself.

There was no pause in the celebrations for some time – not, indeed, until mid-afternoon when the December sky lost what little light it had had and dusk began to fall. Then, at a signal from Rabbi Moishe, he and Rev. Levitt and most of the men withdrew to the synagogue for the recital of the afternoon and evening prayers. The girls who had been dancing were glad of the respite. It was a chance for them to catch their breath and look forward to

372

a new stage in the festivities when the men would return. For the ending of the prayers would mark the beginning of Chanukah, the joyous Festival of Lights, and Rabbi Moishe would light the first of the eight special candles, recite the Chanukah blessing and lead them all into the singing of the Chanukah song, *Maoz Tzur*, 'Rock of Strength'. The women had already moved a table to the centre of the floor, covered it with a clean cloth and got out from a cupboard the large silver *menorah*, its eight whorled branches gleaming under the lights and a taller ninth one protruding from the centre stem. This would hold the *shammas*, from which each evening the other candles would draw their flame, and so it was the only one which would not be allowed to burn out until the last day of Chanukah.

Soon the menfolk began to troop back, smiles of anticipation on their faces when they saw the *menorah* standing by itself in the centre of the floor. Even without a gaily burning candle it seemed already a beacon.

Rabbi Moishe approached, followed by Max Klein whose enjoyment of festivals – sacred or secular – always brought out the child in him. He opened the box of coloured candles and offered it to the Rabbi. As Rabbi Moishe smiled his thanks and stretched out a hand to take one, he paused momentarily, thinking that this was his last Chanukah in Cork, his last religious function. The President met his eyes and read the thought behind them.

'*Leshana habaa b'Yerushulayim* – to next year in Jerusalem, Rabbi,' he whispered.

'God willing,' Rabbi Moishe nodded, 'God willing.'

He took a blue candle from the box and fitted it into the first branch of the *menorah*. Then, turning to the box again, he carefully chose a white candle to be the *shammas*. His choice of a white one always met with appreciative grunts and nods, for its colour and tall spare shape seemed in a way twin of the Rabbi himself with his thin upright figure wrapped in a *kittel*, the long white coat he wore on such occasions. Rabbi Moishe was well aware that his community treasured the comparison and so he

373

never varied his choice, but closer to his heart was the
sentiment that both the candle and he had the same
function – that of giving light to others without losing
any of one's own lustre. This year, however, as he lit the
white candle, the light it made seemed to be mixed with
shadow. He saw a week ahead to the next Sunday when
the remnant of that white candle would be lit for the last
time and to mark the end of Chanukah it would be allowed
to burn down until its flame would gutter and finally die.
And he...?

'*Nu?*'

Max Klein's muttered prompt made him realise that his
mind had been straying. He shook his head as if to chase
away all morbid thoughts and then lit the pure white
candle. Holding it out for all to see he intoned the
blessing: 'Blessed art Thou, O Lord our God, King of the
Universe, Who hath sanctified us with His commandments, and hath commanded us to kindle the lights for
Chanukah.'

Slowly he inclined it towards the lone coloured candle
in the *menorah*, caressing it with glancing tender touches
until its wick began to splutter and then, suddenly
awakened, it burst into proud dancing flame as all the
watchers in company with Rabbi Moishe chanted the
additional blessing recited only on the first night:
'Blessed art Thou, O Lord our God, King of the Universe,
Who hath kept us in life, and hath preserved us, and
enabled us to reach this season.'

Immediately the final word had been said everyone fell
silent, waiting for their Rabbi to commence the special
Chanukah hymn, 'Rock of Strength'.

Rabbi Moishe turned, smiled at their anticipation – and
at his own – and then, with a gesture as of a conductor
marshalling his chorus, he led them into the rousing tune.

> Rock of strength against despair, unto You
>   alone I sing!
> Give me back my house of prayer, and with
>   praise of You 'twill ring.
>   When Your wrath has set me free

374

Of the brass-mouthed enemy
Music's thong, in coils of song, round Your
altar I will fling.

Every man, woman and child in the room, their voices kept in perfect time by Percy Lovitch's loud shepherding tenor, sang lustily.

Labour was my constant dole and sorrow spun
my strength away,
Sickly, sickly was my soul, locked in Egypt's
cruel sway.
Then for us Your mighty hand
Swept the ocean from the land –
Pharaoh's breed, with all its seed, sank like
stones into the bay.

Here Percy's hands made urgent signs for a *pianissimo* opening to the final verse, and as the verse proceeded they churned in ever-widening circles to whip the singers into a final triumphant *crescendo*.

Brought unto Your holy shrine, still my lusts I
could not quell;
Once again strange gods were mine, once
again I captive fell.
All my hope had gone – but when
Life itself was going, then
I was won from Babylon by the power of
Zerubuvel.

As the last resounding notes hung in the air the singers turned to each other in mutual congratulation, laughter on their lips, pride and pleasure shining in their eyes. Percy Lovitch purred with satisfaction at his own performance, grateful for the undimmed vibrancy of his voice and still hearing inside his head the resonance of its sweetest echoes. Max Klein wiped his brow, beaded with perspiration from his exertions and the heat of the room. The more matronly of the men's wives unashamedly fanned themselves and each other, patting their bosoms, puffing out the sleeves from under their armpits, and turning eyes full of nostalgic envy on the still cool-looking younger women.

Rabbi Cohen bent to blow out the *shammas* candle, and the President put a hand on his arm, saying: 'Now, Rabbi, we have a little ceremony to perform – a special surprise ceremony.' He held up his hands for silence and the chatter of the men and women, privy to what was coming, immediately ceased.

'Rabbi Cohen,' Max Klein announced in a loud voice. Then he cleared his throat and started again. 'No, Rabbi Moishe I mean.'

'*Ga recht*, that's right, Rabbi Moishe,' was repeated around him.

'Rabbi Moishe, next Sunday you will be leaving us for *Eretz*, and of course we couldn't let you go from here without giving you something to remember us by, something that expresses our feelings for you and our gratitude for all you have done for us and what you have meant to us for so long. Now, I'm not going to make a speech, but as Chanukah is traditionally a time when members of a family give each other gifts, and as this is the first night of Chanukah, we felt it would be fitting to use this opportunity....'

The President mopped his brow again, this time with relief at having memorised his words successfully and proud to be officiating on such an important occasion.

'Zvi,' he called, but Zvi Lipsky was already at his side, a white cardboard box in his hands. Max Klein took the box from him and presented it to Rabbi Cohen, removing the lid as he did so.

'Rabbi Moishe,' he said, 'this is a Chanukah gift and a going-away gift from your family, the Cork Jewish Community, to you.'

Throughout the President's little presentation speech Rabbi Moishe's head had been lowered to hide both his embarrassment and his emotion. Now he took the box from Max Klein and placed it on the table so as to examine its contents. It held a set of five books, each bound

376

sumptuously in dark blue leather, the title of each volume in gold letters on the spine: *Genesis, Exodus, Leviticus, Numbers, Deuteronomy.*'

'The Torah, Rabbi,' Max Klein said solemnly. 'The very latest edition. With all the Commentaries. We sent to Vienna specially for them.'

Rabbi Cohen looked around at his people, his eyes moist. Then he lifted out the first volume and fondled it. The front was inscribed, again in gold letters, 'To Rabbi Moishe Cohen on the occasion of his departure to *Eretz Yisroel*, from the Cork Jewish Community'.

'*Ai, ai,*' the Rabbi almost moaned, unable to form a word. His heart was pounding, his senses overwhelmed with the emotion of the moment.

'Open it, Rabbi, open it,' Max Klein urged anxiously, but when Rabbi Moishe seemed powerless to move the President turned over the cover to expose the fly-leaf. Written on it was a host of names.

'We all signed it,' Max Klein explained. 'Everyone who contributed signed it.'

Rabbi Moishe took out a handkerchief and wiped his eyes so as to read the list. At the top was the Minister, Rev. Levitt, then the President and the other officers of the Executive Committee. Next came the name Joshua Cohen, and the Rabbi looked up to search for his son. Joshua stood arm in arm with his wife, Judith and Jacob by his side, and when his father's eyes met his he turned away in embarrassment.

Rabbi Moishe returned to the list, speaking the names as he came on them, and with each name he sought out its bearer and bowed his head in thanks. They were all there. 'Percy Lovitch,' Rabbi Moishe read out, 'Samuel Spiro, Benjamin Katz, Reuben Levy' – there was laughter as a voice called: 'Not here, Rabbi, otherwise engaged.' Rabbi Moishe laughed, too, and then bent to resume reading. Suddenly he appeared to falter. 'Abraham,' he read, his voice quivering. Slowly he raised his head until he was looking straight up at the ceiling, as if he was trying to see through it to the heavens beyond.

'Abraham Klugman,' he called.

'Yes,' Max Klein put in, 'poor Abie. He signed it, too, before.... '

But before the President could finish what he was saying Rabbi Moishe called again.

'Abraham Klugman!'

It did not sound like a name. It was more a cry, as of a doomed man, and a ripple of fear swept through the people, followed by gasps and half-stifled screams as the Rabbi's whole body went stiff, the book fell from his hands and before anyone could move he crashed forward on to the table.

Immediately there was pandemonium. Joshua rushed to his father's aid, and with willing helpers the Rabbi was carefully lifted and laid upon one of the benches. His eyes were closed, and his face had gone chalk white.

'What happened? *Vos iz de meisa?*' some of the men asked as others comforted their distressed wives. Ada Neumann quickly went to Bertha Cohen and tried with Judith to assure her that everything would be all right.

'A doctor! Get a doctor!' someone demanded, but Joshua had already called Jacob to him and told him to go for Dr Lee, who for many years had ministered to the ills of most of Cork's Jews from his home near Celtic Crescent.

'Hurry!' Joshua ordered. 'Hurry! And if he's not there find him.'

'My bike is downstairs. It won't take me a minute,' Jacob called back as he rushed out of the room.

As people crowded round the prostrate figure of their Rabbi, Max Klein quietly shooed them away, suggesting that they should go home. But no one was willing to leave until they knew how serious Rabbi Moishe's collapse might be. Instead they moved back to the walls, the women occupying the chairs, the men standing in knots, quietly discussing the alarming development. Would the Rabbi recover in time to go to *Eretz*? they asked each other. Only a week more. And, if he didn't, what would happen to the whole plan? Meanwhile, Rabbi Cohen was motionless on the bench, his eyes closed, his neck bare where Joshua had removed his stiff collar. Bertha and

Judith sat by him, Bertha holding one of his hands.

'He's cold, Joshua. His hand is cold,' she whispered, and Joshua took off his coat and spread it over his father.

From a window someone who had been watching the street suddenly announced, 'He's coming. Dr Lee is coming,' and in the silence all could hear a horse's hoofs as Dr Lee approached, driving the side-car he always used for his calls. In a moment his heavy steps sounded on the stairs and he hurried into the room, black bag in hand, Jacob following on his heels.

He took no more than a minute to examine the Rabbi and make his diagnosis.

'I'm afraid the Rabbi has had a stroke, Mr Cohen,' he said, turning to Joshua. 'It's not very surprising in a man of his age. Maybe he's been overdoing things lately.'

Joshua nodded, thinking of the shocks his father had had to bear in the past week.

'He'll need complete rest for a while,' Dr Lee declared.

'But he's expecting to leave for Palestine next Sunday.'

'Oh, I know all about that, Mr Cohen, but it's out of the question. A stroke is a serious matter. I can't tell for certain how bad your father is until I've had a chance to make a proper examination when we get him to hospital. The sooner the better. I'll try to get an ambulance.'

There was a gurgling sound behind them, and they turned to see the Rabbi's eyelids flickering and his lips moving.

Joshua knelt by him.

'*Vos?* What is it, *tata?*'

He had to put an ear to his father's lips to hear the Rabbi's whisper.

'*Heim! Heim!*'

'He said "Home". He wants to go home.'

Dr Lee shook his head.

'Most unwise. He needs proper nursing attention.'

'You can't send him to hospital,' Bertha broke in. 'Believe me, Doctor, he'd get better more quickly at home. We can take care of him. We could have someone beside his bed day and night.'

Dr Lee understood her anxiety. He was long enough

attending his Jewish patients to be aware that they could not eat hospital food because it wasn't kosher; he knew, too, how important peace of mind was to an old man suffering from a stroke and that, if the Rabbi was to recover, familiar Jewish surroundings and a Jewish atmosphere could have a vital influence. He suspected, however, that Rabbi Cohen's stroke might be even more serious than it appeared. It was a difficult decision, and he needed to make it quickly.

'All right,' he said. 'But you'll need an ambulance to get him home.'

'Don't worry. I've got my motor-car here,' Max Klein put in. 'We could take him in that. It'll be quicker – only five minutes.'

'Dr Lee,' Joshua appealed, taking the doctor by the arm and moving a few steps away from his father. 'Palestine ...?'

Dr Lee shook his head, rubbed his bushy eyebrows and stroked his thick grey moustache. His Jewish patients had been telling him for months about the planned emigration to the Holy Land. He knew what Palestine meant to them, for he was a Bible-lover himself. From his childhood in his Scottish Presbyterian home he had read about the People of the Book. He understood – fully understood – what going there would mean to Rabbi Cohen. But there was no point in raising false hopes.

'No, not next week. Perhaps later. Perhaps not. I'll be able to tell you more when I've examined him properly. Get him to bed and I'll call in an hour.'

Already Max Klein had enlisted the aid of some of the young men present, and together they lifted Rabbi Cohen tenderly in their arms and were carrying him towards the door. Joshua shook the doctor's hand and hurried after them.

'He's a fine old man, your father, a noble old man,' Dr Lee said as he entered the Cohens' kitchen later that evening after spending half an hour examining the Rabbi. 'But he is an *old* man, and a stroke at his age is. ... ' He sighed, put his bag on the ground and spread his hands as if to indicate that the outcome of the Rabbi's illness would depend on a Healer other than he.

'Sit, Doctor, sit,' Bertha urged. 'You'll have a cup of tea.'

'I think someone should be with the Rabbi all the time,' Dr Lee advised. 'And if he seems to get worse or be in any distress with his breathing call me immediately.'

'I'll go up,' Judith said.

When she had gone, Dr Lee sat at the table, and as he munched one of Bertha's *pletsls* and drank a cup of tea Joshua told him about Abie Klugman's death and then the attack on Father McGiff and the shock they both were to his father. He told him, too, about the presentation after the wedding and that the Rabbi's stroke had come when he saw Abie's signature in the book. Dr Lee nodded. All that would certainly have been enough to bring on the attack.

'And how bad is it, Doctor?' Bertha asked.

Dr Lee coughed almost gruffly. Telling unpleasant truths had never come easily to him.

'Rabbi Cohen has had a very severe stroke,' he said slowly, emphasising the last three words. After a pause he added: 'The left side of his body is paralysed—'

'*Oi vey*,' Bertha interrupted. 'That's why his hand was so cold.'

'He's in a semi-coma, sometimes conscious, sometimes unconscious. When conscious he appears to be fairly lucid – that is, I think he knows what's going on, but at the moment he seems unable to speak. However, the power of speech isn't necessarily permanently lost.'

'Will he get worse?' Joshua asked.

'He might. You must be prepared. No one can tell. The next few days will be critical. If he gets through them.... We'll just have to wait and see. Certainly a journey to Palestine in the near future is something you will have to put out of your mind. He would never survive it.'

Joshua made no reply. Nervously he picked at a thread in the tablecloth. Bertha stretched forward and took his hand in hers. At her touch he looked up and hastily rubbed at the cloth to repair any damage he might have done.

'*Nein, nein,*' Bertha murmured, taking his hand again and squeezing it to let him know that it was comfort she was offering, not chastisement.

'Rest and quiet,' Dr Lee said as he dusted crumbs from his fingers and prepared to go. 'Rest and quiet – that's really all the treatment he needs at the moment. And prayer of course – but you'll be doing that anyway.' At the door he turned. 'Hope for the best but – well, be prepared. The next few days will tell.'

Joshua rose. 'We understand, Doctor, we understand.'

'I'll call again in the morning, but if you need me in the night send Jacob around.'

Judith sat by her *zeide's* bed and stared at his face, as if fearful of missing something, some slightest sign of any change in his condition. Like him, she didn't move and hardly breathed. Even thought was frozen – stunned by the prospect of what his illness was going to mean to her. He wouldn't be going to *Eretz* – not next Sunday anyway – and she had promised to go instead of him. What foolishness! Why had she been so irresponsible? She should have thought over his request, taken time to consider it. That her *zeide* would even think of asking her such a favour – such an outlandish impossible favour – that alone should have alerted her. It was as if he had known something like this would happen. Or at least had feared it might. Why had it never entered her mind that she might have to keep her promise? Oh, yes, she remembered – her thoughts had been fixed on a more immediate fear, the fear that he had learned about her and Denis. She had been so relieved to find that he knew nothing about it – yes, that was why she had been taken off guard. But how *could* she go to *Eretz*? And within a week. It was impossible.

She started forward as Rabbi Moishe's eyes opened. Her face was close to his.

'Yes, *zeide*, I'm here. It's Judith. Don't worry, don't worry, you're going to get well.'

She didn't know if he could hear her, if he could

382

understand her, if he even knew her. His right arm moved slowly, and she took his hand and held it.

'Don't worry, *zeide*, you're at home. We're all here. Do you want Father? Is there anything? Do you understand me, *zeide*?'

She thought she felt an answering pressure in his hand. She couldn't be sure. But there was no mistaking the fearful troubled look in his eyes.

He murmured something. It sounded like '*Heim*'.

'Yes, yes, you're at home. In your own bed,' Judith whispered.

This time she was certain of the pressure on her hand, but there was an urgency about it that seemed to want to draw her attention, to need some particular response.

'What is it, *zeide*? What's the matter?' she asked.

His eyes had come alive now, and as they held hers she saw that they were his only voice, that he was trying to make them speak for him. His lips moved again, but no sound came from them. He was trying to shape some message, some word. Could it be the word she thought he had uttered a moment ago? Could it be *heim*? *Heim* ... home. Suddenly understanding flooded through her. *Heim* was home, and home was *Eretz*!

'Yes, *zeide*, yes,' she answered him. 'I know. My promise. I haven't forgotten it. I haven't. Don't worry, I'll keep my promise, and when you're better you'll come to *Eretz*, too.'

His hand opened, releasing its grip on hers, the wildness left his eyes, and the lids closed on them. Judith stared for some moments at his chest to make sure he was still breathing.

What could I do, she asked herself then, what could I say? It was not her head reprimanding her heart. She was consoling herself. She knew there had been no other answer she could have given her *zeide*.

A little later, when Jacob took over the bedside vigil, she went down to the kitchen and told her parents about her promise. For a while they said nothing, showed even no reaction. It was as if they had already been so numbed that no new shock could have any effect on them.

383

Then her father spoke.

'But in a week . . . less than a week! Can you be ready for such a journey in that time?'

He did not question her decision. He knew that this was a promise she had to keep, no matter how difficult keeping it might be.

'I'll *have* to be ready,' Judith said. 'Anyway, it might not be for too long. I mean, I can come back when *zeide* recovers and is well enough to go to *Eretz* himself.'

'And if he doesn't recover?' Joshua asked, thinking of Dr Lee's warning.

Judith shrugged. She couldn't think that far ahead. She couldn't even think to the next morning.

'We'll see,' she replied. 'We'll just have to wait and see.'

Wait and see. Those had been the doctor's words, Joshua remembered.

'*Oi vey*,' Bertha Cohen cried. '*Oi vey!*'

29

JUDITH LAY AWAKE far into that night, trying not to think about the nerve-racking prospect she faced. But the darkness and silence of her bedroom were a void in which her mind, finding nothing familiar to distract it, chased its own terrors, and she was unable to stop herself from grappling there and then with the seemingly endless problems of getting ready within a week to leave her home and family, probably for ever, and journey to a primitive country on the other side of the world.

She tried to concentrate on her *zeide*, to make her concern and sympathy for him divert her thoughts from her own dilemma. But that didn't help, for distorting her concern was a resentment she could neither deny nor ignore. If it hadn't been for him.... That he was an old man, that his life – his long life – was already lived, made her bitterness burn like a fire, for *her* life, still unlived, stretched in front of her and now what could she possibly make of it in Palestine?

Then, as if her *zeide's* spirit had risen from his stricken body and stolen through the walls between them to treat with her, she was suddenly reminded that at a fairly young age he, too, had had to leave his home and build a new life in a strange country. Yes, she argued back, but you were a man, a rabbi, surrounded by people who looked up to you, while I am only a woman, not even a married woman. And the voice in her mind answered: the people you will be with are your own people; you are as close to them as I was to the people who left my homeland with me; I was a man, yes, and a rabbi, yes, but respect, affection, love – especially love – have to be earned; I had to earn all that, and you. . . .

Judith sat up in bed and punched her pillow back into shape, angry with herself for letting her mind concoct such a farcical dialogue. Oh, but if only she had someone real she could talk to, someone with whom she could give way to the terror of what lay ahead of her, pour it all out, her anger, too. Talking about it might change nothing, but not being able to talk about it made it harder to bear. She missed her sister more than ever. Molly would have helped her, given her courage. But Molly was far away, due to have her baby any day, and though Judith was ready to get up even in the middle of the night and write her a letter so that Molly could reply by return of post she knew it would be wrong to worry her at such a time. Indeed, she doubted that her mother would even tell Molly about their *zeide's* collapse until after her baby was born.

No, she would have to face it all alone – except for Denis. But what help could he be when he himself was the black backdrop to all her unhappiness? She remembered promising herself at the wedding that she would go to see him next morning. The recollection added to her self-disgust. She was just too fond of making promises – promises she was forced to keep when she didn't want to, or promises she would like to keep but wasn't able to. There was no point now in going to see Denis. That promise had been made before Rabbi Moishe's stroke. Since then the past had been killed off. She might as well wipe Denis out of her mind. It was over . . . finished. Short and sweet. Short and sweet – hadn't that been another of her so knowing promises to herself? Hadn't that been all she had planned for her affair with Denis, all she would allow it to be? Yes, but not *so* short. Almost better not to have lain with him at all than to have to forget him so quickly. It was too cruel. Heart and body rebelled. She moved her head away from a damp patch that had formed on the pillow and eventually fell into a tortured sleep.

In the morning the familiar sounds of her mother preparing breakfast in the kitchen awakened her. That was always the sign it was time to get up. But as she threw off the bedclothes and was putting her feet down on the freezing linoleum something unusual – some oddness – made her pause and remain for a moment stock still. She listened. What day was it? Wasn't it Monday? Of course it was Monday. Then why were the sounds from the kitchen all she could hear? Monday mornings – every Monday morning all through her life, except for High Holy days – had commenced with the clamour and bustle of the men of Celtic Crescent and the surrounding streets getting ready to go out to the country on their weekly rounds. She would lie in bed listening to the neighing horses, the jingling of their harness, the squeak and rumble of the cart-wheels, and above it all the voices of the traders, some shouting obscure Yiddish curses as they struggled with heavy packs, others calling loud goodbyes to their companions as they set out. But this Monday morning Judith could hear only her mother getting breakfast ready downstairs.

Had she awakened too early? Or too late? It was still dark outside her window, but early or late it would be dark anyway on a mid-December morning. Then the awful possibility struck her. Perhaps Rabbi Moishe had. . . .

Still in her nightdress she rushed down to the kitchen and burst in. Bertha Cohen glanced up from her work at the range.

'*Zeide* – has he . . . ?' Judith gasped.

'The same, the same,' her mother replied quickly. 'No change. Your father stayed with him all night. He's still up there.'

Judith looked at the clock on the dresser. It showed just five past seven.

'What are you standing there for?' Bertha Cohen asked. 'It's time to get up.'

387

'But why is it so quiet outside? Have they all gone off already?'

'Go and look. See for yourself.'

Judith went into the front room and peered through the window at the gas-lit road. What she saw made her draw in her breath in astonishment.

The men were not gone. They were all there, muffled up in their coats, scarves and fur hats, with their horses and carts and cases and packs, all busy manoeuvring the horses between the shafts, harnessing up, gesturing, beckoning, moving one to the other as, bodies straining, they helped with each other's loads. But they might have been a bizarre band of ghosts, no more substantial than the white misty clouds their own and their horses' breath made in the cold morning air, for if they spoke it must have been only in whispers and all their movements were rendered inaudible by the thick carpet of straw they had spread over the roadway in front of the house and for yards on either side.

For a full five minutes Judith remained at the window, watching them finishing their preparations. Then, instead of getting into their carts and traps immediately with their usual shouts and whip-cracks, they quietly led their horses to the end of the street and out of sight before commencing their journeys. As they left she began to shiver – it was not alone the cold of the room at last beginning to pimple her flesh, it was also a shiver of awe at their consideration for their stricken Rabbi. Such tenderness bound her to them with a warmth of fellow-feeling and she was stabbed with the shame of her own self-centredness. If their Rabbi died, she could do nothing to soften their loss; but for those who would have to go to *Eretz* without him it was up to her to assuage the pain of his absence in whatever way she could. Merely to travel with them was not enough; that, she now realised for the first time, was part of her promise to her *zeide*.

She let the curtain drop and slowly went back to her bedroom to dress.

* * *

As she was finishing breakfast her father entered the kitchen.

'You can't go to the store this morning,' Bertha immediately pleaded. 'You've been up all night.'

Joshua rubbed his eyes and yawned.

'No. I'll have a cup of tea and go to bed. Judith, you go in for the morning and then come home to sit with your *zeide*. Jacob will stay with him until then – he has only one lecture this morning and he said he can get a friend's notes of it later.'

'And will you go to the store in the afternoon?' Judith asked.

'Yes. If anyone is looking for me, tell them I'll be in after dinner. Provided your *zeide* is no worse. He had a quiet night, *Gott tzu danken*. He was able to drink some water but he wasn't really awake. Bertha, you'll wake me when Dr Lee calls.'

'*Yah, yah*,' Bertha grudgingly conceded, wishing she could allow her husband a full morning's rest, 'I'll wake you.'

'*Goot*,' Joshua murmured. He smiled at his wife, and as he was leaving the kitchen he put a hand on Judith's shoulder. It was so unexpected that it made her start. She couldn't remember him ever touching her before, and by the time she moved to respond he had turned and gone upstairs.

She was hoping there might be a letter from Molly waiting for her at the store, but there was no post there at all. It wasn't that a letter could have eased her burden but it might have helped her to feel less isolated. Well, it was too much to expect Molly to write when her baby was due so soon. Judith sat in the office, made herself a cup of tea and then forgot to drink it. She hadn't really wanted tea, she just wanted to be doing something instead of facing an empty morning gazing out the little window at grey skies and a dark shed of scrap metal. Now that her anger had begun to drain away, she was beginning to see that she had no alternative but to make the best of things, and the way to make the best of things was to look forward instead of back. She wished she could plunge immediately into her new role. The sooner she could take it up, the less time there would be to brood over it. There was so much to be done. Apart from her personal preparations, there was the task of informing the rest of the community – especially the members of the group going to Palestine – that instead of having their Rabbi lead them it would be his grand-daughter. But no doubt her mother would tell anyone who called to the house that morning and the news would quickly spread. They had all seen Rabbi Moishe's collapse and would hardly be surprised to hear that he wouldn't be able to go with them to *Eretz*. She would tell them it had been his wish that she should represent him, that she should be his link with them, their link with him.

The morning dragged. She wished it would rain – the drops coursing down the window would at least be something moving her eyes could follow, the pinging of the rain on the corrugated-tin roof would be a busy sound she could listen to, and with the gas-fire whistling away and the heat dulling her senses she might be able to forget her worries and feel as happy where she was as anywhere else she might be. But there was no sign of rain, nothing to fill the empty morning ahead of her, so that no matter how hard she tried she could not keep Denis out of her thoughts. Where would he be, she wondered, while she was in *Eretz*, living in a *kibbutz*, helping to build a new Palestine? Would he still be trying to build a new Ireland? No doubt he would – unless. . . . The thought of the danger he was in – the thought that he might be killed – rocked her mind, flooding it once again with the vision she had had when they were in the Pavilion Restaurant together of him lying dead in the street. And she'd have no way of finding out if that happened. If it *did* happen, he'd have gone to his death probably without even knowing that she had left Ireland or why he had never seen her or heard from her again. If, that is, he still cared. Did he?

Impetuously she took her untouched cup of tea, emptied it down the shore, and without even putting a note on the door for any callers locked up and left.

She hurried through the streets, giving herself no time to consider the wisdom of rushing off to see Denis and perhaps be rebuffed by him, but any doubts that might have formed were overtaken by the more immediate fear of the risk she was running in going into the city at all. At the wedding the previous day people had been saying that to venture into Patrick Street now was to take one's life in one's hands. Too late she wished she had brought a basket with her as evidence for any policeman who might stop her that she was going shopping. But the RIC and the military were not the worst of her worries – the most they would do would be to search you or drag you off to the barracks for a couple of hours. It was the Black and Tans who were the real danger. A few days earlier a band of them had snatched the whips from the hands of the jarveys outside the Victoria Hotel and made great sport for themselves whipping every man in sight, young or old – and some of the women, too. If they came along the street swinging their guns, it was best to run out of their way into a shop, but if a lorry-load of them roared down the road they were as likely to be firing indiscriminately as singing their heads off and the safest thing was to throw yourself to the ground immediately. Never mind the muck or the wet, she was told; better to get dirty than to get shot.

But to avoid Patrick Street she would have to make a detour that would put half an hour on to her journey, and Judith was too impatient to do that. She'd just have to conquer her fear – there was no going back or taking the long way round. She had faced worse. What about Wednesday night when there seemed to be no chance of escaping capture by the Tans? She hadn't felt nervous then, so why be afraid now? Of course Denis had been with her and she was so caught up in the pace of what was happening that there hadn't really been any time to take fright. It was a bit like having to go to *Eretz*, she told herself – thinking about it instead of getting immersed in what had to be done was a recipe for worry. Determination, that's what was needed. She'd go to Palestine with a good grace no matter what the difficulties; and she was

391

going to see Denis first, Patrick Street or no Patrick Street, Tans or not.

As if to test her resolution – and her courage – she did make a detour, a short one that took her past the GPO and the bombed newsagent's. The debris had been cleared from the roadway, and the space where the shop had been was a mass of rubble with huge spars of wood propping up the buildings on either side. Pedestrians were passing it without a second glance – burned-out, bombed, ravaged premises were now a commonplace, and no issue of the *Cork Examiner* was without a photograph of what remained after the latest outrage.

The sight affected her less than she had expected. It was difficult to associate herself with what had happened there such a short time ago – as if someone else, not she, had been involved. In a sense it *was* someone else; so much had changed since then, so much more was going to change, that there seemed to be an unbridgeable gap between then and now. It was already part of a past she would soon have to bury, probably for ever. But Denis wasn't yet part of that past – not completely anyway – and she hastened on, excited now at the prospect of seeing him once again, even though it was to be for the last time.

Entering Patrick Street she looked around quickly for signs of danger. She was relieved to see plenty of pedestrians, most of whom were intent on going about their business with little dawdling or gazing in shop windows. Trams, ponies and traps, tradesmen's vans filled the roadway and, though there were more policemen than ever at every corner, the only evidence of military or Black and Tan activity was one of their easily recognisable lorries parked on Patrick's Bridge, a hundred yards away. Gratefully she hurried across the road into the security of the laneways leading to the quays and almost ran the rest of the way to Denis's workplace.

The old assistant in the shop next to the yard recognised her immediately and greeted her as if she were a regular customer.

'Good morning, miss. Not a very nice morning, but what

392

can we expect so near Christmas? Denis Hurley you'll be wanting, is it? Take a seat there and I'll tell him.'

Judith smiled her thanks – it was all she was given time for – but did not sit down. On her first visit she had been a stranger and a supplicant, not knowing what sort of man or welcome to expect; this time, although neither a stranger nor a supplicant, she once again did not know what sort of man or welcome to expect. Perhaps it had been a mistake to come; perhaps Denis's feelings towards her would have cooled and she'd have cheapened herself for nothing.

She clenched her fists in her gloves and stared at the door through which she expected him to appear, but when the door opened it was the old assistant, adjusting his spectacles and saying 'Denis won't be a tick,' before disappearing again.

Oh, what's keeping him, what's keeping him? Judith fretted. He might have to finish a job first. Or – remembering what seemed to have been embarrassment over his work-dirty hands last time she had called -- perhaps he was having a wash. The old man would have told him his visitor was the same young lady and, if the delay was for him to spruce himself up first, could she take that as a sign he still cared?

At last the door opened again, and Denis hurried in.

'Judith!'

'Hello, Denis,' she said, the greeting almost choking in her throat even though his pleasure at seeing her was unmistakable. He put his hands on her arms as if he would have embraced her had they been anywhere else.

'Where have you been at all?' he asked, the weight of concern in his voice broadening his Cork accent.

'I couldn't keep our appointment that Sunday....'

'I know,' he interrupted. 'You had a funeral, hadn't you? I read about it in the paper. But where have you been since then? Why didn't you come sooner? I thought it was the way you didn't want to see me any more after....'

He broke off in embarrassment as the red in his cheeks deepened and spread all over his face. Judith had forgotten how easily he blushed.

393

'No, no, it wasn't that,' she assured him, adding lamely: 'Things have been happening.'

'You're here now; that's all that matters.' In his delight at seeing her he failed to pick up the hint of despair in her words.

'Well, the fact is I've come to say goodbye. I'm going away.'

'Where? When?'

'I'm going next Sunday.'

'How long for? Where are you going?'

'I'm going to Palestine. With the rest of the group from the community. For ever probably. I don't know.'

Denis stared at her and backed away a step. Then 'Are you joking me?' he asked, lightly, unbelievingly.

'Oh, it's no joke. I don't really want to go, but. . . .'

There was silence for a moment. The half-smile on his face slowly collapsed.

'But, if you don't want to go, why are you going?'

Judith shrugged. 'I have to. It's too difficult, really, to explain. But I couldn't go without seeing you and saying goodbye.'

Denis suddenly jerked to attention, like a soldier responding to a command. He propelled Judith to a chair and sat her down. 'Wait there. I won't be a tick,' he said. 'Don't move now.' And before she could protest he had left the shop.

Within a minute he returned through the street door and beckoned to her.

A lorry with the name 'Twohey & Co' painted on its side was parked at the kerb, and Denis was holding the passenger door open.

'Come on, get in.' The invitation was almost peremptory.

'I can't, Denis,' Judith said. 'I've got to get back to the store.'

'Never mind the store. I'll drive you back later. If you're really leaving Cork for ever, I want to hear all about it and we can't talk here. This is no place for us to be saying goodbye.'

His voice was gentle but firm, and Judith recognised in

394

him once more the man of action she had witnessed after his narrow escape from the bomb outside the newsagent's. That time she had gone with him against his wishes; this time she had no desire to oppose him. She gathered the ends of her coat and with his helping hand climbed into the lorry's cabin.

'Where are we going?' she asked as he got in beside her and drove away. 'I have to get back to the store. There's no one there at the moment.'

'Where's your father? He's not ill, is he?'

'*He* isn't, but my grandfather is' – and, as Denis drove carefully past the Black and Tan lorry on Patrick's Bridge, Judith began to tell him what had happened.

Denis made no comment while she spoke nor when she had finished. The movements of his body as he drove frequently threw them against each other, and the brief contacts first tantalised her, then aroused her. The closeness and warmth of the cabin became one with the pattern of narrow streets through which they were driving, footpaths not even wide enough for two abreast, shops, houses, pubs and buildings all squeezed together with here and there an alleyway somehow prised between them. It was a part of Cork Judith had never seen before, and as the lorry wound its way up and around the endless hills she suddenly realised how confined her whole life had been. It was ridiculous that she should have been born in Cork and lived there for a quarter of a century, yet only in the past few weeks have known for the first time such places as the Western Road, the Lee Fields, Casimir Street – places on her very doorstep but a million miles away as far as she was concerned. It was ridiculous, too, that at an age when so many other women had raised a family she was having her first experience of love. Where had she been for so long? What had she been missing, swaddled in the cocoon of her Irish ghetto? Her thoughts pitched her mind forward to Palestine and the future she faced there. Was she just exchanging one ghetto for another? Perhaps. But that would all be changed. Not by the promises of others but by the efforts and determination of the Jews themselves. Karlinsky had said so. They

395

would not be denied. They would be free of the ghetto –
freed from all the ghettos – free to be their own masters in
their own land – to grow up, to mature, to create their own
future. She turned to look at Denis, and like a thunder-
clap it suddenly hit her – those were the very reasons he
had joined the IRA.

The lorry halted, and she came out of her spell.

'Where are we?'

'This is where I live,' Denis told her. 'Come on.'

He jumped down from the cabin and hurried around to
help her out. One step carried her over the footpath and
through a door into a dark and narrow hallway. On her
left was the entrance to the shop proper, but Denis bustled
her past it and up an uncovered stairway between peeling
walls to a room on the first landing. He unlocked its door,
stood aside to let her in, and then locked the door behind
them.

'Is this where you live?' Judith asked, unable to
disguise her surprise at what she saw. In one corner was a
brass bedstead, the bed unmade, the rest of the room being
tidy only because there was nothing in it to make it
untidy. Of furniture there was just an old wardrobe, the
door hanging off the hinges, and a chest of drawers with a
marble top on which a cracked ewer stood in a large china
basin.

'Temporarily,' Denis answered.

'You mean it isn't your home?'

Denis covered up the naked sheets and smoothed down
the bedclothes.

'No, it's just a room I've taken for the moment.'

'But why? What do you want a room like this for?'

There wasn't even a chair – for which Denis apologised.

'You'll have to sit on the bed,' he told Judith. 'I don't
come here during the day. Only to sleep.'

'But why aren't you sleeping at home?'

'It's a precaution. I'll be in action with the unit very
soon, and if the police or anyone should get wind of it and
want to arrest me it's to my home they'd call in the night-
time. That's the way they usually pick us up.'

'What sort of action? You'll be in danger, won't you?'

Denis shrugged. He went to the dressing-table and poured some water into the basin. Then he took off his overalls and started to unbutton his shirt.

'I could do with a wash,' he said, 'if you have no objection. You can turn your back if it embarrasses you.'

'I've seen you with your shirt off before,' Judith reminded him.

Denis was silent for a moment as he stood, shirt in hand. Then, throwing it on to the bed, he said half-casually: 'I saw your father last Friday.'

'Oh? Where?'

'In your store. I went to see him.'

'What for? You weren't trying to kidnap him again surely,' Judith laughed.

'No. But I needed his help.'

Denis soaped his face and hands, drying them on a towel he took from a side-rail. Judith waited, puzzled.

'The assignment we'll be going on soon – it's important, especially to me because it's my first real chance with the unit. We have the arms and ammunition but we needed a safe place to hide them until we're ready.'

He soaped his hands again and began to wash his chest and back. It reminded Judith of the way she and Molly used to take turns to wash Jacob's hair before he was old enough to do it himself. He'd stand at the sink, his thin body naked to the waist, crying about the soap in his eyes until they made him laugh by tickling him under his arms. His boyish laughter was so infectious that they were often reduced to helpless giggles themselves. But the feeling in her body now was one of excitement as she watched Denis's muscles and shoulder-blades move beneath his skin. He raised his head and took up the towel again. She would have offered to dry him had he not resumed speaking.

'I thought your father's yard would be a perfect place to hide the guns and things – you know, just inside that back gate. I could put them there myself during the night – I'd get over the wall easily – and collect them when we'd want them. No one else would know. But I didn't want to do it without his permission. I was hoping I'd see you first so as I could tell you beforehand. I didn't want to do anything behind your back.'

'Well, I'm sorry you wasted your time. You don't have to tell me what my father said.'

'Oh, no,' Denis replied, looking up, the towel draped from his hands. 'You're wrong. He agreed to help me. He even gave me a key to the back gate.'

Judith gasped with surprise. She had no idea what could possible have induced her father to become involved, but what was important was that he had. In her elation she ran to Denis and flung her arms around him. Before he could respond she released him, only to unbutton her coat and struggle out of it before embracing him again.

'You seem very pleased with the news,' he said.

'Why wouldn't I be? If it means less danger for you....' She hugged him to her, her hands moving swiftly all over his back, rubbing dry his still damp skin.

'You know this is the last time we'll be seeing each other,' she said.

It wasn't a question, but she looked up into his eyes as if she was making some entreaty.

He nodded.

'Denis,' she whispered, 'don't ... don't let yourself get killed. Please.'

He did not answer but cradled her head in his hands and kissed her.

'What time do you have to be back in the store?'

'It doesn't matter if I don't go back at all. My father will be going in for the afternoon, so they won't be expecting me home until dinner-time. That's about half-one.'

Just then the bells of Shandon commenced their carillon.

'What's that?' Judith asked.

'My God! Have you never heard Shandon before?'

'I don't think so. I never noticed. I've heard *of* it, of course, but you can't hear its bells where I live.'

'Well, then, aren't you lucky I brought you here today?' Denis laughed. 'Otherwise there you'd be on the other side of the world, a native of Cork and not able to tell all

398

those Arabs and their camels in the Holy Land about the famous bells of Shandon.'

Denis lifted her in his arms and laid her on the bed.

'Listen there now,' he murmured, 'so as you'll remember them well.'

It was eleven o'clock. Judith lay on the bed, eyes closed, with Denis next to her, as the eleven strokes sounded. With each stroke he kissed a different part of her body.

'Oh,' she sighed in disappointment when the echo of the last stroke died. 'They've finished.'

'What does it matter?' he whispered. 'In an hour's time they'll strike again and it'll be twelve times then.'

As he gazed down at her his eyes darkened and he suddenly butted his face into the pillow.

'Oh God,' he moaned, 'I wish you didn't have to leave me.'

'I'm not leaving you, Denis, I'm not,' she assured him. 'Not for another two hours at least.'

30

CAPTAIN SIMCOX wearily scanned again each page of the *Cork Examiner*, hoping there might be some interesting item he hadn't seen before tucked away in a corner. But there was nothing – nothing at all. And not only did he find the main stories and reports of what was happening almost too sickening to contemplate, but also every page carried the same prominent detail that exacerbated his impotent anger: the date, Tuesday, 8 December 1920. Getting on for two weeks since he had escaped from the IRA and he was still stuck in barracks. Certainly it was a consolation to know that he had only another five days to endure and then he'd be off at last on extended compassionate leave, but the few hours of euphoria he had enjoyed on the previous evening when Colonel Windsor told him the good news had worn itself out in a sleepless night and he was once again tense with frustration, impatience and sheer boredom. His leave would take him over Christmas, the Colonel had promised, though both of them knew that if Roddy's application to buy himself out of the Army was successful he'd not be seeing Cork or Ireland again.

'I'm sorry, Captain, that I couldn't let you go any sooner,' Colonel Windsor had apologised, 'but I can't afford to be under strength just now even by one –

especially when that one is a soldier of your experience.'

No smile had accompanied the compliment. His monocle remained glassy and his tone as impersonal as if he were reading a routine signal. Roddy smiled, however, though bitterly. It was typical of the Colonel to ignore the fact that he'd have been under strength by the same one experienced soldier if Roddy hadn't made his escape. Colonel Windsor, of course, was a realist – a fortnight ago was a fortnight ago, and Captain Simcox's services had not then been available to him; two weeks later was two weeks later, and the Captain's services were now restored, so he didn't see any reason to put the clock back and dispense with them.

'Things are coming to a head, Captain,' he went on. 'There's something in the air. I don't know what's going to happen, but whatever it is it's bound to be something we won't like and it might well stretch us.'

'Yes, sir,' Roddy had agreed, 'that's what the men feel, too.'

He had been on the easy list since his return to barracks and had been out on the streets only a few times – once to retrieve his possessions and Elizabeth's letters from the room he rented and to tell the landlady that he wouldn't be needing it again – but, even so, he himself had noticed the change in the atmosphere. He was certain it wasn't his imagination. Nor was it that having virtually nothing to do during the long hours had made him more touchy. He wasn't the only one on edge; the tension that had gripped his fellow-officers was all too obvious. *That* wasn't something he just imagined. Roddy had ample opportunity to observe the effect on them when, off duty, they relaxed in the mess. Except that they didn't relax – at least, not the way they had done before Roddy had been kidnapped. Now the hilarity was more forced and brittle, their serious moments less frequent and more abstracted. Experienced, highly trained, battle-hardened, they had got the scent; they knew – as the Colonel had put it – that something was in the air and it was as if anticipation had made them run a mild fever.

With no duties to occupy hands or mind that would help

401

him fight the contagion and with little to do except mope around, Roddy had been forced to continue the habit developed in captivity of reading the *Cork Examiner* from end to end even though that was only turning the screw more. For it was clear from the glut of arrests, burnings, bombings and killings throughout the country – particularly in the province of Munster, the battalion's own bailiwick – that if the situation didn't cool off very quickly there'd be some sort of almighty explosion any day, but cool off was what the situation showed no signs of doing. Opinion in the mess was that the ambush at Macroom had lit the fuse which would blow the whole tinder-box sky-high. A week earlier, at a village just outside Cork, an IRA Flying Column got a convoy of Tans and RIC cadets right between their sights and left seventeen of them dead. The IRA had lost three themselves, but the engagement had been a resounding victory for them. And they weren't letting anyone forget it. Already there was a ballad going the rounds of the province that some of Roddy's fellow-officers had picked up and relayed to him, not without a touch of satisfaction at the defeat inflicted on the Tans:

> On the twenty-eighth day of November, just
>   outside the town of Macroom,
> The Tans in their big Crossley tenders, they
>   hurried along to their doom.
> For the boys of the Column were waiting with
>   hand grenades pinned on the spot
> And the Irish Republican Army made shit of
>   the whole fucking lot!

Roddy smiled to himself – it was a vicious song but it did have a swing to it. These Paddies certainly had a way with words as well as with arms. The jingle the Tans sang as they drove up and down village streets, firing their guns at random, was like a child's nursery rhyme next to the IRA verse. Roddy had heard it himself:

> We are the boys of the RIC,
> As happy as happy can be.

Well, they wouldn't be feeling very happy now, and it was a safe bet that they'd be thirsting for quick revenge. That was what all Cork was expecting – no wonder everyone was jittery. Roddy prayed that whatever was going to happen would wait until he was gone. He didn't want to be involved. He wanted to get home to Elizabeth. He didn't fancy getting wounded – maybe even killed – at the very last moment. For the first time in his long army career he found fear stalking him. And that was an extra worry, because he knew that if the balloon went up before he left and he had to go out into the field he'd only start trying to be careful; and the careful soldier was a bad soldier and the bad soldier was the one most likely to get hit.

'It won't be long, Captain, will it, until Sunday?' Colonel Windsor had said in an effort to mollify him. 'And with luck we'll keep you out of trouble until then. I have a convoy coming down from Dublin with more stores on Saturday, and the lorries will be going back empty next day, so you can go with them and cross over that night. You'll be home by Monday, eh?'

Roddy had rushed off immediately to write Elizabeth the good news. He thought of telegraphing her but decided not to in case the arrival of a telegram – and in the middle of the night into the bargain – gave her a fright. In her condition a fright was the last thing she wanted. Anyhow, a letter would take that much longer and so she'd have less time to wait for his return.

Tuesday – Wednesday – Thursday – Friday – Saturday. Just five more days to get through safely and he'd be out of it all. For ever, he hoped.

'The critical period,' Dr Lee said as he and Joshua stood outside Rabbi Cohen's door. 'The first few days after this sort of attack always are.' He didn't lower his voice – there was no need to. Two visits on Monday, a third on Tuesday morning, and he could tell that the Rabbi was sinking into a deeper coma.

He led the way down the stairs and took his hat from

Bertha Cohen waiting for him in the hall, his greying beetle brows frowning with concern as he moved to the front door.

'I don't want to alarm you, but he's had a good innings and you should be prepared.'

'You mean . . . ?' Joshua murmured.

'No more than that it's in God's hands. There's little we can do for him at this stage except hope and pray and have faith.'

When he had gone, Joshua went back upstairs to sit with his father. 'Hope, pray and have faith.' The words swam around in his mind, changing places as they stirred some echo he couldn't quite capture. He stared at the outline of the Rabbi's thin frame under the bedclothes, not letting his eyes stray far from the weak rise and fall of his chest. His father's face had no colour, the skin was drawn and tight. Joshua's head began to nod rapidly in silent prayer. What could he do but follow Dr Lee's injunction: hope, pray and have faith? And suddenly the three words – *hope, prayer, faith* – were swept out of his mind as another three clicked into their place: *penitence, prayer* and *charity*. That was what was enjoined on every Jew throughout the ten days between the Jewish New Year and the Day of Atonement when the Lord sealed one's fate for the ensuing year. No matter how desperate one's misdeeds or how black one's sins in the previous twelve months, there was still time to appeal, there was still the opportunity to importune God and ask Him for mercy, there was still a way to influence Him. The New Year liturgy repeated it over and over again: 'Penitence, prayer, and charity can avert the evil decree.'

But the New Year was gone. Three months already. It was too late now. And, besides, it was only the supplicant's own life that might be preserved by penitence, prayer and charity. It was not for one to plead another's cause.

Joshua's head ceased its nodding. He let it drop on to his chest and stroked his chin as a question, hope like a shadow on its tail, stirred his thoughts. Was the Lord so rigid that entreaties would be considered only during ten

404

short days at a particular time of the year, and then only by someone on his own behalf? Ten days out of the whole year! Was God a civil servant? The words of another part of the liturgy urged themselves in support. 'O God, O God, compassionate and gracious, long-suffering and abundant in kindness and truth, keeping mercy unto the thousandth generation. . . .' If the Lord was that merciful, He must be ready to listen at any time. And if He was that merciful, then surely he would allow one man to plead on another's behalf. Neighbour for neighbour, friend for friend. If His people were to mirror His loving-kindness, were these not legitimate appeals? And if these, then surely also a son might plead for his father!

Penitence, prayer and charity. Joshua's head danced. Prayer – yes, he *was* praying, and he would continue to pray with all his strength. Everyone was praying – Bertha, Judith, Jacob, the whole community, even Father McGiff. He had called that morning, distraught at the news of the Rabbi's illness, pushing forward his own broken hands in their slings as if fearing that his inability to touch Joshua might somehow filch his sympathy of conviction. He told Joshua that he had arranged for prayers to be said at every Mass in his church for Rabbi Cohen's recovery. Prayers – heaven would rock with the weight of prayer being said for the Rabbi. Joshua's lips moved rapidly as he lifted his head and looked up, that the Lord might turn His gaze unto him and hearken to his voice.

But, even as he prayed, doubt began to arrest his sudden spurt of hope. Prayer, after all, was not everything. What about penitence and charity?

The question of charity did not trouble his conscience. He gave money every week for the Burial Society, for the Board of Guardians, for the Jewish National Fund. As much as was asked. More than that – whenever it happened that some penniless Jew arrived in their community, a stranger within their gates, he had willingly given extra to help the poor wanderer buy clothes, food, shelter, and his passage to Dublin or London if he did not wish to settle in Cork. No one could say Joshua

405

Cohen was not a charitable man.

But penitence. Joshua stopped praying. There was another part of the New Year service, a prayer in which one recited a long list of sins, beating one's breast for each transgression. Everything was included in the list – sins one knew one had committed, sins one might have committed, sins one couldn't possibly have committed. And also the sin of omission. Was that really sufficient penitence? For the sins of commission, perhaps, if one were sincere. But for the sin of omission?

Joshua shifted uneasily in his chair. He looked at his father's face, at the old dry skin, parched from a life spent indoors in constant study and prayer, at the thick beard now white-haired and straggling. He tried to remember a time when his father had been young, had been live-eyed and dark-haired, had played with him, embraced him, kissed him. He couldn't remember such a time. There had never been one – from the day of Joshua's birth his father had been a Rabbi, a holy man, and Joshua had been brought up to be a holy boy, serious and solemn. Respect, awe, honour had been what bound him to his father. Not love or affection. Not then. The bond of love had come later – too late to be expressed, though all the stronger for having been denied so long. Had that been his father's sin of omission? And had his growing wisdom made the Rabbi aware of this sin, so that when Jacob was born he lavished love and affection on *him*? '*Yankeleh, Yankeleh, geb tzu zein zeide a bonkeleh.*' Was that the explanation of the relationship between grandfather and grandson, a relationship that had enabled the Rabbi to persuade Jacob not to leave college, while the boy's own father remained mute? And if there was no bond of love between Joshua and his son was it because in his childhood there had been no bond of love between his father and *his* son?

A shudder passed through Joshua Cohen's body. All those years he had been so blind. He had been devoted to his family, to caring for them, providing for them – food, shelter, clothes, education – whatever they wanted he worked for and gave them. But love, affection, tenderness, companionship? Did they not want or need these things,

406

too? He couldn't remember. Their young lives were a blank in his memory. He had been too busy giving them the fruits of his labour, but never giving of himself. Not to his daughters, not to his son. That had been his great sin of omission. The sudden recognition of his guilt, the shocking realisation that he had compounded it year after year, made him weak with the weight of remorse that lay upon his heart. Penitence, prayer and charity – all three were needed to avert the evil decree, and Joshua Cohen could see now why penitence was placed first. He sank to the floor beside the Rabbi's bed and prayed – for his father's life, for forgiveness for his sin, but most of all for the grace, the courage and the ability to show his children the love for them that was now flooding his heart.

When Judith came home for dinner her father told her he had decided to close the store for the time being – he would not go in again while her *zeide* was so ill, so she could take the rest of the week off to prepare for her departure to *Eretz*. He would ask her only to go back after dinner and leave a note on the door saying they would be closed until further notice owing to a family illness.

Judith was surprised at her father's decision, but in her preoccupation with her own worries she put the subdued tone of his voice down to his concern over the Rabbi and did not notice that he addressed her as '*mein kinde*', a term only her mother and *zeide* usually used. On her way to the store that morning she had bought the *Cork Examiner* and had spent the hours in the little office going through every one of its pages for reports of IRA attacks the previous night. Even though she didn't think the action Denis was preparing for would have taken place so soon, as she turned each page her fingers almost trembled for fear of discovering a headline reporting IRA losses. She found none, but her fears still left her fretful and tense. She thought of going down to the back gate of the yard to see if she could find any arms and ammunition

407

hidden there; for, if she did, it would mean that Denis had not been in action yet. But, even if she found no arms, that wouldn't prove anything, for Denis hadn't actually said when he intended hiding them. So she didn't look; and as she pinned the note on the door after her dinner and carefully checked the lock she was delighted for Denis's sake with her father's decision. Now, for the next few days at least, maybe longer, the store would be closed, no one could go in, and so there would be no chance for anyone to find arms there, whether they were hidden yet or not.

On her way home again she decided to call in to Max Klein's warehouse. She didn't know if he had yet learned that she was going to *Eretz* in place of Rabbi Moishe; certainly he would need to know. He was the President and he it was who would have to notify Karlinsky of the change of plan. To her relief she found that he had already been in touch with Karlinsky.

'Yes, Judith,' he told her, 'I sent him a telegram yesterday as soon as it was certain that the Rabbi would not be going.'

'And did you tell him—?'

'I did,' he interrupted, his gravelly voice enthusiastically anticipating her enquiry, proud of the way he was coping with the crisis. 'I called to your home yesterday morning and your mother told me you were going instead of the Rabbi. I passed the information on to Karlinsky, and he sent me a telegram in reply. He wants me to phone him at five o'clock today.'

'Why does he want you to phone him?' Judith asked apprehensively. 'Maybe he doesn't think it a good idea that I should be taking my *zeide*'s place.'

'Nonsense, girl, nonsense,' Max Klein assured her, in his sincerity grasping her arm and squeezing it so hard she almost winced. 'Leave him to me. If I say you'll be all right, he'll take my word for it. You won't let your *zeide* down, I'm quite sure. He wouldn't have chosen you if he didn't think you could do the job. You're a brave girl.'

Judith gave a wan smile. She didn't know about being brave – and it wasn't as if there had been anyone else her *zeide* could have chosen. But if she wasn't to let him down there were things to be done. She would have to visit all the others going to Palestine, to reassure them, to let them know that she would do everything she possibly could to help them. She couldn't be their spiritual guide, of course, as the Rabbi would have been, but she would try to be some sort of leader for them, at least on the journey. She would tell each one that. They must be feeling lost and bewildered, so one by one she would visit them all that evening and do her best to gain their confidence.

When she reached home, however, she found that she herself had a visitor.

'Mickey Aronson,' her mother whispered. 'He's in the front room waiting for you. He's been there for half an hour.'

'Waiting for *me*? What can he want with me?'

'Go and see, go and see,' Bertha Cohen hurried her daughter. 'Don't keep the poor man waiting any longer.'

Judith took off her coat and hat and threw a glance in the mirror. She couldn't imagine what business Mickey Aronson had with her. She really hardly knew the man. Even though he had been a neighbour as long as she could remember, she had never had anything more to do with him than smile and say hello when she passed him in the street or saw him in Mrs Neumann's.

When she entered the front room he sprang forward from the chair he had been sitting on and then immediately backed away again.

'Good day, Mr Aronson. My mother said you wished to see me,' Judith greeted, almost questioningly, as if she thought her mother must somehow be mistaken.

'Yes, Judith. Miss Cohen, I mean,' Mickey Aronson replied, flustered and embarrassed. Judith was surprised at his demeanour. He had always known her by her first name – after all, he was already a grown man when she was born – why the sudden deference? Certainly, since Abie Klugman's death he wasn't the perky irreverent character familiar to the whole community, but that it could have changed him into this haunted chastened figure was a shock to Judith. She had heard it said he could not have been more broken-hearted if they had been

409

blood brothers. He had even taken it on himself to say the mourner's *Kaddish* at the synagogue services. True, Abie had left no next of kin to recite the *Kaddish* for him, and in such circumstances it was in order for a close friend to do so – but Mickey Aronson! The one who had always been a thorn in his flesh, who had made fun of him mercilessly! Perhaps, someone suggested, that's why he says the *Kaddish* – as a sort of atonement. Judith felt awkward in his presence. This wasn't the Mickey Aronson she knew; this was a total stranger. She was glad when he spoke first.

'Rabbi Moishe,' he asked timidly, 'how is he?'

'The same,' Judith said. 'There's been no sign of any improvement yet. Won't you sit down, Mr Aronson?' she added.

Mickey Aronson, however, ignored her invitation and remained standing, his hands clenching each other.

'So *you* are going to *Eretz* instead of him. It is true?'

'Yes. That was my *zeide*'s wish. I promised him,' Judith explained, but feeling she would need to give a fuller account to the people she would be visiting that evening.

Mickey Aronson made as if to speak again, but it took him a few efforts to get the words out.

'Miss Cohen, may I go? To *Eretz*? Will you take me with you?'

His eyes pleaded, and his hands now were clenched so tightly that the thin knuckles were white.

'You!' Judith exclaimed.

To Mickey Aronson it sounded as if she thought his suggestion preposterous and he collapsed into a chair, his small frame racked with convulsive sobs.

'I must, Miss Cohen, I must go. For Abie's sake. Instead of him. You are going instead of your *zeide*. Why not I instead of Abie Klugman?'

Judith, almost stunned at his sudden breakdown, fell on her knees beside him.

'But of course you can come, Mr Aronson. Of course. Why shouldn't you? Anyone who wants can come with us.'

Mickey Aronson stopped sobbing as suddenly as he had

started and looked at her half-suspiciously.

'*Sversach?* You mean it, Miss Cohen? You're not just saying it? I *can* go with you?'

Judith rose, then pulled up a chair and sat facing her visitor. His eyes burned into hers with the pain of his anxiety, and his lips trembled with anticipation. His anguish so moved her that she took his hands in hers, as a mother would her child's. They were cold to the touch, shivering. She would *have* to still his doubts, convince him that there was a place for him in the group, just as Rabbi Moishe had stilled Abie Klugman's doubts and convinced *him* that he would be welcome in *Eretz*.

'Mr Aronson,' she said, 'let me tell you something. Mr Klugman came to see the Rabbi a few days before he.... He was unhappy. He thought that because he was simple-minded no one would want him in *Eretz*, that at the last moment they'd find an excuse to keep him out. Do you know what my *zeide* told him?'

Mickey Aronson shook his head and waited.

'He said to him: "Mr Klugman, if *you* don't go, *I* don't go." And I say the same to you, Mr Aronson. If—'

But Mickey Aronson jumped up from his chair and clamped a hand over Judith's mouth.

'No, no. Don't say that.' He snatched his hand away. 'Forgive me, Miss Cohen. But don't say that.'

Judith smiled. 'All right, Mr Aronson. But don't worry. If you can be ready by Sunday, you will come with us. I'll let Mr Karlinsky know. As a matter of fact, the President is telephoning him later today. I'll go straight into town to tell him. I'll speak to Mr Karlinsky myself.'

Mickey Aronson straightened himself, and for the first time since Abie Klugman's death a light shone again in his eyes. But as Judith showed him out she was too full of satisfaction and relief to hear his words of thanks. Mickey Aronson had not gone to Max Klein with his request. He had come to *her*. Without question he had recognised *her* as the new leader of those bound for *Eretz*. And because she was their leader she was no longer Judith, but Miss Cohen.

She closed the front door and stood in the narrow hall,

looking up the stairs and wishing she could rush up to her *zeide*'s room and tell him. If only she could. Oh, if only she could!

31

EVEN THOUGH SHE DIDN'T have to go into the store, Judith woke at her usual early hour on Wednesday morning. She was tired after the previous night's round of visits; she had managed to see every one of the intending emigrants and was relieved to find that not only did they all know of the change of plan, but also they were anxious, even insistent, that she share the burden of her responsibility with them. How could they help? they asked. Give them some task, no matter how big or how little. They would miss their Rabbi, of course, but their concern was not for their own disappointment but for his recovery. And he *would* recover, they assured her – 'God is good, God is good' – but Judith sensed that behind their assurances they feared the worst.

When she got home, after midnight, she found their fears shared by all her family. Dr Lee had called during the evening, had stayed over half an hour, and had told them that there was no doubt the Rabbi was sinking. After that they had not gone to bed for hours – Jacob not at all, he stayed in his *zeide*'s room all night – and no one had spoken much. They felt betrayed by their own hopes. Since Sunday they had lived in a false paradise – they could see that now – and with the hope on which that paradise had been built turned to dust they had nothing to sustain them. They could only wait in fear and disbelief.

As Judith got out of bed she listened for the familiar early-morning sounds. She did not hear them. Sounds there were, but they seemed to be coming from a distance and only by straining her ears could she identify them as those she was used to. An eeriness had taken over the house and its inhabitants, a reluctance to make any noise, to move, talk, perform the normal domestic tasks, as if for them to expend energy was a betrayal of their loved one from whose body both life and energy were steadily slipping away.

All morning the mood persisted. Judith tried to busy herself with some preparations for her journey – clothes had to be sorted out to choose what would be most sensible for the climate she could expect. She consulted notes made on her previous evening's visits, little hints and pieces of advice that those going to *Eretz* had received from their private talk with Karlinsky after he had addressed the assembled community and which they passed on to her. Almost all of them were matters of common sense, things she could have guessed for herself, but it would have been churlish not to have paid attention to their suggestions and she had, anyway, quickly seen that to appear to put herself in their hands, rather than the opposite, was the best way both of distracting them from the loss of the Rabbi and of letting them express their devotion to him by making them take care of her.

During the morning many neighbours called, knocking so lightly on the door that had the family inside not been so quiet they would not have heard. No one came into the house – they called only to enquire – and to each one Bertha shook her head, murmuring, '*Nisht goot, nisht goot.*'

Later in the morning came a very loud rat-tat of the knocker. Its suddenness made them jump in alarm as it reverberated through the stillness. Jacob was quick to rush out and forestall any further knocking.

'A telegram! A telegram!' he said excitedly, coming back into the kitchen.

Bertha Cohen grabbed it from his hands and tore it

414

open. She held it out to read, gave a little gasp, and then sank into a chair, unable to speak for sobbing.

'What is it?' Jacob asked anxiously as Judith took the telegram from her mother.

'"Molly had a baby boy this morning stop eight pounds two ounces stop mother and son fine stop *Mazeltov* stop signed Sol,"' she read out.

She put the telegram down and looked at her mother. Tears were streaming down Bertha Cohen's face as she stood and gathered her children into her arms.

'*Mazeltov, mazeltov!*' they congratulated each other.

'Don't cry, Mother, don't cry,' Judith comforted her, though her own eyes were no longer dry.

Her mother shook her head, trying to draw breath to speak. At last she managed to say: 'Your father. We must tell him.'

Together they went out of the kitchen and started to ascend the stairs. As they looked up they saw Joshua on the landing, peering down at them.

'I heard the knocking,' he complained. 'Who was it?'

'Malka, Malka,' his wife sang. 'A telegram! She's had a baby boy!'

'*Gott tzu danken, Gott tzu danken,*' Joshua breathed as Bertha reached him. He took her hands in his and led her up the final steps so as to embrace her.

'*Mazeltov, buba,*' he said, '*mazeltov.*'

'And you, too, *zeide,*' she replied.

With Jacob and Judith they crowded onto the small landing, hugging each other in joy and celebration. Then Joshua turned his head towards the Rabbi's door. They could see that he was trying to keep back his tears.

'He wanted to go to *Eretz,*' he said, 'and that's been taken from him. And he wanted to be a great-grandfather, and now he is one but he'll never know it.'

'Shush, shush,' Bertha Cohen admonished. 'Don't speak like that. You mustn't give up hope.'

'Father,' Jacob said, 'you go down and have a cup of tea. I'll stay with *zeide.*'

'No, I'll stay with him in case he should open his eyes and I could tell him. Perhaps he'd understand.'

'Yes, you stay with your father,' Bertha Cohen agreed.

'And I'll bring the tea up to you,' Judith said.

Reluctantly they went downstairs as Joshua turned back to his father's room. Their moment of ecstasy was so brief, so clouded – if only they could have all been together in the kitchen, with the Rabbi, all in health and happiness, to talk, laugh, reminisce, cry a little more, really make the most of God's gift. But this they could not do, when at the back of each one's mind was the expectation that the giving of this new life was about to be balanced by the taking of an old one.

It was the Lord's recompense, yes, Joshua told himself, as he resumed his seat by his father's bedside. But the recompense was to him, to his wife, to his children, not to the old man lying silently in the bed. His father had cherished a lifelong wish to go to *Eretz* – that had been taken from him by the Lord in His wisdom. Was he now also to lose the wish of his last days, the wish to know, before he died, that he had a great-grandchild? Why? Why? Could the Lord be so harsh?

Joshua looked up in silent prayer and then sank to his knees by the bed. Nervously he put a hand on his father's arm and lightly pressed it.

'*Tata, tata,*' he begged, 'wake up. It's me, your son, Joshua. Wake up, *tata*. I have something to tell you. You have a great-grandchild, a fine boy. Please, *tata*, wake up. Just for a moment.'

There was no response. Joshua let his head drop onto his arms, pressing into his father's side, as if through the touch of flesh upon flesh the knowledge of his great-grandson's birth might somehow penetrate his father's coma and light up whatever deep dreams were flickering through his mind. He waited thus and prayed to himself for some minutes. Then, almost timorously, he raised his head, examining the Rabbi's face to see if there was any sign of movement, any indication, however slight, that his eyes might open or that some word would issue from his parted lips – anything to tell Joshua that he had heard and understood. But there was nothing: his eyelids were as still as those of a blind statue, and no sound escaped

416

from his lips – not even a whisper from the fading breath in his body. Joshua remained kneeling by the bed for some time until he heard the latch of the front door being lifted and Dr Lee's step in the hall. He wiped his eyes and rose.

This time the doctor spent no more than five minutes with his patient, and when he descended the stairs he seemed anxious to get away. Perhaps he thought the family would consider he had failed them in not being able to coax the Rabbi back to consciousness even for a few moments – for he had hardly been inside the front door when Bertha had rushed to tell him about Molly's child, protesting that if only they could let the Rabbi know she was sure he would recover. Perhaps he was upset that he could only report a further deterioration since his last visit, news which he knew would completely blight their already tarnished joy.

'I'm sorry,' he said. 'I'm very sorry there is nothing I can do. I'm afraid the Rabbi is much weaker.'

'Much weaker?' Joshua echoed.

'Yes. It's only a question of time.'

'How long?' Bertha asked as her husband seemed too affected to speak.

Dr Lee raised his eyebrows and then shook his head discouragingly.

'Not long, Mrs Cohen, not long at all. He might last the night, he might not.'

'*Oi vey*,' Bertha Cohen murmured, clutching at Joshua's arm in support both of herself and of him. As neither of them moved to open the door for the doctor, he lifted the latch himself.

'I'll come back again on my way home,' he said.

They were still standing in the hall, leaning against each other, until the sound of the doctor's horse and trap died away. Judith and Jacob came out of the kitchen.

'We heard,' Judith said, going to comfort her parents.

Joshua turned to his son. 'My boy, go down to Mr Lovitch's shop and ask him to come here. Tell him it's urgent. Tell him what the doctor said.'

'But it's Wednesday,' Judith pointed out. 'Half-day. Mr Lovitch will be closed.'

417

'Yes, yes, I forgot. Then, he'll be at home. Hurry, Jacob.'
Jacob nodded.

'Be careful, *mein kinde*,' Joshua called after him as he wheeled his bicycle out and jumped onto the saddle. 'Let us go back upstairs.'

They returned to the Rabbi's room. Judith brought in a stool and another chair, and in silence they sat and waited.

The news spread quickly and within a few hours a small crowd had gathered in the road outside Rabbi Cohen's home. They were mostly the more elderly men of the community together with those whose livelihood did not require them to go to the country towns and villages. They stood in groups on the path – some with their womenfolk – or leaned against the low wall of the tiny front garden, well muffled up against the cold, talking a little – but quietly – smoking, offering each other a pinch of snuff. Every few minutes someone else would join them and to his questioning '*Nu?*' they would answer with a shrug or a slow shake of the head.

'Percy is in there,' someone might say. 'Since four o'clock.' And the newcomer would nod understandingly.

'And Levitt, the minister, too,' another would add.

'The President? Isn't he here yet?'

'Yes, yes, he's here. His car is parked round the corner.'

'Ah.'

Some of the non-Jewish residents of the area came, too, standing sympathetically on the fringe of their Jewish neighbours. They were joined by Father McGiff, his soutane showing under his big overcoat which had been thrown like a cape over his shoulders and was buttoned at the waist, for the slings on his arms prevented him from donning it properly. As he moved among his parishioners, the empty sleeves flapped forlornly, as if searching for the limbs that should have filled them.

Inside the house a knife-edge of light cut the darkness where the front door had been left ajar, but it was to the upper window that the eyes of the waiting people constantly drifted. There, behind the flickering candlelight that wavered on the drawn blind, they knew their Rabbi was lying. Every now and again someone's shadow would move into that light, making everyone quickly look up, before it moved away again.

Suddenly the sound of church bells was heard, and Father McGiff and his companions took off their hats, crossed themselves, and began to recite the Angelus.

'Six o'clock,' some of the waiting community murmured, while others opened an overcoat button to delve into an inner pocket from which they drew out watch and chain to check the time. In their minds, however, they were wondering: when? when? Or perhaps he will fool them all and live and go to *Eretz*. But they made no such speculation to each other; they did not really believe it themselves. It was, they knew, that in the tension of waiting optimism – foolish though it be – was all that could make the vigil bearable.

Shortly afterwards Dr Lee's horse and trap appeared round the corner and stopped at the end of the street. The doctor climbed down, black bag in hand, and approached the house. As he reached the crowd of people outside the gate, all of whom he had at one time or another attended, he raised his hat and nodded to them silently. They saluted him back but did not delay him.

For some twenty minutes more the people stood and gazed up at the lighted window. There was little conversation now. Each was thinking that the doctor was a long time inside. Was that good or bad?

Then suddenly they heard a sound. Had it come from the room? Was it a sob? They looked at each other. 'Did you hear that? What was it?' But no one was certain, no one would say.

Then came another sound and, though soft, it was clear and recognisable. As it started, Dr Lee emerged from the house and stood to listen. It was the voice of Percy Lovitch singing the *Kol Nidrei* prayer, annulling all one's terrestrial vows, obligations and oaths. Its solemnity and importance were such that it was recited only once in the year, on the eve of the Day of Atonement, but its melody was so moving that a single hearing was sufficient to

419

embed both song and words in the memory of every devout Jew. When sung in the synagogue, the congregation would keep step, reciting the prayer in the background, but now, in the cold still night air, the congregation assembled on the road had no voice. Their voice was that of Percy Lovitch, and as the unbearably sweet anguish that the song and its words engendered pulsed through their blood each one's heart dipped and swayed in the sea of memory.

> All vows, obligations, oaths, anathemas, by whatever name they be called ... we do repent. May they be deemed to be forgiven, absolved, annulled or void, and made of no effect. They shall not bind us or have power over us; the vows shall not be considered vows, nor the obligations obligatory, nor the oaths oaths.

Percy's voice sank to a whisper. The prayer reached its end.

For a full minute no one moved, and then Father McGiff approached the group.

'Tell me, please, what was that? What does it mean?'

'It was the *Kol Nidrei*,' someone answered. 'It means that the body has no more duties and the Lord has reclaimed the soul. It means Rabbi Cohen is dead, Father. Our Rabbi is dead.'

Father McGiff took off his hat and, closing his eyes on his tears, made the sign of the cross.

'May God have mercy on him,' he said. 'He was a saint.'

'It was so quick, Judith,' Miriam said, 'so sudden. You've had only less than a week to get ready.'

Reuben and Miriam had returned from their honeymoon on Thursday afternoon to learn of Rabbi Cohen's death. The news did not surprise them – while in Dublin they had been told by friends who were in touch with Cork that the Rabbi had been in a coma since his collapse and was steadily growing weaker.

420

'There's not much for me to do, really, is there?' Judith replied, grateful that they had called immediately to give her family what little consolation they could and to offer her their help in preparing for her journey. She was touched by the solicitude of this couple who, though younger than she, seemed already by their marriage to have taken on quite naturally an almost parental concern. Her nervousness about going to *Eretz* had, for the present at least, been dissipated. The death of her *zeide* had frozen her responses in the immediate moment, concentrating her worries on the strain the funeral would place on her parents and the loneliness they would face during the *Shivah*, the seven days of deep mourning that would commence on their return to Celtic Crescent after the Rabbi had been laid to rest. They would have Jacob, of course, and there would be constant callers to the house to help ease their grief through the first black days – and they would also have the consolation of looking forward to the visit she was sure they would make to Molly and her baby as soon as the *Shivah* was over. But even all that, she feared, would do little to lift the gloom that would surely descend on them, confined to this house which for so long they had shared with their loved one who was now gone for ever and would then be lying in the cold earth of his Irish hillside grave.

She sat in the kitchen with her mother and Jacob, having seen out Reuben and Miriam, and waited for her father to join them. He was in the front room with Max Klein and Zvi Lipsky, discussing the arrangements for the funeral. She wondered what was keeping him so long – Mr Lipsky had been years running the Burial Society and would know everything that needed to be done – but, then, of course the funeral of a rabbi would be something very special.

'I'll make more tea,' Bertha Cohen said, rising from her chair by the range.

'No, I'll do it, Mother. You sit down,' Judith offered.

'*Nein*,' her mother replied, 'it's better to keep busy. See if your father and the men want another cup.'

Just then, however, they heard Max Klein and Zvi

421

Lipsky depart, and Joshua Cohen entered the kitchen. Judith looked at her father. She expected to see the strain show in his face, but instead there was almost a smile playing about his lips and his head was nodding – just the way, she thought, his own father's used to when he was particularly pleased about something.

'*Vos*,' Bertha enquired, 'what is it?' as her husband stood on the threshold a moment before coming to join his family.

'It is decided,' he announced. 'The Rabbi will be buried in *Eretz*!'

Judith gasped with astonishment, Jacob asked hesitantly, 'Are you sure it is possible?', while Bertha gazed admiringly at her husband, her hands raised to her face in wonder at the plan but also already a little afraid in case somehow it might come to grief.

'This was your idea, Joshua?' she enquired.

'Yes. It is what he would have wanted. I'm certain of it. He lived to be a great-grandfather – though he did not know it. That was one thing he wanted. And he always spoke of ending his days in *Eretz* – you know that. Well, in *Eretz* he will rest.'

Joshua sat down, weary but content.

'There's not much time,' he admitted, 'but it will be enough. The President will arrange everything. He knows people in the City Hall. He will go to Dr Lee, get whatever medical certificates they need. He will telephone Karlinsky. Don't worry, it will all be done in time. Max Klein is a real *gantser macher*. Would he be where he is today if he wasn't?'

The question needed no answer – Max Klein was, indeed, a fixer. Bertha Cohen, who could forget nothing where her family was concerned, felt a twinge of doubt – she remembered that the President had failed to get any of his children into the better secondary schools – but she immediately shook the doubt from her mind. There was no comparison; this was different. He wouldn't fail them. More, he wouldn't fail Rabbi Moishe!

'Here, *mein mon*,' she said to her husband, 'a hot cup of tea. Drink.'

422

My darling Elizabeth,
This is probably the last letter I'll write you from Ireland. Another three days or so and, God willing, we'll be together again at last. There's so much I want to say and yet I hardly know how to start. I suppose the trouble is that there's really not a lot I have to say. It's more what I want to do – to put my arms around you and tell you I love you. Goodness, what would all the hardened soldiers around me think of their tough brave Captain Simcox if they could read these words? The man who defied his IRA captors for two weeks and then succeeded single-handed with a great feat of derring-do in escaping from them! But it doesn't matter what they would think. With any luck at all my soldiering days will soon be over – no more uniforms, no more orders, no more guns, no more Ireland, and no more IRA or Black and Tans.

It's funny how distant those two weeks I spent in my country residence now seem. When I think about them, I see myself in a way enjoying them. Silly, isn't it? Because I don't suppose I really was enjoying them – it's just vanity to imagine that there weren't times when I was really afraid. But, then, conditions could have been so much worse than they were, and Boxer and Joe were such good chaps really. Joe was only a child of course, and Boxer was a simple straightforward sort of bloke. No, I'm not going soft; I know what they and their comrades are capable of, I know they'd have shot me in cold blood if they were ordered to. Every day now when I read the paper and see the terrible things that are happening it sickens me. It's funny, these are the same things I used to read every day when I was a prisoner and used deliberately to avoid in my letters to you. Now it doesn't matter.

because I'll be out of it all so soon. But the tragedy is that these things will go on, God knows for how long. A man shot dead coming out of church, shops burned down everywhere and in one village a shop-owner thrown into the flooded river, an inmate of an asylum shot dead when he didn't respond to a challenge, kidnappings almost daily, looting, some torturing even – all sides are at it. And it gets worse and worse. God, how lucky I am to be getting away from all that savagery. Luckier still to have you to go to, and soon with God's help we'll be a father and mother, parents. When I look around me in this unfortunate island, I can't believe my luck and I thank God for you and also for King and country. I'd better stop now before I start crying into my beer.

Stay well, darling. All my love.

RODDY

Captain Simcox read over his letter before sealing it. It was a bit sloppy and sentimental in places, he thought, but what of it? That was the way he felt. And anyway he was too impatient and light-headed with anticipation to rewrite it.

On that same Thursday morning Colonel Windsor, too, was reading over a letter – not one he had written, but one he had just received. It was from the office of Sir Hamar Greenwood, Secretary for Ireland. It said:

The Secretary for Ireland asks me to thank you for your letter of 25th ultimo. He has noted your comments but does not feel there is anything he can usefully add to his public statements on the situation in Ireland.

424

It was signed by Sir Hamar's private secretary. Brief and formal, as if swatting a fly – a smack on the wrist for him.

Colonel Windsor wasn't really surprised. He could hardly have expected anything else. He fitted another cigarette into his holder, lit it, and then put the match to the letter. As he watched it burn, its flame was magnified in his mind's eye into some huge conflagration, a conflagration he was quite sure each day was bringing nearer and nearer. He dropped the burning letter into the ashtray before its flame could scorch his fingers. For a very brief moment he wondered if he would still be unscathed after that big conflagration he had just imagined. But he quickly dismissed such a thought – it wasn't his style. He had a job to do for King and country. A soldier always had to put up with stupid politicians.

Late on Thursday night, under cover of darkness, Denis collected the arms from their hiding-place in Iron Josh's store and took them to his room. He didn't go to work next day and he didn't visit his home. He remained in his room with sandwiches and a flask of tea, checked over all the guns and ammunition, saw that everything was in working order. Having to stay a whole day in the room made him realise what a lonely ugly place it was, but he knew that – if he lived – he would ever after remember it only as the place he had last seen Judith, the place they had last made love. He didn't dwell much, however, on the memory of those few hours; what he thought about mostly was that next day, after so many, many months of waiting, he was finally going to get his wish. Tomorrow he would strike his blow for Ireland.

Judith, too, thought about Denis during those two days, thoughts that gave neither her body nor her mind any rest. The recollection of their lovemaking in his room – more leisurely, more deliberate than on the first occasion – was still sharp enough to stab her with pangs of desire

425

she could not suppress; and her inability to get a *Cork Examiner* on either day – since she could not leave the house of mourning – made her tremble with fears for his safety. She knew it was foolish of her to be thinking about Denis at all, but she knew, too, that until she boarded the train for Dublin on Sunday, going forward into a new life and leaving behind Cork and what it had come to mean to her for ever, it would be impossible for her even to begin to forget him.

32

SATURDAY DAWNED FINE, dull but dry, and far from cold enough to raise expectations that the Christmas now only two weeks away would be a white one. It was 'real Shabbos weather', the members of the Jewish community congratulated each other as they walked to synagogue for the morning service and home afterwards for the leisurely Saturday dinner of soup with meatballs, followed by the traditional *tsimmes* – a casserole of carrots, potatoes, and a little brisket, sweetened with honey or golden syrup – and, to finish, a glass of black tea flavoured with a slice of lemon and lump sugar. Then, with the glasses drained and the topics of the day exhausted, the *sidurim* were opened – even though none had need of a prayer-book – and the voices around the table began to hum and drone and rise and fall in the serene, song-studded, long Grace After Meals.

The weather was, however, the only thing the worshippers could be happy about: for all it was the first Shabbos ever that the Rabbi's special seat beside the Ark of the Law had been empty; and for a handful it was their last Shabbos in Cork. So the service was muted and the congregation's responses almost perfunctory, as if the common unspoken desire was to hasten the passing of this saddest of sad weekends.

427

Getting through the day was a problem for Denis, too. His orders were to stay in his room until six o'clock and then make his way, with the arms and ammunition, to the meeting-place.

The time passed so slowly, Shandon seeming to take a full hour before consenting to strike each reluctant quarter. Denis wished he had something to read – the morning paper or any old book at all – then told himself that, if he had, he'd probably be too excited to read anyway. He checked the guns a few times before forcing himself to let them be – the less he tinkered at them and cleaned them at this stage, the better. He lay on the bed most of the day, tried to sleep but couldn't even doze, tried to think of Judith but found his nerves and mind too preoccupied and too jumpy even to keep Judith in his thoughts for long.

As darkness enveloped the room in the early afternoon, he began to feel much calmer. This surprised him. He had expected to become more nervous as six o'clock approached; to find the opposite happening gave him both strength and confidence. He remembered now having the same experience when he and Boxer kidnapped Joshua Cohen. The journey to Iron Josh's store, and then the ride into the country with their victim lying under a rug in the horse and cart – these had been the bad moments, the waiting moments, when nothing was happening. He felt it then, and today the thought returned – that all action was like this: a span, long or short, in which one did nothing – could do nothing except be at the mercy of one's nerves – and then *the* moment, the test. . . .

Well, his test had come – at last. He put on his gaberdine and sat on the edge of the bed, waiting for Shandon to strike six o'clock. Immediately the peals started he jumped up, had a last look in his knapsack to check its contents – five revolvers and enough ammunition. He didn't know who had been detailed to make up the column with him but he was confident that his companions would be expert marksmen. They'd need to be, for the attack was to be a close-quarters engagement from the start and they'd be operating in darkness. He knew one of the men

428

would have a bomb prepared by GHQ, but the column had had some unhappy experiences when their bombs failed to explode and, even if this one went off, there were still bound to be plenty of targets left for their bullets. He fastened the knapsack, slung it over his shoulder, put on his cap and quietly left the room.

As he came out of the house, a young man he had never seen before casually wheeled a bicycle across the narrow street and nodded to him. Denis took the machine, jumped onto it, and pedalled away.

Not long after six o'clock Jacob Cohen was also out on his bicycle.

'Out? Where? What for? Where have you got to go?' Joshua had asked testily, affronted by Jacob's tentative suggestion that he might go out for a while – if his father thought it would be all right. But with the Rabbi's body coffined upstairs, ready for its journey to *Eretz*, Joshua's immediate reaction was that it certainly would not be all right for anyone to leave the house. Jacob wasn't surprised – he had guessed that his father would consider it disrespectful, almost unnatural, for any member of his family to want to go out at such a time.

'I wasn't going to go anywhere special, Father,' he said. 'And I'm not calling on anyone. It's just that, being stuck in for so long, I felt. . . . But it doesn't matter; I'll stay here.'

And then Joshua remembered. He remembered the bond that had existed between his father and Jacob. He remembered his own revelation, the chilling recognition of his sin of omission in never trying to foster a similar bond between himself and his only son. He remembered that Jacob was a young man – a young man? no, only a youth – and that this was his first experience of death. He remembered that as soon as his father's body was carried out for the start of its long journey their seven days of deep mourning would commence and they would be unable to leave the house once during all that time. Was his son's request so outrageous after all? Joshua remembered and relented.

429

'*Gei, gei, mein kinde,*' he said, his voice for a moment awkward with remorse. 'But be careful. Don't go near Patrick Street at this hour. And don't be late.'

Jacob had looked in surprise at his father. Joshua turned his head aside in the shy gesture that his son recognised. But the warmth in his voice and the note of solicitude in his instructions struck a chord.

'Thank you, *tata*,' Jacob said, not seeing, as he left the room, his father's eyes light up.

He cycled slowly, keeping a course westwards, away from the centre and the main thoroughfare. He had no special destination in mind; he didn't need one, for the history and geography of his city had so gripped his imagination that wherever the humming wheels of his bicycle took him would, he knew, call up some local legend or item of recorded knowledge that, rousing the ghosts of time, would make the place more than just bricks and mortar. He was happy to be back again with his first love. For weeks Cork had been relegated to the background, merely a setting for his infatuation with Deirdre. Her image still filled him with warmth, but to his surprise it was a warmth that had the flavour of nostalgia rather than of desire. The realisation disturbed his self-esteem. Was he so fickle? Could he be getting over her so quickly?

As he turned into South Terrace and passed the synagogue, now closed and dark, he thought of his *zeide* and recalled their last conversation, when the Rabbi had convinced him that it would be foolish to leave university and Cork, and go to Palestine. Jacob could see now what his *zeide* had been doing. He hadn't merely been talking about the present and the future; he had, in his wise old way, been helping his grandson to grow up. How many others in the community had his *zeide*, at one time or another, guided towards the right decision when confronted by some seemingly impossible choice? Jacob guessed that there were few who hadn't as much cause as he – as much and more – to remember their dead Rabbi with gratitude and love for his humanity and wisdom, as well as with respect for his holiness. No wonder it had been decided that when his coffin set out on the next morning its route to the station would be diverted to pass the synagogue, an honour accorded only to a deeply venerated Jew on his final journey to the grave.

Jacob felt exhilarated as he cycled on, seeming to float through the almost empty streets. It was a perfect night for a spin – no hint of rain and no strong wind to make his progress laborious. Along George's Quay he could hear the bristling of the Lee as it flowed past Morrison's Island and under Parliament Bridge. Then, continuing on to Sullivan's Quay he had a view, across the river, of the Grand Parade with the Berwick fountain that to Deirdre had seemed 'just a fountain'. And beyond the fountain he had only to raise his head to see, against the starry sky, the lofty spire of Christ Church Cathedral, where the poet Edmund Spenser married his Youghal sweetheart, Elizabeth Boyle, the river then becoming their Lido as they stepped into a ribbon-bedecked boat to be rowed the short distance to their honeymoon house in North Main Street.

From there Jacob turned north, deciding now exactly where he was making for, and after weaving through a maze of silent cobbled laneways he emerged face to face with Washington Street's Court House. More awesome by night than it ever was by day when the constant scurry of people climbing its steps and disappearing behind its pillars into the cavernous doorways made it seem a place where justice might be tempered with mercy, now, deserted, and with the moon bathing it in a cold light, it appeared to Jacob full of menace, promising at best only blind justice and no more, at worst retribution. But in the moon's spotlight he was able to appreciate why Thackeray on his Irish tour had said that its portico 'would do honour to Palladio' – the ten noble pillars rising out of the many-stepped stone patio were stark, stern and beautiful.

West again it was but a short ride to his old school, Presentation Brothers College, the scene of his mother's great triumph. He smiled now at the recollection of her tenacity but he was proud of her, too, for although the single-minded purpose she displayed had sprung from her fierce ambition for her own son it had in fact opened the

431

doors of Presentation Brothers College to other Jewish students after him. Less than half a century since a community of Jews had settled in Cork and one of the main barriers to their advancement had been removed. Was that a long time for what had been, after all, only a local barrier? How much longer was it going to take to remove a much greater barrier – for example, the one preventing the Jewish people from having a home of its own in Palestine? True, the Zionist movement was now world-wide, but there were also world-wide forces ranged against it. Yet given the followers, given the time, and who could say what might not be possible in the Holy Land – a Jewish home, a Jewish country, perhaps even a Jewish State? But at what cost? Jacob knew that such an upheaval could not possibly be achieved without bloodshed. It would be naïve to imagine otherwise. He had only to contemplate his own city to see that land was never won easily. Whether it was a land not yours and you wanted it, or a land that *was* yours and you wanted it back, you had to fight for it. Look what such a fight was costing the Irish. Centuries of time, thousands of lives!

Jacob cycled a little further, coming to a halt between Presentation College and the nearby entrance to the University, and turned his face to look southwards. What he saw helped to banish the turbulent images from his mind.

Across the road, a few yards away, was the familiar Cork & Muskerry Light Railway line, its slender tracks gleaming in the darkness. Beyond that he could hear the night song of one of the Lee's many chattering tributaries meandering on its lazy course; and beyond that again was Gilabbey Rock.

Gilabbey was, indeed, a huge outcrop of jagged rock that the local urchins delighted in trying to climb. Some three hundred yards across and over fifty feet high, it rose up from an area of overgrown wasteland to a plateau that was part of one of the hills rimming the valley in which the city lay. To Jacob, as his gaze ranged over the whole span with the moon etching black and gold bars on its

432

craggy face, it was a view that always filled him with emotion, for there, over thirteen centuries earlier, Cork had been born. On the top of that sheer ledge, a monk had established a monastery which drew students and acolytes in such numbers from all over the world that soon the wattle and mud huts of the scattered families subsisting on the marshy land below multiplied and grew to form a city. The city was named after the Irish for a marsh, Corcach, and the monk became St Finbar, its patron saint.

As Jacob looked at Gilabbey Rock, he saw in his mind's eye not only the hallowed stones and primitive cells of that famous monastery, quiet apart from the drone of prayer and study, but also time's transformation of the first settlements into the elegant storied city that he loved. He had been born here, he had grown up here, it was a part of him, almost physically, certainly spiritually. It wasn't the same sort of spiritual bond that had made Rabbi Moishe all his life an exile, yearning for a plot of land on the other side of the world where his bones might rest. Jacob did not feel an exile. He felt at home. Had he been leaving Cork the next day he knew now how desolate he would have been. His *zeide*'s spirit would be happy in *Eretz*; his would be happy in Cork. They had both got what they wanted.

Jacob turned his bicycle and, retracing his route, made his way back towards Celtic Crescent. He cycled slowly, rehearsing each street's historic associations, peopling the houses with the ghosts of former tenants, and smiling to himself at the way the city's name, like a cork, bobbed about in his mind.

And then, as he was crossing the bridge over the Bandon railway just round the corner from his home, he looked north and saw something that brought him back to reality. It was a glow in the sky, a glow such as had become familiar to the citizens of Cork. Somewhere in the heart of the city another building was on fire, and like tears of blood its red flames were shooting into the sky.

* * *

It was nearly seven o'clock by the time Denis reached the meeting-place on the Old Youghal Road, some ten miles from the city centre. It was a farmhouse set in the furthest corner of a field beside the road, and as Denis went through the open gate he could see a number of bicycles lying against a side-wall, their frames gleaming in the moonlight. Guessing he was the last to arrive, he put his machine with them, surprised that everything was so quiet. Were it not for the smoke issuing from a chimney in the thatched roof and for the heap of bicycles, he would have thought the place deserted.

A volunteer stood inside the open door of the farmhouse.

'Good man. You're here,' he muttered as Denis approached. 'They're all inside' – and he jerked his head towards a room on one side of the narrow stone hall.

Inside the room the members of the column had gathered in a group at the window, some staring out onto the dark fields, others nervously whispering among themselves. The OC sat at the bare table, in the centre of which an oil-lamp burned beside some mugs and a bucket of tea.

Denis saluted and handed his knapsack to the OC, then greeted the other men. A few of them threw jocular reprimands at him for taking so long, but their voices, instead of being light, had the strain of tension. Denis guessed their sallies were meant to ease their own nerves, for they'd have known that the back lanes and boreens he had to keep to on his journey were what had slowed him down.

'The priest is across,' the OC told him. 'The rest of us have been.'

Denis nodded. At the other side of the hall a door was ajar. He pushed it open and looked in.

Beside a bed was a three-legged stool on which a candle stood in its own congealed wax. In the flickering light Denis saw two chairs. A priest was sitting in one and when he saw Denis he patted the seat of the other invitingly.

'Good evening, Father,' Denis greeted him, taking off his cap.

'Come in, my son. Is there any more after you?'

'I don't think so, Father. I think I'm the last.'

The priest was not young. His hair had more grey than its original dark colour, his eyes were hidden behind thick spectacles, and the hands fingering rosary beads were fleshless and scored with thick veins that swelled out on his brown-spotted skin.

Denis knelt on the cold floor, resting his elbows on the seat of the empty chair. He joined his palms in front of his face and in a low voice made his Confession.

When he finished, he rose and thanked the priest.

'You're not afraid, are you, my son?'

'No, Father, I'm not afraid,' Denis replied. 'A bit nervous – excited like. If I was afraid, I wouldn't be much use.'

'Your cause is just, my son, and the Lord is always on the side of justice. He will watch over you. Good luck to ye all, my son.'

'Thank you, Father,' Denis murmured.

The priest gave him his blessing, and Denis turned and rejoined his comrades.

When he entered the room, they were standing to attention, anxious to be on their way, a gun in each one's hand. The OC gave Denis the last weapon and led them out to the front door.

'You know the plan,' he said.

He pointed down to the end of the field at the low stone wall separating it from the road.

'In about ten minutes a Tan lorry is due to come along that road on its way to the barracks. When it gets to that sharp bend just below us – you can see it clearly – it'll be going dead slow and as it takes the bend the back of the lorry will be turned to the wall. That's where we'll be – behind the wall – and that's the moment when Con throws the bomb. Keep down until you hear my whistle. Then up with you, pick your targets and fire. The bomb might get some of the Tans, but any left will be exposed, so they'll have to jump out of the lorry to get to the cover on the other side of the road. They'll be no more than a few yards from us and that's when we can get them.'

435

'How many will there be?' someone asked.

'Ten or twelve at the most, so we'll be outnumbered. Unless the bomb does for a lot of them. If Con can land it right in the lorry, it might. But we don't know for certain if there'll be a follow-up lorry behind. That means we'll only have time for a short sharp attack. Then when you hear my whistle a second time belt it back to the house one by one so that there's always some of us left to keep them busy. Leave your guns up where the bikes are now and scatter. And remember – keep a distance between ye, no two cycling together. Is all that clear?'

The OC's calm, almost conversational tone succeeded in stirring up in the men the same enthusiasm and confidence they had felt in their training sessions. Tension was replaced by determination. Each man's courage bolstered his comrades, and the excitement passed from one to another like an electric current. Denis licked his dry lips and wished he had remembered to take a sup of tea before leaving the farmhouse.

'Right, then, lads, take up your positions. Good luck! And for God's sake keep your heads down until I whistle.'

They moved off quickly down the field, some of them bending low as if to avoid observation. Con walked at an even pace, the bomb in a shopping-bag held out in front of him, the OC beside him. When they reached the wall they crouched down behind it, no more than fifteen feet between any two of them. Denis was fourth in line, then Con, then the OC. They waited.

No one spoke, and the silence was broken only by the odd suppressed cough or the noise of shuffling as someone manoeuvred his body into a more comfortable position. Denis sat back against the wall, the gun in his lap, his right hand tucked under his armpit to keep it warm. He hoped the Tan lorry would come quickly. Sitting out for long like this in an open field on a sharp December evening would soon freeze a man's bones and slow his reactions. Neither he nor his comrades were wearing overcoats – running or cycling at speed in an overcoat wouldn't have been easy. If anyone who didn't know what was going on saw them – huddled down behind a wall, each in his everyday suit, a peaked cap pulled tight on every head and a few with a scarf wound round their throats – he'd surely think they were like a band of overgrown children playing Hide and Seek. Denis smiled to himself at the thought. It *was* a sort of Hide and Seek – but it was no game. They might be quiet as waiting children now, each counting the seconds, but in a matter of minutes they'd be fighting men, all hell would break loose, and afterwards....

Afterwards ... he knew what was in store for himself and his comrades. Some of them might be wounded, some of them might even be killed, God forbid, but the action would be so short and sharp that the most likely thing was they'd all escape. The family up at the farmhouse wouldn't escape, however. The house was their home, and they knew what would happen to it. With a thatched roof it would burn quickly. That was the usual Tan retaliation – along with making them sing 'God Save the King' while they watched their home burn down. That's what had happened a few weeks before after a similar ambush. Well, at least they wouldn't have to stand in the rain, as the other poor family had.

'Ready, boys.'

The OC's whispered call startled him from his thoughts. In the distance a motor engine could be heard. The men prepared themselves.

Denis had to restrain himself from raising his head above the wall to see if the approaching vehicle was their quarry.

'It's coming, lads,' the OC hissed again. 'Keep down now.'

Denis tried to picture the lorry. It would be travelling at a good speed, but already he could hear the engine's lower note as the gears were changed for the sharp bend. The headlamps would be lighting up the bit of road ahead and soon, too, the wall behind which he and his comrades were waiting, guns ready. The Tan bastards would be sitting in the lorry, feeling safe now because they were so near their barracks. They might be singing – maybe the engine was drowning their voices – or perhaps the driver

437

in his cabin was singing. The noise was louder now, much louder. They must be almost level. It sounded as if the lorry was taking the bend.

Denis was conscious of a slight movement from the OC, a signal to Con. Out of the corner of his eye he saw an arm curve up lazily, almost in slow motion, like a swimmer doing a few casual pre-race strokes. As the arm reached the top of its arc, something dark and round lobbed from the opened hand and out of Denis's sight. He waited, his heart thumping with anticipation, his ears almost willing the crack of the explosion.

Even behind the thunderous roar of the lorry's engine he was able to distinguish a sharp rap. The bomb had hit something. But where was the explosion? If it was going to go off, he should hear only the bang. Christ, had something gone wrong?

Before he could sort out his impressions, the OC's whistle sounded a piercing blast and in the very same moment the shattering noise of the bomb exploding made him jerk back on his haunches. He pushed out his free hand, grabbing the wall to save himself from falling backwards altogether, and in the same action pulled himself up to fire.

In the split second before his gun-hand was raised, he saw what had happened. The bomb had struck the side of the lorry and fallen down onto the road before it detonated. The force of the explosion had slewed the lorry around so that now, instead of presenting its passengers to the men's open sights, it had come to a stop broadside on and, like seals flopping off a rock into the sea, the Tans were flinging themselves over its side to take cover behind it.

The men blazed away. The Tans were disappearing so quickly that there was no time to take aim. The noise of the shooting and the shouts of the Black and Tans filled the air, and already some of them were returning fire. Their bullets screamed as they ricocheted off the wall. Then came a blast on the OC's whistle and the man on the end of the line turned and ran off, his body bent double. Within ten seconds came another blast and the next man

438

followed him. Denis wished he hadn't emptied his gun so quickly. He should have reloaded and kept firing at the Tans so as to give his retreating comrades cover.

Suddenly he realised it was his turn to make his escape. He ran – never in his life had he run faster – he didn't fancy a bullet in the back. He wondered if they had got any of the Tans at all. Some of them could have been lying dead on the roadway behind the lorry. It was impossible to tell. If they were, he hoped at least one of his bullets had found its mark. But he would never know that, either.

Gasping for breath he reached the farmhouse, quickly threw his gun down beside the others and grabbed his bicycle. He pedalled away, his lungs gulping in huge draughts of air. His head was light with the mixture of excitement, elation, relief. He had been in action at last and he had come through.

The road rose in a hill against him and he pressed down hard on the pedals. Reaching the crest, he freewheeled down the other side, gaining momentum with every yard. The starry sky, the whirring wheels, the wind in his face – it was all exhilarating, sheer bliss. He lifted his legs from the pedals, whooped like a Red Indian, and then, snatching his cap from his head, flung it with a mad and mighty throw far into the night.

Jacob lingered on the bridge, appalled by the sight of the fire burning in the city but unable to drag himself away. There was an eeriness about it, as if seeing the flames leaping up but not being able to hear their hiss and crackle or feel their heat should have made it possible for him to imagine that it was all just a vision. But it was no vision – other passers-by were joining him, aghast at the spectacle, and now they could all hear, plainly though distantly, the clang of bells as fire-engines raced through the streets.

'Lord save us,' a man said, 'that's the worst yet.'

'Where do you think it is? Could it be South Mall,' Jacob speculated, 'or is it further off?'

439

'Oh, yes,' came from a youth standing with his girl, 'it's further away than that. In Patrick Street somewhere. Could be any of the big shops. One thing is certain – the Tans are having sport.'

'Come on, Sean,' the girl pleaded, 'come away. I'm afraid.'

The young man, reluctant to leave, put an arm around her. 'Sure there's nothing to be afraid of. We're safe enough here.'

As the crowd, growing larger all the time, pressed closer to the iron rail of the bridge, Jacob left his bicycle and joined them.

Some of the women made the sign of the cross and started to pray.

'God protect us,' wailed one, pulling more tightly around her the black shawl and hood still worn in the country villages. 'Lord save any poor soul caught in that.'

'Tan bastards,' the men muttered to each other, and 'Up the IRA. Our lads will pay them out for this.'

Even as they spoke, a ball of flame suddenly erupted into the sky from another building beside the first fire. The people on the bridge drew back in horror as both fires joined in a massive conflagration.

'Jesus, what are they doing at all?' a voice protested.

'That's Patrick Street for sure,' an old man asserted, taking off his cap and holding it in front of his face as if to protect himself from being burned. 'The northern end, I'd say, up by Roche's Stores and the Statue. You can tell by the distance from the Court House roof, away to the left.'

'You're right,' Jacob agreed. 'I can see the Court House now.'

In the almost garish light the city's whole skyline was clearly recognisable, and the green dome of the Court House stood out as a landmark and reference-point.

'I knew something like this was coming,' a bespectacled young man told them. 'I was reading in the Library this afternoon when a Protestant Unionist friend of mine came up to me and told me to go home at once, as he had been told there was to be bad work tonight.'

The information caused no surprise. Few in the crowd

440

thought that destruction on this scale could be anything but planned.

'Sure didn't we all know?' someone added. 'You could sense all week that something was going to happen.'

Jacob stayed watching for another ten minutes. By then further fires had turned the whole area into an inferno, police whistles and fire brigade bells sounded constantly, and now the smell of burning was being carried to them on the breeze. If this continued, there'd be nothing of Patrick Street left – nothing of Cork left. Jacob could stand it no longer. He retrieved his bicycle and rushed home.

Immediately he opened the front door Judith and her mother ran from the kitchen to meet him.

'Where were you? Where have you been?' Bertha Cohen flung at him, her voice a mixture of anger and concern.

'I was just out for a spin. I told Father – he said I could go.'

'Were you near the store? Did you see your father?' Judith asked agitatedly.

'What would I be doing near the store? Father told me to keep away from Patrick Street. Isn't he here?'

'No. He's gone to the store. Patrick Street is on fire. The Black and Tans are burning it.'

'I know,' Jacob told her. 'It's terrible. I was watching it from the bridge. But what's Father gone to the store for? He shouldn't have gone. It's dangerous to go anywhere near there.'

'I know, I know,' his mother wailed. 'I couldn't stop him.'

'He said he had some documents in the office that are important,' Judith explained. 'He wants to get them quickly in case they set fire to the store.'

'Documents! Documents!' Bertha shouted. 'Pieces of paper. Could they be more important than his life? He'll be killed – your father will be killed.'

Jacob backed his bicycle out the door. 'I'll go after him. Is he long gone?'

'Ten minutes or more,' Judith replied. 'You'll never find him, Jacob. You'll only get hurt yourself.'

441

'No, no, I'll find him,' Jacob assured them. 'Don't worry, Mother, I'll find him. If he's gone to the store, I'll get him there or meet him on the way back. Don't worry.'

As Jacob rushed off, Bertha Cohen put a hand to her mouth, not knowing whether she wanted her son to go or stay. What good could he do, even if he found her husband? Joshua was so obstinate; if the documents were that important to him, he wouldn't come back without them. But at least with Jacob there he'd have someone to help him, he wouldn't be alone. Jacob was young and strong.

Judith tried to comfort her mother, but her emotions were even more confused and her dilemma more agonising. She knew why her father had rushed to the store but she had to pretend, she couldn't tell anyone. There were no precious documents – she was certain of that. She guessed her father was afraid that if the Tans broke into the store they might find the guns and ammunition Denis said he was hiding there. Even if they didn't, the store might be set on fire, and if the ammunition started to explode her father would end up in trouble just the same. The worst of it was that Denis might have changed his mind – he mightn't have hidden the arms in the store at all. Or, if he did, he might have removed them by now. With the Tans burning the city, her father was taking his life in his hands – and it could all be for nothing.

'Don't worry, Momma, don't worry, he'll be all right. You'll see, he'll be back in no time, and Jacob with him,' she told her mother, putting an arm round her and guiding her back into the kitchen.

Bertha Cohen looked at her, her eyes full of fear and doubt. Judith made her own eyes smile reassurance, but the same fear and doubt had their grip on her heart.

Joshua could hear himself panting as he hurried across the South Mall but he was not concerned for his health. He had had to stop running – the exertion was too much for him, and perspiration was streaming down his forehead. The air was thick with smoke, and when he wiped his hand across his eyes it became streaked with soot. He

442

was annoyed with himself. So hastily had he rushed out of the house that he had forgotten to put on his bowler hat, and when the running had made his *yarmulkah* slip he had had to take it off and stuff it in his pocket. Now he had nothing to cover his head and he'd get all soot in his hair.

He could see above the roofs of the Mall the flames from the buildings in Patrick Street towering into the sky. He had thought the neighbour who rushed around Celtic Crescent shouting that the Tans were burning the city must have been exaggerating. His only worry at the time had been for Jacob out on his bicycle – he had warned him to keep away from Patrick Street, but who could tell where he was?

'They're burning every shop,' the neighbour had sworn. 'Burning and looting. The whole centre of the city!'

Oi vei, savages, animals; and then – only then – had he remembered about the arms and ammunition Denis Hurley was to hide in the store. All week it had slipped his mind completely, as if Hurley had never even come to ask his permission, as if he had never given him a key to the back gate. No wonder he had forgotten! How could he remember such a thing – how could he think of anything else all week except his father's collapse and then his death? But he'd have to do something. He knew what the Black and Tans were like. They'd break in anywhere for loot, no matter how unlikely-looking the place. Saturday night, they'd probably be too drunk to know the difference. If they broke into the store ... if they started to search it. ... They'd hardly get as far as the back gate and find the arms. But if they set it on fire – the fire could reach the ammunition. Denis had said 'guns and ammunition' – Joshua remembered it all now. He couldn't take the chance. He'd have to get rid of them somehow.

Reaching George's Street he was relieved to find it deserted and quiet, but being so near Patrick Street he couldn't be certain some drunken marauding Tans wouldn't find their way there. He'd have to hurry.

He took a key from his pocket, but his hands were so slippery from perspiration that he had difficulty in opening the door in the big wooden gate. He could clearly hear

443

the bedlam in Patrick Street – above the roar of the flames there was the sound of revolver shots, shouting and screaming, fire brigades, police whistles. Determined to ignore it all he ran into the yard and hurried towards the back gate. That's where Denis had said he would hide the arms – just inside the gate. That's what he had said.

As he ran, the smoke made tears stream from his eyes and he stumbled from side to side, knocking his shins against piles of scrap. Breathless, he reached the gate and feverishly started lifting heavy iron bars and rusting metal lying against the wall.

He heaved piece after piece out of the way, his heart thumping madly. Wherever he searched, he found nothing. It looked as if the arms had been taken away already, but Joshua had to make sure. He knew he had to search everywhere near the gate. If the arms were there and he missed them. . . .

Suddenly he heard a commotion from the front of the yard. There were rough voices, shots – and was it laughter? He couldn't make out any words. Could it be the Tans? He thought of running back to the front to see but knew immediately that that would be foolish. If the Black and Tans *were* there, he'd run straight into them. Anyway, the arms and ammunition – that was what was important.

Joshua searched on, panting from the heavy weights he had to move. The noise from the front of the yard continued, and then – *Gott in himmel* – a shot, and another shot, followed immediately by a muffled explosion and the whole place was suddenly bathed in a flood of light. Joshua swung around. He guessed what had happened. He was right. Flames were shooting upwards, and he knew that his office and all the front of the yard was on fire.

He took a handkerchief from his pocket and wiped the perspiration from his brow. What should he do? He thought of his family waiting for him at home, of his father's coffin ready to start its journey next morning to *Eretz*. Should he give up his search? He had looked everywhere already, and there was no sign of any arms.

444

Surely he'd have found them by now if they were still there. Get out – go home – that was the only thing to do. It was madness to delay. He couldn't escape the front way – the burning office would have made that too dangerous – and anyway the Tans might still be there. He'd have to go out the back gate. And then he realised – he didn't have a key. Apart from the spare key he had given Denis, he had one other, but he used that so seldom that it was always kept hanging on a bunch in the office. And now the office was on fire. He was trapped.

Joshua sank to the ground and leaned his back against the wall. His head was reeling, his eyes were burning from the smoke and his clothes were sticking to him. He had to have a few seconds' rest, to calm himself, get back his strength, decide what to do. The only way out of the yard seemed to be over the wall. But it was high. Did he have enough strength left? His arms were shaking with exhaustion from moving so much heavy scrap, and his muscles felt like water. He could stand on something of course – that way his fingers could reach the top of the wall. But could he pull himself onto it? He looked up. In the light of the flames it seemed to tower above him as he sat on the ground. And, even if he did get to the top, there was still the drop down on the other side.... He might break a leg, lie there injured, hurt himself so badly that he would not be able to accompany his father's coffin to the station. But he couldn't miss that last journey with his *tata*. Perhaps the Tans had left the front – perhaps the fire wouldn't be too bad – perhaps he could get out that way after all. He'd go and see. With God's help he'd escape that way. He'd go and see.

Jacob pedalled madly along the South Mall, going as fast as he could while at the same time trying to keep a watch on both sides of the road in the hope of seeing his father. Pedestrians were running from the area and, although the whole sky was by now incandescent with firelight, the tall buildings around him kept most of the Mall in shadow. The shouts of the people fleeing and the horrifying noise from Patrick Street struck fear into him, but he

445

had to go on. Thank God that at least there were no Black and Tans in sight. He guessed they wouldn't be wasting their time on the South Mall where there were only offices and no shops to loot.

Swinging off the Mall to face the top of George's Street and the last few hundred yards to his father's store, he had to brake sharply. Ahead of him were three Tans right at the entrance to George's Street. Their backs were turned to him, but he didn't dare continue – he knew he'd never get past them. There was only one thing for it – he'd have to go round by Patrick Street to get to the lane at the back of the store. His father must still be there. A minute was as long as Jacob would be in Patrick Street; less than a hundred yards and he'd be able to turn down one of the side-streets to the lane. Dangerous or not, he'd have to risk it. On a bicycle he'd have a good chance of getting through. There was no alternative.

He turned, sped up Oliver Plunkett Street, and took the next corner so fast that he was nearly catapulted onto the road. He managed to get the machine under control again as he rounded Cudmore's cake shop and entered Patrick Street. The shock of what he saw made him cry aloud.

All the way up to the statue of Father Mathew was one immense conflagration, as if the whole block had been turned into a gigantic furnace. Cash's huge shop and Roche's Stores were like a hell-pit with flames engulfing them. Their show windows had been smashed, and the goods on display were piled in the middle of the broad street, well clear of the flames, from where swarms of Black and Tans were busy carrying away as much as they could. Near the Statue a tram was burning fiercely. Two Crossley tenders were parked near it, and their occupants were spilling out to dance around the tram, shooting wildly and screaming oaths. Black and Tans were everywhere, some with cans of kerosene, others, carrying as many bottles as they could, reeling drunkenly and firing at pedestrians. Most of the latter were fleeing in terror, but a few tried to help the firemen. A fire engine had pulled up outside the Munster Arcade, and men were rushing to reel out the hose. As Jacob flew past he heard

446

one of the Tans shout: 'At your peril don't turn the hose on that fire. Let it blaze.' When the officers continued their efforts another Tan ran up, bayonet in hand, and slashed the hose to pieces.

Jacob could not bear to look on the devastation. He put his head down and raced on. Out of the corner of his eye he saw an arm grab at him as he steered the careering bicycle between sofas and armchairs stacked in the road, praying he wouldn't get a puncture from the broken glass that littered his path. The hiss and crackle of the burning buildings were hideous sounds, and the heat and smoke, combined with the terrifying sizzle as walls collapsed, made him feel as if he was swimming in a vast boiling cauldron. Shots were ringing out on all sides, but he ignored them. Most of the Tans were too drunk to aim straight. What would be left of Cork after this? What would be left of the city he loved? The thought barely flashed through his mind as he turned the corner that would take him away from the horror of it all and on to the lane behind his father's store. His father was his only worry now. Please God, let me find him, he prayed. Please God let him be safe.

Patches of smoke had gathered between the high walls of the narrow lane and the air was heavy with the acrid smell of burning. There were no street-lamps, but the reflection from the glowing sky provided Jacob with sufficient light. At the back gate he jumped off his bicycle, rested it against the wall and carefully climbed onto the saddle. From there he was able to reach the top of the wall and pull himself up until he straddled it.

'Oh my God!' he breathed as he saw the flames that had engulfed the front of the yard. The office, the shed, everything there was ablaze.

'Father! Father!' he screamed. If his father had been in the office when it was set on fire, how could he escape?

In panic Jacob jumped down from the wall, not caring that he might land on something that would turn his ankle or even break a bone. His father might be burning to death. He had to see.

He landed on his knees with a thump that knocked the

447

breath out of his body but at least he wasn't hurt. Picking himself up, he started to run between the piled-up scrap now shining and sparkling in the light of the fire. As he ran, the smoke made him cough and obscured his vision. He thought he could see someone ahead of him. He wiped the tears from his eyes and stopped running so as to focus more clearly. Yes, there was somebody there, running towards him. Could it be...?

'Father?' he called.

He looked again. Out of the swirling clouds of smoke the shape suddenly took form. 'Jacob!' it was calling. 'Jacob!'

'*Tata! Tata!*' he shouted back as his father, gasping and dishevelled, stumbled into his arms. '*Tata*, you're safe' – his tears now those of joy and relief as much as from the biting smoke.

'Jacob, Jacob,' Joshua sobbed as he hugged his son. 'What are you doing here?'

'I came to find you, Father. Judith told me you were here. Come on, come on, we must get away.'

As Jacob started to make for the front gate Joshua restrained him. 'We can't get out that way. The office is on fire and we'd never get past it. I've just been there.'

'Then we'll go out the back way,' Jacob answered, urging his father on towards the gate.

'I have no key,' Joshua panted, almost overcome. 'The gate is locked and I haven't the key.'

'We'll get over the wall. We must, Father, we must. I can help you.'

Jacob ran to the wall and piled up a number of large stones against it.

'Now, Father, come on. If you stand on these, you can get a hand on the top. I'll get underneath you and push.'

Breathing heavily and with constant encouragement from his son, Joshua pulled himself up until he was sitting on the wall. Jacob then stepped onto the pile of stones, calling 'Stay there,' and with a quick leap joined his father.

'Wait now,' he ordered. 'Don't try to jump down.'

'What are you going to do, Jacob?'

448

Jacob turned carefully, lowered his body and dropped down into the lane. He ran to get his bicycle and quickly wheeled it to a point underneath where his father was sitting.

'Now,' he said, looking up. 'Take it slowly, Father. Hold on to the top and let your body down. I'll guide your leg on to the saddle.'

Grunting with exertion, Joshua eased his body around and slid himself down. He felt Jacob catch his leg and direct it until it rested on the bicycle's saddle. It took Jacob all his strength to hold the machine steady under the pressure of his father's weight.

'Now the other leg. Easy, easy.'

Slowly, his faith now resting completely in his son, Joshua put his other leg on the saddle and turned his head. The ground was only a few feet away.

'Jump!' Jacob shouted.

Joshua jumped, catching onto Jacob's shoulder for support, and both of them were flung to the ground. Shaken but unhurt they sat up.

'Bless you, *mein kinde*, God bless you. You saved my life.'

'Are you sure you're all right, Father?' Jacob asked anxiously.

'*I'm* all right. You?'

'Yes, yes. But we must get away from here. Can you walk?'

Joshua rose to his feet and leaned against the wall for a few moments.

'Why should we walk?' he asked, still panting. 'We have your bicycle.'

Jacob looked at his father in puzzlement.

'Before you were born, my son, I used to ride a bicycle,' Joshua said. 'When I first went to the country to make a living, I often had to cycle.'

He took hold of the handlebars and swung a leg over the saddle. He seemed to have found new strength.

'Come, Jacob, you sit on the crossbar. You've never given your college friends a ride on the crossbar?'

'Of course I have,' Jacob replied. As he lifted himself on

to the bar, he suddenly realised that there was something different, something unusual about his father's face.

'*Tata*,' he pointed, 'your head.'

Joshua quickly put a hand up.

'What's wrong? Is it cut?'

'No, no. But it's uncovered.'

'*Ai, ai*,' Joshua laughed. 'I forgot.'

He searched in his pockets, found his *yarmulkah* and slapped it on his head.

'Now, let us go. Hold on, Yankel. We'll soon be home.'

Hesitantly he pushed the bicycle into motion. Jacob held his breath, clinging on grimly as they wobbled for some yards until his father at last had the machine under control. Then, with the inferno still raging behind them and the awful din still in their ears, they rode away.

I'm a lucky man, Joshua thought, a very lucky man. Twice in a month I've escaped death. The first time I could tell no one, so I could not recite the special prayer. But this time I can tell everyone that my son, Jacob, saved my life and at the *minyan* tomorrow morning I can say the prayer at last. God has been good to me.

As he bent to the pedals his head kept moving close to his son's, so close indeed that he was able to brush his hair with his lips.

'A very lucky man,' he muttered under his breath. 'A very lucky man.'

33

IN HIS DREAM Max Klein was banging for silence, but no one would pay him any attention. He banged and banged until he realised he was no longer dreaming. He was awake, someone was banging on the knocker and Myra was shaking him.

'Max, Max, wake up. There's someone at the door.'

He sat up confusedly in the darkness.

'What time is it? Light a match. See.'

Myra lit her bedside candle, and Max Klein lifted his large gold watch from the chair beside his pillow.

'Five o'clock! *Mein Gott*, who could it be at five o'clock on a Sunday morning?'

The knocking continued as he clambered into his trousers, not even waiting to take off his pyjamas, and pulled the braces over his shoulders.

'I'm coming, I'm coming,' he muttered as his wife nagged at him to hurry. Going down the stairs he tried to clear his throat of the phlegm that had accumulated during the night.

At the front door he peered out through the glass. He could see a figure standing on the doorstep, but it was too dark to make out who it was. Cautiously he opened the door.

'Mr Clayne?'

It was the voice Max recognised.

'Colonel Windsor? What is it? What is it?'

'May I come in, Mr Clayne?'

'Of course, of course. Come in. Please.'

Max led his visitor into the parlour. The room was freezing. He lit the gas-mantle and then without a word went into the hall, coming back in a moment attired in his heavy overcoat.

'Very wise, Mr Clayne,' Colonel Windsor smiled. 'I'm afraid I always seem to be disturbing you on dark cold mornings. But this is important – to you.'

'Important to me? Sit down, Colonel.'

Colonel Windsor looked around, then sat in the same chair he had occupied on his first visit. As Max saw him take out his cigarette-holder, he hastened to place an ashtray beside him. The Colonel inserted a cigarette and lit it before speaking.

'After last night's trouble—' he began, at which the President put his head on one side and interrupted him.

'Trouble? What trouble?'

'You haven't heard?'

'Heard what, Colonel? I was here all night. I went to bed early.'

Colonel Windsor blew out a mouthful of smoke and adjusted his monocle.

'Well, to be brief, Mr Clayne, there was quite a to-do in the city last night and I'm afraid half of Patrick Street was burned down. Those Black and Tan gangs of course.'

Max whistled in astonishment.

'Half of Patrick Street? Burned down?'

'Gutted, I'm sorry to say. Only shells left.'

As Max shook his head from side to side, unable to credit the news, Colonel Windsor continued. 'But the point is that as a result the railways are on strike. Completely shut down. No trains will be running at all, I'm afraid. Which is what brings me here.'

Max Klein looked at him strangely. He hadn't yet properly absorbed the news about Patrick Street, and now the Colonel was talking about trains on strike.

Colonel Windsor noticed the President's confusion.

452

'It *was* this Sunday, wasn't it, Mr Clayne?' he said. 'Your people – going off to Palestine.'

Max Klein sprang to his feet and gasped. He was fully awake now.

'No trains!' he exclaimed. 'But there must be. They have to get to Dublin today. They're all ready. What will they do? They'll miss the boat . . . everything.'

Colonel Windsor took his monocle from his eye and clicked his tongue reprovingly at Max's loss of composure.

'Sit down, my good man. Keep calm. That's why I'm here.'

The edge of authority in his voice had the required effect. The President resumed his seat.

'Now,' Colonel Windsor explained, 'this gives me an opportunity to make some reparation to your community for that unfortunate incident a few weeks ago involving one of my officers.'

'You mean . . . Abie Klugman?'

'Quite. Mr Klugman. Your people are due to go to Dublin this morning by train, but there are no trains. As it happens, I have some empty lorries – part of a convoy that reached me from Dublin yesterday – due to drive back there in a few hours. If you wish. . . . '

Max Klein jumped to his feet again, relief spreading over his face.

'If I wish! You will take them to Dublin – all of them?'

'How many are going?'

'Fourteen.'

'Capital,' the Colonel said. 'We'll make them as comfortable as we can. A few can travel with the drivers, the rest on seats in the lorries. Now, you'll need a few hours to notify all of them and gather them together. Supposing we aim to start at – ten? That should get them to Dublin well in time to catch the boat.'

'Wonderful, Colonel, wonderful. Couldn't be better,' Max smiled. 'I'll have them all ready by ten o'clock, I promise you.'

'Where, Mr Clayne? Where is the most convenient place to rendezvous?'

453

The President was about to answer when his eyes suddenly closed in dismay and he sank back into his chair.

'I said fourteen, Colonel Windsor, but I was wrong. It's fifteen.'

'My goodness, man, that's no difficulty,' the Colonel laughed. 'One extra? We have room for far more than that.'

Max Klein shook his head.

'But the extra one.... ' He paused. 'The extra one.... It's the body of our Rabbi.'

There was silence. The Colonel jammed his monocle back into his eye.

'Explain, man,' he almost barked. 'What do you mean?'

Max Klein explained, the Colonel listened, the smoke curling up from his cigarette.

'So you see', the President finished, 'Rabbi Cohen has to go, too. No one would go without him.'

The Colonel extracted the end of his cigarette from its holder and stubbed it out in the ashtray. He smiled at Max.

'Mr Clayne, his Majesty's soldiers are not exactly inexperienced in transporting coffins. I think you may safely leave that problem to me. Rest assured, your Rabbi will not be left behind.'

Max Klein was about to take the Colonel's hand but thought better of it, instead putting his own hands together and rubbing them in satisfaction.

'Where is your Rabbi's coffin at the moment, Mr Clayne? Wherever it is, I take it that would be the best place for all to meet.'

'Yes, yes, indeed, Colonel. Celtic Crescent. You know it?'

'Not personally,' Colonel Windsor said, rising to leave, 'but no doubt my men will find it. Celtic Crescent – ten o'clock, then?'

'Ten o'clock,' Max Klein agreed. 'But—' He turned aside sheepishly for a moment before facing the Colonel again. 'There is one other thing.... Oh, nothing big – just a small favour. But important. *Very* important.'

'That is?'

'An old Jewish custom, Colonel. When a very holy, very special Jew is going to his last resting-place, it is usual for the funeral to pass the synagogue on its way. It's a very rare honour, you understand. We had decided—'

Colonel Windsor interrupted him.

'Your synagogue is in South Terrace, I believe. Is that far from Celtic Crescent?'

'Five minutes. Only five minutes, I promise you, Colonel.'

'And that *is* everything, Mr Clayne? We just pass the synagogue, do we? You don't have to take the coffin in?'

'No, no, I assure you, Colonel. Just stop for a moment for one short prayer, and then go on.'

Colonel Windsor smiled.

'Right-ho. Celtic Crescent at ten, slow march to the synagogue, a minute there, and then the convoy can be off on its way. You'll be there yourself at ten o'clock, Mr Clayne?'

'Of course, of course.'

'It's all arranged, then.'

The two men shook hands.

'Thank you,' Max Klein said, 'thank you. You are performing what we call a *mitzvah*. That means a good deed, but a very special good deed, Colonel.'

'Just squaring the account, Mr Clayne,' the Colonel rejoined as he reached the front door. 'Just squaring the account.'

He turned, marched smartly down the path to his waiting car, and the President hurried back to his bedroom to dress.

By a quarter to ten Celtic Crescent almost overflowed with people. Most of the community had gathered outside the Cohens' house to accompany the cortège on its journey to the synagogue. News of the change of plans had spread rapidly. No one was surprised that the trains were on strike after the previous night's destruction –

455

some of the men had already been in to Patrick Street to see for themselves its smoking remains, and their reports of the devastation were greeted with horror. Now they stood in the road, conversing in groups, their horses and traps lined up by the path with their families sitting patiently inside, thankful the morning was dry. Others leaned on their bicycles, while a few with no means of transport were going from man to man trying to find a spare seat. Rev. Levitt, with Zvi Lipsky, Percy Lovitch and other officials, had already gone ahead to the synagogue in preparation for the arrival of the Rabbi's coffin.

As Max Klein drove round the corner into Celtic Crescent he was feeling well satisfied with the way he had handled everything. His satisfaction was marred, however, when he saw all the transport lined up by the footpath.

'Fools,' he muttered, 'ignoramuses. Don't they know they must leave room for the lorries?'

He parked his own car on the other side of the road and ran over to the men, arguing angrily with them.

Immediately there was a flurry of activity as they led their horses across the road, shrugging their shoulders at the President's irascibility.

Recovering his dignity, Max Klein approached Judith Cohen who was standing with the departing group outside the house, their cases and luggage piled by the wall.

'No sign of them yet?' he asked.

'Not yet, Mr Klein.'

'They'll come, they'll come. Colonel Windsor won't let me down.' There was a note of pride in his voice, as if to imply that he was on close terms with the Colonel and could be confident of relying on him.

Inside the hallway Joshua stood with Bertha and Jacob beside his father's coffin, which had been carried down from the bedroom. Christian neighbours dressed for Mass in their Sunday best, with Mrs Burns at their head, tarried at the end of the street, anxious to pay their last respects and intrigued by the rumour they had heard that the British Army was going to take the Jews and the body of their dead Rabbi to Dublin. They murmured restrainedly among themselves – funerals were solemn occasions.

Punctually at ten o'clock three army lorries, preceded by Colonel Windsor in his staff car, rumbled round the corner into Celtic Crescent and pulled up beside Max Klein, awaiting them on the footpath. The Colonel jumped out smartly and shook hands with the President.

'All ready, I see, Mr Clayne. Good chap!'

'Yes, we're all ready, Colonel. The coffin is just inside the hall here. Which lorry will we put it into?'

'It won't be in any of them, Mr Clayne. I have something else to transport it. Come, I'll show you.'

The Colonel led him to the second lorry, to the back of which a gleaming gun-carriage had been coupled.

'You are going to put our Rabbi's coffin on that?' Max Klein asked incredulously.

'Of course. Why not?'

'Not fitting,' the President replied tersely. 'Not fitting. Out in the open. Exposed. Not fitting for a Rabbi.'

'My good man,' the Colonel explained patiently, 'gun-carriages are used for funerals only of very special people, like great leaders. It is a tribute, Mr Clayne, a mark of respect. You can't hide your Rabbi away in a lorry for his last journey.'

Max Klein looked doubtful.

'One moment, Colonel. I'll have to consult the family.'

He went into the house, and after a minute Joshua and Jacob emerged onto the front step and from there gazed at the gun-carriage. Satisfied, Joshua nodded to Max Klein, who went to tell the Colonel. Then at a signal from him four members of the Burial Society entered the house, carried the coffin out and placed it on the gun-carriage. While soldiers helped to secure it, Colonel Windsor turned to Max Klein.

'Now, who is leading the group?'

'Miss Cohen, Judith Cohen. I'll introduce you, Colonel.'

'*Miss* Cohen? A woman?'

'The Rabbi's grand-daughter. It was his wish that she should go instead of him.'

Surprised, the Colonel allowed himself to be introduced to Judith.

She began to thank him for helping them out of their difficulty when he cut her short.

'No need to thank me, Miss Cohen, no need at all. Now, are there many ladies in your group?'

'Three more besides me,' Judith replied.

'Ah, good. I suggest the men go in the back of the lorries with all the luggage and the ladies ride in the drivers' cabins. As the leader, Miss Cohen, perhaps you would ride in the first vehicle.'

Colonel Windsor signalled to a figure sitting in his staff car. Roddy Simcox stepped out and approached them.

'May I introduce you, Miss Cohen? This is Captain Simcox, who is accompanying the convoy to Dublin.' Then, turning to Roddy, he said: 'Captain, Miss Cohen is the leader of the group. She will be with you. Now, we should nearly be ready' – and he gave the Captain a signal.

Roddy went to the car, took what seemed to be a bundle from the back seat and carried it to the coffin now resting on the gun-carriage with soldiers waiting beside it.

'What's that?' Judith asked.

Captain Simcox opened it to reveal a huge green, white and orange flag.

'It's the Irish flag, Miss Cohen,' Colonel Windsor told her. 'We frequently find them in searches of Republican houses. Confiscate them of course.'

'What are you going to do with it?' Max Klein put in.

'Drape it over the coffin of course. Coffins on gun-carriages always have a national flag over them. I didn't think you'd want a British flag.'

'But an Irish one?' Judith protested.

'If you have a Jewish one, of course, Miss Cohen....'

'A Jewish flag?' Max Klein laughed. 'We have no country, Colonel – how could we have a flag?'

'Then, it will have to be this. Besides, it's rather a good protection. It's a long journey. I don't want to alarm you,

458

but British army convoys have been ambushed before, you know. If the IRA saw us with just a coffin they might think it was some trick. But a coffin with an Irish flag – I don't think they'd shoot at that. At least it should confuse them for long enough to allow the convoy past. Rather clever, really.'

'I'm sure you're right, Colonel,' Judith agreed, 'but I'll have to ask my father.'

'Do be quick, Miss Cohen. We can't afford to delay.'

Judith went to Joshua, spoke briefly with him, and with a smile returned to Colonel Windsor.

'He says yes, Colonel. He thinks his father would have liked the idea.'

In a minute the emigrants and their luggage were helped aboard the lorries, accompanied by soldiers to protect them. As the flag was placed over the coffin there were gasps, the men and the non-Jewish neighbours clustering around to examine it and wonder. Max Klein had a word with one of the youths on a bicycle, telling him to hurry on to the synagogue and prepare them for the gun-carriage and the flag. Then he ushered Joshua, Bertha and Jacob into his own car and nodded to Colonel Windsor.

The Colonel took his seat beside his driver, looked out to make sure everything was ready, and then his car moved off, slowly leading the way. Behind him were the three lorries with the gun-carriage in the middle, behind them came Max Klein's motor-car and then the host of bicycles and horses and traps, with a knot of walkers bringing up the rear.

'How long will the journey to Dublin take?' Judith asked Roddy Simcox in the first lorry.

'Five or six hours. But we'll get you there in time, don't worry.'

'We don't go anywhere near Patrick Street, do we?'

'No, no. We go in the other direction. Anyway, you don't want to see it. It wouldn't be a pretty sight after last night.'

Judith had no desire to see Patrick Street but she had heard talk already that morning that the burning was in

459

reprisal for an IRA ambush on the Old Youghal Road. Her heart had grown cold at the thought that Denis might have been involved. Perhaps Captain Simcox would know more about it.

'I heard there was trouble last night before the fire – somewhere on the north side of the city.'

'Yes, I believe so, Miss Cohen. A lorry full of Tans was ambushed. There was some shooting.'

'Anyone hurt?'

'They killed one Tan, I'm told.'

Judith held her breath. 'What about the IRA? Did they have any casualties?'

'No bodies left. But of course if they had any wounded they'd have carried them away.'

'I see,' Judith said. She knew she shouldn't feel concern, but what was the use? How could she forget so quickly?

'So you're the leader of the group going to Palestine, Miss Cohen,' Roddy said conversationally.

'Not the leader,' Judith replied, roused from her thoughts. 'I'm in charge. But the leader is the man in the coffin, our Rabbi. He was my grandfather. As far as I'm concerned, he's still our leader.'

Captain Simcox glanced at her quizzically and relapsed into silence. A rum lot, those Jews, a rum lot.

In the synagogue Rev. Levitt waited with Zvi Lipsky, Percy Lovitch and the other elders of the community. Outside a young man had been posted as a look-out and when he saw the cortège appear round the corner of South Terrace he called to the men.

Immediately, all the lamps in the synagogue were lit and the three front doors opened wide. Then the group gathered on the steps, watching the slow approach of the army lorries. A priest waiting across the road came over and asked to join them. It was Father McGiff, one arm still in a sling.

They stood in silence.

460

Zvi Lipsky shivered inside his coat. The cold was getting to him. Maybe his age, too. When this was over he would have to sit down and think seriously about his future. It was time.

Percy Lovitch did not feel cold but he did feel melancholy. With Rabbi Moishe and some dozen others gone from the community it was like the final curtain falling on an opera. The community would go on of course; and there'd be other operas. But Percy wouldn't ever be singing in an opera again and he wondered if he should seriously consider joining the little settlement of Cork Jews in *Eretz*. Well, there was time enough to think about that. Wait until they send back reports of what it is like there. Wait until the Carl Rosa come back to Cork next year. Perhaps Barry Brandreth will still be manager and perhaps.... No, no – Percy shook his head; no use all this hoping, all this wishful thinking. Just wait. Wait and see.

By now the cortège had reached the synagogue and halted directly outside the open doors. Rev. Levitt recited the *Kaddish*; Percy's tenor, sounding its sweetest in the open air, led the responses. The prayer ended. Max Klein got out of his car, hurried to the head of the convoy to thank Colonel Windsor and then stepped back. The lorries moved off again, the ends of the flag on Rabbi Moishe's coffin flapping in the slight breeze.

The cortège was in sight for only a few more yards, for it immediately turned round onto Union Quay to proceed towards the Dublin road. As it went, the group on the synagogue steps, the people in their horses and carts and on their bicycles, Max Klein still standing out on the road, and the Cohen family in his car – all had a clear view into the backs of the lorries at their departing loved ones. But no one waved – no one except Father McGiff, and he quickly lowered his hand when he realised he was alone.

The President returned to his car to take Joshua Cohen with Bertha and Jacob back to their home. They were sitting in the back seat, Joshua in the middle. He put an arm around his wife, the other around his son, and pulled them close to him. They would go home to start their seven days of deep mourning with the customary

461

'Recovery Meal' of hard-boiled eggs, to symbolise on-going life, which some of the women would have stayed behind to prepare for them. For a week they would stay indoors, with all mirrors covered, sitting on hard low seats, praying, receiving the daily visitors bringing their comfort and sympathy to the house of mourning.

'*Nu*,' Joshua said. 'He is gone. To *Eretz*. As he wished. God is good. Next week *we* go to Leeds, the three of us, to see Malka and her son. Yes?'

'Yes, *tata*,' Jacob replied, while Bertha rested her head on her husband's shoulder.

Max Klein turned the car and started back. He was thinking that tomorrow was Monday, a new week, and before dawn in Celtic Crescent the host of horses and traps and cyclists now following him would be gathering again with their cases and packs, loaded with goods, to go out to the country. Business as usual. That was life. And perhaps there'd be a letter in the post for him from the Rabbinical Court in London, a reply to the one he had sent them some weeks before asking them to let it be known to Jewish communities all over Britain that Cork, in Ireland, where for years the great Rabbi Moishe Cohen had ministered, needed a new Rabbi.